He reloaded the Browning.

The rain would silence guns and muskets alike. Thick smoke from the firepowder lay across the entire battle area. Archers could not see a hundred paces into the gloom, and had no targets.

The battle would be won by whoever could bring home a charge, infantry or cavalry. There could be no strategy, and in this smoke weapons that struck at a distance were useless.

Vothan favors the side with the greatest numbers. Ganton had heard that as a child. Today it might be true.

The enemy trumpets sounded again.

Also from Orbit by Jerry Pournelle:

JANISSARIES
JANISSARIES: CLAN AND CROWN
BLACK HOLES
KING DAVID'S SPACESHIP
FUTURE HISTORY
HIGH JUSTICE

JERRY E. POURNELLE
and
ROLAND GREEN

Janissaries 3:
Storms of Victory

Futura

An Orbit Book

Copyright © 1987 by Jerry Pournelle and Roland Green

Maps by Diane Duane and Noreen Fogel

First published in Great Britain in 1989
by Futura Publications, a Division of
Macdonald & Co (Publishers) Ltd
London & Sydney

ISBN 0 7088 8298 6

Printed and bound in Great Britain by
Collins, Glasgow

Futura Publications
A Division of
Macdonald & Co (Publishers) Ltd
66–73 Shoe Lane
London EC4P 4AB

A member of Maxwell Pergamon Publishing Corporation plc

Acknowledgments

We gratefully acknowledge the editorial consultation of Barbara J. Clifford, without whose help this book would probably never have been completed.

For Violette Yvonne Green

A Political Glossary

The Galactics

The Galactic Confederation is a loose federation of non-human races, governing Earth's region of the spiral arm of our Galaxy. Its member races include the **Shalnuksis,** the Ader'at'eel, the Fusttael, and the Finsit'tuvii. The **Council** is the supreme governing body of the Confederation; the **High Commission** is a subordinate body, in charge of relations with non-member races, particularly humans.

Tran

The Five Kingdoms is a confederation of northern kingdoms (including Ta-Meltemos, Ta-Lataos, and Ta-Kartos) under a High Rexja.

Drantos is an independent kingdom under its own Wanax, although it has been claimed by both Rome and the Five Kingdoms. **Chelm** is part of Drantos.

Rome is a (self-proclaimed) empire, descended from Romans of the time of Septimius Severus (c. 200 A.D.) brought to Tran by the **Shalnuksis.**

The City-States are an array of independent cities lying south of Drantos and south-west of Rome. Their most prominent members are **Vis** and **Rustengo.**

The Sunlands is the general term for everything south of the City-States.

The Westmen are nomadic horse barbarians from beyond the High Plains, ultimately descended from Scythians.

Dramatis Personae

The Galactics

Inspector Agzaral—Confederation High Commission law enforcement officer.

Jehna Sae Leern—Courier for the Ader'at'eel.

Karreel—*Shalnuksi* merchant, in the Tran trade.

Les—Human pilot in *Shalnuksi* service; Gwen's husband.

Wilno—Retired Confederate naval officer, classmate of Agzaral.

The Starmen

Private Jack Beazeley—Mason's right-hand man.

Sergeant Harold Bisso—Elliot's right-hand man.

Private Alexander Boyd—Gengrich's chief of staff.

Sergeant William Campbell—Professor of Engineering at the University.

Private Lance Clavell—Rick Galloway's ambassador to Nikeis.

Sergeant Major Rafael Elliot—Top kick of the mercs; Provost of the University.

Rick Galloway—Captain, U.S.A.; Colonel of Mercenaries, Eqeta of Chelm, Captain General of Drantos, War Leader of Tamaerthon.

Corporal Arnold Gengrich—Leader of mutinous mercs; Lord of Zyphron.

Private Alan MacAllister—Expert sniper.

Sergeant John McCleve—Medic; Professor of Medicine at the University.

Major Art Mason—Rick's right-hand man; Marshal of the Captain General's Household.

Sergeant Ben Murphy—Bheroman of Westrook.

Corporal Mortimer Schultz—Master of Foot in Rustengo.

Gwen Tremaine—Rector of the University.

Warrant Officer Larry Warner—Chancellor of the University.

The Alliance

Ajacias—Bheroman of Drantos, in the Sutmarg.

Apelles, son of Lykon—Priest of Yatar.

Balquhain—Drumold's son and heir.

Drumold—MacClallan Muir: Tylara's father.

Enipses—Bheroman of Drantos.

Ganton, son of Loron—Wanax of Drantos.

Hilaskos—Bheroman of Drantos.

Mad Bear—Chief of the exiled Silver Wolves clan of the Westmen (the Horse People).

Maev—Merchant's daughter, handfasted to Apelles.

Monira—Leader of the war-trained Children of Vothan.

Morrone, son of Morron—Companion to the Wanax Ganton.

Pinir, son of the smith—Master Gunner in the Royal Artillery of Drantos.

Rudhrig—Eqeta of Harms.

Lady Siobhan—Art Mason's fiancée and Gwen Tremaine's office manager.

Teuthras—Colonel of First Tamaerthan Hussars.

Traskon, son of Trakon—Bheroman of Drantos.

Tylara do Tamaerthon—Rick Galloway's wife; Eqetassa of Chelm and Justiciar of Drantos.

Yanulf—Highpriest of Yatar and Chancellor of Drantos.

The Romans

Titus Licinius Frugi—Legate, commanding the Fourth Legion.

Lucius—Freedman and confidant to Marselius Caesar.

Gaius Marius Marselius Caesar—Emperor of Rome.

Octavia Marselia Caesar—Wanaxxae of Drantos; Publius's daughter.

Archbishop Polycarp—Founder of the movement for the united worship of Yatar and Christ.

Publius Caesar—Marselius's son and heir.

Marcus Julius Vinicianus—Exiled Roman nobleman and chief spy for Gengrich.

The Enemies

Prince Akkilas—High Rexja Toris's sole surviving legitimate son.

Issardos—High Chancellor of the Five Kingdoms.

Matthais—Highpriest of Vothan.

Phrados the Prophet—Religious fanatic opposed to the united worship of Yatar and Christ.

Crown Prince Strymon—Heir to Ta-Meltemos.

Prince Teodoros—Strymon's younger brother.

Toris—High Rexja of the Five Kingdoms.

Volauf—Captain General to Matthais.

Walking Stone—Paramount war chief of the Westmen.

STORMS OF VICTORY

the Frigid Lands

NIKEIS

THE EMPIRE

TAR KARTOS

ROMA

GARIOCH

TAMAERTHON

N

Roman
Provinces

BATTLE OF THE OTTARN

Ottarn River

Swamp

Ford

Village

Village

High Road

Allied Camp

1st Division — Scrymon

2nd Division — Teuthras

3rd Division — Rudhig

Ganton

Reserves (incl. Starmen)

① Deurhian's attack
② Tyrkanus attack
③ Tylara's charge
④ Ilack's charge

⋀ hill
✗ cannons
swamp
◤ village

PART ONE
Searching

CHAPTER ONE

"Turn out the Guard! Corporal of the Guard, Post Number Twelve!"

Rick Galloway turned toward the window and frowned. Sounds of shouting and running men floated up from the cobblestoned courtyard six stories below. "What in hell?" Rick muttered. Then he shrugged. "Guess I'll find out if I need to know. Okay, Art, what's next?"

"Next you get your armor on. Flak jacket first, then the mail."

"Christ, Mason! I'll roast. Look, I don't have to wear this tonight."

Art Mason spoke slowly and carefully. "Colonel, why do we have to go through this every week? You're not leaving this room without armor, not without you sending me to the brig first. Look, we've got that nice Kevlar jacket Les brought you. Only thing like it on this planet. And don't ask me who's going to shoot you. You know damn well the little king has that Browning."

"Ganton wouldn't shoot me." Rick held out his arms and let Mason help him into the Kevlar vest, then the fine chain mail shirt that covered it.

"I grant you that, Colonel. But I can think of some in his court who'd be glad to borrow that pistol. With or without royal permission." Mason tugged on the straps. "And I grant you that Wanax Ganton needs you. The problem is, he knows he needs you. Kings don't like that. Neither do teenagers. We got a teenaged king, and if you know what he's going to do, you're doing better than me."

There were more shouts from below. "Sergeant of the Guard! Post Number Twelve. Officer of the Guard! Post Number Twelve."

"That sounds serious," Rick said.

"Yeah, maybe I better have a look." Mason glanced at his watch. "Better not. Can't let the troops think I don't trust them. Follow procedures—"

"Yeah. Follow procedures." Rick laughed, then went to the table and poured two glasses of wine. The table was massive, carved from a wood that had never grown on Earth. The goblets were gold, hammered with scenes of men riding centaurs and hunting strange beasts. Rick handed one to Mason. "Here's to proper procedures."

"Yeah." Mason sipped at his wine, then frowned as Rick drank his in a gulp. "Colonel, you drink too damned much."

"You sound like my wife. Are you my wife?"

"No, sir."

"I could say it's none of your business."

"No sir, you couldn't," Mason said. "Very much my business. Anything happens to you, and I'm supposed to be in command. Only you know damned well it won't work that way. Sergeant Major Elliot will choose your successor, and it may or may not be me."

"Well, nothing's going to happen to me tonight," Rick said. He poured another goblet of wine and sipped at it. "We were drinking to proper procedures. Ever think where we'd be if we'd followed procedures? What the hell *is* the procedure for meeting a flying saucer?"

"Yeah. Well, we managed all right," Mason said. "Bloody good thing it came along."

"Yeah. I guess."

"Guess, hell, Colonel. We were goners, and you know that better'n me." Mason swept his hand in a wide gesture to indicate the stone walls, tapestries, fireplace, and primitive furnishings of the room. "This may not be all we ever wanted, but it's sure as hell more'n the Cubans would have given us."

"Yeah, I know, Art, but..." Rick let his voice trail off as he heard more shouts from outside. "Think we ought to look?"

"No, sir," Mason said. "Fact is, that's your biggest problem. Colonel, I grant you we'd have been finished a dozen times without you, and not much gets done except it's in your name—but that doesn't mean you got to do it all yourself. Procedures. Make policy, approve procedures, and then let somebody else do the work. You're going to wear yourself out if you keep on the way you're going."

Rick sat at the massive table and fingered a stack of documents. An ornate dagger served as a paperweight. "Think I wouldn't like to? Only how in hell can I make policy on stuff we've never done before? None of us have any experience handling primitives. And Romans. And barbarians. And—"

"Well, yes, sir, but—"

"And not even the locals have any experience living with a rogue star coming. Just legends." Rick tossed off his goblet of wine and poured another. "Policy! Procedures! The whole goddam planet's going to hell, and all they've got is a bunch of legends. Legends and us. And we don't know what we're doing."

Mason shrugged. "Colonel, for somebody who don't know what he's doing, you've done damned well. You must be doing something right, even if I do think you work too hard and drink too much."

"I'll—"

There was a loud knock at the door.

"Yeah?" Mason called. He took out a .45 automatic and glanced at the loads before returning it to its holster. "Who's there?"

The voice belonged to Rick's orderly. "The Star Lord Les wishes to speak with the Marshal of Drantos."

Mason looked at Rick. Rick shrugged, then nodded. Mason went to the door, looked through the peephole, then opened it.

The man who entered was shorter than Rick, about

Mason's height. He didn't look much different from the other two. A starman, Rick thought. A real one. Not a cheap imitation like me. So how should a starman look? God knows his bosses look weird enough.

"Hello, Les. Wine?" Rick offered.

"Hello. Yes, small glass—and, Major Mason, if you don't mind—"

"Let him stay. He's my deputy," Rick protested.

"It's all right, Colonel. I better go check out that commotion in the courtyard. I'll be back to walk you to your meeting."

"Don't bother. Jamiy and the Guards can do that."

Mason nodded. It wasn't hard to read his expression. Since Tylara's man Caradoc had been killed in street riots, there weren't as many locals Rick could trust to guard his back. Come to that, a lot of other things had changed for the worse.

"I'd rather you found out what the problem is down there."

"Okay." Mason threw half a salute and left without waiting for Rick to return it.

Rick poured wine and handed it to Les. They sat at the table and Rick lifted his goblet. "Cheers."

"Cheers."

They sat in silence. Finally Les spoke. "I'll be leaving in a day or so."

"Back to Earth?"

"Yes."

"I don't suppose I can talk you into taking us with you."

Les shook his head. "No. You wouldn't want me to." He wasn't smiling.

"Try me."

"You wouldn't. What would you do? Go to the authorities? Tell them you were kidnapped by a flying saucer and taken across light-years to another planet just so you could grow drugs?"

"Well, that would have the great merit of being true—"

"And the serious demerit that no one would believe you,"

Les said. "It would be worse if someone did. Either way you'd irritate the High Commission, make a deadly enemy of Inspector Agzaral, and spend the rest of your life dodging us. No, my friend, you do not want to be returned to Earth."

"What if—suppose we promise to lay low? Never tell what happened to us?"

"No," Les said.

"Yeah, well I suppose you can't believe us—"

"Even if I did, I couldn't hide the fact that I took you back to Earth. I could probably hide it from the Commission, but not from Agzaral. I don't know what he'd do about it, but I don't want to find out." Les sipped at his wine. "There's another reason. You may be safer on Tran."

"What? Come off it! This planet is coming apart! It's going to be fried by a rogue sun, the ice caps melt, coasts under water, migrations sparking wars everywhere, and your *Shalnuksi* friends are probably going to bomb the survivors back to the Stone Age anyway—and you say—"

"I say it may be safer than Earth," Les repeated. "Things happen so fast. Atom bombs. Space travel. Big colliding beam accelerators. Huge lasers. Leave things alone and pretty soon Earth will have real space travel. There are factions on the Commission that don't want that."

"And they'd really bomb Earth?"

"I don't know. They could."

"You said Earth is the breeding ground for—for wild humans."

"Wild. Not like me," Les agreed. "Not slaves."

"Slave soldiers. Janissaries."

"I'm not a soldier," Les said. "But yes, that's as good a description as any."

"And you run the whole damned empire—"

"It's not an empire."

"Confederation. But humans run it. You have all the military power, but you're still slaves. It doesn't make sense."

"Put that way, maybe not. But you don't have to make sense of it. Lay off, Rick. Just lay off."

"Lay off. Look, I have to know. Are they going to bomb Earth? Us? Both?"

Les shook his head. "Rick, I don't know. I don't understand Federation politics. Agzaral may know what's going on. He claims to. But he hasn't told me."

"You haven't told me much, either," Rick said.

"I know. Look at it my way. It's all the *Shalnuksis* need, to find out Tran natives are discussing Federation politics! They'd sure know who told you."

"How will they find out?"

"The next time one of their ships comes here they'll see changes. More water mills. Your semaphore towers. They just might pick up some locals for questioning. One of your mercs. You, even. They're pretty lazy. They probably won't. But they could."

"Do they own this planet, then?"

"It's complicated," Les said. "The Commission has rules about dealing with primitives, but they don't seem to apply to this place. Most records of Tran have been lost. I expect the *Shalnuksis* paid plenty to lose them. There are rules, my friend, but who'll enforce them?"

"Agzaral?"

"Maybe. If it's to his interest."

"What is his interest?"

Les shrugged and held his glass out to be refilled. "I do not know. He doesn't tell me."

"But—"

"But I do as he says anyway," Les said. His voice fell and he grew more serious. "Agzaral's all I've got. I think he's doing his best to look out for humans. All humans, everywhere, and especially Earth. Think, hell. I don't think it, I *know* it. He's doing his best. Whether that's good enough is another story, but he is trying."

"Okay. But about the *Shalnuksis*—"

"They don't exactly own the planet, but you better act like they do. And if Tran looks like it's about to spring an industrial and scientific revolution, the Commission has some hard choices to make. They'd have to set up permanent sur-

veillance, with an inspector. Like Agzaral's operation on
Earth's Moon. That could be expensive. There'll be some to
argue that it's cheaper and simpler to blast Tran back to the
Early Iron Age."

"Like they did before—"

"Like the *Shalnuksis* did before," Les corrected. "Two or
three times before. But that was their own work. If the
Commission orders it, the bombardment will be a lot more
thorough."

"Will they do that?"

Les shook his head. "Insufficient data. The *Shalnuksis*
don't have as much influence in the Commission as they
used to have. That's the good side. And there's Agzaral's
plan."

"Whatever that is—"

Les nodded firmly. "Whatever that is. Because it's about
all we've got."

By the light of the Demon Star the dead sentry looked
uglier than the run of corpses. Lord Morrone knew that
there was no such thing as a handsome corpse; for all that
he had not seen his eleventh name-day he had been in
enough battles to learn that. Even so, the sentry was an un-
wholesome sight, his face dark, tongue protruding, and his
clothes fouled and stinking. *It's not his look, it's what this fore-
tells.*

Morrone and his Guardsmen whirled, hands to swords, at
the sound of footsteps.

"Belay that."

The voice was soft, but there was no mistaking it. "Lord
Mason. Well come. I feared it was another." Well come indeed, Morrone thought. Now work your star magic and discover who has done this—

"Who found him?"

"Guardsman Echaino. An accident. He came into this

passage to relieve himself, found the sentry where you see him, and summoned the Guard."

"Did you leave the corpse, Echaino?"

"No, my lord."

"Touch anything?"

Echaino shuddered. "No, my lord."

"Good man." Mason knelt by the body and took its wrist in his hand. He moved the dead arm back and forth. "Not dead long," he muttered. He poked at the body for a moment and stood. "How many men have you got with you?"

Morrone's lips tightened. That tone of command was not the proper way to address a Companion to the Wanax Ganton. Morrone let it pass. He had seen enough of the starmen and their peremptory ways. Strangely effective ways. There might yet be a reckoning over the place of the starmen in Drantos, but this was not the time for it.

"Twelve Guardsmen and three of my own men-at-arms. You have brought nine. I fear we shall need more, if we are to search the Outer Bailey without making each searching party too small to defend itself."

Mason nodded. "Right." He turned to one of his men. "Lugh, take a message to Lieutenant Brionn. The ready platoon is to turn out in full kit and report to Lord Morrone at Hestia's Fountain. Tell them to move quietly, and tell anyone who sees them that this is a drill."

"Sir!" Lugh clicked his heels and hurried off. Morrone knew that Brionn would obey, for all that he was the son of a knight and his orders came to him by the son of a carpenter. A year ago Mason might have had to go himself to bring the platoon, but much had changed in that year. For the better or for the worse?

It couldn't matter. The urgent need was for a thorough search. That wouldn't be easy. Edron was the royal seat of Drantos, but it had never been planned as such. What had begun as a fortress tower had grown into a full castle, then into a city. The Outer Bailey was no open courtyard with a few buildings set against the walls, but part of the city of

Edron itself, walled off by the Wanax Ganton's great-grand-father to provide more quarters for his men-at-arms, servants, and (so the tales ran) mistresses. Except for one broad street leading from the Outer Gate to the Great North Gate of the castle itself, the Outer Bailey was as much a warren as any part of the city outside the walls.

In war the defenders would fire this area and retreat behind the flames to the castle. That was hardly the answer here, though Morrone was tempted. "What plot is afoot?" he asked.

Mason chuckled. "Must be fifty of them, wouldn't you say, my lord?"

"True enough." The royal wedding of Wanax Ganton and the Roman Lady Octavia Caesar had drawn lords, Senators, merchants, barons, knights, soldiers, and wealthy magnates from a dozen lands, half of them at war or nearly so with each other.

"We'll be until the True Sun rises searching this lot," Mason said. "Who's out here?"

Morrone shrugged. "Am I a clerk? Those of rank who could not find room inside. Lords, retainers. Clergy. Great ones. Any might be the target of a plot." Or be plotters themselves. "Wanax Ganton will not care to have his guests turned out on his last night unwed. Nor, I think, will Caesar care for the complaints of his Senators."

"Yeah. It's a problem. Got any suggestions?"

Morrone looked up at the sky, but Yatar Dayfather did not appear with an answer to his dilemma. Only the baleful glare of the Demon Star—which did give enough light to make the searching easier, for all that its growing power over the nights on Tran meant that the Time was coming nearer. . . .

"I think it would be well if I turned out the rest of my men-at-arms who are fit for duty," Morrone said. "Also—do you know who is quartered in this house?"

"Am I a clerk?" Mason said, but he was laughing, and turned to one of his Guardsmen, who produced a paper.

It was a list. Morrone took a mild pleasure in seeing that even starmen did not tax their memories with details more fit for clerks and scribes than for warriors.

"Nobody seems to be assigned to it," Mason concluded. "But the one to the left is for Councilor Daettan of Dirstvaal, who's Ambassador from Lord Gengrich. The one to the right is for the Lady Gwen, Lord Warner, and the rest of the University people. The one across the street is for Fabricius Maximus Valens, Marselius Caesar's ambassador, but he hasn't arrived yet. Too bad about that; I'd have liked to have seen these bastards take on some legionaries."

"Do you doubt the valor of the men of Drantos?"

"Not at all. It's just that if a legionary had been killed, we could have found more reliable troops for the searching parties without having to spread the word of what happened."

"Indeed." Lord Mason sounded sincere and spoke good sense, and there was no helping the starmen's fondness for the Romans. The other Rome on the starmen's home world —once our ancestors' home world, the starmen say!—had passed down much wisdom to the starmen, particularly in matters of war and statecraft. It was still just as well that Publius Caesar, the heir of Rome, saw the starmen as a new kind of "barbarian" and openly distrusted them; if starmen and Romans made an alliance only the gods could help Drantos.

"Okay, let's get at it," Mason said. "You take charge here. Post some guards. Maybe they killed that sentry to keep him from seeing something. Make sure there's men enough to see anything the sentry would. Then search this place as best you can."

"And you?"

"I'll wait for the duty squad, then somebody's got to tell Lord Rick and the King. Want that job?"

"No. No, the arrangement is satisfactory. Armsman Garrakos, take three companions and torches to search this house. The rest of you, move to surround it." Morrone shuddered. "I like it not, this skulking about in the dark. It makes me feel like an assassin. There can be no honor in it."

"Now there's something we can agree on," Mason said. "But there's not much more in letting the Wanax's guests be slaughtered on the night before his wedding. Steady up, my Lord. I'll be back when I can come."

Morrone sent off a messenger for his men. "Now, Garrakos. Let us go see what we find."

The autumn night was chilly even though the wind had died, but Morrone felt himself sweating under his mail and arming doublet as he had not since the Battle of the Hooey River. "I like it not," he muttered to himself. "An evil omen. I like it not."

Art Mason unbuttoned the flap of his shoulder holster and wished that the nearest tobacco wasn't ten light-years away. There was a kind of aromatic grass that grew in the High Cumac, and some of the troopers made it into cigarettes; Mason had tried it once. The stuff was probably related to madweed. It gave a mild high, nothing like enough to compensate for the awful taste.

Morrone was trying hard not to fidget or look nervous, but you could tell he wasn't too happy over the prospect of somebody's hired goons screwing up his friend's wedding. A lot of people on this planet believed in omens. The sentry was bad enough. If some high muckety-muck did get offed—

"Happened on my watch," Mason muttered. Not that all crime was his responsibility, but this was no burglar caught in the act by the sentry. Thin cord around the man's neck, dagger in just the right place. A professional job. "Damn professional," Mason muttered. "Green Berets?"

It was worth thinking about. Most of the Earth troops here on this screwy planet had some training in the dirty tricks department, and some of them had been Green Beret before the CIA hired them off to go mucking about in Africa.

All our troops are accounted for, Mason thought. But there's a dozen off with Gengrich. Gengrich's ambassador in yonder house. Says no starmen with him. None I recognized. But one could have been smuggled in—

Or, what the hell, there's no shortage of local talent good enough to do that job.

Wish it hadn't happened on my watch.

"Watch ho!" someone called. Mason heard the Outer Gate guards respond. There were sounds of horses and centaurs.

"Who is there?"

Mason couldn't make out the words of the response, but one of the voices sounded familiar. The gate opened, and a smaller number of horses and centaurs came through the wall into the Outer Bailey.

A small mounted party guided by two Guardsmen with torches appeared at the gate end of the street. Five armored men, a couple of unarmored ones, and a banner-bearer carrying the red raven banner of the Bheroman of Westrook.

By God, Mason thought. Ben Murphy. Grown pretty big for a private. Of course I was only a corporal when we came here.

Ben Murphy had defended Castle Westrook and its lands after the Westmen rode down out of the High Plains. When the Westmen killed Lord Harkon and most of his knights, the King had created Murphy a real honest-to-Yatar Drantos nobleman, so that on the local scale of rank he was senior to everybody else from Earth except the Captain himself....

"Hello, Art. How are things?"

"I'll be damned!"

"I hope not." The lead rider reined in, dismounted, and came over to Mason. It was Ben Murphy all right—no mistaking that big Irish nose or the way he walked. But until you got up close and saw the shoulder holster with the .45 in it, you couldn't tell him from your standard Drantos iron-hat.

"Like I said, Art, how are things?"

"Could be worse, could be worse. Everybody and their Aunt Ermentrude's come to town for the wedding, so if you're looking for a billet in the castle—"

"No way. My—Lord Harkon's son Jan's—grandmother wants to look me over, see if I'm the right sort to be raising her daughter's son. She's the Dowager Eqetassa of Rhuinas, so what she wants she gets, and what she's got is everybody I brought with me billeted in her townhouse. The men-at-arms are stacked up like cordwood in the stables, but at least we've got a roof over our heads. I was afraid we'd have to camp outside the walls, along with the Romans. Did Publius really bring a whole legion to the wedding?"

"Two cohorts, under our old friend Titus Frugi."

"Oho. Little Caesar can't be too happy about that."

"No." Titus Frugi had commanded forces loyal to the old emperor. Now he was loyal to Marselius Caesar. Not necessarily to Marselius's son Publius. "No, I don't expect he is. Belay that. How are you getting along?"

"Not too bad, all things considered. The Tamaerthan archers who've settled the vacant farms pretty much make up for the people the Westmen killed. None of them have turned bandit, either."

"Lady Tylara will be happy to hear that. And how's Honeypie—I mean, Lady Dirdre?"

"We're going to be married, soon as I get back from the King's wedding. He's already given permission, but I want to swear fealty to him for Westrook and get an update on the charter before we make it legal. That way Dirdre inherits with no trouble if something happens to me on the way home."

"Yeah. Say, Ben, how many men do you have with you—here and outside the gate?"

"Six here, ten more outside. Why?"

"I got a problem and maybe you can help me solve it.

Somebody killed a sentry just a few minutes ago."

"Blood feud?"

"Looked more like a professional job. Somebody's up to something, and I've got the reserve platoon of Guards on the way. But I'd like some more reliable men on hand before they get here. If you help, I think I can persuade the Captain and the Wanax that they owe you one, like maybe letting you billet some of your people in the castle."

"Sounds all right. Who's in charge?"

Mason jerked his head in Morrone's direction. Murphy frowned, raised his eyebrows, and lowered his voice. "Does he know what he's doing?"

"Close enough. He's got more guts and charm than brains, but he's not one of the real hard-core ironhats."

"Jesus, I hope not. Most of them were out for a short beer when God passed out the brains."

"Sure. Which is how you got your job."

Murphy grinned.

"Anyway. Bring in your men, and I'll pick my escort and go bring the Captain up to speed."

Murphy grinned. "Escort? Come on, Art. You getting nervous in the service? I thought everybody knew by now that tackling an armed starman just gave Graves Registration some business."

"Some people are slow learners, and I'm pretty sure our killer isn't alone. Besides, I'm a great noble now, Lord Mason, Marshal of the Household to the Captain General of the Realm, Major of Guards, Scrubber of the Official Chamberpot of Chelm, and Yatar knows what else. I have to swank around. Hell, Ben, you should know that sort of stuff better than I do."

"Maybe a little. Oh well, it sure beats being stuck on a hill in Africa, with Cubans all around and the only way out a friggin' flying saucer."

"Damned straight."

CHAPTER TWO

Rick's party entered the long corridor leading to the Council chamber. There was a low whistle, then another group came down the stairs to his left. Rick's guards advanced slightly. The leading guards of the other group fell in behind. This group moved down the corridor.

Rick waited. After a moment Tylara came in. Silently she fell in beside him. When she was exactly even with him, they followed the forward guards, while the others merged behind them.

"You are well, my husband?" Tylara said formally.

"I am well. And you?"

"Very well, thank you."

Are you well? Very well. What in God's name has happened to us? Rick wondered. *How long has it been? Weeks. Months.*

He could remember when the sight of her was enough to make his heart leap. *God, she's beautiful, she's still beautiful, and I love her still, but we meet in corridors with guards and witnesses, we speak in formalities, we haven't been alone in weeks.*

When? How did it happen?

After the last campaign. After Les came. After Caradoc was killed in a street riot. Could that be it? Was she in love with Caradoc? Her bodyguard, her captain, her rescuer? She knew him long before she knew me.

No! She had plenty of opportunities with Caradoc, before we met, after we met. She never showed that kind of interest in him. Or anyone else. We were in love, and now we are not in love, and I don't understand it.

"I understand the Wanax will not join us tonight," Tylara said.

"Eh? But the summons to Council—"

"Was withdrawn," Tylara said. "We meet with the Eqeta of the Riverland." She smiled at his puzzled look. "It is an ancient convention. No decisions can be taken if the Wanax is not present. Thus Wanax Ganton chooses to be represented by the Eqeta of the Riverland. Who is of course Ganton."

"Oh. Something of that sort was done on Earth. Perhaps it's as well. I don't know what to recommend anyway."

"Doubtless you will think of something," Tylara said.

And she says that as if she believes it. As if she still believes in me. But she won't sleep with me, won't even see me alone. Now we go in there, and Gwen will be there.

Gwen. Could that be it? Tylara always was afraid of Gwen Tremaine. Could she know about that one time—nonsense. No way. It happened long before—before she started acting funny. And no one knows, except Gwen, and she sure won't tell.

Jamiy, Rick's orderly and chief of guards, rapped on the Council room door. In response to the challenge from inside he answered, "The Lord Rick, Eqeta of Chelm, Captain General of the Host of Drantos, Lord of Star Lords."

Rick glanced at Tylara. She winked.

So she still has a sense of humor. And knows I do. So what in God's Name is wrong?

Gwen Tremaine finished her presentation and waited while the young man at the head of the long table stared at the map on the whitewashed wall. Finally he spoke.

"Then is there no hope for us, or at least no more than there was before the starmen came? Have they in fact shed so much blood only to put us in greater peril of *skyfire* than we were before?"

Rick frowned. Who'd been talking to the king? Ganton had every damn reason in the world to be grateful to Rick

Galloway and his troops, and why was he taking that tone? Rick was about to speak when Tylara laid her hand lightly on his arm. "She speaks. Let her," Tylara whispered.

Feminism? Not hardly. Or does she hope Gwen will stumble? Damn. I used to understand Tylara. Not now.

The others waited expectantly as Gwen paused to marshal her thoughts.

She had painted a grim picture of the future. The dwarf sun that everyone on Tran called the Demon Star was approaching. At perigee it would add more than ten percent to the planet's illuminance. That didn't sound like much, but it was enough. Ice caps would melt. Weather and climate would change, and all for the worse.

And now it was all happening. The seas were rising, and the southern zones of this hemisphere were hot. Drought there. Rain here. Floods everywhere. Tribes, whole nations and populations fled northward....

Rick saw that Tylara wasn't the only one staring at Gwen Tremaine. She'd told them the worst. Now the entire Inner Council waited for her to give them some shred of hope.

Yanulf, Highpriest of Yatar and Chancellor of Drantos, sat impassively. Nothing Gwen had said would surprise him. The Yatar hierarchy had preserved the legends of previous visits of the rogue star. They knew what the Time would bring, and wanted only to prepare for it. So long as the ice caves were filled with grain and other food, Yanulf would be happy.

Sergeant Major Elliot. Career soldier, U.S. Army, on loan to the CIA for an African adventure. Now a long way from home. Trustworthy, Rick thought. So long as I don't screw up. But his loyalty's to the outfit, not to any individual. And if push came to shove, as many of the mercs would take his orders as they would mine.

Warrant Officer Larry Warner. They called him Professor when he was a private. Now he was Chancellor of the University, and a good job he was doing. Gwen as Rector, Warner as Chancellor, and they were teaching the locals everything from the calculus to how to make paper and soap. With luck, knowledge would be spread so wide this time that nothing the damn Demon Star could do would stop it.

Lucius, in theory no more than Marselius Caesar's freedman. Lucius had been tutor to Marselius's son Publius, and every Roman Senator had heard the old scholar referred to as Caesar's oldest friend. A delegation of Senators had been sent as the formal representatives of Rome. Perhaps some of them believed Caesar read their dispatches with as much attention as he gave Lucius. Perhaps.

And the others. All waiting, like the young king, for Gwen to say what good would come from this alliance with the starmen.

Gwen swallowed and brushed back into place a few blond curls that had escaped from her wimple. In her Gown of Office she looked remarkably like an old-fashioned nun—a misleading impression if there ever was one—

And that was no safe thought, not with Tylara sitting right beside him!

"Your—my Lord Count," Gwen began. "I know you speak in anger and grief for those of your subjects you will not be able to save from the Time. Yet in truth much has already been done that will make this Time different from all those before."

Sure, Rick thought. Different. Provided that Les was reading Agzaral right, and Agzaral knew what he was doing, and the crazy-quilt union of races that governed this end of the galaxy didn't decide to take matters into its own hands. And a lot of other ifs. We can't talk about any of that here.

"Tell of this," Yanulf said.

"Blunt bastard," Rick whispered. Tylara touched his hand with dagger-sharp nails.

"The servants of Yatar have ever foretold of the Time," Yanulf said. "Often have we been ignored. It is well that as this Time approaches all believe us. But how else will the Time be different from the past? What has been done?"

"Much for this Realm," Gwen said. "The starmen's

weapons and knowledge of war have saved this Realm. Not once only. The Lord Rick has cast down in succession Sarakos the Usurper, Flaminius Caesar the Dotard, and the Westmen. Drantos itself survives because of them."

Yeah, Rick thought, but what have we done for them lately?

"And there is more. There is knowledge," Gwen said. "They have taught the servants of Yatar the skills to heal the sick and wounded."

Yanulf nodded sagely. He hadn't known of the small devils that lived in septic conditions, which could be killed by boiling and ritual cleanliness. The knowledge made the priest healers enormously more effective.

At a cost, Rick thought. Yatar heals, Vothan the Chooser of the Slain takes fewer guests to his hall. The Vothan cult has no great reason to love us—

"And with the balloon they have made accurate maps where there were none before, maps that even the Romans envy. Iron plows turn the earth deeper, increasing yields, so that there is more to store in the Caves of the Preserver. There is paper, for records, so that the knowledge of the Time will be preserved, and the Wanax can know all that is known about his Realm. With the new healing knowledge, fewer wounds fester and fewer mothers die in childbirth, so that the number of His Majesty's subjects increases.

"My lord, the starmen are not gods. They do not claim the powers of gods. Yet they have much power, and all that they have has been freely used in the service of the Wanax and the Realm of Drantos. Much has been done. There will be more."

Someone shouted in the courtyard below. Ganton glanced at the window, then back at Rick.

"You speak well," Ganton said. "I am certain that the Wanax knows of his indebtedness to the Star Lords. Yet he also has obligations to his barons. And to all his subjects."

Rick looked to Tylara and got an answering nod. So that's it. The bheromen always did resent us. Ganton's father lost his throne when the barons deserted him. Ganton won't make that mistake. Meaning that we'd better be more careful than I thought.

"I know this," Gwen was saying. "I have told you what I know. Now the Captain General should speak."

Damn Gwen, Rick thought. *She could have given me a little warning.*

As he took the pointer from Gwen, he caught a whiff of her perfume. It was the same herbal essence she'd been wearing the day—no time to think of that. He glanced nervously at Tylara.

Begin with what they know. No matter that Gwen just told them. Tell them again. If enough of us tell them often enough, maybe they'll believe it. Maybe I'll believe it.

Tran was a planet in a triple-star system, consisting of the True Sun, the more distant Firestealer, and the Demon Star. Every six hundred Terran years—the Tran year was 1.7 of those—the Demon Star's eccentric orbit carried it close enough to Tran to affect the climate. For the two years of closest approach there would be few crops harvested.

But. As the Demon Star approached, the warmer weather did some good. In the years before closest approach crops were better, growing seasons longer. There was another effect. The increased sunlight made the plant the locals called madweed grow very well indeed—and madweed was much in demand as a recreational drug in interstellar trade. "Tran Natural" commanded an excellent price, and the *Shalnuksi* merchant adventurers had a monopoly on it, so long as they could get kidnapped human soldiers to collect it for them.

And they've been doing that for three thousand years I know of, and Gwen says more like five. The *Shalnuksis* had brought in Achaean Bronze Age warriors. Romans from the time of Septimius Severus, and again from the Byzantine period. Franks. Celts. Scythians. Cultures mixed together, and none allowed to develop, because as soon as Tran threatened to become civilized the *Shalnuksis* bombed them back into a new Dark Age.

Not this time. Damn all, not this time! They can destroy technology, but we'll spread something more powerful than technology. We'll teach the scientific method. They can't bomb that out! Only we have to live through the next few years.

That wouldn't be easy. If anything, it was going to be worse than Gwen's lecture indicated—and that was worse than any of them except Yanulf had expected.

The rising seas would swallow most of the coastal cities, adding their people to the hordes of refugees already heading north. Storms and tsunamis like the one that had already mangled Rustengo's waterfront would scour the coastal areas. Tylara's homeland of Tamaerthon would become a rocky island. Rome would be reduced to the highlands, which could only support a fraction of its people. The Romans were well organized, but no organization could make a single ton of grain feed a thousand people for two years.

What Tran needed was the miracle of the loaves and the fishes. How fast did fish grow here? Weather changes would stir the water. Nutrients should upwell from the sea bottom. Ocean plant life would bloom. How long before the fish population rose significantly, and could anyone take advantage of that? Another task for the University.

"I see two choices," Rick began. "Both involve the Five Kingdoms. Drantos is inland. There will be flooding, but not so bad as in the coastal regions. Still, we will have famine, and there will be refugees from the south. Hordes of them, some well armed and desperate. We will need armies to hold them out lest they eat everything we have.

"Famine and border war will weaken our army. The High Rexja of the Five Kingdoms has already invaded Drantos and nearly unseated our Wanax Ganton. Had his son Sarakos been more concerned with rule than destruction, Drantos might today be one of the Six Kingdoms."

Ganton frowned. "I think I would not care to remind the Wanax Ganton of too many painful matters."

Rick shrugged. "Yet these things must be said. The High Rexja has not given up his claim to Drantos. In the early years of the Time his lands will have better crops as ours have worse. We stand as his defense against the refugees—"

"Give them safe passage to the north," Tylara said.

"If we could. But they would have to be fed and transported at a time when we will have little food for our own men and horses. I do not think it possible." Rick spread his hands. "Eventually Toris or his ministers will realize that Drantos is his for the taking, and come south with an army."

"Star weapons," Ganton said.

"Star weapons," Rick agreed. "But never enough. I have fewer than a score of starmen. We will never have more. I have little enough ammunition for our weapons. We can get more of that, but to do so we must continue to grow and harvest the madweed. That takes great effort—"

"More than you know," Yanulf said. "Slaves and convicts to grow the crops. Cavalry to guard the slaves so they do not run away."

As I would, if I could. Growing and harvesting that stuff is the worst work in the world.

"Soldiers to watch the guards, men and wagons to bring in the food for slaves and their guards and soldiers. And those who grow the food and bring it must themselves be fed."

He's learned well. "Precisely," Rick said. "But we have no choice regarding madweed. If the—great Star Lords—do not get the madweed they want, not only will they cease to bring us tools and ammunition, they may well throw *skyfire* in their anger."

"So we are told," Yanulf said. "A tale I believe. We have temple records, and everyone has heard how dangerous it is to deal with the demon gods who come with the Demon Star."

"You say, then, that they will grow stronger as Drantos grows weaker," Ganton said.

"Yes."

"And two choices."

"Yes. Either we invade the Five Kingdoms now, or we make peace with them now."

"It is not time to talk of war," Yanulf said. "The Time approaches. We must have peace."

"Yet an alliance of Rome and Drantos might take the Five," Ganton said. "If Drantos will grow weaker during the Time, will not Rome be harmed more? With lowland fields flooded—will not many Romans need shelter, here and wherever we can find food for them?"

"It would be well to have that choice," Lucius said. "My Lord Marshal, you have said there are two choices, but you have not said which you favor."

"Peace," Rick said. "The gods themselves conspire to bring death and destruction. Should we add more?"

"Well said." Yanulf nodded approval. "Well said."

And Lord knows if we do march into the Five we'll leave enough devastation in our wake. Tran armies live off the land, and discipline means they only rape the women.

The north is the right place to be at the height of the Time. And it's better to trade than fight. Trade iron, war-horses, maybe eventually gunpowder, for food. Teach the High Rexja how to set up his own University and send a cadre of people to help. Try to turn the High Rexja into an ally, instead of an enemy to be fended off or destroyed....

"Can we make peace?" Ganton demanded.

"We can send a reliable commission to try."

"Nothing else?" said the Wanax/Count.

"At this time, no," Rick replied. "We do not wish to appear too eager. That would make the High Rexja suspect that we were weak or fearful."

"Since we are neither, why should the Wanax not wish to put forward his own claim to the High Throne?" said Ganton. "His grandfather's sister was wife to Toris, and because of this Sarakos put forward his claim to the throne of Drantos. Why should not such a claim travel north as well as south?"

"Because making it would mean yet another war," growled Yanulf. "The Time approaches, with the gods only know what perils and horrors yet unrevealed, and this Council would advise the Wanax to throw away blood and treasure on a petty dynastic quarrel!"

"If it gives us the land that it seems we shall most surely need, how can it be petty?" said Ganton.

"We might lose," Yanulf said. "If we can gain what we need in peace, can any cause be great enough to be worth yet another war? We must certainly send an army south to deal with those fleeing toward the city-states. We are certain to hear more from the Westmen. Will we advise His Majesty to the folly of new wars when the old ones may not yet be done?"

"That may be wisdom," Ganton said. "What say our Roman allies?"

"I do not think that the High Rexja will give us more than a pittance, without our paying a price greater than we can afford."

"Greater than another war?" muttered Yanulf.

"More than likely," said Lucius. "Toris may have given no further offense, but neither has he made peace. If he sincerely wished it, he could have had it anytime during the past year."

Ganton looked thoughtful. "True. If an offer had been made we—the Wanax would have put it before the Council. None was made, yet we have no further quarrel with the High Rexja."

"As I thought." Lucius spread his hands. "Then it seems most likely that the High Rexja only wishes to choose his own time for avenging Sarakos. Why should the Wanax wait for the blow to fall, rather than unsheathing his own sword and ending the menace of the Five Kingdoms at a blow?"

Not at a blow. And what's your game, anyway? Rick wondered. One guess: peace between the High Rexja and Drantos might turn into an alliance. Would turn into an alliance, if Rick gave the Five Kingdoms any star wisdom, let alone a University. That was an alliance that could turn against Rome—and for all that Lucius was trustworthy enough to be sitting on the Inner Council, he was still friend and counselor to Marselius Caesar.

Marselius was growing old, his son Publius was a good soldier but had more than his share of enemies. Ganton had been hailed by a Roman legion as "Imperator"—worthy to command Romans—and was about to marry Caesar's granddaughter.

An alliance with the Five Kingdoms could tempt the Wanax of Drantos to the purple, unleashing another civil war on Rome with the Time closer than ever. A war between Toris and Drantos, on the other hand, could keep Rome's two most formidable rivals chewing on each other for long enough to let Marselius put things in order. Perhaps long enough for Marselius to retire in favor of Publius.

You knew Lucius wouldn't give disinterested advice. Disinterested be damned, is it good?

Rick turned that question over in his mind as the debate went around the table. Lucius was pro-war. Yanulf of course was against it. So were Gwen and Warner, although the Professor seemed rather lukewarm for peace. Why? Warner liked his post at the University. What else did he want?

Another question they never raised in ROTC classes on leadership, and one with no answer for now.

Elliot was in favor of war, as long as they first settled accounts with Gengrich and the rest of the mutineers who were still in the south. Rick had the feeling that Elliot didn't much care whether that settlement left Gengrich and his men alive or not. The Sergeant Major was loyal to Rick and his plans and knew Gengrich's ten men might make a difference in carrying them out. He was also too good an NCO to be very happy about depending on men who'd already mutinied once. In his books they couldn't be trusted not to do it again.

Tylara was blunt. "It will take more than one defeat to make Toris give up the idea of taking our lands. Every High King for two centuries has known that Drantos and Chelm were once a sixth Kingdom, and dreamed of making it one again."

"Toris is old and by all reports feeble," said Yanulf. "Will such a man do more than dream? Will he not rather concern himself with assuring the peaceful succession of his last surviving son, Prince Akkilas?"

"He will best assure that by taking Drantos and avenging Sarakos," said Tylara. "His eqetas and bheromen will not swallow their defeat forever. If Akkilas comes to the High Throne as the Conqueror of Drantos, his way will be easy. If not, the warriors of the Five Kingdoms may turn to one who will give them that victory. There is Prince Strymon, heir to Ta-Meltemos, and he is only the most formidable out of several captains."

"War now. Peace now," Ganton said. "Can we win if we strike now? How much aid will Rome give us?"

He's forgotten the myth about being Count of the North or whatever. That's the King talking, and a nervous one at that. And what the hell's keeping Art?

"I can convey a request to Caesar," Lucius said smoothly. "But I cannot make promises—"

"Convenient enough," Tylara said.

"But what shall we do?" Ganton demanded.

"Send commissioners to Toris," Rick said. "And others to Rome. After tomorrow it should be more difficult for Caesar to refuse a request from our Wanax."

"He cannot honor a request for soldiers he does not have," Yanulf said. "Rome must look to the south. As must we."

And that's for sure. Plenty of danger there. Not only the hordes of refugees. There were also rumors of a fanatical religious leader, who was welding the horde into a crusade against the new idea of Christ as the Son of Yatar. Rick hoped the rumors were just that; religious warfare was one ingredient the Tran stew didn't need.

"There is another thing," Warner said.

"Yes?"

"By all reports, the Westmen are marching north as they agreed, after the Wanax's great victory at the Hooey River."

"True enough," Rick said.

"I'd guess they'll bounce off Margilos and head right into the Five Kingdoms. Toris can probably beat them, but I bet it'll take a year to drive them out."

"A year in which the Five do not become stronger," Tylara said thoughtfully. "This is welcome news. We have, then, a year—"

There was a knock at the door.

Elliot got up with a frown. He came back to stand next to Rick. "Beg pardon, Colonel. Art Mason's outside. Wants to talk to you. Seems like there's trouble in the Outer Castle."

"What kind of trouble?"

"Assassins. One sentry's dead already. He's alerted the ready platoon and Ben Murphy's on hand with a bunch of his men."

"Good. Who'd he leave in command?"

"Morrone."

"Oh, crap."

"Yeah."

"I better go look. We're not going to decide anything here anyway."

And Tylara won't care where I am. God, what happened to us?

CHAPTER THREE

"Okay, Art, what is it?"

"Damfino. Look, Colonel, I wouldn't have called you but you said I should if I didn't know what's going on—"

"And?"

"And I don't. There's a dead sentry. Professional job of killing him. Too damn professional to be a blood feud. But we've looked, and we can't find one damn thing."

"Looked. Looked where?"

"Well, you know, all around out there. It's the Outer Bailey, it's a warren. Nobody ever found anybody in that place. Look, you wanted me to tell you what's happening. I did. Now get back to your meeting. I can handle it."

"Sure you can, but I'm damned sick of meetings. Let's go look."

"Well—I guess I got enough troops."

Rick laughed. "Art, if we don't have enough firepower between us to handle anything this bunch of primitives can throw at us—"

"Primitives."

Okay, so I don't talk that way usually. So I'm getting sick of some of the Mickey Mouse crap. "Let's go look."

"Whose quarters?" Rick demanded.

"Nobody yet," Mason said. "Not this house. But over there is Daettan of Dirstvaal, and over there is the place Gwen and Warner share—"

"Eh?"

"Gwen and Warner. And some of the other University people."

"Who's in there now?"

"Hell, Colonel, I don't know. Their people I suppose—"

"Let's go check."

"Eh?"

"Call it a hunch." *Call it that Tylara's acting funny, and she's scared of Gwen, but I'm damned if I'll tell you that.* "Let's look."

"Okay. Lugh."

"Sir."

"Take some troops around back of that house. Lord Rick and I are going to search it."

Lugh's eyes widened slightly, then he grinned. "Sir."

"Don't think anybody but us could get away with looking into *her* place," Mason said.

"Rog. Maybe not even us. But here goes." Rick waited until Lugh and his Guardsmen had deployed around the house. "Okay."

Mason banged on the door. "Open in the name of the Guard."

He waited and banged again. "Nobody home."

Rick lowered his voice. "Bullshit. She's got half a dozen servants. So does Warner. Somebody's in there to unbolt the door."

Mason whistled, low. "Sumbitch. Goddam, Cap'n, you're right. So what do we do?"

"Knock one more time and we act like we're going away."

"Right—" Mason pounded once more. "Nobody home," he said loudly. "Let's go—"

They walked around the corner of the vacant house. The dead sentry still lay there, now covered with some Guardsman's cloak. "Sir?" Mason said.

"First. Get five mercs back to the Council room, and nobody leaves there until I get back. Nobody. Alert your Guardsmen and have them take over the corridors, but when I get back to that chamber I want Elliot and the troops with rounds chambered."

Mason nodded slowly. "You sure—"

"Who gives a shit about sure? Better to be ready and not need it—"

"Sir."

"And who the hell did you send down here to take charge? Not Morrone—"

Mason looked pained. "No, sir. Murphy held the fort until I could get Henderson. He's in back—"

"Right. Get him over here and get on your way."

Rick watched Mason go around the house. *It's probably all bat turds. But suppose it's not?*

"Colonel?"

"Right. Henderson, go get me one of the Daughters of Yatar. In full robes. A short one."

"Sir?" Corporal Henderson frowned. "Uh, Colonel—"

Rick consulted the papers Mason had left him and pointed. "Down there. That house. There ought to be a dozen of them. I just want one. Get a couple of footmen while you're at it. And don't forget, a short Daughter of Yatar, in robes."

"Sir? Yes, sir." Henderson bolted off. Rick chuckled to himself.

"Okay, here's the drill," Rick said. "My Lady Iris walks behind the troops. Lady Gwen copied her robes of office from the Daughters of Yatar. In this light nobody's going to know it's not Gwen come back from Council. You two footmen, go up, bang on the door, and shout to open in the name of the Lady Rector. Then get the hell out of the way."

The footmen glanced at him nervously. Then they looked at the squad of determined Guardsmen and Star Lords, and looked resigned.

"If anything happens"—he turned to Lady Iris—"anything at all, forget your dignity and get the hell behind somebody and stay there."

"Certainly. I take it you do not mind if I pray?"

Rick looked at her closely and laughed. "For all of us, if it please your ladyship. Okay, troops. Let's do it. And remember. We want live ones."

The footmen went to the door and knocked. "Open for the Lady Rector."

For a moment nothing happened, then a light flared inside the house. Shutters above the door opened, and a torch was thrust out. A muffled voice shouted, "My lady!" and the shutters closed again.

So. There is someone in there. He waited until he heard the door unbolted. It seemed to take forever, then it opened. He dashed forward and threw himself against it. "Inside! Move!" he shouted. He felt the door slam into whoever had opened it.

That one's out of action. He left him for the followers and dashed to the next room. Rick heard motion and whirled. Somone had been standing at the doorway and had swung a bludgeon at him. "Stand!" The man raised the club.

Rick lowered his aim point and fired at the groin. The .45 flared in the dark, and the man doubled over. *That's two. How many?* He moved on through the room. The last room was the kitchen, and it was empty.

Behind him his troops poured into the house. "Gotcha!" Henderson shouted.

That's that one. Rick found the stairs. *They'll be alerted and ready. I should wait for troops. Or burn the place and be done with it. We've got two, and both will live long enough to answer questions.*

And you're a track star.

This is stupid. He darted up the stairs. At the top he continued, but kept low, diving across the floor to hit and roll. Two figures loomed behind him.

Rick fired once between them. "Move and get your testicles shot off."

Everything froze for a moment. Henderson and the others were running up the stairs. Then one of the men turned—

Rick moved without thought, diving into the man, knocking his outstretched arm up. Three gunshots thundered in the enclosed space. Henderson and his troops came fast. There was another shot, and one of the Guardsmen fell. Henderson threw Rick's opponent against the wall. Someone swung a club and the other enemy went down.

A torchbearer climbed the stairs. Long before he got to the top Rick looked at his prisoner, nodded, and said, "Private Rand, I believe—"

"You can talk to me, or the royal executioners. Just one thing. Once I turn you over to them, I can't get you back."

"Hell, Captain, I'll talk to you. Just give me a second to catch my breath."

Harvey Rand didn't look much like a Star Lord. He was bearded like most Tran nobles. His clothes were the remnants of Tran finery, but they had seen much better days.

Rick fingered the Walther PPK they'd taken from him. It was clean and well greased. "How much ammo does Gengrich have left?"

"Not a lot, but he don't tell me—"

"Mason, maybe you better alert the executioner."

"Captain, damn it, I'll tell you what I know!" Rand shouted. "You don't want me to make things up—"

"Don't," Mason said.

"So what were you doing here?" Rick demanded.

Rand looked resigned. "Trying to—look, it was a snatch job. Kidnap the lady that runs the University."

"Gwen Tremaine. Why?"

"Look, can I have a drink?"

"Sure." Rick gestured to Mason. "And have a seat." He indicated the bench beside the oak table. "Just remember, my office is a hell of a lot more comfortable than where they'll take you if I get tired of listening. Now what's all this about?"

"Arnie wants to come in."

"Good. We want him. What's that got to do with Gwen Tremaine?"

"What do we come in as?" Rand asked. "Not just us. Our friends. Wives. Relatives. There's a lot of us."

"And Gwen?" Rick kept his voice deceptively calm.

"Bargaining chip. Figured if we had her you'd listen while we talked status."

Rick's orderly came in with a pitcher of wine and goblets.

Rick poured three. Mason shook his head and stood in the corner. "I'll pass."

"Christ, Art, you don't have to worry about me," Rand said.

"It's Major Mason."

"Well smell—yes, sir. Major Mason."

"And don't play games, Rand." Art Mason sounded tired. "Bargaining chips are fine, but who did you mean to bargain with?"

Rand looked scared.

"Thought so. Colonel, they want to grow goddam madweed and sell it direct."

"Cut out the middlemen, so to speak," Rick said. "That true, Rand?"

Rand gulped wine. "Yes, sir."

"What made you think it would work?"

"We—"

"Who?" Mason demanded. "One of my troops?"

"I don't know—"

"Bull shit. You've got a spy in the University. Right in Lady Gwen's office, probably," Mason said. "That's one of mine, and I want the son of a bitch dead. If I can't have him I'll take your balls to make a purse out of."

"Damn it Major, I don't know! Gengrich knows, but I don't."

"And he sent you—"

"No."

Mason started to say something, but Rick gestured him to silence. "What do you mean, no?"

"Gengrich don't know nothing about this."

"I think you'd better explain."

"I'm trying to! Look, we're all in the same racket, right? Only you're doing better than the rest of us. But we're all in the same damn boat."

"On the same planet," Rick said. "So?"

"Captain, we never deserted from you. After Parsons ran you off, we ducked out on him. By the time you were back in charge we had things going down south. Now you get stuff from that flying saucer, and we get dick. Damn it, that ain't fair."

Mason snorted.

"Well, okay, Ar—Major. You ducked out with Captain Galloway. Smart move. We cut cards on that. Remember?"

"Damn all. He's right, Colonel. I forgot. Rand was one of them that volunteered to go with you, only Elliot wouldn't let but one go."

"Okay. How does that change things? Who the hell are you working for?"

"Some locals. Daettan of Dinstvaal."

"Gengrich's ambassador."

"Well, yeah, only—look, Colonel, there's a lot of them. Locals. They're scared. They figured if they had Gwen, they'd have a chance. We could trade her to Gengrich. Or you. Or something."

"In other words," Mason said, "Gengrich is running out of ammo, has a lot of locals mixed in with his troops, and ain't got a pot to piss in."

"Pretty close," Rand said.

"And he didn't approve this operation."

"Christ no! But he does want to talk."

"Right. Mason, take over. I'd better get back to the meeting."

"What do I do with this one?"

"Damn it—Major—I got a name and you know it. Look, okay, it was a fool stunt and we lost, but I got a right to hire out. Don't I? What the hell am I supposed to do in this stinking place?"

Good question. "Just talk to him, Art. Hang in there, Rand. We'll think of something."

Rick left the office. A dozen Guardsmen fell in around him as he went down the corridor to the Council chamber.

Clavell and Beazeley stood outside the Council chamber door. Both held battle rifles. A dozen Guardsmen with drawn swords were with them.

"Alert's over," Rick said. "We got them. Remember Rand?"

"Harv Rand," Clavell said. "Yeah, he was in my squad back in Africa. Good man with a garotte."

"Too good for one of our sentries." Rick spoke in English too rapid for any local to understand. "Anyway, we got him. And the others. You can stand down."

"Yes, sir."

Inside the chamber things looked about the same—except that Elliot, Warner, and Gwen all had pistols lying on the table. Ganton's Browning was still in its holster, but the strap was undone.

Rick glanced at Tylara. No weapon in sight. But her right hand was in her left sleeve....

Larry Warner was reading from a long document. After a moment it was obvious what it was. The official history of the coming of the starmen.

"Alert's over," Rick said.

"You say no more than that?" Ganton demanded.

"No more to say, my Lord Count. Some thieves attempted to rob the house assigned to the Lady Gwen. They have been captured. Two Guardsmen were killed, and one wounded." *That'll do for now.* "If you'll continue, my lord?" Rick gestured to Warner.

"Yes, sir."

Warner read with animation. In ten minutes he had killed Sarakos in a village boobytrapped with a ton of gunpowder, married off Rick and Tylara, delivered their daughter Isobel, and was starting on Marselius Caesar's rebellion.

Not really rebellion. After our raids into Marselius's prefecture he could either revolt or let Flaminius the Dotard kill him. Not much choice there.

"So Marselius Caesar, Tamaerthon, and the Realm of Drantos became allies against Flaminius. Their host marched into the Dotard's land and fought a great battle against the Romans under the Legate Titus Licinius Frugi. The Romans fought gallantly, but to no avail against the star weapons, the balloon, and the valor of the men of Drantos and Tamaerthon. A wise captain, Titus Licinius Frugi yielded to save his men, and thus ended the Roman civil war."

Ganton smiled. "I see that Lord Rick follows the custom of Drantos, and does not boast of his deeds. The tale of that battle passes over his capturing Titus Frugi with his own hands."

"It is enough that you know, your—my Lord Count."

After the Roman alliance came Bishop Polycarp's vision. One night he had dreamed that Yatar came to him and proclaimed that Christ was His Only Begotten Son, borne of Hestia, who had taken the form of a mortal woman. So the followers of Yatar and the followers of Christ should be as brothers to one another.

For some people on both sides the vision came as a blessing; there was a real "ecumenical movement" growing up on both sides. For others it was like throwing a hand grenade into the middle of a cocktail party. There were the rumors about that madman in the south, and the priests of Vothan hadn't been heard from yet. Rick didn't like to think about what the priests would have to say.

The rest of the story was mostly the campaign against the Westmen, ending in Ganton's great victory at the Hooey River and the withdrawal of the Westmen to the north. After that came a note on Caradoc's death in a riot, another on the betrothal of Ganton to Octavia Caesar (who'd come to Drantos as a hostage but would remain as a queen), and a wish that Yatar and Christ His Son might bless all who read these words.

Rick led a round of applause.

Warner had the grace to blush. "Thank you, my lords and ladies. Does this mean I can put the scribes on to making copies?"

Ganton nodded. "Speaking for the Wanax, I say yes. I am sure he will want as many of the wedding guests as possible to carry away this wisdom when they depart."

How many of them would call it wisdom and how many would call it heresy, God (any or all, take your pick) only knew, but they had to start somewhere. In fact, Rick wondered if that might not be a good, if unofficial, motto for the House of Galloway—"You have to start somewhere."

Lucius dipped his gull-feather pen in the ink and continued writing. No doubt the young men learning to write now would find the new iron-tipped pens child's play, but he was too old a dog to learn new tricks.

Also a rather weary one, with little hope of getting a decent night's sleep before the wedding. The Demon Star was already sinking toward the hills beyond the Roman camp, the wedding would begin shortly after noon, and yet this letter to Marselius had to be completed before he could rest.

> The Lord Rick told the Council that thieves invaded the University. They could be no ordinary thieves. My agent with the Guardsmen tells me that one of these thieves had a star weapon, and spoke in a strange language with the Lord Rick. The man was of the party sent by the Star Lord Gengrich. We may be safe in assuming this was no ordinary robbery attempt. I could speculate on the real purpose, but my guesses will be no better than yours.
>
> Could there be opportunity here? It may be that Lord Gengrich would welcome new allies. Certainly we could use assistance in recovering the lost southern provinces, and Gengrich is there.
>
> It was the Wanax's wish that Lady Octavia be told of the night's events at once. He grew angry at the suggestion that she might not bear the news well, saying that it was to insult his bride and Caesar's House to suggest she lacked the courage to hear bad news.
>
> It fell to me to be the news-bringer. Lady Cyra, chief among Octavia's new Drantos attendants, attempted to bar my path until I had given her the message, which I was strictly instructed to bring only to Octavia's ears. When Octavia did appear, Lady Cyra refused to depart, and only force could have moved her.

When I gave the news to Octavia, Lady Cyra screamed aloud and flew into a great passion, crying that it was an evil omen for the Wanax's marriage. Lady Octavia flew into as great a rage as I have ever seen in her, and said that Lady Cyra was a fool. It was a very good omen, that those loyal to the throne of Drantos could so easily defeat an attack by one of its enemies. She would pray to Christ and his Father Yatar that the throne should face no worse enemies in the years to come.

She then asked if the dead Guardsmen had wives or children. When told that one had a daughter of three and a second child to be born in midwinter, she swore before Yatar, Christ, Hestia, and all the saints to provide the daughter with a dowry when she came of age and to stand godmother to the unborn child.

This silenced Lady Cyra, a feat I had thought impossible. With her present I could not linger, but I assure you that I have never in my life felt so proud of Octavia.

I do not know if Lady Cyra is naturally lacking in good sense or seeks to wield power over the Lady Octavia. I also do not know if such a desire is her own, or given to her by her husband Bheroman Kilantis. He is a leader among those lords who swore oath to Sarakos and were afterward pardoned. Not a few of those are less than pleased with the Roman alliance; they fear that a Wanax of Drantos with legions at his command may seek to rule without the consent of his nobles and knights, in the manner of a Caesar. The fear is all the greater, because Ganton's father Loron did exactly that, and so brought much suffering to Drantos.

And it is time you bring this letter to a close, Lucius! You are telling Caesar things that he already knows. Next, you will be telling him that his son Publius does not much care to have Titus Frugi commanding the cohorts charged with his safety at the wedding....

Lucius spread sand on the parchment, shook it off, rolled the parchment into a wooden cylinder, and sealed it. Then he stamped the still-soft wax with his signet and rang for a messenger.

CHAPTER FOUR

Archbishop Polycarp wore his pearl-studded mitre and his robes of cloth-of-gold. Highpriest Yanulf wore his robes of blue *garta* cloth and carried his great silver staff set with Father's Eyes. To Apelles, neither priest appeared half as splendid as the royal couple kneeling before them.

The Wanax Ganton wore his finest robes under a cloak of ermine and the Great Crown of Drantos. Its rubies and amber threw back the light from the hundreds of candles blazing around the altar, until it seemed that the Wanax wore a crown of flame.

Lady Octavia was dressed more in the Roman style, with a mantle of cream-colored *garta* trimmed with gold over a bronze-hued gown of the finest linen trimmed with pearls. She also wore a veil hanging from a circlet of silver flowers, in the manner of the women of the skyfolk. At the end of the ceremony, the Wanax would lift that veil to kiss his bride.

Apelles knew this and many more details of the royal wedding, down to the very undergarments the Wanaxxae would be wearing on this day. As Yanulf's right hand, he had been set to more labors than Hercules in the matter of the wedding.

Once he had ventured to ask, "I know that the Lord Publius Caesar has no living wife and that his sister is not well enough to make such a long journey so late in the year. Yet could not much of what has fallen to me have been done as well by the Eqetassa of Chelm or the Lady Cyra?"

"Lady Tylara will be chief among the bride's attendants at the wedding," Yanulf had replied. "Until then, her duties as

Justiciar of Drantos and mistress of the Captain General's household will prevent her from doing as much as I am sure she would wish to do.

"As for Lady Cyra, she too has much to occupy her in the Lady Octavia's household. Also, she knows little of Roman customs and might give offense without meaning it."

It was then and remained now Apelles' opinion that Lady Cyra knew a great deal about Roman customs and was utterly opposed to seeing any of them introduced into the Court of Drantos. The Chancellor's tone of voice had spoken whole scrolls about the unwisdom of saying this aloud.

At least his labors had obtained for Apelles a good place in the hall, into which half the Realm seemed to have crowded and in which half the Realm had certainly sought places. The only people closer to the altar than the row in which Apelles stood were the attendants of the bride and groom and the Guardsmen double-ranked across the hall between the altar and the guests. *A long way for a swineherd to come.*

Incense rose in a cloud. So did Polycarp's thin voice.

"Dearly beloved, we are gathered here today in the sight of Yatar Dayfather, Christ His Son, Holy Hestia the Mother of Christ, and this noble congregation, to join this man and this woman in Holy Matrimony, which is an honorable estate—"

Apelles felt someone prodding him in the ribs. The dignity of the occasion kept him from prodding back. Instead he turned his head as far as he could, to see Eyan son of Fnor, the Guardsman assigned him as a messenger. At least that was Yanulf's tale; after seeing how many other "messengers" were scattered through the crowd, Apelles suspected they were really there to keep watch on those guests out of sight or reach of the Guards before the altar.

"What of Vothan?" Eyan muttered. "I like not this casting out of the Warlord."

"What casting out?" said Apelles. "It is written, that when the Christ was upon Earth, he said, 'I come to bring not peace, but a sword.' Who else would say that, but Vothan? It is also written that he was hung upon a cross and seemed to die, yet rose again wiser than before. Is that not also said of Vothan?"

"They also call the Christ 'Prince of Peace,'" said Eyan.

"Has this ever kept the Romans from fighting?" replied Apelles. "Or made them fight less fiercely when they marched against us?" Eyan shook his head with a wry grin.

"Even the starmen are Christians," Apelles went on. "And do they not enjoy the blessings of Vothan?"

"The starmen are Christians?" Eyan frowned.

"Yes, and from his first day in our land the Lord Rick has always honored Yatar and Vothan as well as Christ."

"That is true," said Eyan slowly. He seemed to want to say more, but Apelles saw the looks their whispered conversation was beginning to draw. He waved the Guardsman to silence.

Very likely he had awakened as many doubts in the man as he'd laid to rest. Not just in Eyan. *I am no warrior, but it would be a harsh world indeed if brave men had no hope of guesting with One-Eyed Vothan after dying in battle.*

Polycarp droned on. "—but reverently, discreetly, soberly, and in the fear of Yatar and Christ, duly considering the causes for which matrimony was ordained.

"First, It was ordained for the increase of mankind, according to the will of Yatar and Christ, and that children might be brought up in the fear and nurture of Them, and to the praise of Their Holy names...."

Tylara shifted restlessly.

"Thirdly, it was ordained for the mutual society, help, and comfort, that the one ought to have of the other, both in prosperity and adversity.

"Into which holy estate, these two persons present come now to be joined..."

If the Lady Gwen had not been standing close beside her, Tylara would have shut her eyes. *That is as it should be. As it was. And I have forfeited the love of the gods, and worse, of my husband.*

I have betrayed them all. Yet what could I have done?

The thoughts raced through her head in well-worn grooves, raced endlessly. Caradoc. Loyal to Tylara and her house. Married to the faithless Gwen. And Gwen's true husband returning from the stars, returning with a star ship and *skyfire*. With the means to lay waste all Rick had built.

What could I do?

Kill the Star Lord Les? And as he died his ship would send *skyfire*. So said Rick. And she had seen the ship. It could do all Rick said, and more.

Kill the Lady Gwen? *I owe her nothing. Yet the University is more than nothing. It may be the only inheritance I can leave my children. So say the legends of the Time. So says Rick.*

But Caradoc and Les must not meet.

It had been simple enough. Coded orders to the Children of the Eighth House of Vothan. And waiting, which was worse than any battle, wait and wait and—

And comes the news, of a riot and a horse that stumbled, and her protector and rescuer—

Rescue. Sarakos had read her aright, curse him; in the end she would have broken, begging to please him if that would earn her a swifter end.... Until Caradoc came, and with Yanulf led her through the caves of Yatar, and away.

And now he was dead. Of an accident. And none knew. *My husband probably does not even suspect; he does not think like a Tran lord.*

None but me. And it will be me the gods judge. Not my instruments. Yatar forgive the Children. They acted for me. They know no better.

If anyone learns. Blood feud with those most loyal to our house. And no matter. I have brought cold and ruin to our marriage. And what right have I to "mutual society, comfort, and help," in the eyes of the gods or anyone else?

She did not close her eyes, but she kept them fixed on the

rush-strewn floor, fearful of what she might see if she looked up.

"Octavia Marselia Caesar, wilt thou have this man to thy wedded husband, to live together according to the laws of Yatar and Christ in the holy estate of matrimony? Wilt thou love him, comfort him, honor, obey, and keep him, in sickness and health; and forsaking all others, keep thee only unto him, so long as ye both shall live?"

"I will."

Publius's frown deepened. He had been frowning ever since Yanulf began to speak. It was infuriating that a Roman archbishop should have such a pitiful excuse for a voice while a barbarian priest could thunder like a centurion drilling an entire cohort. Now this damned promise by Octavia to *obey* her husband!

The barbarians must have put that in their new marriage ceremony on purpose, to cut away his own authority over his daughter. Matters should have been left so that in any dispute between Drantos and Rome, Caesar's house could invoke the *patria potestas* it held over Drantos's Queen.

They would have been left that way, too, if someone among the barbarians hadn't as good as read Publius's mind and added that little word! Or was it someone among the barbarians?

Frugi. Yes! That contemplative smile must hide treachery; that gilded legate's breastplate hides a heart gone over to the barbarians. Who else could it be, but the man who had allowed the Fourth Legion to hail a barbarian king as "Imperator"?

Frugi. You command here. Once in Rome it will be different.

And yet. He is loyal to my father, and he is a good general. Rome has need of generals. Flaminius the Dotard killed his best commanders—and now his bones wash down the Tiber.

And I have no heir. None but Octavia. She will have need of generals no less than I.

So. Live, Titus Frugi. And I will watch you, and send you where I have need.

Publius smiled thinly, hoping that a time would come when he could tell Lucius about this moment. His old tutor had always urged him to think before he spoke, and often doubted that he would ever learn.

"Forasmuch as Ganton son of Loron, Wanax of Drantos, and Octavia Marselia Caesar have consented together in holy wedlock, and have witnessed the same before Yatar, Christ, and this noble company, and thereto have given and pledged their troth to each other—"

Gwen Tremaine felt her eyes ready to overflow.

Stop it, you twit. Do you want Tylara to see you crying?

I always cry at weddings.

How many have you attended?

Well, there was Beth Allison's, there's this one, and both of my own.

You call marrying Les a wedding?

You want to argue with Yanulf? Or Les?

The voice was silent. Gwen blinked, thinking that maybe she wasn't going to cry after all but glad that here on Tran there was no mascara to run if she did. Drantos women used no makeup, although they did use perfume. They were better off than the Roman ladies, who used cosmetics McCleve had said were mostly lead-based. A good thing Octavia seems to be adopting the Drantos custom, but then at nine Tran or fifteen Earth years old she hardly needed makeup.

Octavia and Ganton made a handsome young couple, no doubt about it. Octavia would never be beautiful. But she's tall! With that red hair and those legs everyone notices her. And she may not be through growing! Ganton looked almost too hefty in his royal robes, but Gwen had seen him working out in the courtyard with that battle-ax of his; she knew all that bulk was iron-hard muscle.

The tears threatened again as Gwen thought of Octavia's luck—from hostage to Queen in a single year, and from a dynastic match to a love match. She'd been more or less handed to Ganton like a suckling pig on a platter, but she'd found she could love him, and now she would have him by her side every day and night.

Gwen had picked her own husband, got on board a flying saucer because she loved him, and now she was going to have him with her about a month out of every two Earth years.

Not fair, dammit! So who said the universe is fair? Or cares?

"—I pronounce that they be man and wife together, in the name of Yatar Dayfather, Christ His Son, and the Blessed Hestia Mother of Christ. Amen."

The tears overflowed. Gwen didn't fight them, because she saw that Tylara was crying too.

The wedding party flowed out to the sound of drums and trumpets. A Guards captain shouted importantly.

"Gunners! Salute!"

Goddam twenty-one gun salute. Sure wish I had that much gunpowder at Westrook. I got a feeling I'll need it.

The cannon drowned out the thump of the Guards' boots and the thud of their musket butts as they formed a double line from the cathedral door to the waiting carriage.

Ben Murphy waited, hand on the hilt of his sword, until the man beside him started to move toward the aisle formed by the Guards. *Lord Enipses, I think. I sure better start learning all the names and faces and estates. Another part of good manners I never thought of. But bad manners can sure get you killed. And I always thought being a landlord was easy.*

It looked as if half the high muckety-mucks in the kingdom were coming to stand between the Guards. Not just the Drantos nobles, but Romans too, Publius and Titus Frugi, to start with. Mercs. The Captain, Elliot, Art Mason, and the rest. Except for the guys with scoped rifles up in the towers.

Ganton and Octavia reached the top of the great stone stairway. Rick nodded to Elliot.

"Wedding party—draw—swords!"

Murphy drew, pulling the draw slightly to keep from ramming the sword's point between Hilaskos's teeth. What sounded like a whole battery of guns went off. Murphy could smell powder smoke. Then people were cheering, Ganton was lifting the veil from Octavia's face and kissing her a lot more enthusiastically than ceremony required, and the newlyweds were marching down the stairs under the arch of swords.

Murphy kept eyes front but knew when Ganton and Octavia reached the courtyard gateway and the crowd out in the capital streets saw them. Even Elliot couldn't have outshouted that cheering. Then each pair in the arch in turn sheathed their swords, as Yatar and Polycarp came down the aisle. It looked as if Yatar was supporting the Archbishop, but both of them were smiling and looked as if they'd just married off favorite children. Murphy found himself reaching for rosary beads he hadn't worn since he was a boy as he went through a Hail Mary he hadn't said more than a couple of times since.

Maybe old Polycarp had really had a vision from Somebody Upstairs. Even if there wasn't anybody upstairs to send visions, it made sense if Rome and Drantos were going to be allies.

It's got to be better than Ulster. Lord God. Anything is.

The Roman buccinae bellowed, the drums rolled, and the Praetorian cohort just ahead of Art Mason stepped off. He looked back along his mounted Guardsmen formed up in a column of fours. *Sharp troops. Maybe not up to what the Romans can do, but sharp enough considering they were plowboys a year ago.*

"Pass in review!"

The crowd cheered as the Praetorians came out onto the

field. Sounded just like a football crowd back home—and come to think of it, they'd have called this real good football weather, back home. With a little imagination Mason could think he was in the grandstand, watching the Sailors take the field for the kickoff.

Make that a lot of imagination. The sky was the wrong shade of blue, the hills beyond the Edre were the wrong colors, the smell on the wind was roast meat, gunpowder, wood smoke, and unwashed people, and the music wasn't any brass band that ever showed up at a football game.

The signal gun bellowed. Thank God they were just using a little one-pounder and weren't firing the bombards anymore. They must have used up half the gunpowder in Drantos in salutes.

Art Mason raised his sword and swept it forward in command. "Drantos!" He gave a touch with his spurs and the horse moved into a swift trot. The Praetorians were taking their own sweet time, as if they wanted to tell all the barbarians that nobody made them move faster than they wanted to. For a minute Art was afraid he'd have to order the Guards down to a walk. But then the Praetorians were clear. The bright tapestries of the reviewing stand were coming up on the right.

His sword went up, trumpets blared, and the platoon sergeants shouted, "First Guards, eyes—right!"

Mason's sword dipped in the royal salute, until the point was aimed at the ground. As the Guards trotted past the reviewing stand, he wished he'd seen more movies with cavalry parades. *Guess those Hollywood budgets didn't run to enough trained horses. Or riders...*

There was the little king, in armor now with that gold helmet he favored. They'd never let him give it up even if he wanted to; after the Hooey River everyone thought it was lucky. Same thing with that battle ax of old Camithon's.

Octavia—she looked like she was walking on air, with a smile too big for her face. Publius was grim, Titus Frugi was smiling, and they weren't looking at each other even though they stood side by side. The Captain looked worried, but on a big day like this he always did. Lady Tylara—she looked like she'd been crying....

And no guesses. Mason had gone as far as he could with guessing. *Maybe too far. Damn all.*

A coded message. In a code none of Mason's clerks could read. None of Apelles' people either. And none of the Captain's. What in hell was Lady Tylara doing, sending a message the Captain couldn't read?

Lady Tylara at Armagh to Castle Dravan—and just in time for somebody to reach that town where Caradoc was killed. In a damn funny riot.

I don't much believe in that riot.

And now what? Tell the Captain he's maybe married to Lady Macbeth? Shut up and soldier!

They were coming up to the corner of the reviewing field. Kitchen lads and girls were running from the roasting pits to the Guardsmen's tables. They all stopped to cheer, and Mason acknowledged.

"Left wheel!"

The Guards pivoted expertly, from column of fours to company order, each quartet of horses turning as if they were tied together.

A damned good outfit, and the Second Guards were shaping up almost as well. Their cadre had missed the Hooey River and nobody was letting them forget it, so they were training the Second Guards as if they were going to have to win the next big fight singlehanded.

A good outfit. *I'm married to the outfit.*

Maybe it's time for more than that. We're not going home. No way. Tran or no place, and damn I'm getting lonesome.

And suppose you find one like the Lady Tylara?

There's something to be said for being single.

Tylara stood at the edge of the bed. Her fur-lined chamber robe covered her from her throat to the floor. Rick remembered better times, when she'd worn a sheer *garta* cloth nightgown. Of course the weather was warmer then, and she'd had three goblets of good wine, but—

She smiled lightly. "My husband. You have not properly celebrated the Wanax's wedding." She held out a wine goblet.

He tried to smile in return as he took the goblet and touched hers with it. "Thank you."

"You are troubled."

"Some. Mostly trying to decide what to do with Harvey Rand."

"Rand. The Star Lord in the attempt on the Lady Gwen."

"Him. I think I have a solution, but as Justiciar of Drantos any case involving a nobleman could end in your court."

"Yes, if he demands."

At least you don't question that he's noble. I'd hate for that question to come up. "We can't just hang him."

"To be sure. It would be work for the headsman."

"Not that either. He's got friends."

"I had thought he might," she said.

"And there's Gengrich. I need every soldier I can get. Thing is, if you have enough problems they can solve each other."

She looked at him quizzically.

He grinned. "I thought it might work this way. Harvey gets fined the blood price for the dead sentry, and double that for not thinking ahead. Since he hasn't got anything but his uniform, I'll pay the fines. Then he owes me." Rick drank half the wine. "Good stuff."

"What will you demand in repayment?"

"Well, I thought a Tran year in the madweed plantation garrison. Nobody wants that job, but it has to be done. Even Rand's friends can see that."

"He will also be a long way from the men of Eqeta Rudhrig." Her smile had faded.

"Exactly. So when Gengrich comes in, he'll want to bargain. Rand can be another chip I hold. If Gengrich wants his title recognized he'll have to assume responsibility for

Rand. Pay his fines." Rick shrugged. "There's even some justice in it. Madweed guard duty's nothing soft."

Tylara stepped back a pace. "A wise solution, my lord. You have learned the laws and ways of the great lords very well indeed."

"Yeah, I thought—hey, what's wrong?"

"What makes you think there is something wrong?"

"I don't know, you just seem—"

"There is nothing wrong, my lord."

Rick got up and went to her. He put his arms around her and tried to draw her to him. After a moment he went back to the bed. "Sure. Nothing wrong."

She snuffed the last candle and lay down with her back to him.

Now what? Another nightmare about Sarakos? She was all right for a minute there. Did I put my foot in it about the laws? Or what? "Tylara, what have I done *now?*"

"Nothing. Good night, my lord."

Something about Gwen? I should put a medal on Rand for trying to snatch Gwen?

He lay in the dark and tried to sort memories, of Tylara and Gwen, and finally he got up and found the pitcher of wine his orderly had left for him.

"My lord husband!" Octavia put down the hair brush but did not giggle, as much as she wanted to. She knew that Ganton did not like women who giggled.

"Yes, my lady?"

"I have won my wager with the Lady Gwen."

Ganton frowned. "A wager?"

"Yes. I fear you might think it unseemly, but—"

"We both owe the Lady Gwen much. Even if it is unseemly, I will hold my tongue."

"Your word of honor?"

"By Yator, Christ, the honor of the throne of Drantos, my love for you, and my feet which are beginning to freeze, I swear to do no harm to the Lady Gwen by word or deed."

"Very well. She wagered that you would wear your Browning when first you came to my bed."

Even in the candlelight she could see Ganton's face turning red. Then he threw back his head and howled with laughter. When he could speak again, he shrugged.

"The Lady Gwen has a most unwomanly mind. I think I am well enough armed."

"So it would seem. But any weapon must be well wielded."

"It shall be, and at close quarters."

"Then let the contest begin!"

CHAPTER FIVE

The narrow streets of the Outer Castle were better lit than usual tonight, although not like last night. Then there'd been bonfires on every corner, candles in every window, and torches in the hands of half the revelers staggering from drink to drink. *Big send off for the royal wedding. Not so big for me, on my last night here.*

One house was brighter-lit than most. Les stopped below an open window. Voices were singing in English.

> What shall we do with the Wanax Ganton?
> What shall we do with the Wanax Ganton?
> What shall we do with the Wanax Ganton,
> Early in the morning?
>
> Give him a ladder as a wedding present.
> Give him a ladder as a wedding present.
> Give him a ladder as a wedding present,
> Early in the morning.

The Earth mercenaries, of course. With Jack Beazeley's song about Ganton's wedding. Beazeley had been more than a little nervous when he got a royal command to sing it for Ganton. By the time he got to the verse that went, "Wrap their kid in a purple diaper," Ganton had been laughing so hard he had to call for wine when he got his breath back.

Four Guardsmen saluted at the door to Gwen's house and passed him inside; two more escorted him up the stairs. As he knocked on the door to the private chambers, Les was beginning to wonder if they were going to tuck him into bed. Then he heard Gwen's voice.

"Come on in. I've given Lady Marva the night off."

Les swept Gwen into his arms. It was quite awhile before he could say anything that wasn't muffled in her hair. Eventually he broke away and poured wine. "Have you heard about the Great Council meeting?"

She nodded. "Larry Warner was by earlier and told me all about it. They're up to letting a woman be Rector of the University, but not up to letting her represent it on the Great Council."

Les's wine cup paused on its way to his lips.

Gwen frowned. "Les, are you jealous of Larry Warner?"

Les emptied the cup and he set it down with a steady hand. "You wouldn't be flattered if I said I was. I wouldn't be telling the truth, either. I may let myself be jealous someday, when I can be a full-time husband, but now, when I'm on Tran once a year if I'm lucky..."

"Sorry. You must have been thinking about that even more than I. Here." He put an arm around her and let her cry on his shoulder. When she stopped, he kissed her. "You've just made my point for me. When I'm fifty light-years away and you need a shoulder to cry on, why not Larry Warner's? It's a damned sight safer than Captain Galloway's."

"Ugh."

"My sentiments exactly. I don't know if Tylara's a good friend, but she's a bad enemy. You know she's been trying to pump me about the Galactic Confederation, outside of the Inner Council?"

"No, but I'm not surprised. She is one shrewd lady."

"My opinion is you could put her down in a howling wilderness, and inside of five years she'd be running the place. She might have to convince the local headman that he needed a raven-haired concubine, but that wouldn't stop her."

"She'd probably create a vacancy among the concubines. What did you tell her?"

"Not much. I'm not convinced she's given up trying to hijack my ship. Rick has already told her more than I would." He shrugged. "Not that I know much to tell. That's Agzaral's department."

"If you're not careful she'll learn more than you know."

"Yeah. Look, maybe I don't think enough about local politics. Somebody tried to kidnap you last night."

"No, that was thieves—"

"No. Not thieves. One of them was from Earth. One of Gengrich's people. Galloway has him in a cell. Gwen, Gengrich, or somebody close to him, wanted you."

Her eyes seemed twice as large as usual. "Why?"

"Because you're such a damned good university administrator? Hey, it's all right. I don't know why. The Earth guy says it was so they'd have a better bargaining position with Rick. Me, I think they wanted your transceiver as much as anything. So they could bargain directly with the *Shalnuksis.*"

"Oh. But—Gengrich couldn't have hoped to get away with that."

"They aren't sure he had anything to do with it. Right now Galloway suspects the captain of the ambassador's guards, Aidhos do Viz. They don't have any evidence that would justify arresting a diplomat, but they're pretty sure he was in on it. He'd be high in Lord Gengrich's favor if he got you, and if he failed Lord Gengrich could disavow him."

"Gengrich is going to be dangerous, if he commands loyalty like that."

"Captain Galloway thinks so too."

"All right. And they asked you not to tell me. Right?"

"Right."

"Thanks for not listening to them."

"I did listen to them, for a while. Then—well, everybody talks about Lady Tylara's pride, but they don't know you the way I do." He kissed her.

She held him until he broke away. "Look, we have to talk," he said.

She held him. "So talk."

He broke away and went to the door to look outside. The four Guardsmen were at the end of the hall. "My lord?"

"Nothing. Stay on watch."

"Les, what—"

"Want to be sure no one's listening."

"The Guards don't understand English—"

"It isn't the Guards I'm worried about." He lowered his voice almost to a whisper. "Look, I think I've worked out a plan. I can take you back. You and the kids. To Earth."

She ran toward him, then stopped at his look.

"There's a catch. I could never see you again. But I could set you up. Not so rich that people would notice, but comfortable. Gold—"

"Gold. You trying to buy your way out?"

"No! I mean—"

"What do you mean?"

"It's just something I thought of. I couldn't hide you from Agzaral, but I think I could talk him into letting you alone."

"But I'd never see you again."

"Probably not."

"So. I go to Earth and hide, live on your money and not see you. And do what? What would I be? Les, even a kept woman gets to see her lover once in a while." Then she laughed. "Besides, if you're going to send me back to Earth, I want more than gold."

"What?"

"Do you know they have a complete Ptolemy's *Life of Alexander the Great* here on Tran?"

"You mean Arrian's?"

"No, Ptolemy's. The one written by Alexander's own best general and half-brother after he was King of Egypt. Arrian probably used it, but on Earth it's been lost for centuries. Octavia gave Ganton a copy as a wedding present. There are a thousand other pieces of classical literature I could sell for a fortune. Do you know I spent a whole afternoon reading a Latin translation of Aeschylus's *The Myrmidons?* Mary Renault got it almost exactly right in *The Mask of Apollo,* when Nikeratos puts it on at Delphi."

"Now I know you're crazy."

"Why? Who would know? I'm sure classical scholars and universities would put up a fine smokescreen against any awkward questions."

"Maybe. Maybe not. If it wasn't fine enough—Agzaral

wouldn't hesitate to send agents to Earth to kill you and the children. Kill you and disintegrate your bodies, so nobody would find anything suspicious in the kids' DNA."

"He wouldn't!"

"Maybe he wouldn't. Maybe. But somebody would. Gwen, I don't know what they're going to do about Earth, but if your people learn about the Confederation it could— Look, one faction wants to destroy Earth now.

"Even if nothing happened to Earth, the secret of Tran would be out. Then the *Shalnuksis* would have to cover their tracks. Gwen, they have a weapon that could make the True Sun go nova."

"Good God. You're—no, you're not joking. Anyway, it doesn't matter. I'm not going back."

Thank the Light. "Why not?"

"Because I'd rather have you once every couple of years than never, you goose."

She came to his arms and he held her tightly.

Tran's your home, and you're important here. But maybe I am part of it.

"Just come back. Please."

"I'll always come back."

The nightmares were still close, but they knew what would drive them away, for a while. Dreams and nightmares alternated through the long Tran night.

Gwen woke to find an empty bed and a pillow wet with tears she was quite sure weren't all hers.

I've lived through plenty of mornings without you. What's one more?

She slipped out of bed and stepped into the outer chamber. Marva was asleep in her bed and the children in theirs, with the maids on their pallets.

Gwen clapped her hands. "Up, up, everyone. Rise and shine."

CHAPTER SIX

The mist was closing in and the track underfoot was even worse than Gengrich remembered it. Well, he hadn't approached Castle Zyphron this way since early summer, before the Westmen invasion up north, and there'd been a hell of a lot of rain since then. No wonder the track had potholes you could damned near bathe in!

Alex Boyd, riding beside him, frowned at the hills slowly disappearing behind the gray wall of mist. "Arnie, if I remember right the track runs along the side of one of those hills. There's woods upslope, enough to hide a whole battalion."

"Ambushes?"

"Could be."

"What about riding downhill, off the track?"

"You could swing it in good weather. I've done it myself, riding light. With the grass wet, the ground soft, and the horses tired—no way."

It seemed like a good idea when they started off in the morning, on the last day's march homeward. Why not approach Castle Zyphron from the west, to smoke out any bandits who might have thought there was safety in a place the Lord of Zyphron would never think of looking? They'd certainly chased enough of them out of other places; the city council of Valus would be happy as a grig with the heads they'd sent in.

It had seemed like a good idea at the time. Now that the autumn rains had started the notion didn't look so good. Progress came a yard at a time, even when they dismounted and led the horses through the worst of it. Now it was mid-afternoon, visibility was going to hell, they were still seven klicks from the castle, and there wasn't a dry campground in sight. No dry wood, either.

They'd better move on and try to make it home tonight, or there were going to be seven hundred men thoroughly pissed off at one Lord Gengrich do Zyphron, former Corporal, U.S.A. Come to think of it, he was fairly pissed off at himself. *This stuff worse than the 'Nam highlands. Should have expected it.* "Alex."

"Yeah?"

"The men won't like sleeping out in the wet this close to home. Take Clayton and Green and a double load of ammo and fifty men and ride up ahead. Picket the road every couple of hundred meters. If that smokes out an ambush, we can come up and bail you out. If it doesn't, we can push on through."

Boyd nodded slowly. "If you say so—"

"What's buggin' you, Alex? The ammo?"

"Yeah. I don't mind shooting it off, but risking its being captured..."

"Got any better ideas?" Boyd shook his head. "Then move it. We sure don't want to be out here in the dark."

"Aaaa-men, brother."

Gengrich watched as Boyd rode off to round up the other two mercs for his fire team and pick a half-company of locals. He spat into a clump of sheepdog bush beside the track. *Never knew what officers did. Until I had to be one.*

Christ, for a nickel I'd give it up. Except that doesn't work either. Bad enough taking care of two thousand people, but damn all it's worse being alone. Goddam crummy planet.

A snatch of song ran through his mind. Something he'd seen on an arts channel movie. "And it is a pleasant thing, to be a pirate king."

Flipping bull shit it is!

At least the harvests hadn't been too bad, which had bought him a little time to play what was now really his only card. He didn't know what good would come of sending an embassy north to Ganton's wedding, but old Daettan had a reputation for being a pretty smart bargainer.

No harm asking. Maybe the Captain will take us all back. Only what happens if he wants just the mercs and none of the locals? What in hell do I do then?

When Alex's patrol rode through Gengrich ordered the others to dismount and lead. "Save the horses." There were grumbles, and some arguments. One of his NCOs shouted and he heard blows.

No flipping discipline, and what do I do about that? Pirate king my ass.

It was just enough darker to notice when Gengrich heard the shots. Six that sounded like one of the H&Ks and another that sounded like a .45. That meant trouble unless it was Green firing; he had a bad rep for being trigger-happy.

"Red alert!"

Gengrich heard the order relayed as he swung up into his saddle. If it was Green wasting ammo again, he'd just made a real good down payment on being the first merc to really smoke for screwing up—

"Bandits!" somebody shouted, invisible in the mist ahead. Then two more bursts and a lot of wordless yelling, some of it not even sounding human.

Gengrich felt his hands quiver the way they always did when he knew a firefight was coming. It never bothered him once he was doing some personal shooting, but sitting and watching or even worse listening always got to him.

"First and Fourth Companies, mount up! Second and Third Companies, take the flanks and advance for dismounted action!" Please God the horseholders knew their business and all the bandits were up front and not lurking down here ready to grab the mounts.

Gengrich drew his sword and dug in his spurs. Gravel flew as he came level with the captain of Fourth Company. As the mounted column got into motion, it made enough noise to alert any bandits for miles around. Not enough to drown out more bursts of firing up ahead. Gengrich concentrated on controlling his horse with one hand. He could now manage a horse if he kept his mind on it, although he suspected that most of the born-in-the-saddle types among the locals still sniggered at him behind his back.

He was so busy with his mount that he didn't notice the battle noises getting louder. Suddenly they were all around him, and he saw Alex Boyd down on one knee behind his dead horse, one arm dangling useless, firing his pistol with the other hand.

Gengrich opened his mouth to shout to Boyd. Before he could take a deep breath not just the battle noises but the battle itself was all around him. A stand of scrub oak spewed ragged figures in all directions. The captain of the Fourth Company flipped backward out of his saddle, his face mashed into jam by a flail. Someone leaped into his saddle and started to turn his mount's head, then screamed even louder and fell under its hooves as Boyd shot him in the belly.

Two other bandits closed in on Gengrich. He slashed down at the head of the one in the lead. The man's long dagger gashed his boot as the sword came down. The man tried to slash again as he reeled back, his skull split open, then crumpled. The other bandit let out a scream that turned Gengrich's stomach and leaped like a frog, left hand gripping the bow of the saddle and the right the horse's reins. As Gengrich realized the bandit was a woman, she brought the knife in her right hand around toward the horse's neck. His swordcut only gashed her shoulder, but it broke her grip in time to save the horse. He made another wild slash at her and felt it hit something, but didn't see what happened to her after that. The bandits who'd run past him came running back, and after them some reinforcements from the First Company.

The bandits didn't wait around for the full four companies to come up; they scattered with what they'd managed to grab or strip from the dead. Gengrich was just starting to think of casualty reports when he heard four evenly spaced rifle shots from back where the horses of the dismounted companies were being held. He was turning his mount when he heard a horse's scream, another shot, then silence. He waited while the silence dragged on, then sighed. Whatever it was back there, it wasn't a full-scale attack on the rear.

What the bandits up in front had done was bad enough. Joe Green was going to have to be trigger-happy with his left hand; somebody had hacked off the first two joints of his right index finger. Alex Boyd would be out of action for a while with a broken arm; that was a mace. Twelve of the locals were dead and about twenty had reported wounded, which meant probably twice as many needing the medics. The local habit of proving your guts by not reporting wounded wasn't quite as bad as it was before Gengrich trained the medics in antisepsis; now you could prove your guts by letting boiling water be dumped on your wounds. You still got a lot of people walking around with legitimate Purple Hearts and never saying a frigging word!

The bandits left fourteen bodies behind, and any of them who lit out with a bad wound was probably going to die, but they'd also made off with a dozen weapons and five horses. No star weapons or ammo, thank God; Gengrich still knew that Alex Boyd had come too damned close to being a prophet instead of just a casualty.

A scribe was getting the figures down on a wooden tablet when Private Alan MacAllister rode up the track. "That's wrong," he said, pointing at the figures.

"Yeah?"

"I got five more back there. They tried to come through the horses. I think they were in a hurry."

"They probably were. We weren't exactly running a resort up here."

"I know. Like I said, I got five more back there."

No time to send somebody for a body count, and no need either. MacAllister was about the surliest merc in the whole outfit and always had been. He was also the best and coolest shot Gengrich had ever known, and was real sticky about an accurate count of his kills.

So that meant nineteen bandits dead in return for a

dozen locals down plus two starmen and twenty-odd locals hurt. With the loot they'd snagged, the bandits might be calling it a victory.

Victory. Right. Who was that guy who said, "Give me another victory like this and I'm dog meat"?

The rising wind whipped the flames of the torches on the gate towers but the light rain wasn't enough to put them out. Helmets and shield bosses glistened as the sentries presented arms. Gengrich returned their salutes and rode on through the smelly darkness of the gate itself into the courtyard of Castle Zyphron.

Behind him rode the mercs, the wounded with the medics and stretcher-bearers, and his own personal bodyguard. The rest of the column would probably already be settling down in New Zyphron, which was their fancy name for the walled camp at the foot of the hill.

At least they'd take care of their horses and armor before they went looking for wine and an audience. He'd made it a rule from the first, that a man who neglected his mount joined the infantry and a man who neglected his armor or weapons joined the bandits. He'd had to fight twice, once against six men, before he made that rule stick, but that was the last bit of trouble.

Frank Guilford came up, saluted, and went off to triage the wounded without waiting for a reply. After him came the seneschal, Master Arranthos. *Master Arranthos. Damfino master of what. Some city guild until politics got him. He sure don't talk about it.*

"Master Khemos thinks that the south gate must be braced, at least, to see the winter through."

"Can't he finish the repairs?"

"The foundation on the left side needs work. The ground will be too wet for safe digging until the frosts come."

After that it would be too hard, of course. A sweet set of choices—override a master mason, start work and risk Khemos quitting or people getting killed; block off the castle's escape hatch to mounted men for the rest of the winter;

or do nothing and watch the gate fall on somebody's head in the first blizzard.

"Give Master Khemos my compliments and tell him to brace the gate." *Read that in a novel once. Sure comes in handy.*

This far south a light-infantry army that didn't need forage for cavalry or a siege train could campaign damned near all year 'round, but that wouldn't be a menace to Castle Zyphron. They couldn't be in real hot water before spring, and then if they did have to get out in a hurry it'd be for good and damned sure they wouldn't be riding!

"Yes, my lord. The Lord Holloway says he expects the forge to be fit for the making of—guns—in another ten days. He asks whether you wish iron or bronze guns."

Now that was almost good news! Siggie Holloway was just as good a blacksmith as he said he was, and ready to bust his tail into the bargain. Once they'd decided that their gunpowder was good enough to use in guns, he'd rounded up the people and the tools without anybody having to ride herd on him.

Bronze or iron was still a question. Iron they had, but nobody on Tran seemed to know how to cast it, except maybe the Romans. They'd have to use guns hammered together out of wrought-iron bars; they'd be heavy mothers and likely to blow up in your face if you gave 'em a dirty look.

Bronze could be cast, and that meant lighter, stronger guns that wouldn't rust. But both bronze and the bronzesmiths would have to be imported from Rustengo. *Who in hell do we know in Rustengo besides Mort Schultz? Have to ask around. Guess we'll have to make peace with Schultzy. But not just yet.*

"Iron, I think. We have the men with the art of working it, and it is easier to come by. We'll need a lot."

Arranthos gave Gengrich's H & K a pointed look. "The star weapons seem to wield great power, though they are small."

Why try to bluff? "That is true. They are also made with starmetals that may not exist on this world, and with magic that none of the starmen know, not even the Lord Rick."

Arranthos looked thoughtful. "Very well. Lady Helena asks that you see her as soon as your duties permit. Your son Dan has been sick with the lung-fever these past three days. Lord Guilford does not hold out much hope."

"Oh, Christ."

Gengrich briefly closed his eyes and tried not to sway in the saddle. It was all just too damned much. Dan was such a likable baby, with his mother's blond hair and his father's dark eyes, and Helena had gone through hell having him. She was so proud, too, because Erika had a girl, then miscarried so that she couldn't have any more....

Pneumonia didn't care whether you liked somebody or not. All it cared about was whether there were any drugs to fight it off. There weren't and there weren't going to be any, and that was that, although Frank had done some pretty good work with home remedies picked up from the local midwives.

"Forgive me, my lord, that I brought—"

"Oh, it's not your fault. Tell Lady Helena I'll be with her as soon as I've prayed to Hestia." *And washed up, but I can't get them to understand about that.*

"Yes, my lord."

Gengrich dismounted and strode off toward the shrine of Hestia without noticing if his squires caught his horse. *Please, God or Hestia, or Somebody, don't let Dan die. What did he do to anybody?*

Maybe Hestia would answer.

And maybe Elliot would fly down from the sky in a balloon with a case of penicillin and a case of Lone Star beer.

Dan died just before True Sun-rise the next morning. The last thing on Tran or any other world Gengrich wanted to do was stay in the sickroom looking at his son's body. But Helena was crying so hard he didn't want to leave her alone.

Hell, even Erika was crying. Maybe that meant he wouldn't have woman troubles with Erika crowing over her rival's losing Dan....

By late morning Helena was cried out. Gengrich staggered into his chamber and collapsed on the bed. He didn't bother taking off his boots, but he did grab a jug of Guilford's Private Stock. It was about eighty proof and tasted even worse than Gengrich felt.

He'd thought one drink would be enough to send him off, but he was on his third when he heard a knock at the door.

"Go to hell."

"It is Lord Severianus, Lord Gengrich."

"He can go to hell too."

"My lord," came a more educated voice. "I fear this is worth disturbing you. When you have heard me, then if you wish I will go to hell."

Gengrich groaned. "Let him in."

Marcus Julius Vinicianus strode in. He'd been a drunk ever since Flaminius exiled him ten years ago for some satirical verses on Caesar's inability to make up his mind. The booze had left his nose, eyes, and cheeks permanently red and given him a potbelly, but he still walked and carried himself like a drill sergeant.

"All right. What is it?"

"Forgive me for breaking in on your grief. May Christ and all His Saints keep your son, and send you and Lady Helena—"

"I can hear condolences some other time. What else?"

"Some news from the north. I fear that we have misjudged one of the men we thought we could most trust, and much evil may come of—"

"Marcus, if you want your neck wrung like a chicken, just go on trying to be polite. Spit it out."

Uninvited, Vinicianus poured himself a cupful of whiskey and drank. "Captain Aidhos do Vis assisted by the starman Harvey Rand made an attempt to carry off the Lady Gwen Tremaine and bring her south to you."

"Christ! Why?"

"He thought she would be of value, to force the Star Lord Les to help you speak to the skyfolk. Or perhaps she could help you do that herself. Either way, you would be able to trade madweed for star weapons and tools. For medicines. Aidhos no doubt expected that you would be grateful for this, and give him honor and wealth."

"Jesus Christ." *What have they got me into?* "That's what he tried. What happened?"

"Four of his men were killed or captured, including the starman Rand."

He's no loss.

"Two confessed under torture and were executed. No one seems to know what happened to Rand. Lord Rick spoke harshly to Master Daettan in Council and accused him of bringing thieves to a royal wedding."

"Thieves?"

"Yes. Except for the Inner Council of Drantos, all are being told that the men were only thieves. Nor had Captain Aidhos been arrested at the time the message left Edron."

That could have long since changed, of course. But if Aidhos was going to be let go to protect the Captain's cover story ... "Marcus. Do you have any reliable informants in Vis?"

"Need you ask?"

"Not really." Vinicianus had informants everywhere. *Including in my household, I expect. But he's useful.* "Have them learn all they can about Aidhos's friends and kin. I do not want to be at feud with half of Vis for taking Aidhos's head, but if I can do so safely, I will have it."

"To what end?"

"As a present for the Lord Rick."

"It will take more than that to make peace with him."

"What makes you think I want to make peace with Lord Rick?"

"I predict that we will have no choice by spring."

"When I want predictions, I'll hire a soothsayer."

"Very well. You know better than I, whether the 'magic' of the star weapons will last beyond this winter without being renewed."

There wasn't anything to say to that. "Sure, I'd like to

make peace. I'll be his ally if he'll have us. All of us, everybody who follows me. Anyway, we can't wait until spring."

"We agree, then."

Damn nice of you. "So. You look into Vis and I'll send somebody to talk to Schultz in Rustengo."

"An alliance with Rustengo will anger the Prophet Phrados."

"Tell Phrados to kiss my arse."

"Impractical. How does one compel the master of a hundred thousand soldiers?"

"The man who says he has a hundred thousand soldiers."

"Yes. It is not quite the same thing. But he certainly has a large host, and we have no spies in it."

"So I'll keep it a secret that I'm talking to Schultz. For God's sake, leave me alone!"

"As you wish."

"Stop." The liquor and the exhaustion were hitting now; Gengrich felt as if his arms and eyelids were weighted with lead. "Sometimes I don't know what I'd do without you, Marcus."

"Today you would go to bed with your boots on," said Vinicianus, expertly heaving Gengrich's legs onto the bed and starting to unlace the boots. A snore was the only reply. He pulled the boots off and piled furs over the sleeping Star Lord.

"Sleep, my friend, and God give you peace if men cannot."

CHAPTER SEVEN

Master of Foot Mortimer Schultz stood up in the sternsheets of the boat. The boat swung to port as the helmsman put the tiller over to avoid the submerged ruins of a wall. Schultz spread his legs to balance against the sudden motion. They glided into open water. Two crewmen furled the sail and hoisted the leeboard. A moment later they slid aground on a muddy bottom that had once been a hillside above a fishing village east of Rustengo.

"Well done," Schultz said. The helmsman grunted something that might have been "thanks." The sailors of Rustengo were a close-mouthed lot at best, and the helmsman no doubt suspected the Master Schultz knew little of ships. He was right; before Schultz joined the Army to escape going to rabbinical school his only acquaintance with ships had been the Staten Island ferry.

Schultz's four guards splashed ashore and took up positions where they could cover the hillside with their crossbows. Schultz followed them, then called back to the crew, "If we have not returned by darkness or if anyone attacks the boat, you must bear word to the house of Mahros."

"Master—"

"I don't doubt your courage. But if we meet danger today, it will come from more men than the three of you could fight, were each of you an Achilles."

"As you wish, Master Schultz." For the helmsman, that was an oration. As Schultz led the guards up the hill the crew were already breaking out poles to push the boat back into water deep enough for safe anchorage.

Not that he expected trouble, even if the Prophet Phrados was a *gonef* of the worst sort and his envoy no better. Four guards hand-picked from the Bronzesmith's Cohort would make easy and silent assassination impossible. *He can't kill me without the City finding out. Is that enough? Hell, I'm engaged to the daughter of the Master of Bronzesmiths. That has to be enough.*

Not even Phrados would be mad enough to start a new war with the city Guilds.

Up the hill, over the crest, and down the other side. The point man had out his brush-cutter, a big curved wooden stick like a boomerang with a cold-worked bronze edge riveted to the inside. It was getting a workout. This path had got pretty nearly overgrown during the summer, now that the tidal wave and the rising sea had swallowed the village below it. The vegetation was dying back with the coming of autumn, but enough fleecevine and hydras bane was left to occasionally give Schultz the feeling he was back in the Mekong Delta.

The path dipped sharply fifty yards beyond the crest. *Ha. Used to be level here.* The whole hillside was sliding down into the sea. *Quake or undermined by water? No matter. This is our last trip here.*

He slipped on a patch of mud and caught himself with the rifle butt. Once again Schultz thanked the Lord that Gengrich and Warner had managed to snag H&Ks for everybody when they led the mutiny. M-16s would never have stood up to this kind of punishment and skimpy maintenance. He patted the plastic butt for luck.

The old path now wound down to the water's edge and vanished. A new path branched off to the left, following the new shoreline to a sprawling building of logs and driftwood with a thatched roof. A crudely lettered sign over the door told the world that this was "Charon's Rest."

A while back the river running down through this little valley was something you could wade across on a summer day. Then the earthquakes and tidal wave dumped a hill across its mouth; the rising sea did the rest. The valley was flooded a good eight or nine klicks back into the hill. Between the end of the valley and the next good road to the north was a lot of rugged hills and more bandits than anything short of a century would care to tackle, although Gengrich was supposed to be getting on top of those bastards.

Right now, though, anyone coming along the coast road had to pay the owner of Charon's Rest for a ferry across the valley. If it was too late for the traveler to reach Rustengo before the gates closed, a traveler could also pay stiff prices for bad food, worse wine, and vermin-ridden beds. Before the rising sea washed Charon's Rest away, its owner was going to be a rich man—if an earthquake didn't dump the whole thing into the water.

The sign's rusty chains squealed in the rising wind as Schultz led his men in through the door. The owner's wife greeted him.

"Your friend has already arrived. He is in the back room."

Schultz handed her two Roman silvers and five Rustengo brasses. She bit one of the silvers, then nodded. "He is alone there. Another man came with him, to tend their horses."

That pretty much ruled out treachery. "What does he look like?"

"He dresses like a merchant from just north of the Sunlands, but he does not look like one. More like a soldier. He also speaks with the tongue of an educated man of the north."

"Thanks."

A lot of people running around these days weren't what they looked like—and that included Anna Schultz's son Mortimer. *Northerner. Could be. Wonder if he knows what's happening up there?*

Schultz nodded to the guards. "Follow me."

Matthias, Highpriest of Vothan, watched the starman enter. He was no taller than most men of this world, but his strange green and brown tunic and trousers made him look otherwise. He also carried both a large and a small star weapon.

Two Rustengan soldiers followed him into the room. One stood by the door, holding his crossbow so that it was ready to shoot without appearing so to an inexperienced eye. That pleased Matthias. It suggested that the starman was accepting him as the merchant he said he was.

Best not to accept things too calmly, however. "I asked that we meet alone, Master Schultz."

"We will, once my men have searched this room for spies. Would you trust the owner to hold his tongue? Either gold or less gentle means might give our secrets to God knows who."

So Schultz believed there was only one god. That meant he was a Christian like the other starmen. A pity. It would have been agreeable to learn that he lived apart even from Lord Gengrich because he worshipped other gods, even if they were not the true ones. Something might have been made of such a quarrel.

The Rustengans knew their business. After the search one pronounced the room "clean" and went outside to stand by the door. The other vanished, to return shortly with sausages, cheese, and wine, then join his comrade. Schultz closed the door and poured out the wine.

"To prosperity for all honest traders."

Matthias doubted there was such a thing, but it was a toast the man he pretended to be could not have refused. He drank, then picked up a sausage and cut a piece of cheese with his knife.

Schultz ate no sausages, only cheese, and mixed his wine with water from a strange flattened metal jug at his waist. Their talk wandered over many matters—whether there was any profit to be found in the rebuilding of Rustengo's walls, how many guards a caravan needed to be safe from bandits, what were the best (or at least the safest) inns for outland merchants, and much else.

Matthias felt that it fouled his tongue to speak of such

matters. He also knew that he had done as much in the service of Vothan, and would do worse in the service of Issardos, High Chancellor of the Five Kingdoms. "How tender a conscience can we allow ourselves, when we fight men who seem to have no conscience at all?" was the Chancellor's question, and many nights of fasting and meditating at Vothan's shrine had given Matthias no clear answer.

At last matters turned to rebuilding certain temples of Yatar fallen or damaged in the earthquake. "Some say it is wasted effort, with the Time so close and other needs so pressing," said Schultz. "Others say that it is never a waste, to honor the gods. Even some of the Christians say that they wish to help honor the Father of Christ, although what they would say if their own churches had not largely escaped I do not know."

"Then the vision of Archbishop—?"

"Polycarp."

"That vision, it has won converts in Rustengo?"

"Does this surprise you?"

"No, since I know that the followers of Christ and the followers of Yatar have long been at peace with each other in Rustengo. Yet I warn you, this will not please the Prophet Phrados."

For a moment Matthias was in fear that the Star Lord would draw his weapon. It would be godless treachery, but if the Star Lords thought themselves so close to the gods that they need not fear them...?

The moment passed, but the unfamiliar and unwelcome taste of fear did not leave Matthias's mouth. He drank more wine, glad to find his hand steady.

"I thank you for your warning," said Schultz. "It is not unknown, that the Prophet Phrados seeks to defend the honor of the gods by smiting those who believe in Polycarp's visions. I will return the favor by giving my own warning. Rustengo has ruled itself in such matters even when it was under the Empire of Rome. It will do no less now. Anyone who seeks to dictate the City's religions had best bring an army with him."

"The Prophet has just that."

"He is *said* to have just that, my friend. Surely you have heard of enough ghost armies to believe only what you see."

"I have. The Prophet marches with a host the like of which no living man has seen. With my own eyes I have seen ten thousand men swearing themselves into his service. I have counted thrice that many already sworn. More come each day."

"Rustengo has ships, men, and walls enough to defend herself against any who seek to break the Great Peace."

"Ships and men, perhaps, but walls?"

"What has fallen can be raised again."

Matthias shrugged. "May Yatar watch over Rustengo, and Vothan strengthen the arms of its defenders."

The wine was surprisingly good. Matthias drained the last and set down his cup. "It is said that the men of Lord Gengrich also follow the new way of Polycarp's vision. Or so I was told in the camps of Phrados."

Schultz's expression told nothing. "I have no great quarrel with the Lord Gengrich, but I cannot say that I am much in his confidence either. The Star Lords themselves are worshippers of Christ, but like all wise men they honor His Father and the Warlord as well. I do not know what gods Gengrich's men worship. I am told that all who will obey his orders are welcome in his service."

"Even outlaws and bandits?"

"Outlaws, very likely. Bandits, I much doubt it. I know that he has fought bandits side by side with the soldiers of half the city-states and a good many of the mercenary bands. Most speak well of him, although they also say he is a hard man in bargaining for pay and a dangerous man to cheat."

"He will hire himself to anyone?"

"I have not heard that he refused any offer, unless he was already in another's service or the pay was too low."

Those were the words from Schultz's lips. What Matthias heard in his mind was, "Why don't you come right out and say what would be Phrados's price for Lord Gengrich's men?"

Once again Matthias reminded himself that a merchant would not show a nobleman's anger. "It may be to Lord Gengrich's—profit, to have made no alliance with those whom the Prophet calls enemies."

"I am sure that the Lord Gengrich will hear that message. As to what he may do afterward..." The shrug was not only a dismissal of the matter, it was very nearly a dismissal of Matthias.

Matthias did not rise in anger, but swore that the next time he spoke to Master Schultz the Star Lord would learn to respect one who served Vothan and was also kin to the Crown of Ta-Lataos! Aloud, he said only, "Shall we order more wine?" and nearly sighed with relief when Schultz shook his head.

Schultz huddled amidships, back against the straining mast, trying to stay under his oilcloth cloak. Every so often the boat stuck her nose in deep enough to throw spray, and his boots were already wet from what was sloshing around in the bottom. They'd have to start bailing pretty soon, and it was getting dark....

They were sailing across what used to be swamp. Now it was open water with a few treetops. Fewer of those every day.

The helmsman shouted. Schultz saw a wavering glow in the twilight about a klick off to starboard. That must be the new lighthouse, and it was a lot brighter than the last time he'd seen it. They must have got the reflectors installed. Last time he'd passed, the light from the fish-oil lamps was so dim that a good-sized ship would damned near run aground before anybody aboard saw the light.

The helmsman shouted again and the boat heeled as she came about. Schultz threw one arm around the mast and held on. He'd a lot rather have an arm around Diana, but he'd have that in another hour, now that they were on course for the harbor.

Schultz smiled as he thought of Diana waiting in her white robe with her blond hair unbound and flowing down over her shoulders. She'd lead him to the bath, of course. Funny how the Rustengans weren't hung up on the virginity of their daughters. Guess it came from having been under the Romans without ever really turning Christian. Roman baths and willing girls made up for a lot of things, like having to deal with that wacko ambassador from the Prophet who called himself a trader.

What *was* that *momser*'s game, anyway? With Rustengo, it was pretty clear. If the city did anything against the Prophet Phrados, they'd be in trouble—as much trouble as the Prophet's army could make for them.

That could be a lot. The city's walls really weren't in too great shape; a general who didn't care about casualties could probably storm the city outright. The Rustengans couldn't march out and fight in the open either, not if the other side had any good cavalry. From what Schultz knew about the Sunlands and the rest of where the refugees came from, the Prophet wouldn't have any now, but if he got some of the better local mercenary outfits on his side...

Maybe that was why he wanted Gengrich. Arnie had some fair to middling cavalry of his own. More dragoons than cavalry, but not bad. He also had a lot of contacts with other mounted mercenary outfits.

Mort, you better get up north to Castle Zyphron and lay all this on Gengrich, before that Prophet gonef sends him an offer he can't refuse.

It would be a lot harder to make peace with the Captain if Gengrich signed up with somebody fighting the Captain's new religion. *Arnie has to know that. If he doesn't—*

If he doesn't, we're both finished.

Damn the Prophet anyway! Going north meant leaving Diana. It meant leaving the shop right when things were about to click on moveable type—and *that* would guarantee him red-carpet treatment from the Captain. For him and anybody he wanted to bring along. It meant leaving his century, right when they were beginning to shape up....

Arnie, you're going to owe me one. Hope you figure that out.

It was so dark under the trees that Matthias didn't see the sentries' lanterns until a moment before they challenged him.

"Who is there?"

"The true servant."

"Thank Vothan! We were beginning to worry, my lord. Is all well?"

Matthias dismounted without answering, and took a bowl of hot soup from a man-at-arms. Tonight's march would be no easy task, but there was no other way to get safely into the hills by daybreak. Bandits would not trouble eighty armed men. At least no small band of them would, and Lord Gengrich and his allies had left few large ones.

A good war captain, Gengrich, by all appearances. Could he be turned against his Captain General? Then the Five Kingdoms could crush the starmen and their allies one by one. But it must be done quickly, before everyone was overtaken by the Time.

The cult of Yatar had its records of the Time. So did the Priests of Vothan, although they did not boast of them. In the Time, the lands of the Five Kingdoms would grow strong—and the hordes from the south would come. So said the records.

As the men-at-arms began beating out the campfire, the horses suddenly neighed in a ragged chorus. The air grew still. Matthias felt a moment of dizziness. Then the ground quivered. It felt as if he stood on the back of a large animal.

"Forget the campfire!" he shouted. "Lead the horses out of the trees!"

By the time they were out of the trees, the campfire was

only a dim glow in the distance. A hasty count showed that all the men and horses were safe. Anyone coming on the remains of the camp would think bandits had struck.

Matthias swung into the saddle and led the way north-ward. His head held confusion. When the very earth under men's feet betrayed them, was this a time to do the will of men who seemed to worship nothing but their own magic, and led others to do the same?

And if their magic is a gift from the gods?

He rode on without answers. The trail led steeply uphill, and it took all his skill and attention to keep his seat.

No more earth shocks came, but when they reached the open hills, it was snowing.

Interlude
LUNA

The man Rick Galloway knew as Inspector Agzaral studied the telltales on the device clipped to the underside of his desk and smiled to himself. For the next hour anyone listening would hear only meaningless pleasantries. When the office door opened he rose and went more than halfway to greet the woman who entered. He raised her hand to his lips, an act that would have astonished both humans and nonhumans who knew him. It would not have surprised those who knew of his relationship with Jehna Sae Leern, but there had been no such persons of any race in forty Terran years.

"You haven't changed much," she said. She glanced at his desk.

"We can talk," he said. "Or—"

"Later." She smiled.

"How was the Council meeting?"

"To anyone but us, entirely routine."

"So. There was pressure on anyone to declare their position on the future of Earth."

"Nothing overt."

"No faction believes it has won, then."

Jehna smiled. "You can see the sun by daylight. And yet, I sensed that some were waiting. To pounce, to change sides —I don't know. Is there anything in those decanters?"

Agzaral chose a Waterford decanter and two Scandinavian glasses in the shape of dragons. "A new sherry. I think you'll find it drinkable."

"I'd rather have whiskey." They raised their glasses. Jehna tossed hers back stiff-wristed. "Free stars."

Agzaral glanced at the telltales on his desk. "Free stars! Are you mad?"

"I think not. If I read the meeting right, we may have opportunities. Better than in the past five hundred years."

"A long time."

"I mean it. At least three of the Five Families might be glad to see Earth humans burst into space on their own. It's all on the tape. Listen, then tell me."

"I'll listen. But why might they want that?"

"Ennui. Look at it through their eyes. A lifetime of centuries with everything the same at the end as at the beginning. They don't even have to work at it. You and I do it for them.

"War as a cure for boredom. Interesting. But the Ader'at'eel are beyond that."

"Are they? Listen to the tapes and say that again. I don't say they want war. They're just bored, and not too concerned about the Confederation. Did you ever see a film made on Earth called *La Dolce Vita*? It may be a disease of ruling families of every race. Everywhere."

"Are the Ehk'mai among the three Families who feel this way?"

"Ah. I think you do understand."

"Perhaps. Have they prepared to take advantage of the instabilities— Hah. Put wild humans in space and none of us can know what will happen."

"Isn't that what we want? The only really predictable thing is stasis. Anyway, I don't know what the Ehk'mai have planned." She grinned. "You expect me to know a lot. Courier First-Rank isn't even the highest human rank in the service of the Ehk'mai."

"But can you find out?"

"I have some access to both humans and Ader'at'eel at the proper level. Is it wise to ask such questions?"

"We have to know. It will be dangerous to ask?"

"Of course, and since when have you become protective?"

"Merely concerned with timing. One wishes to choose the most profitable moment to go—'in harm's way' is the phrase an Earth sailor once used."

Jehna smiled. "K'yar, you are not deceiving me, let alone yourself. You are worried—for me, and for what the Ader'at'eel might be plotting."

Agzaral sipped his sherry. "That may be." He looked thoughtful, then decisive. "At all events, this is not the proper time for you to go in harm's way. You wouldn't learn enough. The time will come, and now I think sooner than we expected."

"You sound almost—pleased."

"Does this surprise you?"

"Somewhat. You have always been the perfect cynic. Now you seem to be welcoming a situation that could force you to choose sides."

"You are surprised that I can see the sun by daylight?"

"It isn't that clear to me."

"Perhaps it will be clearer once you have seen a film I have for you."

"A film?" She raised one eyebrow. "From Earth?"

"Not that kind. You would not believe how Terran erotica has deteriorated in the last few years. Most would nauseate anyone but sadists, and bore them."

"You intrigue me!"

"I'd be a poor host if I didn't." He turned off the scrambler and rose. "Come. The caviar isn't Persian, but the smoked salmon is Fortnum's best. There's an extra side of it for you."

The film had been shot against a green-sprayed wall of lunar rock. Les was holding up a photograph as he talked.

"Gwen isn't the only one who bounces back when she's knocked down. Take Jack Beazeley. His hobby is folk singing, and he's missed having a guitar. So he learned to play the lyre, and rescored a lot of songs for it. Then he sat down with an instrument-maker and described a twelve-string guitar. You see the results. I don't think any Earth folk singer would recognize it, let alone be able to play it, but I've heard Beazeley give a two-hour concert on it. Next time I'll bring a tape of his less ribald compositions."

Les stopped smiling. "I think the *Shalnuksis* badly underestimated what they turned loose on Tran. There've been a few duds like Parsons, but most of Rick's people are turning out to be the sort you don't want mad at you. And they've been turned loose on a planet that was settled with fairly tough people to start with—people who've been systematically selected for survival qualities by a hostile environment and periodic doses of A-bombs.

"If I were one of the *Shalnuksis*, I'd be frightened, but I'm not one of those sons of bitches. I'm proud to be human and proud to be Gwen's chosen mate. I'll always be proud of these things, whatever happens to me or to Tran."

The screen went blank. Jehna picked up a forkful of sachertorte, then put it down.

"So that's Les."

"An interesting specimen, isn't he? Not particularly discreet, but—"

"I'd like to meet him."

"To see if he's irresistible?"

"Jealous, K'yar?"

"Envious, rather. Les—I believe the phrase is 'has to beat women off with a club.'"

"In that case I'd rather meet Gwen. He's obviously found *her* irresistible." Jehna finished the torte and rubbed her stomach. "I shall have to fast halfway to Aderat to lose the weight your hospitality has put on me."

"If you find yourself a trifle full—"

"Satisfying one appetite doesn't satisfy all of them, my friend. You knew that once. Have you forgotten?"

He rose and stood behind her, his hands on her shoulders, and took her neck in his teeth. When she gasped he put his hands on her hips. "No, I haven't forgotten."

"I see you haven't."

She slipped out of her robe and he saw that she still swam

and sunbathed nude; the long limbs were as brown and supple as ever. He moved against her. They both knew that they were in danger, and as usual this was exciting her.

Danger was too constant a companion to excite him but he didn't object to its effect on Jehna. He would not forget their interlude in Seoul in 1950, the last time he and Jehna went Earthside together....

As desire replaced thought, Agzaral could not help wondering whether Les had stumbled on an important truth. Had the *Shalnuksis* conjured up a danger to the whole Confederation?

Interlude
GWEN TREMAINE'S DIARY

25/Mists/Ganton 2—Routine University business all day—inspecting the firewood and coal supplies and sending for more, reading reports, sitting on a court of inquiry on two legionaries found drunk in the women's quarters, etc., etc., *ad nauseam*.

Day only redeemed at the end by dinner with Larry Warner. He's got a positively courtly manner now, and a slight potbelly that he's fighting by working out with the Romans every morning. He's also obviously still interested in me, but not pushing it.

Just as well. The loneliness hasn't hit yet, but it will, after the child comes.

Should I have told Les about the child? He was frank enough with me about the kidnap attempt. I just don't know how much he will tell me. He says he doesn't want me to worry. If he keeps enough secrets about the Galactics I won't have to worry, I'll be dead! I don't know, but at least there won't be any question about whose kid this one is!

So far no morning sickness, so I haven't had to tell anyone but Marva and Sergeant McCleve. He's going to be
really handy to have around if I have another hard time;
he's reinvented obstetrical forceps. That could do almost as
much for a population boom as antisepsis.

Back to the dinner. Larry read me a letter from Lance
Clavell, our new Ambassador Extraordinary, Plenipoten-
tiary, etc., to the island city-state of Nikeis. It sounds like a
cross between Venice and Mont-St. Michel. Better than Venice. High ground. Won't sink. Or get flooded in the Time.
I'd sure like to see their Arsenal. Larry heard they can work
on a dozen ships at a time.

For the record, Nikeis is governed by a Council of Guilds
and merchant houses. Sounds like Venice again. They've got
a figurehead Eqeta and some theoretical allegiance to
Drantos, but I notice Drantos doesn't collect taxes there!
And the last time their Eqeta defied the Council they got a
new one. The old one and his heirs went off a cliff as a
special sacrifice for good weather....

The Nikeians import most of their food, but they do grow
some in terraces. Larry got figures for yields so high we
don't really believe them. If it's true, we want to know how
they do it. They use fertilizer, mostly from guano deposits
on the Glacier Coast. We've asked Clavell to negotiate for a
shipload for the University experimental farms. Larry
Warner says he wants to see Marva's face when she learns
she has to find storage for ten tons of seagull dung!

Clavell says that his assistant and chief of staff Clarence
Harrison is "getting enough action for a whole platoon." It
seems Nikeis was once saved by an admiral who also had lost
his left hand. Not many people believe Lord Harrison is
really this character come back, but a lot of people think he
has mana.

There's a rumor that Gengrich had Captain Aidhos do
Vis executed for "dishonoring" the Embassy to Ganton's
wedding. I said "Good riddance to bad rubbish" before I
could stop myself, which made Larry give me a really odd
look. I'd completely forgotten I'm not supposed to know

that Aidhos was trying to kidnap me. I will not kick all over-protective men in the shins. I will not kick all overprotective men in the shins. I will not kick all overprotective men in the shins. . . .

Anyway, Larry said Aidhos probably deserved what he got, but he hoped the man didn't have any family who'd think they were now at blood feud with Gengrich. From what I've heard of Gengrich he'd check that. How could he have lived this long and not known that much about local customs?

Larry knew Arnold Gengrich in Africa. After he talked about him for a while I said Gengrich sounded like an intelligent street gang leader. That got me another funny look, then Larry said that's just what Arnie used to be. Sounds like he'll fit right in, if Rick can talk him into coming back.

We ended the dinner when the candles began to gutter and smoke. Larry says he's trying to invent a clean-burning candle, and I promised to remember anything I could about candlemaking to help him. Oh, if we only had a couple of copies of *The Way Things Work. The Foxfire Book* would be even better.

PART TWO
Discoveries

CHAPTER ONE

Mason squinted against the glare of the sun from snow-covered hills. Then he raised his hand against the icy wind. "First and Second Platoons, form a mounted perimeter around the farm. Third and Fourth Platoons, prepare for dismounted action. Platoon leaders, this is a battle warning."

Mason pounded his numb hands together as the order passed back along the column. Tran cold-weather clothing was pretty damned good for a medieval society, and the Guards and starmen got the best. Mason had better: a polystyrene leotard and vapor barrier aluminized cloth over that. Put that under furs and you'd be warm in a blizzard.

The perimeter platoons moved out at a walk. They churned up fresh snow that fell back like sprays of tiny jewels. *Come on, come on. Let's get this over with.*

He kept hoping he was wrong about this old manor farm. *Maybe nobody's here. Or they bugged out already. They had time since the scouts found this place.*

A manor not on the registry, with no clear ownership. Land not only not cultivated but gone to thorns. Nothing else like that within a day's ride from Castle Dravan. No manor lord, it had to be directly held by the Eqeta. Or the Eqetassa...

Let's hope they bugged out. It could get sticky if they're still here.

"What the hell is this place, Major?" Jack Beazeley had no real trouble saying 'sir' to Art Mason, for all they'd been friends before Mason's commission. He'd say 'sir,' but he'd still ask questions.

"Jack, I damn well don't know. I got a hunch—"

Beazeley waved to indicate the Guardsmen surrounding the place. "Sir, you got more than a hunch. Just how much trouble do you expect? Sir."

"None at all, or maybe a lot."

"A lot. Lot as in mercs with ammo?"

"Huh? Naw. Not that. Locals, but damn good locals."

"Okay, as long as I know what to expect."

"I'll go in first."

"Like hell."

"Corporal, I'll go in first."

Beazeley shrugged. "Yes, sir."

The perimeter was formed, two lines of Guardsmen. One line faced in, the other outward. More troops held positions as reserves. Musketeers unslung their weapons while their loaders drove in the rests and nervously counted the charges on their bandoliers.

"We're set to take on a whole damn army," Beazeley said.

"Yeah. And it won't be that." He rose in his stirrups. "Sergeant Bisso!"

"Sir."

"Stay out here. You're in charge. Anything happens, report to the Colonel. Take live prisoners if you can. That may not be easy."

"Sir."

Bisso was a sergeant when I was a corporal. Don't seem to bother him a lot, but anything he knows, Elliot's going to know. Just as well, I guess.

Mason dismounted, drew his .45, and checked the loads. Then he signaled to Beazeley.

"Jack, follow me. Anybody in there knows we've come loaded for bear. If it's what I think, they're going to fight. I want prisoners. Live ones. Just remember that."

Beazeley tilted his head to one side. "Yes, sir."

The farmhouse showed signs of recent repairs, rough but sturdy. The only unusual thing was an image of Vothan One-Eye painted on the door.

"Another orphanage of the Children of Vothan?" Beazeley asked.

"That's what it says."

"But why out here?"

"Good question. Now shut up." Mason rapped on the door with the butt of his .45.

Silence.

Mason knocked again. After a moment there was a click, and movement behind Vothan's eye.

"Who seeks entry to the House of the Wolf?" The voice was unlettered.

"Open in the Name of the War Leader of Drantos."

"There is plague in this House, my lord."

Mason and Beazeley exchanged looks. "All the more reason to open the door. I bring starhealing and medics."

"My lord, we—"

"Open in the name of the Wanax and the Captain General of Drantos!"

Silence.

"Prepare to batter down the door."

Beazeley handed his M-16 to an orderly and took out a grenade. "Blow it in?"

"If it needs it."

"Right. Here goes." Beazeley tied a string to the grenade pin and wedged it against the door. "Stand back."

They heard the sound of bolts thrown back. Beazeley retrieved the grenade and his rifle and moved to cover the door as it opened slowly to reveal an unshaven man in peasant dress.

"I am Bartolf, my lord. A sick child and I are the only ones in this house. The plague took the ones who did not run away to seek better healing than I can give. The gods grant they find it."

"Indeed. Now if you will show me through the house."

"My lord, I beg you, do not expose yourself—"

"Now, Bartolf." Mason shouldered his way through the door. "Stick with me, Jack."

"Sir."

Bartolf led them off to the right along a low hallway lit by a pair of rush dips. There wasn't enough dust to show footprints.

"Damn fast plague," Beazeley muttered.

"Yeah."

"The boy is in here," Bartolf said, gesturing toward a curtained door. Beazeley tapped the opposite wall with a rifle butt. The wall was solid. Beazeley backed against it as Bartolf raised the curtain.

Inside was a row of pallets. A blanket-shrouded figure tossed and moaned on one of them. Bartolf led the way in. Mason raised his pistol and slipped through the door sideways. *It may be just what it looks like. But I might as well give Jack a clear field of fire.*

The moaning stopped and the blanket fell away. The small figure on the pallet held a crossbow. Mason ducked and fired. The .45 slug showered plaster over the pallet as the crossbow bolt ripped through the hood of his coat. A club smashed across his mailed shoulders and sent him sprawling onto the pallet.

Who? Bartolf was in the doorway, but there was someone else in the room and no time to think about that. The boy flung the crossbow away and pulled a dagger from under the pillow. Mason ignored the new man behind him. *Leave him for Jack!* Art dove toward the boy feet first. His boots smashed against the kid's elbow sending the knife flying across the room.

Art kicked at the boy's head and turned on Bartolf.

Bartolf threw up his hands. "My lord—"

Whatever he was going to say didn't matter. Mason chopped at the older man's throat, and when Bartolf raised both hands to ward off the blow Mason came down hard on both insteps. Bartolf grunted and Mason slammed him against the doorpost, kicked at a kneecap, and turned back toward the boy on the pallet.

Bartolf's fall left the doorway clear. Beazeley came through. The third man leaped at him with a short sword.

The blade hacked deep into the jacket Beazeley had wrapped around his left arm. Beazeley feinted high to bring the man's arms up, then drove four stiffened fingers into his attacker's solar plexus with a blow that lifted the man from the floor.

That's one. As Mason turned the boy leaped toward him. He held the dagger. Any inhibitions Mason had about cold-cocking children vanished. He stepped sideways and slammed the blade of his right hand into the base of the boy's neck. As the child thrashed, Mason braced two fingers under the boy's chin and dug into the carotid arteries. He held on as the boy's other hand flailed against him. In fifteen seconds the boy slumped. Mason held the grip another ten seconds and then drew his Colt.

The only other person on his feet was Jack Beazeley.

Mason shook for a second while his mind accepted the fact that it was over. "Thanks, Jack."

"Any time. Now, what the hell was that all about?"

"Later. Right now, you go out and give Bisso—" The Sergeant and five Guardsmen burst into the room.

"We heard shots. No action outside, and I've got the First Platoon in tight around the house, so—"

"No need, Bisso. There were two sick people instead of one. Wrap 'em up like mummies. Jack, you come with me."

Mason and Beazeley sat at a table in what must have once been the manor's bedroom. "Jesus." Mason waved to indicate the pile of objects on the table. "All that stuff."

There was a lot. Noose. Garrote. Bastinado. Fishskin buskins for climbing. Masks and scarves and hoods. Daggers. Crossbows, and the quarrel the boy had shot at Mason. There were also a dozen clay pots with lead stoppers. The crossbow quarrel and all the dagger points were stained with a dull green oil. "Want to bet those are poisoned?" Mason asked.

"Don't have to bet. I've smelled hydras bane before. Art, what in the hell is this place?"

"I'm still not sure, but—Jack, you ever hear of ninjas?"

"Jap assassins. Every now and then some merc claims to have ninja training. Never met one who knew anything. But yeah, I heard of them. Supposed to be able to walk up walls and turn invisible."

"I think that's what this place is. A training ground for the Tran equivalent."

"Humph. That kid can't be more than twelve. And all this gear is kid-sized. Apprentices? Maybe it makes sense."

"They're more than apprentices. Look how much trouble I had taking that one. A lot of good troopers got killed in 'Nam by kids no older than him."

"Yeah, I'll buy that, but Jesus, Art—Major—teeny-bopper ninjas? Whose?"

"Who do you think?"

"I don't get paid to think. But since you ask, let's see. Not the Romans. Not Ganton, he's not old enough. This place has been going since before he got crowned. Not the Captain. He doesn't think that way. So who?"

"This is a House of Vothan. Who founded them?"

"God damn! Major, you think the Captain knows?"

"I *know* he doesn't know. Next question. Do we tell him?"

"Why not? So his wife keeps a herd of trained juvie assassins. So what?"

"So one of them offed Caradoc."

Beazeley whistled. "Shee-it. You sure? Sir?"

"Wasn't until we took this place. Sure now."

"Okay. I guess I believe. Now what do we do?"

"We tell people. Start with Bisso and Elliot. That's enough so that if the mean little kids come after us somebody's left to tell the Captain."

Mason fingered a wine jug. "I sure want a drink, but—"

"Right. I wouldn't touch nothing from this place. Okay, we spread the word. What do we do with Bartolf and the others?"

"Good question. This place belongs to the Lady Tylara. Who's our boss, sort of. Makes them hers. But damn all, she's got no right keeping a herd of private killers."

"So what do we do?" Beazeley demanded.

"Turn them loose. I'll swear not to harm them or this House, if they swear to harm only the proclaimed enemies of the Crown of Drantos. If they go with that, we can leave them alone. I'll make that Bartolf write a report for our great Lady Eqetessa, explaining what we know, and what we made them promise. That ought to make her go easy on everybody."

"You hope. Sure it won't hit the fan anyway? Sir?"

"Hell, it probably will. Most of the kids got clean away. And there's fresh snow. We sure as hell can't track them. Look, we take this lot back under guard or we turn them loose under oath. I don't think of any other choices."

"So do we tell the Captain?"

"Shit. Ask Yatar. Ask Christ. Ask Ghu, but for Christ's sake don't ask me—"

"Still your job." Beazeley chuckled. "Major, I'm sure glad *I'm* not an officer."

The room was small and had earthen walls. The only entrance was hidden behind the coal bin, but tubes ran to all the rooms in the House of Vothan. Chai listened to Mason and Beazeley and smiled. He hadn't understood all of what they said, because they often spoke in star language; but when they called in Bartolf and the boy called Bennok they had to explain again.

So, he thought. The starmen were not going to burn out the Children root and branch. They were not going to reveal what they had learned to their soldiers. They had not even slain any of those who attacked them.

Yatar be thanked we shed no starman's blood.

The prayer came easily, and brought a wry grin. He had not always been called 'Chai,' and he had once been a consecrated priest of Yatar. That was before the infernal starmen with their new wisdom caught him stealing temple revenues. A change of names and tasks seemed preferable to an appointment with the Eqetassa's hangman.

Chai pulled a piece of sausage from inside his robe and munched it cautiously. It might have to last him for several days until the starmen led their Guards away.

Let it be soon. Chai had long practice in hiding, but being able to endure it was not the same as enjoying it. For many reasons it would be best if the Guards departed swiftly. The Lord Mason had found that four of the children's rooms had been empty far longer than the others, but he hadn't understood. Now it was too late. The four who went south would surely complete their mission....

Still, one must be sent to warn the Lady Tylara that this House had been found. When the messenger and the four who went south returned, all the Children of the Wolf could move to the other House, the house on the Littlescarp that no one would ever find. Then let Mason rage.

Oaths? What were oaths to those destined for Vothan's Hall, chosen by Vothan the Chooser to do His will in this world?

CHAPTER TWO

Gengrich looked up at the gray sky. The villagers standing in front of him would probably think he was praying to Yatar for the wisdom to give fair judgment. Actually he was trying to guess if it was going to rain before he reached home.

The sky said nothing about either rain or judgment. He could wait on the rain, but the judgment had to be given now. The villagers had given up half a day's work to bear witness before their lord; they would resent no judgment almost as much as a bad judgment.

Here goes nothing.

"I have heard all the witnesses from the villages of Fallen Eagle and Oak Creek. I have prayed to Yatar for guidance. Now I, Lord Gengrich do Zyphron, do give this as my judgment in the matter of the strayed cow of Oak Creek.

"I judge that the cow was indeed found unlawfully in the pastures of Fallen Eagle. I also judge that the cow strayed because of negligence by the herdboy, Bemis son of Nestor."

The faces of the Oak Creek people looked as grim as the sky. "I also find that the herdboy was trying to herd the cow back home when the men of Fallen Eagle came upon him. Therefore they had no cause to beat him so that he has been unfit for work these past ten days. They also had no cause to hurry the cow along so that she miscarried of a heifer calf."

"That old screw would've miscarried if we'n tapped her w' a feather!" shouted someone from Fallen Eagle. "Everybody knows that!"

"That cow was as healthy as yer big wind, Kuris!" came an equally loud reply from the Oak Creek side.

Now voices were raised on both sides, and a few fists. It would be knives and flails next. Gengrich signaled to Boyd, who shouted:

"Silence for the Lord's judgment!" and signaled to the guards. The thump of pike-butts striking the ground brought results.

"I therefore find that the offense of Fallen Eagle is the greater, and they owe a fine of four silvers plus two silvers toward the cost of healing the herdboy. I have also learned that this is the cow's third miscarriage. I will therefore buy her from the village of Oak Creek for eight silvers, that she may be slaughtered and provide a feast for both villages. If at that feast they will also swear peace with each other, I shall send bread and wine from my cellars."

Gengrich studied the crowd and was relieved to see long faces turn to smiles. A few villagers from Fallen Eagle still looked sullen, and a few of the Oak Creekers made rude gestures, but it looked as if the feud had been headed off.

"I thank you for your loyalty in bringing this matter before me. Yatar grant you warm beds this winter and good crops and sleek beasts next year."

Fat bloody chance, he added to himself. Aloud, he called for his horse.

They were riding past the stumps of the oak trees that had given Oak Creek its name when Boyd pulled close to him. "Arnie, how'd you know about the cow's miscarrying? She looked like it to me, but you're a city boy. No offense meant."

"I'm a city boy who knows how to use spies. One of Vinicianus's people went in disguised as a traveling shoemaker. He kept his ears open and his mouth shut until he got home."

"Oho."

The bridge over the creek had fallen during the last bunch of earthquakes, but it hadn't rained for a couple of days. They forded with the water no higher than the bellies of the horses, and were checking their gear on the far side when four men in Gengrich's colors rode up leading one of his warhorses.

"Lord Gengrich! A message from the Lord Vinicianus. He begs you to return at once to the castle. He has sent a fresh mount."

The horse was Buster, Gengrich's favorite. If Vinicianus had risked sending *him* out, it must be something worse than a flooded privy. Still, he was supposed to hear cases in three more villages. . . .

"What is it?"

The messenger lowered his voice. "He says it is an important message from the north."

"Very well. Alex, take fifteen men and ride on to the other three villages. Hear the witnesses—"

"Me? I'm no feudal judge!"

"You're the best they'll get today, buddy. Or do you want to spend half the winter patrolling their fields for barn-burners and cattle thieves?"

"You put it that way, no. Okay, hear the witnesses, and then—?"

"Tell each of them to send a man to Castle Zyphron. I'll give my judgment tomorrow."

Gengrich waited until Boyd had picked his men. *Alex has his problems. But he takes orders and you don't have to watch him every minute. It's worth a few bribes to husbands and fathers.*

Bloody tears ran from the staring eyes of the man in the bed. The fingers of his bandaged hands all ended at the first joint. His cheeks and nose were blackened ruins, stinking with infection and decay.

His moans rose to a gasping scream as Guilford unwrapped the bandages from one foot. Gengrich turned away, his stomach twitching. The foot was black halfway to the heel. The toes dangled in shreds of flesh, and the smell was beyond anything Arnie Gengrich could have imagined.

He forced himself not to be sick as Guilford snipped away the dead flesh, amputated the ruined toes, doused everything with antiseptics and ointments, and put on fresh bandages. When Guilford started on the other foot, Gengrich bolted for the door. As he went out he heard the screams turn into words:

"Evil—bandits—thought she sent them—didn't know—killed—killed . . ."

Gengrich stopped. "Eh?"

Guilford shook his head. "No point in you staying, Arnie. That's more sense than he's made in the last couple hours. Go on, before I have to tend you too!"

Gengrich nodded and stumbled through the door.

He stood on the castle wall and drew in deep lungfuls of damp chilly air. He watched the carpenters at work on the south gate. The castle had come off pretty well in the last quakes. Not like Rustengo. The big port city was supposed to be one-third in ruins now, with a lot of the rest ready to fall down if you sneezed hard.

He wondered if that would take some of the wind out of Schultzy's sails. Last time Mort had come for a visit he'd acted like a royal ambassador. Maybe he did have clout in Rustengo; he'd always been good at looking out for himself. Lucky too, and Gengrich had learned that luck counts for a lot.

Time, Mort. For you and me. We got anything the Captain wants, time to produce it. We ain't either one of us going to hold on down here much longer.

"Arnie?"

Guilford was standing behind him. "Yeah, Frank?"

"I gave him a knockout dose of babble juice. If he's lucky, he won't wake up."

"That bad?"

"That bad. If I was a real M.D. with the whole nine yards

I still couldn't save his hands or feet. As it is, the gangrene's spreading, he's got hemorraghic fever, and he's developing pneumonia. I'm surprised he got far enough for our patrols to pick him up."

"He's from up north?"

"Far as I can tell. From what he said before he went out of his head, he was some kind of clerk at Castle Dravan. Something made him think he and a couple of his friends were in danger. They cooked up a story about a dying mother and rode off in the middle of a snowstorm. They figured nobody would try to track them. If they didn't come back at all, everybody would think the storm got them."

"It did get one of them, and that's where—Karl, I think his name is—started the frostbite. Bandits killed another one south of Vis. Karl was going on sheer guts when he ran into one of our patrols."

Guilford rummaged in his bag and pulled out an oiled-leather packet sealed with wax. "He had this sewn into the lining of his coat. I thought you ought to see it first."

Gengrich drew a knife and slit the leather pouch open. A folded piece of parchment dropped out. He caught it and started reading.

"Jesus H. Christ!"

"Last time I called him, I got put on hold—" Guilford stopped at the look on Gengrich's face. "Trouble?"

"Yeah, but—Frank, you really didn't read this?"

"You had to cut it open, didn't you? Is it hot?"

"Too hot to talk about here. It's trouble, but maybe not for us. I need to talk with friend Marcus."

The long-expected rain was turning to wet snow. Gengrich hoped Alex and his men would make it home safely. Meanwhile he was fighting the chill with a roaring fire and a jug of Guilford's homebrew.

Marcus Julius Vinicianus sat across the table from him. He turned the parchment over and over in his fingers. He hadn't taken a drink since he began to read. Finally he shook his head. "I find it hard to believe that Lady Tylara would employ assassins to kill the man who saved her from Sarakos."

"Not just Caradoc. They suspect she offed Dughuilas. She set up somebody else, too."

"And I am probably looking at him?"

"Got any better candidates?"

"No. You hold your people together as an organized force. Without you to control them your Earthmen would fight. Your local recruits would be divided and many would desert. By spring the Lord Rick could set any terms he liked for taking your surviving men back under his rule."

"Just what I was thinking." Arnold Gengrich drained his cup and refilled it. "Which means I have to stay alive. That's a real interesting proposition, seeing as how I also have to let these thugs try to assassinate me."

Vinicianus looked down into his cup. "Does the wine speak, or did I hear you say you must allow an attempt on your life?"

"You heard me right."

"Then—may I say that I honor your courage, but your judgment...?"

"Is okay. Look, Marcus. This is something that can blow the Captain's alliance up north to little bits. If he stands by his wife, he's at blood feud with Caradoc's clan. If he dumps her, he's not Count of Chelm anymore. No land of his own. That'll make it hard for Ganton to keep him on as Captain General. And old Drumold will take his archers home. What's he got left?"

"Anarchy. And the Time drawing closer. The priests of Yatar will not be pleased either."

"*Nobody's* gonna be happy if this gets out. The worst of it is we don't *know* anything. All we have is this paper, and it's not signed by anybody. No proof she did it."

"But you believe—"

"I don't believe in coincidences. Not big ones. If Caradoc hadn't went west, things would have come apart."

"I reached the same conclusion. Caradoc's death was very

convenient. Too convenient. What has this to do with letting them attempt your life?"

"Hard evidence. We let 'em try and catch one in the act. Give the kid to the Captain for a present."

The Roman looked thoughtful. "That would work. But you must catch your rabbit before you make a stew. You leave yourself as bait for assassins whose numbers and skills may be greater than we know."

"Give me a better idea and I'll take it."

"Stay guarded."

"How? I have to ride circuit to give judgment. And I can't live with guards under the bed. Marcus, I am damned if I'll sit on my ass in this room all winter!"

"I sympathize. But I would not trade places with you. Given the Lady Tylara's reputation I would suppose she would not employ any but the most competent assassins.

"So. You seek evidence of the plot in order to trade with the Lord Rick. What else do you offer him?"

Gengrich shook his head to try to clear out the wine fumes. "I don't get you."

"I think we should be able to aid Lord Rick as well as threaten him. Threats alone might not move him, but if we have both carrot and stick..."

"With luck I'll have the stick. What's the carrot?"

"The craftsmen of Rustengo. The Lord Rick's University designs many new and useful devices, but there are few craftsmen in Tamaerthon or Drantos to make them. The Romans would gladly help, but Lord Rick does not altogether trust Romans."

"Smart man."

Marcus gave a tight smile. "The Lord Schultz has influence among the Guilds of Rustengo, if he is telling the truth."

"He's probably exaggerating, but Schultzy's no B.S. artist. If he says he can swing the Guilds, at the least they listen to him."

"Excellent. Then let us offer to guard all those Rustengan craftsmen who wish to seek new homes in the north. I imagine that many would have already done so, except for the winter storms at sea and the bandits on land. We can do nothing about the weather or the lack of ships. We have already done much about the bandits, and allied with the Lord Rick we can do more."

"That makes sense. Hell, Marcus, he might go better than that. To get a couple of thousand craftsmen for the University's shops he might even spring for enough ammo to fight Phrados's whole damned army!" Gengrich lurched to his feet and gripped Marcus's shoulder with the other. "Friend Marcus, let's drink a toast. To you and me never being enemies!"

CHAPTER THREE

"Present—*arms!*"

Twenty soldiers banged pike-butts on the stone floor. Two officers drew swords. A herald dressed in a moth-eaten scarlet robe strode forward.

"Who comes before Arnold son of Maximilian, Lord Gengrich, Lord of Zyphron?"

Schultz nodded to his own herald. The boy hitched up his robe, which was too long for him and made of plain blue cloth, though without moth holes. Then he stepped forward and shouted, while Schultz prayed his voice wouldn't break:

"Master of Foot Mortimer Schultz of Rustengo, speaking for the Great Guilds of the Free City of Rustengo."

"Bear you proof of this?"

"I do."

The boy's voice had been steady. Now his hands were too as he pulled Schultz's credentials out of his purse and handed them to the other herald. Schultz made a mental note to praise the boy for doing so well his first time as a herald. The job should have been filled by somebody more experienced, but the Great Guilds hadn't been able to agree on whom. So it went to young Dylos, who was some sort of cousin umpteen-times removed to Diana. He'd lost most of his family in the last quake, and landed on Schultz's doorstep with nothing but the clothes on his back. He couldn't just be turned away, so it was good to know he might really earn his keep.

In fact, the Great Guilds hadn't been able to agree on damned near anything other than sending this embassy. Schultz hoped Vinicianus's spies weren't as good as they were supposed to be, otherwise Gengrich would know too damned much about what a poor hand old Schultzy held.

The other herald turned toward the dais where Gengrich sat. "By my own honor and that of my office, by Yatar and Vothan, I swear that these are the true seals of the Great Guilds of the Free City of Rustengo."

Gengrich took the parchment. "Then I greet you, Master Schultz. How does the Free City?"

"Well enough." That was actually pretty close to the truth. The Rustengans were a tough lot, and were already pulling themselves together even before the last of the quake's thousand dead were dug out and buried. If the walls hadn't been so badly damaged that the city couldn't be made defensible before spring came and with it Phrados's army—

"We honor the men of Rustengo, and join you in mourning your dead. Yet if matters are well in the Free City, what do the Great Guilds ask of us? And why do they send an ambassador who will not submit to having his weapons peacebonded?"

Dylos's mouth dropped open. Schultz put a hand on his shoulder before he could say anything. "Lord Gengrich, two strong men may yet find themselves still stronger by joining forces. That could be the case with the Free City and the Lord of Zyphron."

"Indeed."

"As to why I refused to submit to peacebonding—I do not wish to insult your valiant men, but I could not be sure they had their orders in this matter from you. If it was indeed your wish that this be done . . ."

Schultz let his voice trail off and fixed Gengrich with a look. *I can play cockamamy games too.*

It was an old argument in this area: did a Master of Foot of a Free City rank as a noble with the right to be received in formal audience bearing an unbonded weapon? Or did he rank as a merchant, whose weapons had to be bonded?

It didn't make much personal difference to Schultz. He still had his holdout gun and boot knife. It was obviously important to Gengrich. His people wouldn't let him back down.

It would also stick in the craw of the Great Guilds if they had to put up with contempt from an ally. In fact, they might refuse the alliance. But if Schultz flat-out refused the peacebonding, the alliance might never even be offered.

The thought of Diana being crushed in the next quake or turned over to Phrados's men settled Schultz's mind. "Lord Gengrich, to honor custom I shall submit to the peacebonding of my sword. You have but to give the order in my presence, and I will say no more."

Gengrich nodded graciously. "I see that the Great Guilds have chosen their ambassador wisely. To honor him and that wisdom, I will peacebond Master Schultz's sword with my own hands."

Schultz relaxed. That was an honor often shown to men who were noble in their home countries but not here— Romans of equestrian rank, for example.

Gengrich stepped down from the dais. One of his guards handed him a yard-long leather thong. He wound it several times around the hilt and guard of Schultz's short sword, then began an elaborate knot. As he tied it he bent down until his mouth was next to Schultz's ear.

"Schultzy?" The whispered question was in English.

Schultz nodded.

"Don't say anything. Don't give up your holdout gun, but don't let anybody see it. How are things in Rustengo, really? Not so bad?"

Schultz nodded again.

"Not so bad that you're beggars?"

A third nod.

"I didn't think you would be. Well, I don't think I'm going to be asking for anything you can't give." He tightened the knot. "Someone with my signet ring will come around to your quarters about a candle after sunset. Follow him. Don't take anybody with you—"

Schultz shook his head.

"Okay, take your herald. But that's all. Understand? Otherwise no deal!"

A nod. Gengrich finished the knot and straightened up.

"Let this peacebonding be a sign of the strong peace between Zyphron and the Free City in days to come. Long live the Free City!"

The cheering was ragged, but with a couple of drums thrown in there was enough noise to hide Schultz's sigh of relief. He'd made it to first base without giving up anything important. Now Arnie wanted to talk for real.

Schultz backed away from the dais. *I could turn, but it doesn't cost anything to be polite. But I'm sure going to be in armor when Arnie's messenger comes with that ring.*

Gengrich sighed contentedly as the bathmaid poured another bucket of hot water into the tub.

"I think it's time to start warming the oil."

"I've already warmed it, my lord. Then I wrapped it in a hot towel."

"Good, Risha. You're learning your work very fast."

The girl blushed and looked down. She was the shy kind, never speaking unless you spoke to her first. Probably that busted nose and the scars on her chin and her left ear made her think she was ugly. She had a real nice figure, though, and with that head of blond hair—well, if he hadn't valued peace with his women, Gengrich would have asked her to shuck off her gown and hop in the tub with him.

It was a Japanese-style tub, one of the little comforts he'd insisted on introducing to Castle Zyphron. Originally it had been founded as a Roman camp, back when this was part of the Roman Provinces, but that was so long ago that you'd need a steam shovel to dig out the Roman baths. The tub leaked a couple of gallons every bath, but it still beat standing bare-assed in a stone-cold room and taking a sponge bath—

Someone was shouting outside the bathroom door, then Gengrich heard running feet. Fists pounded on the door.

"Lord Gengrich! Lord Gengrich!"

"The lord is at his bath—" began one of the guards at the door.

"Fire in the kitchen!" someone shouted.

"Damn!" said Gengrich. He stood up, sending water sloshing over the rim of the tub. A fire in the kitchen could be dangerous, with all the grease and oil ready to go up. Even if it didn't spread, it could fill the whole place with smoke and force everybody outside on a miserable cold wet night—

"One of you go down and help fight the fire," he said to the guards. "The other stay here, but leave the door open in case we have to leave in a hurry. Risha, you'd better go too."

"Thank you, lord, but with you here there is no danger."

Gengrich grinned, not quite sure if he'd been flattered or insulted. Better warn her not to try any remark like that on Alex Boyd....

One of the guards ran off to join the fire-fighting. The other wedged the door ajar with the lid of an oil pot and stood facing the opening. Risha went over to the hearth and picked up a cloth-wrapped bundle. Gengrich heard more shouting in the distance and sniffed for smoke.

Running feet echoed in the hallway. A man wearing a sodden cloak peered around the door. "Lord Gengrich! There's a fire at the south gate! The scaffolding—ah!" He broke off with a gasp. Then he clutched at the back of his neck and fell.

As he hit the floor Gengrich saw Risha's blue eyes blaze open. The look on her face turned her from a pretty teen-ager to a demon.

"Look out! The girl!" Gengrich shouted.

His warning was too late for the guard. Risha flung the oil pot straight at his head. Gengrich heard the crunch of bone, then the guard was down on top of the worker, writhing and clawing at eyes blinded by hot oil.

Risha reached under her gown and came out with a knife that looked two feet long.

He was already climbing out of the tub as she reached him. She stabbed upward toward his groin. Gengrich twisted and the thrust missed its target, but his violent movements upset the tub. It went over with a crash, and sent a wave of oily water across the floor. The water reached the hearth; the fire hissed, spat, and poured out a cloud of choking smoke.

Risha lost her footing on the suddenly slippery floor and went down. Gengrich stood and turned to run. She rolled and bounced to her feet like a trained athlete. She slashed at his leg and the knife left a thin line of red.

"Ho, guards! Assassins! To your lord!" Then, as Risha dashed between him and his sword he shouted again. "Help!"

The knife flicked across Gengrich's left arm, leaving more red—and now he felt more pain in his leg than a light cut like that should have left. Poison on the knife? God, what a hell of a way to go, cut to bits by a teenaged girl!

"God damn you!" He struck at her and missed, feinted to the left, then kicked as she turned. She was fast but not fast enough to escape entirely. His bare foot whacked solidly against her left arm.

He feinted again, and stepped on a broken piece of oil pot. *God damn it!* He felt himself going over, and dived into a roll toward the girl. She slashed at his thigh, but that brought her knife hand in reach of his left. He grabbed the wrist, squeezing and twisting and heaving all in one motion. She let herself rise, then came down with her heel just missing his groin. He clamped his legs together on her foot without letting go of her hand, then rolled. She went down, but her thick pad of hair saved her skull.

"Give up, damn you!"

She didn't answer. Her left arm wasn't working. She clawed at his eyes with her right hand. "Enough," Gengrich shouted. He locked the fingers of his free hand into her hair and smashed her head against the floor. She moaned but still struggled. He smashed her head down again. Then a third time, for luck and hate.

She was still breathing. He took a deep breath and resisted the impulse to stamp on her throat.

Schultz turned the corner behind the guide and cursed the cold and damp. He was sneezing before they reached the end of the corridor. *Damn and blast.* Colds were no fun on a planet ten light-years from nasal spray and Kleenex!

Maybe it would have helped if he hadn't worn armor. He could feel the chill of his mail shirt even through the arming doublet. Now a couple of extra layers of wool might have done a nice job—

"Look out!" The shout made the guide draw his sword and sprint down the hall toward a half-open door on the left side. He'd covered maybe ten feet when the shadow of a beam seemed to turn solid and stick a knife in him.

At least that was the way it looked to Schultz. "Dylos, stay behind me—!"

"Ho, guards! Assassins! To your lord!" Smoke poured out of the door. "Help!"

The solid shadow came at Schultz with a knife in its hand.

Schultz's 9-mm Star was in his hand before his attacker got to knife range. He squeezed off three rounds before he took time to wonder why the man looked so small. Schultz fired once more as he fell. *That's one.* He turned warily.

A crossbow twanged from farther down the corridor and a quarrel sprouted from Dylos's chest. Lord, why hadn't the kid worn armor? Schultz fired twice into the darkness and was rewarded by a scream and the sound of a falling body. *Six rounds. Two left.* He wished for his 9-mm H&K with its fifteen rounds, and groped his way into the alcove.

Small fingers with an iron grip clamped around his wrist. At the same time a knife thrust toward his thigh. It struck the tail of Schultz's mail shirt. He heard a high-pitched curse and the grip on his gun hand tightened.

The attacker was small enough to lift from the floor. Schultz picked him up by the groin and threw him against the stone wall. The grip relaxed and he brought the Star to bear, thought better of it, and smashed the barrel into the attacker's throat. *Not too hard. Not to break anything.* Then he brought the butt of the weapon down on top of the assassin's head.

Suddenly the hall was filled with guards. They eyed his pistol warily.

"Schultzy?"

"I'm okay, Alex. I heard Arnie call from in there. Tell these jokers I'm not an assassin."

"Oh, shit. Joe, stay here and square it. You can see what Schultzy caught." Boyd ran on down the corridor.

"What did you catch?" Green asked. He lifted the hood from the nearest attacker. "Christ, he can't be more than twelve."

"Twelve or fifty, he damn near killed me," Schultz said.

The other two were maybe a year older. One was a girl. Both were dead or dying.

"Good shooting," Green said.

"Yeah. Sure."

"Like Cui Nol." Green turned to the guards and pointed at the younger boy. "Tie him up good. If he dies I'll kill the man who killed him. If he gets away I'll go after families."

"Rough," Schultz said in English.

"Arnie's been after a live one. We owe you, Schultzy."

"A fat lot of good that's going to do Dylos," was the answer Schultz wanted to give. He swallowed it. Instead he bent over the dying boy. The crossbow was only a little one, the kind used for small game, but the quarrel had gone deep into Dylos's unprotected chest.

"You did well, Dylos. Your family will be proud."

"No family, Mas— No family. Only you. So—didn't want to dishonor—you. Herald's honor too. Can't—distrust men by—wearing—"

Blood trickled from the corner of Dylos's mouth and his eyes rolled up in his head. The hand Schultz was holding twitched a couple of times, then went limp.

Schultz was still holding that hand when Boyd came up beside him. "There's another of them in there with Gengrich. Girl about fifteen. She's alive. Good figure, too."

Alex always did have woman problems. That was just too bad for the girl; nobody forced her to make a living sticking knives into people.

"How's Arnie?"

"The girl nicked him a couple of times with a poisoned knife. Frank's in there with him now. Says it doesn't look serious.

"It looks like the girl was the primary," Boyd went on. "These three were back-up and guard. They came up the wall on a rope with a hook on the end. Set fires in the kitchen and the south gate with volcano-bush resin in cubes, then used the confusion to make their move."

Schultz wasn't sure whether he was hearing things or Boyd had gone crazy. "Alex, they're kids! Just what the hell is going on around here?"

"Schultzy, we'll tell you as soon as we know ourselves."

Gengrich winced as Frank Guilford pulled the last strip of bandage off his left arm. "Can you make a fist?" the medic asked. Gengrich winced again but succeeded.

"Good."

"What about delayed effects?"

"Not with hydras bane sap in this dosage. You'll have scars, but you got off real light."

Gengrich hoped Frank knew what he was talking about. His arm and thigh looked and felt as if a red-hot poker had been laid along them.

"It's the oil," Frank said. "That sap dissolves in oil. Your fancy bubble bath saved your ass, or anyway your leg."

Gengrich sipped from a cup of hot wine and gritted his teeth as Guilford cleaned the wound and applied a freshly boiled bandage. Finally the medic was done.

"You won't be wrestling anybody for a couple of weeks, and I'd go easy on the wine. Now I'll go make up more babble juice."

"I still say wring the little bastards dry without any juice," said Alex Boyd. "Give me the girl."

"For Chrissake let's not start that again," Gengrich shouted. "I want them alive. Not just to talk, alive to take to the Captain, damn it."

"I won't kill her," Alex said. "She might wish I did."

"Maybe you would," Guilford said. "Alex, you didn't get a good look at that girl when I was treating her. I don't know what happened, but she's been to hell and come back. I'd bet you'd lose interest before she said a word—"

"Now listen, you goddamned—" began Boyd.

"Can it, both of you," said Gengrich wearily. It was an old quarrel between Guilford and Boyd. "You got anything else to say, Frank?"

"No, sir."

"Okay. Dismissed."

Guilford went out. Gengrich ignored medical advice and poured himself more wine. Over the rim of the cup he saw Schultz and Vinicianus trying to pretend they hadn't heard Guilford and Boyd shouting at each other.

At least it was a change from trying to pretend they didn't see each other. Vinicianus didn't want Schultz in this little council of war. *And bull shit. Schultzy saved my ass. He can sure as hell find out what he saved it from.*

Vinicianus still looked daggers at Schultz when he thought Gengrich didn't see.

"Okay. We've got the goods on the Lady Tylara and her mean little kids. But damn all, the only way the Captain's going to believe this is to talk to those kids. I mean it, Alex, we got to keep them alive. That means no rough stuff, and no 'killed while trying to escape.'"

"That could mean asking people to get killed to save those little bastards."

"So what? Give 'em a hero's funeral. But keep those kids, because that's our only ticket into Galloway's service. And don't you forget it. We are agreed, aren't we? We go north as soon as the Captain will let us?"

"Yeah, sure," Boyd said.

"What's in it for the Guilds?" Schultz demanded.

"Safe passage north. We'll escort as many craftsmen as will come. And negotiate with Galloway for you."

Schultz thought for a moment. "We can live with that."

"Right. Face it, the Captain had three times the balls and twice the brains Parsons thought he did. Now we've got us an ace in the hole, 'cause the Captain's lady has screwed up but good. Here's to Lady Luck, also known as Tylara do Tamaerthon, Eqetassa of Chelm and Mrs. Rick Galloway."

They drank the toast. By the time Schultz went over to the fireplace to heat more wine, they'd roughed out a text of the letter that would go north.

"I'll write it myself in Tex-Mex. Larry Warner knows that and I don't think anybody else does. Certainly none of the locals. Larry's got his head screwed on the right way; he'll see that it gets to the Captain. Marcus, your people can get a letter into the University without too much trouble, I suppose?"

Vinicianus smiled thinly. He had stayed soberer than usual when the wine was flowing freely; Gengrich could recall his taking only two cups. Was having a rival going to cure his boozing?

"If they cannot, then I have spent much gold to very little purpose."

Over the second batch of wine they roughed out a treaty between the Lord of Zyphron and the Free City of Rustengo and any allies that either party wanted to include.

"Your people and Rustengo," Vinicianus said. "But not the Roman provinces."

"Which are?"

"The boundaries are not agreed. But if you include as your allies people Marselius Caesar thinks are his subjects, it can do no good and may do much harm."

"Leave 'em out," Gengrich said. "Don't cost much. We don't control much of the old Roman territory anyway." He hiccoughed and drank again. "The thing is. The thing is, find out what people want and push where it gives. And maybe you'll get lucky. We just did."

CHAPTER FOUR

"...problemas formidables por el Capitan. Yo creo que el Capitan es un hombre muy sensible, y el Capitan esto tambien comprende. Es imposible que el Capitan no vide una ruta que no me permitera la silencia sobre la muerta de los caballeros Cara—y Duig—. Usted sabe que los fueron.

Su amigo
Arnold G

Larry Warner laid the second page of Gengrich's letter on top of the first. This was the third time he'd read it. The initial shock had worn off, but his hands weren't any steadier. *Problemas formidables indeed. For the Captain, the University, and everybody else.* He didn't need much help from either his imagination or the chilly room for his hands to shake.

At least he could do something about the chill.

"Hamar!"

The boy's head popped around the door. "Yes, Lord Warner?"

"More wood for the fire, and a pot of McCleve's Best."

"At once, my lord."

He didn't really want to get drunk. *Can we trust Arnie?* He tried to remember what he knew about Gengrich. Not a lot. Good man in a fight. Medium on leadership. Talked us into running away from Parsons, but couldn't hold the group together. Not officer material. *Hah. Maybe not, but he's sure got an officer's problems now!*

And so do I. What the hell do I do with this thing? Who do I tell?

The candle on Warner's desk burned steadily, without guttering or flaring. Funny how something as simple as twisting three strands to make a wick could make such a big difference. It had all been trial and error, too; he couldn't have explained exactly what difference it made to save his life. Didn't matter. University-made candles brought a hell of a profit, and would until the local chandlers figured out the secret. *They will, too. That's one bit of knowledge we don't have to try to spread.*

Warner realized he was holding the two sheets inches from the candle. A little closer to the steady flame, and this particular hot potato would be ashes. *And what the hell good would that do? If Arnie can write a letter in Tex-Mex to me he can write one in English to the Captain. Or in local to any damn body he feels like.*

One thing sure. It's no bluff. Gengrich named too many people, places, and dates to be making this up.

Warner put the letter down and looked up at the sooty ceiling. He knew he probably had what Gwen called his "Why me, God?" expression on his face. That was certainly how he felt.

Speaking of Gwen—what about telling her? Warner got up and began to pace the length of the room. *It's her fault. In a way. Marrying Caradoc, then running straight back to Les when he showed up.*

She'd screwed up, and got a damned good man killed. That would always lie between her and Warner now. He'd be polite to her, no problem with that, but nothing else, and she'd notice it. She'd start to worry, then maybe start to prod, and if she didn't get answers would they be able to work together? The Captain was going to have a few things to say to both of them if they mucked up the University.

A knock on the door.

"Come in, Hamar."

The boy set the pot of homebrew on the desk, piled the armful of logs on the fire, then came back to fill Warner's cup. It was silver, commissioned from a Roman soldier who'd been apprenticed to a silversmith before he joined the legions. Lovely work, with centaurs and horses chasing each other around the rim. Probably cost a thousand or more back home.

Back on Earth, you mean. Tran's home now, Tran or nothing. *And Tran's not so bad. Consider the bracing climate, the quaint customs of the natives, the chance to sample genuine medieval living, the spice of danger to keep you from going soft, the headaches caused by women who can't keep their pants on . . .*

Warner swigged down his wine. Oh well, there was always one thing to do with a hot potato: pass it up the chain of command. That meant Elliot. Let the Sergeant Major worry about it. Let *him* tell the Captain.

"Here's to the chain of command!"

Mason pulled his chair out and turned it so that he could sit with his feet toward the fire.

Elliot handed around cups of herb tea well laced with McCleve's Best. "Not bad stuff, Professor," Elliot said. "I expect the Major can use a bit more of that."

"Damn straight. The passes are full of snow. They say this is a mild winter." Mason drained half the cup. "Hate to see a bad one. Now what's all this about?"

"In a minute," Warner said. He refilled the cups.

"Where's Gwen?" Mason asked a couple of swallows later.

"Interviewing her new—guess you'd call it office manager," said Warner. "Not a secretary—that means a scribe to the locals, and that's not work for a noblewoman. This girl's a granddaughter of old Camithon."

"Is she good-looking?" asked Mason.

"What's the matter, Major?" said Elliot. "Another suit fall through?"

"Top, it never got off the ground in the first place," Mason said. "What I really need is a professional matchmaker. Or better yet, a Polaroid camera."

"You'd have to be careful taking pictures," said Warner. "Somebody could decide the camera was stealing their souls."

Elliot laughed. "The Ay-rabs believe that. Least the Yemeni did. Hadn't heard they think that here."

"Neither have I," said Warner. "But an awful lot of the locals still believe that what was good enough for great-grandma is good enough, period. Hell, talk to some of the local chandlers about my new candle wicks. I figured they'd copy them just for the money, but naw, they're waiting for a sign from Yatar—"

"Okay, you got good candles. And I didn't ride through half the snow on Tran to hear about them. Spit it out, Professor."

Warner sighed. "Yeah." He pulled out two sheets of parchment covered with tight handwriting. "It's in Tex-Mex, so you'll have to trust my translation."

"I can read that lingo too, Professor," Elliot said.

"I guess Arnie didn't know that."

"Arnold Gengrich doesn't know anywhere near as much as he thinks he does," Elliot said.

"So one of you read it to me."

"I'll do it." As Warner finished each sheet he passed it to Elliot.

Art Mason got up and poured another cup of tea. "Read that way to you, Top?"

"Yes, sir."

Yes, sir. Elliot's all of a sudden glad he's not in charge. Mason turned to Warner. "Think he's bluffing, Professor?"

"No, sir."

"He's not. I found out a few things on my own." He looked significantly at Elliot, who nodded. "No bluff, and he's got all the proof he needs."

"Does the Captain know yet?" Elliot asked.

"Not yet. Unless Larry sent in a report—"

"Not me," Warner protested.

"We have to tell him."

"Yes, Sergeant Major, we have to tell him."

"Major, we ought to have told him the instant you found that damned Wolf House."

"Maybe. Warner, who else did you talk to about this?"

"Nobody."

Mason raised one eyebrow. "Not even Gwen?"

"No, sir. I figured this one was too big for me to handle."

"You figured right," Elliot said. "You go on keeping your mouth shut around Gwen and I'll begin to think you're as smart as you say you are."

Art Mason paced the length of the room. "Okay. Larry, you're coming to Edron with us. Find yourself a good reason. The Captain will be there if we leave now. You know Gengrich better than the rest of us. How much time do you reckon we have?"

"Awhile. Until spring, I'd guess. Arnie knows we can't march in the winter. He wants to come back, not mess us up."

"It could mess things pretty good if we say 'Come back, all is forgiven,'" Elliot said. "He set up on his own. Did a good job, too. Bring him back and he gets a lot more firepower. Do we trust him with it?"

"Don't know, Sergeant Major. But what are our choices? Suggestions, Top?"

A long silence. "None, sir."

"Okay. Another thing. No semaphore messages on this. None. If any more code clerks desert, the system comes apart."

"Yes, sir," Elliot agreed.

"Anything more? No?" Art held out his cup. "How about a refill, Professor. Leave out the tea."

They were a long way from Earth and military formalities, but Warner, Elliot, and Mason stood at attention in front of Rick Galloway's desk. Rick laid the parchment sheets aside and regarded them coldly.

"Okay. You aren't the first to hide something from the Old Man. I don't need excuses or apologies. What I need is answers. Mason."

"Sir."

"You say the House of the Wolf was abandoned just after you went in there. They didn't care dick about the oath you made them take. Right?"

"Looks that way, Colonel."

"Any chance of finding the Children?"

"No sir. The trail's cold and there's been new snow. I put Beazeley and the Intelligence people on it, and that's about all I can do without turning out enough manpower to make people curious."

"So they could have gone anywhere. Including south."

"Yes, sir," Elliot said. "Which means Gengrich may have more to worry about than he knows."

"Holy—we can't alert him," Warner blurted. "Least I don't know how. The semaphore system—"

"I thought of that," Rick said. "But thanks for bringing it up. You three made one good move there. None of this goes onto the semaphore. Elliot, we've got to restructure that system. Beef it up. I want it tougher, and more secure. And under *our* exclusive control."

"Yes, sir. I'll get on it."

"There's maybe one way to find them," Mason said. He fell silent.

"Spit it out."

"If we knew where to look."

"Oh." Rick thought about that. "She would know, wouldn't she?"

"It's a safe bet, sir."

Art looks relieved. Why? Because I'm taking it so well. Oscar time, Galloway. "The question is, do I let her know that we know?"

"Nobody can decide *that* but you," Warner said. Elliot glared at him.

"May I say something, sir?" Mason asked.

"Yes."

"Like I told Beazeley, Lady Tylara has a short fuse but she isn't crazy. It's why I didn't stake out the place and round up the Children when I had a chance. I don't know what she's planning—"

"But you think it might be useful."

"Yes, sir. Exactly."

"I'm sure she'd appreciate the compliment."

"There's something else," Elliot said.

"Yeah, Top?"

"You already know it, Colonel. We put too much effort in this and the story'll leak out. God knows what happens then, but it won't be good."

"Blood feud. Not just Lady Tylara, but her father and his whole clan," Larry Warner added. "Against Caradoc's people. That sets a good part of the University garrison into civil war."

"So we have to see it doesn't get out," Rick said. "That's priority one. What can we do if it leaks out anyway?"

Art Mason shook his head. "Colonel, you know as well as me. Lady Tylara would have to disown her little assassins, and turn them over alive to Caradoc's relatives. Or put their heads on pikes."

Which she won't do. If she gave the orders, she'll protect the kids who carried them out. I think. I sure as hell can't assume she won't. Jesus Christ, no wonder she won't sleep with me! "And even that won't work."

"Probably not," Warner said. "It's too big for blood money. This was—was—"

"Cold-blooded betrayal of a loyal subordinate," Rick finished for him. "Yes, Mr. Warner, I'm aware of that." *And I shouldn't talk to him like that.*

"There's another problem, Colonel," Mason said. "Caradoc commanded the Mounted Archers. Some of our most loyal troops. If they find out—"

"Who watches our backs," Rick finished. "Thank you for reminding me. We don't have any choices. So. Assuming we can keep secrets—"

Elliot drew himself up to say something.

"And we can, it boils down to Gengrich. How smart is he? Mr. Warner?"

"Colonel, I thought about that all the way here. I'd say plenty smart enough." He spoke in a rush. "He'll have given himself insurance. Told some people. Too many for us to off. Not enough that it'll get out if we cooperate with him."

"Sure of that?"

"Pretty sure, sir."

"Elliot?"

"Yeah, he'd try to do it that way."

"Can he bring it off?"

Elliot hesitated. "Yes, sir. I think so."

"So. Gengrich wants full pardons for his people, and confirmation of his field promotions. Can we live with that?"

"No problems with the pardons," Elliot said. Mason nodded agreement. "Promotions may be stickier."

"They're also more likely to be negotiable," Warner said. "You can be sure that Arnie asks for more than he thinks he'll get."

"We can promote our own people," Rick said. "Rank inflation. Everybody moves up a couple of notches." *And it helps that we've got about a dozen organizations and everybody has different ranks in each.* "All of Gengrich's mercs will be Star Lords."

"Which will mean one hell of a lot more here than down there," Mason said.

"Will it?" Rick asked. "We live better, but we've also got discipline. Elliot, what kind of problems is Gengrich bringing?"

"Boyd's the biggest one. Lot of ability, but he chases. Chases anything, married or not."

"He'll keep it in his pants here," Rick said. "See to it."

"Sir."

"That's settled, then. Next question. Gwen. How much does she know?"

"I said I didn't tell her, Colonel—"

"I know what you said, Mister Warner. Are you sure that's the only way she has of finding out?"

"The letter was sealed."

"And in Tex-Mex," Elliot said.

"Gwen knows Latin," Rick said.

"Oh, shit, of course she does."

"So how sealed?" Rick asked.

"Looked good to me. Sewed up and sealed in leather, Arnie's high school class ring stamped in wax all over it. Colonel, I'd bet a lot nobody opened that before me."

"We are betting a lot. If she knows and we don't know it—damn, I'm almost tempted to tell her myself."

"Might not be a bad idea," Warner said. "This might be a strain—"

"Three can keep a secret if two are dead," Mason said. "Colonel, there's enough know this now. It's sure to get out, no matter what we do. The longer that takes, the better. Long enough and it's just another rumor."

"Okay. We don't tell her." *You don't. Maybe I will. Be a good reason to go see her.* "Anything else?"

"No, sir."

"Good. Dismissed."

Rick waited until the others had left. *Les always thought Gwen would marry me. I suppose he thought I'd be civilized about things when he came back.* He lifted the wine cup, and stared at it a moment. Then he threw the wine into the fire.

Interlude
GWEN TREMAINE'S DIARY

—the first day I felt like being up and around since Caradoc's birth. I still don't have enough milk to nurse him, but
he's thriving on what the wet nurses give him, and otherwise
he didn't give me much trouble. That's one hard delivery
and two fairly easy ones. Maybe I'm getting the knack. If
I'm going to be Fertile Myrtle on a planet with medieval
obstetrics and gynecology, I'd better.

The name won't fool anybody into thinking the boy is
Caradoc's, at least anybody who can count. It doesn't matter
that much. It would have if I'd remarried and gotten pregnant barely two months after Caradoc was killed. Funny
how charitable people are now that my long-lost Earth soldier husband is back from the dead.

The weather is mild enough to make you think spring
really will come before you're old and gray. One thing about
being pregnant in the winter: it makes cabin-fever even less
endurable. But it does look like the winter will end.

Larry Warner came by for lunch. He's still as wound up as
he was before he went up to Edron. What does he know that
he's not telling me? I tried to find out, but he started talking
about the guano shipment from the Nikeian islands. . . .

Damn whoever or whatever made Larry so nervous
around me! It's spoiled my only real open friendship on this
damned planet.

It doesn't help that Marva has accepted Campbell.
They're going to be married when Rick comes through on
his way south, so we'll have plenty of high-ranking witnesses
and sponsors. Marva's going to keep working, at least until

the kids start coming, but now she'll pass things on to Campbell that maybe he shouldn't know. One more problem.

I thought Lady Siobhan would be able to take Marva's place, but now it looks like Art Mason has staked a claim. He writes to her, and the last time he was here he started giving her English lessons. Of course he'll probably let her go on working. The University is one of the safest places around. But she's only seventeen. Who'll have her loyalty—the University or her husband? Foo. Another confidante lost. She'll be the next thing to Rick's spy here.

Rick. I asked Larry how he and Tylara are, and got the oddest look. Not surprise, exactly; but—I wish I knew what Rick is thinking. Last time I was there, he and Tylara weren't what you'd call chummy. Suppose—No. I cannot think about that. I simply cannot.

Les, I miss you. Don't sideswipe a black hole or anything stupid like that.

PART THREE
Prophets

CHAPTER ONE

It was spring at Castle Armagh. Spring meant there was no more ice. The roads were slow because of mud. In a normal year that would get better as summer came on, but Rick wasn't betting on it.

"We can march tomorrow," Art Mason reported. "Nobody likes it, but we can do it."

"Then we will. Plan on an early start." Rick inspected the field gear laid out on his work table. In addition to armor and weapons, there was elaborate sleeping gear, and a hot-draft stove that burned twigs and pine needles and could boil water for tea in minutes. "Sure a lot of stuff to carry around."

"Only we don't have to carry it," Art Mason said.

"Yeah. Makes me feel a little funny. We don't let the troopers take this much gear."

"Rank Hath Its Privileges. Colonel, there's not a man in the army would begrudge you a few comforts."

"You sure?"

"Yes, sir. I'm sure."

"Okay. Hoped you'd say that. Jesus, Art, I'm tired of campaigning."

"So skip this one—"

"Can't. Too many complications. Religious war. Gengrich. The Rustengo artisans. Roman allies. The religious merger. Just too many balls to juggle."

Mason sighed. "I read it that way, too, sir. This one needs you."

There was a knock at the door.

"Who?" Mason asked.

"Tylara."

Rick raised an eyebrow. "Come."

There was no one with her. She was dressed in a long gown of *garta* cloth dyed an off red. *Doesn't really flatter her,* Rick thought. *But it's sure expensive.* She was also wearing a malachite necklace Rick had given her.

"My Lord Mason," Tylara said.

"Good day, my lady. I was just leaving." Mason ducked out and closed the door on the way.

"You come unescorted. Is that wise?"

She laughed. "It is safe enough. Who would harm us in our own castle?"

You'd know that better than me. "What brings you—"

"You leave tomorrow."

"Yeah."

"There was a time when that would have been more than enough reason to see—for us to see each other."

"I suppose that's true," Rick said.

"As you say." Tylara smiled. "But my reasons are not entirely frivolous." She took a small packet from her sleeve.

"For me?" Rick unwrapped the cloth and unrolled a long pair of woolen knitted stockings. The Chelm crest-of-arms was worked into it, and the wool was extremely fine. "Should fit, too. Thank you. This must have taken a long time."

"I had some help." Tylara smiled again.

Help. Right. Always there when you need it. He felt the stockings. *Poisoned thorn in the toe? Don't be ridiculous.* He stuffed the socks into the pouch on the leg of his coveralls. "Thanks, then."

She frowned puzzlement. "Rick, I—"

"Dammit, where the hell did Mason go?" He brushed past her with relief to go to the hall, then stopped. *No! She came to make friends, why am I so suspicious?* But when he turned back, she was already leaving through the other door.

"Hey! Get your ass out of the saddle and lead that horse!"

Apelles drew himself upright into a dignified pose. Who—

"Hey! I'm talking to you! You in the blue bedgown! You and your servant get down and lead your horses. Nobody rides across this bridge, not Caesar himself."

The commands had come from a Roman centurion who stood at the near end of the floating bridge across the Dnaster River. Apelles pressed his knees into his mount's flanks. The road was muddy and he wasn't a very good rider. The horse moved forward at a walk.

"Halt or be stopped!" The Roman raised an arm; several archers who'd been lounging on the bank rose to their feet.

"Are you mad?" Apelles halted and slid out of the saddle. There was no one to hold his horse or stirrup, and he very nearly fell. The mud was deep over the tops of his sandals.

"Centurion, I am Apelles, Priest of Yatar and Nuncio of—"

"Apelles?" said the centurion. His tone changed. "I'll be damned!"

"I hope not, Quintus," said Apelles, much relieved. Quintus Pollio of the Eleventh Legion had been captain of the Roman fire department at the University. His was the first familiar face Apelles had seen in days.

"That's as Christ and St. Michael—and Vothan—will have it," said Quintus cheerfully. "But none of them will save me if I let you or anybody else ride across the bridge. Take a good look at it, friend Apelles, and see if you don't agree with me."

Apelles tossed his mount's reins to his freedman and followed Quintus down the bank to inspect the bridge. The plank roadway was less than two yards across and there were gaps a hand's breadth wide between the planks, which rose and fell as the boats under them jerked and bobbed on their anchor cables in the swift current of the Dnaster. "Uh —friend Quintus, is it safe to cross at all?"

"Walking. If you're careful," Quintus said. "We only lost three parties today. The ferryman downstream picked up two. Hydras got one."

"Hydras."

"Actually that was yesterday. I think we got all the big ones. Bent sword points into hooks, and—"

"There's a ferry? I'll take it."

"Not a chance. Wagons only. Everybody else goes by the bridge."

"Archbishop Polycarp is expecting me by nightfall—"

"Ho. Why didn't you say so?" Quintus said. "You walk. I'll see your horse gets across."

"The blessings of Yatar on you," Apelles said with feeling.

Apelles reached the other bank ready to kneel and kiss the muddy ground. The bridge had swayed every bit as much as he'd feared. Two corpses had floated under it while he was crossing. *There can't be any hydras left. No big ones, anyway.*

Apelles' spirits revived when he was mounted again. In his own village of Nial's Mercy, only three men outside the household of Bheroman Rhegmur had horses. *Even on this slow-gaited dun hack, I'm the equal of a knight. Well, almost.*

In fact he had far more power than any knight, and more than most bheromen. As assistant to the Chancellor of Drantos, Apelles could send warrants and writs the length of the kingdom. His pen and inkwell held life and death for mere knights.

Apelles had never seen an army in the field. He had expected the host's camp to be one vast city of soldiers. Instead he found over a dozen smaller camps. Each squatted on its hilltop or in its valley, some completely undefended, others behind ditches or rough walls of sharpened logs. None showed the elaborate work he had heard that the Romans put into building a camp.

"Where?" his freedman asked.

"Palomas, you talk too much. I should never have set you free."

"We are lost, then."

It was true enough. He knew only that Polycarp's tent lay in Caesar's camp. Where was that?

"We should have asked the centurion," Palomas said.

"Yes, of course, and be silent or I will billet you with the kitchen apprentices."

"That may be better than we'll have tonight."

"Ask those women."

The two women carried buckets and sacks of washing. Palomas rode forward. *He rides better than I do. He has never said how he was enslaved.*

"Ho, goodwives," Palomas said. "Can you tell us how to find Caesar's camp?"

One of the women looked him up and down and then gave him a gap-toothed grin. "Don't think you'll find much pleasure there, my friend. Publius the Satyr keeps it all for himself. We can show you a better time—"

"Chara, that one's a priest," said the other woman.

Chara shrugged. "He's no bishop or highpriest. Stay with us, friend. Chara of Glinz has a name—"

"There are no soldiers quartered in Vis, then," Apelles said.

"Only officers," Chara said. "How did you know?"

"You tempt me, fine lady that you are," Apelles said. "But I must find the tent of Bishop Polycarp by dark. Can you direct us?" He clinked copper coins.

"Ah," said Chara. "See that hill off to the west?" She flung out one large red hand. "Caesar's camp is just beyond it."

Apelles followed the gesture with his eyes. "Thank you." He tossed her two coppers.

Her look told him he'd paid her too much.

The candles on Archbishop Polycarp's camp table neither guttered nor smoked. Their flames seemed as steady as Polycarp's gaze.

"The centurion refused to allow you to ride, and denied you the ferry?" Polycarp demanded.

"Yes, my lord."

"He will regret that."

"My lord, it is no matter—"

"You are Nuncio from the Highpriest of Yatar. You are deputy of the Chancellor of Rome's most powerful ally. Caesar's officers must learn respect."

My office demands dignity. I do not. But in a moment he will give orders— "I learned much, my lord. Do you know that the merchants of Vis have bought hydra flesh? Not merely the fishermen, who use it as bait."

Polycarp had stood. Now he sat again. "There is famine in Vis, then."

"It seems."

"I will speak to Caesar's supply officers. Vis is an important city. We cannot—you are certain of this?"

"Aye, my lord."

Polycarp smiled. "I think my colleague of the Temple of Yatar has chosen his servants well." The smile faded. "Or I would, had I not yesterday received a letter from the Highpriest Yanulf. He speaks of the young woman called Maev."

How in the Name of Yatar did he learn that? "Yes, my lord?"

"What is your relationship with this woman?"

"We—we are betrothed by handfasting, before the shrine of Hestia Christ's Mother."

"Ah. Your superior feared much worse."

Hah. Maev would never have let me within a stade of her bed without—

"Are you aware that when the Instrument of Union is signed, married priests will not be eligible for the higher offices within the united faith?"

"I am." Yanulf himself had told him Polycarp insisted on that provision. "It is not our intention to marry. At least not yet."

"Indeed." Polycarp turned away for a moment, and Apelles thought he heard muttered prayers. Then he turned back, and Apelles would rather have faced a hydra than the Archbishop, for all that his voice was still calm.

"Apelles, you give every appearance of being guilty of what in a priest is an even worse sin than lust. You are ambitious. You wish to rise in the service of God and do your duty to Him, yet you will not do your duty to others who have claims on you. And do not insult me by saying your duty to God comes before all others. To honor Maev and the child she may bear you is also a duty set you by God."

It was told of Polycarp that in his youth he had been a zealous persecutor of the worshippers of Yatar, able to ferret out any secrets and strip away any lies or disguises.

"My lord," Apelles said, and to his surprise his voice was steady, "it was the thought of a child that made us swear before Hestia. We neither of us wished Maev's child to bear the name bastard."

"Then—she is carrying your child?"

"She was not when we parted."

"Christ has blessed you, then. There is still time to pray for guidance and perhaps even to find it."

"Guidance?" Apelles was not feigning bewilderment.

"Toward what you truly wish, for yourself and for Maev."

"Even if I truly wish to become a highpriest rather than to marry her?"

Polycarp frowned. "Were you listening when I spoke of the sin of ambition in a priest?"

"I was, but I did not hear you say what it is to be ambitious. Is it ambitious to wish to serve God where one may do it best? And if one has it in oneself to make a good highpriest or bishop, does one serve God best in a lower position?"

"It is vanity to think one has that ability."

"Is it vanity to think that one *may* have that ability? And if I do, should I deny God any service I may give Him?"

"It is—," began Polycarp. Then the Archbishop laughed softly. "Stop, my son. I believe you could talk the Devil into giving up Hell without a contract."

"Forgive me, my lord. I meant no disrespect—"

"I saw none. Yanulf was right. You sometimes do not

think before you act, but you will not wittingly harm anyone. It is well to know that the Chancellor of Drantos is a good judge of men."

"My lord, I am grateful—for your mercy and for Yanulf's trust in me."

"God has found good servants in far worse than you. There is one further matter before I dismiss you. Have you made a testament in Maev's favor?"

"I did not think—"

"Do so before the battle."

"Yet I have heard that Phrados is no captain. Certainly no match for either Ganton or Publius."

"God will give us victory over this servant of the Devil, but He does not promise who shall be alive to enjoy it. Find parchment and pen. I will witness what you write."

Apelles' hands were steady enough as he wrote out his will, but afterward he felt very ready to pray. He and Polycarp had just knelt when they heard the sound of Roman horns and Tamaerthan drums. A large force of cavalry was moving out.

A messenger dashed in. "My Lord Archbishop! Lord Gengrich's men and the Rustengans have been sighted. The Tamaerthan Hussars and a cohort of the Fourth are going south to escort them."

"Yatar and Christ be praised! Let us continue our prayers."

Matthias stifled a sneeze. The incense and herbs in the braziers were losing their fight against the smells of the camp. Unwashed humanity. Campfires—too few for such a host, because too many draft animals had died to allow for large wood-gathering parties. Cooking meat. Kitchen middens. And over it all, the reek of rotting human corpses. Eight of them hung in chains on a gibbet high above the camp where all could see them.

Best pay attention to Phrados or I'll be the ninth.

"—has gone too far north without giving me his allegiance. Therefore he will not give it. Therefore he has betrayed the gods and must die."

"Let Gengrich die," shouted the twelve Defenders standing six on either side of Phrados.

"Let Gengrich die," shouted everyone in the room. "Let Gengrich die. Let—"

"Cease!" shouted a Defender, crashing the butt of his spear against the floor. Phrados rose from his stool and advanced on the men standing before him. Although he was half a head shorter than the least of them, none of them met his eyes as he walked along their line.

"Tyras," Phrados said, stopping before the tall headman of a southern town whose earthquake-shattered ruins must already be yielding to the forest. "You did not shout as loudly as the others."

"I feel as strongly as you or they, Prophet." He licked his lips. "Yet—forgive me—"

"I will not forgive you if you seem to hide your thoughts. I may forgive those thoughts." Phrados raised a hand; four Defenders raised spears or swords.

Tyras swallowed again, then the words poured out. "Should we not wait to see how Gengrich is received by the other starmen? If they give him only a traitor's welcome, he may yet be forced to turn to us with all his men."

"You would stay the smiting of a traitor to the gods?"

"I would not be so quick to condemn the Lord Gengrich as a traitor to gods he was not born to worship, Prophet. I think—"

"You have thought too much, Tyras, and known too little of God's truth. Gengrich has been condemned. So have you."

Before Tyras could take another breath, a hand signal brought four of the Defenders around him. Two grasped his hands and held them behind his back, while a third cut his throat. As his body thudded to the floor, the last Defender thrust his spear into Tyras's chest. The smell of blood joined the other smells in the room.

From first to last, Phrados had not raised his voice above a conversational tone.

"So perish traitors to the gods," shouted Matthias.

"So perish traitors to the gods," the others shouted. One or two voices sounded a trifle unsteady to Matthias; he did not dare look to see who the waverers might be. When Phrados dismissed them, Matthias walked as steadily as the others, and never looked back.

The Prophet is mad. Tyras was not the first condemned to death on a whim, but he was the first of Phrados's old followers from the south. *Sooner or later we will all die.*

Prayer and meditation had once been Matthias's answer to all doubts, but it had been many days since they did any good.

By the time Matthias passed the scaffolding, Tyras's body had joined the other eight.

CHAPTER TWO

Alex Boyd lowered his binoculars. "Here they come. Still think it's just scouts?"

"We'd be seeing the infantry if the main body'd come up," Gengrich said.

"Pretty heavy for scouts," Boyd said. "Some of those patrols we sent out last night, they might have found the infantry but not got a message back."

"You're a pessimist, Alex."

"Yeah. I'm also still alive."

Exactly what that proved Gengrich wasn't sure, but he was willing to admit it proved something. All of the mercs who'd started north from Castle Zyphron were still alive, but over two hundred of the local troops and several hundred dependents weren't. They'd have lost more if the Rustengan infantry hadn't been pretty much out of the fighting. The Rustengans had medics to spare and space in their wagons for the sick and wounded, and as long as their own people didn't need it they were generous.

The Rustengans had lived close enough to the Romans to get Roman notions of camp sanitation, which meant no plagues and not too many fevers. *We still lost too many,* Gengrich thought. *Old folks and kids dead of fever. People who lost their draft animals and couldn't keep up. And we can't slow down, not with Phrados and his horde dogging us.*

They would have lost a lot more if Gengrich hadn't used ammunition at a prodigal rate. *No point in saving it. When we reach Captain Galloway we get new supplies. We don't reach him, we're dead.*

"More coming," Boyd said.

"Yeah." Gengrich lifted his binoculars. Two groups of cavalry, both about eight hundred strong. The leading group was a mob, but the second group kept good formation behind blue and silver banners. Most of its lancers wore broad-brimmed helmets and back-and-breasts instead of fur jackets or leather jerkins.

"That second outfit looks like some city's regulars," said Boyd.

"Yeah. Alan!"

An arm waved from a stand of scrub oak in the center of the position. The oaks looked natural enough among the native chaparral, but they'd never evolved on this planet. *Lord knows how those trees got here. Acorns scattered by the* Shalnuksis? *Planted by some pig farmer a thousand years ago?*

"When that second outfit gets in range, start with the banner-bearers!"

Another wave. MacAllister was perched where he could see without being seen and snipe in all directions, with a hundred rounds to snipe with. That was one-sixth of the remaining ammo and some people weren't too happy about that, but nuts to that; if they wanted a bigger ammo allowance let 'em learn how to use it like Alan—

"Heads up!" said Boyd. He signaled to the horse-holders to bring their mounts forward. By the time they'd mounted the first outfit was in good shooting range. MacAllister squeezed off six rounds, picking off six horses at intervals in the first line. Gengrich waved his thanks, then signaled to the other mercs. By the time they'd each used up their six, there were more gaps than horses in the first line. The second and third lines bunched up just beyond bowshot. They were ragged enough that you really couldn't call them lines anymore.

The whole second outfit was still coming on too. The orderly formations were just at the rear of the first mob, and didn't so much cut off the mob's retreat as push it forward. By the time the archers had a good target the second outfit had turned the first one into a kind of shield.

"Anybody from that front outfit lives through this, he's going to be mighty pissed at the guys behind," Gengrich said.

Boyd nodded agreement. "Yeah, but let's make sure we're around to be invited to the party."

He's got a point. Gengrich's archers were no longer very well equipped to take on massed cavalry. The caltrops were long gone, the stakes running short, and today there hadn't been time to drive them anyway. *Better get the archers in with the pike squares.* A lot of the archers had started off the march on horseback and turned into infantry when their mounts died. If they got cut to pieces in their first fight as infantry, they wouldn't have any morale worth mentioning by the time they joined up with the Captain.

"First Company, rally on the oaks! Second and Third Company, rally to the pikes on the left and right!" One nice thing about fighting on a medieval planet: most of your men could be in range of your voice when you had to give an order in a hurry. Of course there was a legend of a battle lost because some lord had a cold, but better than busted or jammed radios any day!

The archers were moving now. The enemy didn't have any horse archers in range, so Gengrich's archers had it all their way. They could move by platoons and stop to shoot every few yards. Arrows fell into the leading enemy formation. *Can't call it a formation. Just a mob. They'd break if that second outfit wasn't pushing them on.*

"Snipers, take out officers in the second group. Leave that first outfit to the archers," Gengrich shouted. He heard the orders passed down the line. Banners began to fall. There were still twelve hundred and more horsemen coming at him.

The mercs were coming in toward the oaks. They fired as they ran. Joe Green was fumbling a fresh magazine into place as he moved; had the son of a bitch shot himself dry already? The archers on the left were almost safe behind the pikes; the oaks hid what was going on to the right. More banners were in range now. MacAllister took out three, wham, wham wham, three shots, and Gengrich and Boyd threw in four rounds apiece before putting their heads down and their spurs in. When he reached his new position among the oak trees he could spare time to see how much time they'd bought.

Maybe enough. The Rustengan infantry had moved into position. The Rustengan militiamen were hungry and they weren't used to fighting in the open. On the other hand, they'd fight. They were all that stood between their families and Phrados.

MacAllister shot off half a magazine right over Gengrich's head and suddenly there were a lot fewer banners out front. It didn't help enough. That first outfit was still taking most of the fire, and they were going down but they weren't breaking. Maybe it was guts, maybe it was fear of Phrados or the guys behind them....

A couple of hundred men and horses down now; Gengrich tried to shut his eyes and ears against how they looked and sounded. Horses wouldn't step on corpses or wounded, but there was plenty of bare ground and that second outfit looked to be good riders even if their mounts were a little thin-flanked.

A wave of mounted men from both attacking groups broke over a platoon of archers; Gengrich saw men using their bows like clubs as they went down. Beyond the horsemen he saw the pikes dipping. Arrows soared from inside the pikes.

A second wave, mostly from the second outfit. This time it broke against a platoon of archers helped by star weapons. More arrows flew from the oaks. The southern bow wasn't the Tamaerthan longbow, but at a hundred yards it would punch through any armor these characters were wearing.

The survivors of the platoon moved toward the oaks. They hadn't broken; they still had their bows and some of them had stopped to pick up enemy swords and helmets. Gengrich counted them; he'd passed twenty when he saw one carrying an H&K and two more with a limping figure between them.

"Larry!"

Joe Green sprinted out from the trees. He'd covered half the distance to his buddy Larry Brentano when the third wave came up the slope. Green went to one knee, snapped up his rifle, and let fly on full rock and roll. Gengrich, Boyd, and MacAllister slammed rounds into the cavalry as if there was no tomorrow and no shortages.

There were just too many men and horses. Even some of the riderless mounts were part of the mass that poured over Green before it melted away under the arrows and bullets. Gengrich used every obscenity he knew, then gaped as the last few archers picked their way through the shambles, still carrying Brentano.

"I good as tripped over my own feet, Arnie," he said. "Busted an ankle, twisted my wrist. Did Joe...? Oh hell," as Gengrich's expression answered him.

And still more of the blue-bannered bastards! Gengrich cursed the bad luck that had disabled their last onager three days back. The massed cavalry would have been a sweet target for a barrel holding ten pounds of black powder and ten pounds more of scrap iron and small stones.

"Hey, corp!" shouted MacAllister. "Somebody new's joined the fight!" From his perch in the tree he was the only one who could see over the heads of the attackers.

"Let 'em come," Gengrich shouted. "There's enough party for everybody." For about one more attack, that is, and after that we'll be out of bullets and damned low on arrows, and thank God Erika and Helena and Chrissie are back behind the Rustengans and Schultzy's Diana is looking after them—

"Hey! That's a Tamaerthan banner! Our friends have arrived!"

Gengrich slung his rifle with steady hands; this was one fight where he'd been too busy to get the shakes. Then he breathed a silent prayer of thanks.

Gengrich and his men were spectators for the rest of the battle. A few minutes after the Tamaerthans hit the enemy from the rear, a cohort of Romans rode through the Rustengan line and took them in front. After that Gengrich's men were in more danger of being trampled by their allies' horses than of being overrun by their enemies.

Gengrich and Boyd watched the Romans mopping up the last of the blue banners.

"They do fight," Alex Boyd said. "Wonder why?"

"Phrados has those Defender goon squads in their homes?" Gengrich mused.

"Or they got no homes at all. Yeah."

"Listen," Gengrich said. "M-16s I'd swear."

"Schultzy's got an H&K .308—"

"Yeah. Captain Galloway sent those troops." Gengrich wanted to shout.

"Maybe it's himself."

"Either way, he cares. We don't forget that."

The fight was nearly over, but knots of the enemy fought on. They were badly outclassed, caught between Roman legionaries with their horse archery and Rick Galloway-trained Tamaerthans. When the survivors finally broke and rode for their lives, they left more than a thousand behind.

"Okay, Alex, what's the butcher's bill?"

"Green KIA. Brentano will be out of action for a week anyway. Thirty-four locals KIA. Twenty-seven wounded, and three missing."

"Not as bad as it might be."

"Nope. And this chap wants to see you."

Boyd indicated a young Tamaerthan nobleman cantering toward him. If the guy had been astride a choppered Harley and wearing a leather jacket instead of a mail coat, he'd have been a dead ringer for Panzer Klewicki, back on the Southwest Side. Was Panzer still riding, or had he busted his neck?

And did it matter, if you were never going to find out? For a moment Gengrich felt desperately homesick for Earth.

"Lord Gengrich?" The Tamaerthan reined in.

"The same. Who do I have the honor of thanking for his timely arrival?"

"Teuthras, son of Kevin, of Clan MacClallan. Coronel of the First Tamaerthan Hussars and cousin to Tylara, Eqetassa of Chelm," he added.

"We are grateful. I do not doubt that we would have prevailed in the end, but with your help we have smitten our enemies far harder."

"Indeed. They were a worthy foe. Have all of Phrados's men fought so well?"

"These were the best. Although I do not know if all of the others had orders to press home their attack."

"We can talk more of this later. I have orders from the Lord Captain General to welcome your return to his service. He has sent the Lords Bisso and Beazeley with new strength for your star weapons, firepowder bombs, medicines, and strong waters.

"We hoped we would be able to join you and give your weapons their new strength before this battle. However, when we reached you the enemy was already attacking. It seemed better not to wait. The Lord Rick often quotes an old commander of his, the High Rexja Napolyon—'Ask me for anything but time.'"

So the Captain was claiming to have served under Napoleon, was he? When bigger and better whoppers are told ... Anyway, that explained the other star weapons. Wonder how many rounds the Captain sent, and what orders he gave Bisso about issuing them?

All around the battle was dying down. Most of the Romans had ridden off in pursuit. A lot of the Tamaerthans had dismounted, to loot the bodies and if necessary make sure the bodies were properly dead. They'd posted about half a squadron of sentries, though, and they were bringing the loot to a central collecting point. The Captain had done a good job with these people, which was really no surprise but nice to see all the same.

For the first time in longer than he wanted to think about, Gengrich felt safe.

They were bringing in Joe Green's body tied over a mule.
As they did, Schultzy rode up, with blood on his Rustengan
armor. He gave Boyd a sour look as he dismounted; Gengrich wondered if Alex had been sniffing around Diana
again. Better ask, but not here. Right now Gengrich wanted
to say good-bye to Joe Green. Joe hadn't been any Audie
Murphy, but wasting ammo was his only real vice. Otherwise
he'd been reliable and hardworking and sensible, never
making any trouble. *Damn all. Another hour—*

Gengrich walked up to the mule carrying Green's body. A
man in peasant clothing stood on the far side, another at its
head. A couple of boys were playing kickball with a bound-
up leather jerkin whose owner would never need it again.

"Bring the body to Lord Brentano, fellows. He and Lord
Green were comrades."

"Yes, my lord—"

"Look out, Lord Gengrich!"

The high-pitched shout had Gengrich jumping back from
the mule before the man on the far side came under its belly
and out with a knife in his hand. The blade leaped up, seeking a path under Gengrich's armor and into his belly. As the
blade rose, one of the boys suddenly flung the kickball. It hit
the man in the head, making the knife thrust miss.

The man at the mule's head had also drawn a knife, but
now the mule was rearing. It threw him off balance. By the
time he was steady on his feet, Gengrich had his Colt out.
He shot the man in the chest as the first man closed for
another stab. The boy ran up to the mule, vaulted over it
with his hands on Joe Green, and slammed his bare feet into
the back of the first man's head. The blow knocked the man
sprawling. The thongs holding the body broke, and body
and boy together tumbled down on top of the man. Gengrich stamped hard on the man's wrist. The knife dropped
to the ground.

Now two more men were running toward Gengrich, and
a third was unlimbering a crossbow. Teuthras spurred toward the archer, sword swinging down, and flew out of the
saddle with a quarrel sticking out of his chest. His fall wasn't

all bad; it gave Boyd and Schultz a clear field of fire at the other two. Who hit which man first was never clear and didn't matter anyway; both went down.

This left the archer, who was ten feet from a stray horse and already on the move, reloading and recocking his bow as he ran. Too many people around him for gunplay, too, and none of the dumb bastards were lifting a finger to stop him!

"Grab that man, you—!" yelled Boyd.

The other boy caught up with the fleeing man as he reached the horse. The crossbow twanged and a quarrel tore into the boy's belly, but he already had his arms around the man's thigh. Then his teeth sank into the leg, through leather and into flesh. The man screamed and beat at the boy. For a moment his head was clearly silhouetted—and a moment was all MacAllister ever needed for a clear shot at longer ranges than this. The man's head snapped back and he fell off his horse on top of the boy.

"Medics!" yelled Schultz.

Gengrich said nothing. He really wanted to go off somewhere and have that case of the shakes. He knew he ought to see how Teuthras was—although any man who was sitting up already and swearing like that couldn't be too badly hurt.

What he was going to do was ask a couple of pointed questions of a young lady named Monira. Brushing off Boyd's hands and several other people asking questions, he strode toward his horse.

"The one by the mule was Alanis, from what you say. The other was Cyra."

Was there a moment's hesitation in the level voice, or a flicker in the steady blue eyes? Gengrich thought he detected both. And did that mean the disguised girl who'd taken out the crossbowman at the cost of her own life was somebody Monira didn't know? From another House of the Wolf?

The idea that more of these pint-sized assassins were running around loose made Gengrich ill. Should he dose Monira with more babble juice?

No point. It would be Captain Galloway's problem soon enough. But there was one question Gengrich had to ask.

"Why did—your friends save me?"

For a moment it looked as if Monira was really going to smile. But she only shrugged. "It was our duty, now that it serves Lady Tylara that you be alive. We swore an oath."

We swore an oath. And because they'd sworn an oath, some of those kids had come all the way south to take him out, and others had come south after them to hide among his men, watching him without being detected ever since last winter. How many were there? He knew he'd never get an answer to that question.

At least there was one question he didn't need answered. What would have happened to him if they'd decided it was their duty to keep trying to kill him? He knew that too well.

He started to say "Thank you, Monira." The words stuck in his throat. He had to get out of here, out of this dark smelly wagon where Monira and Euris sat half-naked in moldy straw with about as much expression as a couple of goddamned temple statues!

Gengrich was twenty yards from the wagon and bumping into Schultz before he knew where he was. Schultz grabbed his arm.

"Good Lord, Arnie. You look like your own ghost." He lowered his voice. "Find what you were after?"

"Yeah. I guess."

"You look like you could use a drink. Here." He held up a flask and pulled out the cork. "McCleve's Best Panther Piss. I traded Jack Beazeley for a couple of jugs."

"Thanks. Ah. Good stuff. How's Teuthras?"

"Frank says he's got a couple of cracked ribs and a concussion. He got those falling off his horse. The crossbow just gouged the skin over his ribs. Frank's disinfected it already." Schultz grinned. "The guy nearly took Frank's head off when he said he might miss the big battle. Said that was to call him as weak as a woman." The grin faded. "I didn't tell him the 'boy' who avenged him was a girl."

"How—?"

"She asked for the knife. We let the other one use it. Mind if I have that back?"

"Be my guest."

Schultz gulped from the flask, then stoppered it. "Arnie, do you suppose you could lean on Alex to stay away from Diana, before I have to? If I don't, her family will take a hand."

"I told Vinicianus—"

"Screw our Roamin' Roman. Diana says the last couple of times Boyd dropped around, Vinicianus was with him. Didn't lift a finger to stop his hassling her, either."

"Schultzy, if you're trying to make trouble—"

"Arnie, Horny Alex's already doing that, with your Roman adviser backing him up. I'm trying to stop trouble."

Gengrich reached for the flask again. "I'd better talk to both of them."

"Yeah, you do that."

Gengrich drank. Maybe it hadn't been such a good idea, to play Schultzy and Vinicianus off against each other for the job of—oh, call it grand vizier. If Vinicianus was putting Boyd up to something that could get him shot—not that Alex ever needed much putting up where women were concerned....

Not my problem anymore. The prodigal's home and Daddy, you take over!

CHAPTER THREE

"Welcome, Lady Tylara. Did you have a good journey?"

Tylara stopped at the threshold of the Rector's private chambers and let Lady Siobhan take her cloak. It was the first time she'd visited the University since Les's return; had Gwen added any more luxuries and would it say anything if she had?

I must not *go about looking upon Lady Gwen as an enemy whose strengths and weaknesses I must spy out. She is no fool; if I do this she will know and tell Rick. And if by some strange working of fate she is in truth not my mortal enemy...*

A strange working of fate that would be, indeed, unless my husband is not as other men are.

Tylara forced a smile, before the silence grew too long. "Well enough. At this season it is no great hardship to travel any distance. I confess I will not be unhappy to live to see the days when Tran has the—*freeways*—of Earth."

And that is to admit a weakness, and to Gwen! Must I seem a witling?

"Let's hope we all live that long. Would you like some tea, or would you prefer wine? I have some sherry I've been saving for an occasion, and I think this is one. It's a dark, sweet wine, stronger than ordinary vintages."

"Thank you, my Lady Rector. I will have a glass."

One glass of anything should not weaken my wits or lower my guard, unless the gods have already seen fit to do it.

"Lady Siobhan. Two glasses of the Bristol Cream—oh,

and bring that letter you received yesterday from Lord Mason." The girl went to a carved cupboard by the window and pulled out an Earth bottle and two Roman glasses.

"She reads English very well now," Gwen continued. "I wish I had half her talent for languages."

Do you need that, when you have—other talents? No, that is not just. None of the men she seems to attract can be wound around her finger by no more than a whore's arts.

That is why it is so hard not to fear her. Bedsport is one thing. A true meeting of minds is far more. And since Rick and I have not had either since midwinter...

"Thank you, Lady Siobhan." The sherry was indeed stronger than common wine. Tylara sipped cautiously, not sure she cared for the sweetness. "Is Lord Mason well?"

"Oh yes, my lady. Or at least, he was when he penned the letter, some twelve days ago. I pray that nothing has happened to him in that time."

The look on Siobhan's face was unmistakable. So Lord Mason's suit is succeeding, is it? Well, both could do far worse, she one of the greatest of the Star Lords and a good man for a husband, he a granddaughter of faithful old Camithon for a wife. And my husband—

For a moment Tylara could not complete the thought. Then she forced her wits onward, like forcing a skittish horse across a swift-flowing stream.

My husband will be happy. Did he not say once, "Art Mason's got to limit himself to officer-class ladies from now on. No more barmaids. In fact, he really ought to get married."

And am I so lost to loyalty and good sense that I wish my husband to be unhappy? Especially in a matter so nearly concerning one of his most trusted men, to whom I owe no small debt myself?

"Pour yourself a glass, Siobhan, and sit down," said Gwen. "Let's not stand too much on ceremony."

"Thank you, my lady." The girl didn't take the drink, but sat down, unfolded three pieces of paper, and began to read.

"To my dear Lady Siobhan, greetings and hopes that you are as well as I am.

"By the time you read this, we may have fought the great battle against the horde of the Prophet Phrados. Certainly it will be fought sooner rather than later. They have eaten the country bare behind them, and have no way to go but forward. Nor can they move east into the Roman Provinces, not without leaving us free to strike at their flank and rear.

"Publius Caesar seems to doubt this last. He has kept three of his six legions in the Provinces, together with several cohorts of garrison troops and some thousands of militia. To do him justice, he may fear rebels or bandits as well as Phrados, and does not wish to admit it. In his position, I suspect I would do much the same."

Hah. He fears unfriendly eyes will read his message. Unfriendly, or a stranger. Who in Caesar's camp knows English? A starman hired from the south, one of the deserters? It could be. And Gengrich.

Will Lord Gengrich be truly loyal? He has been pardoned, but will he do treason anew? And if he is, what does that say about my husband's notions of how to deal with traitors?

And mine?

As before, the answer was silence.

Siobhan went on. "However, we have enough here to do the business. Two legions of cavalry, one of pikemen, the Tamaerthons, the Drantos knights and infantry, Gengrich's men, and contingents of infantry from Rustengo, Vis, and a baker's dozen of other towns and small cities, plus the—my lady, what is—?"

"The artillery. That's the large firepowder weapons."

"The artillery, the star weapons, the balloon, and a few tricks the Captain General undoubtedly has up his sleeve. That's forty thousand men and a lot of weapons most of the horde has never even heard of, let alone faced. They have a hundred and twenty thousand, or so we've heard from the last batch of scouts, but only about a quarter of that is much more than an armed mob. . . ."

As Siobhan continued, Tylara more and more ceased to

listen. Instead she tried to imagine her husband's face as he planned the battle. As hard as she tried, she could imagine nothing except the cold mask that he had worn since midwinter. Aye, worn even those few times they shared a bed, as though only his body touched hers, while his mind was somewhere else, with someone else....

What else could he be hiding behind that mask, other than such a shift of allegiance? If by some mischance the secret of the Children of Vothan had been discovered, surely he would have had the wits to see that this was a matter they could discuss as equals. They had a common interest in seeing that their plans and the future of their children were protected from the consequences of Gwen Tremaine's not being a chaste woman—or at least being chaste only by the customs of an Earth she would never see again.

If Rick had been silent for so long, there could be only one reason—that what was dividing him from her was a matter on which no words would make the slightest difference. There could be only one such matter.

Am I helpless in the face of this change of allegiance?

Perhaps not. But I must move cautiously. If Rick has hidden his heart so well for so long, it could be that he is now as skilled in dissimulation as any Tran lord. Skilled in our ways of intrigue. How otherwise could he have devised so wise an end to the problem of Lord Rand? The man who saved me would not have been so wise.

If wise as Tran lords, then—as ruthless? It has been known, to use the children by the first wife as hostages to secure acquiescence in a second. As long as the second is fertile. Which, Yatar help me, Gwen certainly must be....

Has my husband finally succeeded in frightening me?

The gods have mercy, yes.

She shivered.

"Lady Tylara, are you cold? Here, Siobhan. Pull the shutters and make up some tea."

Even worse, I must endure this intriguer's hiding her triumph behind a mask of graciousness!

The bonfires at either end of the bridge and the torches held by the sentries showed the last wagons more than half-way across. The floor of the bridge was sagging to within a foot of the water, but with the extra boats tied in place a few days ago the bridge was holding.

Rick still didn't uncross his fingers until the last wagon had rumbled off the bridge onto the north bank of the Dnaster. He turned, to see Drumold looking at him with what seemed suspiciously like a smile.

"Ye have the air of a man who is hoping that a man ye have to trust really knows what he's doing."

"Is it that obvious?"

"To one who knows ye well enough, Rick, I canna say that you are any great hand at hidin' your thoughts."

I am better than you think, my friend, or you and I would not be standing on this hillside, having this amicable discussion.

"Well, I'm not surprised that Lord Holloway knows his business. He's almost as good an engineer as Lord Campbell. I was surprised how many suggestions he made. He wasn't the only one of Gengrich's men who did more than I expected."

"Mayhap Gengrich knows that his fate is now linked to yours, and would rather stand than fall."

"Likely enough. He never was stupid." *Maybe, just maybe Gengrich would be smart enough to play it straight from now on, and the secret he held would never come out.*

That's hoping the horse will learn to sing with a vengeance, and is there going to be anything left of your marriage even if Gengrich keeps his big bazoo shut for all time to come?

Don't work yourself into a stew over that, or Drumold will notice enough to ask questions you'd rather not answer.

The torches were now moving onto the bridge. Some of

the sentries were kneeling, tools in hand, while others held the torches.

"We're going to dismantle the bridge into four sections tonight. Tomorrow night we tow it downriver and reassemble it under the walls of Vis. It would be too hard to defend where it is. Also, if we fight where I expect to and we do need to retreat, we'll have a shorter and more easily defended route to the bridge.

"Best not mention that to Publius Caesar."

"What kind of fool—?"

"Can you no tell a jest when ye hear one?"

"Sorry." *Got the wind up. Shouldn't show that, to Drumold or anyone else.* "Has Publius said anything new that he shouldn't have?"

"Not since the last Council of War." At the last Council Publius had brusquely suggested that all the contingents of cities and towns claimed by Rome should fight under Roman command or not at all. He'd at least had the sense to leave it as a suggestion, but tempers had been frayed all the same.

"Publius cannot control his tongue." Drumold looked thoughtful. "Yet he might do us no small favor if ye asked him fairly. I have read over the muster roll of Gengrich's men. He has some twelve-score men of the Clan MacBrayne and the Red MacBeans among those who follow him."

"I'm afraid that doesn't mean as much to me as it should, Drumold."

"No shame to ye, Rick. Ye have so much wisdom in war that did I not know ye well, I would be among those who called you wizard. Ye have less knowledge of the clans of Tamaerthon, and indeed who outside the hills does not?

"It is only that the MacBraynes and the Red MacBeans have been at feud with Mac Clallan Muir since my grandfather bore the title. It little matters who gave first offense, and indeed it may well have been my grandfather. His temper made him enemies from the cradle to the burial-mound. Very surely, though, the two clans he outlawed shed much blood in reply. They are now at feud not only with me and mine but with the MacBretachs and so many others it would be past dawn before I'd numbered them all. . . ."

"I'll take your word for it. I gather you'd rather not have the two clans anywhere near the rest of the Tamaerthons?"

"Not unless ye want them shot at from both the front and the back."

"Good God no! So where should we put them? Gengrich won't be too happy with losing them altogether."

"Aye. Yet if he's no a fool, he'll know ye canna leave him with such an army loyal only to him. What matters it if his men start leaving before or after the battle, so long as they go to good service. If Publius would offer to enlist them as auxiliaries, with the hope of earning Roman citizenship in time, would Gengrich not think he was being honored? And if Publius will no offer, can we not ask Titus Frugi—?"

"Don't get within a mile of Frugi without Publius's permission! Frugi's the senior legate. He has to be Publius's second-in-command. But you may have noticed that Publius keeps a whole Praetorian cohort around his tent, to make sure Frugi doesn't succeed to the command. . . ."

"If Publius doesn't stop looking for assassins under the tiles of his tent, he may well find one where he's not looking for it."

"You know that. I know that. Publius doesn't know it." God, was there no end to intrigues, plots, and double-crosses? Probably not, and now he couldn't even hope to find a refuge from them at home. Quite the contrary. Rick found himself looking forward to the coming battle. It would be a horrible business, pretty much a straightforward killing contest, but it would be simple.

"My lords?" A slightly diffident voice spoke from behind Rick. He turned to see Apelles, Yanulf's young assistant. "Yes, Apelles?"

"Archbishop Polycarp sent me. He will hold a united service of worship in half a glass, in his tent. He would be honored if you would attend."

And insulted if we didn't. Not to mention all the rumors

that would fly around that Lord Rick's heart really wasn't in this union of the two religions and that he was a secret worshipper of Christ or Vothan or Ronald MacDonald . . . !

I'm a politician. I kiss babies, eat blintzes, and go to masses. And if need be put on Indian feather bonnets and get adopted into tribes. Right. "Thank you, Apelles. We shall be present. Where have you been assigned for the battle?"

"With the vanguard of the Drantos cavalry, Lord Rick. I am to send the healers where they are needed and to write down the dead and the hurt."

A combination medic and staff officer, but he'd be in the thick of the fighting even if it went well. If it didn't—well, there was something to be said for the fatalistic notion that Vothan One-Eye would have a man he wanted, however far he had to seek or however young or old the man might be. Come to think of it, Apelles wasn't all that young—getting on for twenty-four Earth years, and Rick hadn't been much older than that when he signed up with the CIA for what turned out to be a trip to a really "unknown destination."

Rick Galloway, you are getting too old too fast, and you know the reason.

Goddamnit, Tylara. WHY?

CHAPTER FOUR

"The horse will be divided into two equal parts. One will advance on the left. The other will advance on the right. The foot will advance in the center. The honor of the gods will be avenged."

"For the honor of the gods!" shouted the Defenders standing three deep around Phrados the Prophet.

"For the honor of the gods!" shouted all the captains sitting on their horses in a wider circle around the Defenders.

Highpriest Matthias shouted as loudly as any. It would not be within reason for the Defenders to drag him off his horse and cut his throat now, in the very presence of the enemy—but many things Phrados had ordered in these past few days were not within reason. Tyras now had plenty of company in whatever land a madman's victims went to after death.

Even those who had grown used to capricious murders had been shaken by the slaughter of the women and children of Myreis. Over a thousand of them butchered in a single night after Phrados learned of their men's surrender to the skyfolk.

Clearly Phrados had intended that his soldiers fear him and the Defenders more than the enemy and his magical weapons. Had the Prophet accomplished this? Matthias doubted it, but it was a measure of how much fear Phrados had sown that Matthias dared not speak to anyone about these doubts.

He also doubted that the fear would much outlast the Defenders. If they perished in the battle, whether it was won or lost, not one in ten of the host would thereafter blindly obey Phrados. From such a situation, a man prepared to counsel the captains, as nobleman, warrior, and priest, might draw much to the advantage of both himself and his masters.

But that was pricing the unborn calf. Matthias made a gesture of aversion with his armored gauntlet and gathered up the reins. He wanted to lead his men into position on the right, as soon as Phrados finished giving more precise orders for the battle.

Now the bearers of the Prophet's litter were coming forward. Matthias realized with dismay that no more precise orders would be given. He wondered if the other captains were also dismayed, but those whose faces were visible under their helmets might as well have been wearing masks.

Prophet or no Prophet, it was tempting the gods to make such scanty plans for a battle on which so much depended. The skyfolk and their allies were outnumbered three to one, but even their foot was better than most of the Prophet's. Two-thirds of their horse were the armored knights of Drantos and Tamaerthon or the still more formidable legions of Rome. With or without star weapons the Prophet faced a formidable foe—

And there would be star weapons. The tales of their work in the battles against the Rustengans and Lord Gengrich had lost nothing in the telling, but it seemed to Matthias that the star weapons were indeed formidable. Would they be less formidable if one did not gather one's men in great masses and hurl them at the starmen?

No matter. Such a stratagem was not within the power of the Prophet's host. It had too many captains, too many who did not know their work, and none Phrados would trust to fight except under his eye.

Also, even if a captain did move his men to find a place where the star weapons were weak, would he not be seen at once by the balloon? There it was, hanging in the sky over the hill at the rear of the starmen's host. Smoke trailed from the basket under it. From this distance Matthias could not see the men in the basket, but he knew from the stories of last year's battles that they would be there.

Was the balloon a living creature from Earth? There were no tales of such things in the time when men first came to Tran, but that was long ago. The art of taming balloons might not have been known then.

Or was it a creation of magic? Or—and these tales persisted, though they seemed altogether improbable to Matthias—was it a mere machine, like a wagon or a ship? Could anyone master the art of making balloons and thereafter gaze down upon his enemies with an all-seeing eye?

Perhaps they would find out today, if the gods smiled on the Prophet in spite of his folly. Meanwhile, there were ways to lessen that folly. If he could move his men to the left instead of the right, there would be captains willing to listen to him once out of hearing of the Defenders. He could do something to make sure that the village on the High Road was held, that the High Road itself was held where it left the forest, and that no one advanced down the High Road into what would surely be ambushes.

Beyond that, he could offer even his best friends among the host of Phrados nothing but his prayers.

The vanguard of the knights of Drantos had beaten off their third attack by the enemy's horse when the Roman tribune rode past Apelles. The priest looked to see that the bandage he'd just finished putting on a man-at-arms's leg wasn't too tight, then watched the tribune. He made a very fine sight in his molded and silvered armor, with his escort of twenty almost equally splendid soldiers of the Praetorian Guard.

The tribune rode up to the banner of Rudhrig, Eqeta of Harms, and saluted in the Roman manner.

"Hail, Lord Rudhrig. Publius Caesar hails your victory and the valor of your knights, and bids you withdraw your knights to the slope of the hill just above the edge of the forest and there await further orders."

Even from where he stood, Apelles could see the Eqeta's face change color. "The knights of Drantos do not give up ground they have held thrice over. We will await our orders here."

"Publius Caesar commands—"

"Publius Caesar can command you to come and babble to us of dishonoring ourselves. He cannot command us, unless he comes himself."

"An order brought by a tribune of Caesar is—"

"A fart in a wine cup, as far as it concerns me. Now, tribune, will you take that message to Publius Caesar or not? It matters little to me."

What the tribune might have said in reply was lost in the blare of enemy horns signalling a new attack. Apelles saw the tribune's face twist with conflicting desires—return to Caesar or stay and prove that he would not at least turn his back on a foe.

"They come!" one of the acolytes gibbered. "The enemy comes, and we will be abandoned!"

"Calm," Apelles said, although he felt little enough calm himself. "Not all of them come. They are not clever enough to attack all at once. We defeated them before. We will again. The honor of the bheromen of Drantos protects us. They will not leave us." Or at least they will not leave their dead and wounded. "Now. You neglect the cleansing. Let us wash our hands together, and say together the prayers of exorcism."

When Apelles looked up again he saw that the Roman tribune had joined in the counter stroke. The swiftness of the enemy attack had left him small choice.

"I think they have no one captain in command," Apelles said to a knight as he poured—*disinfectant*—into a deep thigh wound. The leg was broken and would have to be set.

The knight grunted in pain. "This captain seems clever enough. He has pressed home his attack—"

And that he has, Apelles thought.

The enemy horse archers swept around the Drantos left and reached the scrub on the fringes of the forest. For about as long as it would have taken Apelles to drink a cup of poor wine, the ground to the rear of the Drantos vanguard was beaten by enemy arrows. Some fell close to the wounded, and several mules and packhorses went down.

Then the Tamaerthan archers appeared at the edge of the forest. A trumpet sounded. They were too far for Apelles to hear their commander, but in his mind he heard the cry anyway. "Let the gray gulls fly!"

Three hundred arrows arched toward the Prophet's men. Then three hundred more, and in a breath another flight. The horse archers went down. A brave few spurred toward the forest, but no more than a score came close enough to loose their own arrows. Then they too were shot out of their saddles.

The rest of the enemy withdrew. Before they could escape, horse archers and lancers alike were shattered by a Drantos charge. Eqeta and tribune rode boot to boot into the enemy's ranks.

Once the road to the rear was open, the tribune and his surviving Praetorians took it. The Eqeta led his men back past Apelles, dropping off five more dead and fifteen more wounded on the way. Apelles ordered one of the acolytes to divide the wounded into the gravely and the lightly hurt, and a scribe to record the names of the dead.

It was a good thing that so far there were fewer than two hundred wounded, and many of those were tended by their squires or servants. Apelles could have used three times as many acolytes and twice as many scribes.

I am an *administrator*, not a healer, he thought. Neither Yanulf nor Polycarp disputed that, but still he was sent to take his turn in the field hospitals. *They say it is a lesson in humility. It is certainly that.* When he was in his office, surrounded by files and papers with a dozen clerks on call, he was a man of consequence. Here the knights were all too ready to forget that Yatar had made him a priest, and to remember that he had been born a swineherd.

Yet it does no harm to learn the arts of healing, and an administrator *must know something of war.*

Few of the wounded this time needed more than a cleaning of their wounds and a bandage. Apelles had time to gaze around him, and notice that the mass of foot in the enemy's center had grown larger. It also had a vanguard of men in armor, or at least helmets and breastplates, and armed with shields and swords or spears.

It seemed to Apelles that there was wisdom in Publius Caesar's orders. Certainly the eight hundred lances of the vanguard had done well, slaying or unhorsing half again their own numbers. Yet if the enemy choose to support their next attack with some of that mass of foot, would the knights find it as easy to clear their retreat? Apelles did not call himself a man of war, but he knew that heavy cavalry could not easily retreat through a forest and that eight hundred lances were far too many for Drantos to lose.

Not to mention the wounded and dead, whom he could not abandon to an enemy who took no prisoners.

Apelles was just beginning work on an arrow sunk three fingers into a knight's left buttock when horns and hoofbeats made him rise and stare. For a moment he thought it was another attack, but these horns were the deep-toned Roman ones and the horsemen riding up were Roman Praetorians. Roman Praetorians, a whole cohort of them— and in the middle a familiar small figure in gilded armor, with a deep red cloak flowing back from his shoulders.

Publius Caesar had come to give his orders in person.

Apelles signaled to the apprentices to busy themselves in their work. It would not do for them to stare. He himself moved closer, so that he would miss nothing. *If healing is part of my training, so is this.*

"After the Hooey River I thought you well-born witlings knew how to fight," Publius roared. "Titus Frugi even doubted that you were barbarians. Now I know that he was wrong, and you remain barbarians who know nothing except how to die with honor."

"Who is the barbarian?" replied the Eqeta. "Those who

know how to die with honor, or those who have never heard of honor at all?"

The quarrel went on from there. No doubt it helped that five hundred Praetorians were enough to quell any ideas of laying hands on Publius but not enough to give Publius ideas of forcing the knights to move.

"You would not obey my order when I sent it to you," Publius finished. "Now I *bring* it to you, at a time when I and my Praetorians could as well be fighting our common foe. You said you would obey me. Whether you live or die, you will not seem very honorable if you do otherwise. Now—I command you and the vanguard of Drantos to withdraw to a position I will choose for you."

Lord Rudhrig's hesitation lasted only a moment, although it seemed like half a glass to Apelles. Then he nodded, and with a wave of his hand sent messengers riding down the line to carry the order to retreat.

"Here." Apelles indicated a ditch that would be the outermost boundary of his new field hospital at the rear of what everyone was calling the Great Redoubt. Acolytes came to erect the tent, with its solid roof for shade, and its thin netting that gave ventilation but prevented flies and borers from entering. More star lore, but it seemed to work. *Something* worked. Exclude the small devils that hid in dirt from entering the body, and more often than not wounds healed. And certainly flies and borers and carvers carried dirt on their feet....

"I have never heard anyone speak so to an Eqeta." Fnarg was senior acolyte. His father had been a silversmith and town councilor.

"Nor I," Apelles said. "And if we are wise we will not remember that *we* ever heard such."

Apelles knew that Publius Caesar was right, but his heart was with the knights of Drantos. Perhaps they had not chosen the wisest way of proving their honor, yet what honor was there in calling them "barbarians" to their very faces?

Moreover, was the Roman kind of obedience really what

he wished to see in Drantos? Publius had ordered eight hundred lances of Drantos knights led by one of the five greatest nobles of the Realm as if they were spitboys or sweepers. Not even the bheroman of Apelles' native village would have dared order his father about so—at least where it was a matter of knowledge of swine and where they had the right to feed.

As with Maev, Apelles found he was not quite sure if what he'd thought he wanted was in truth his real desire. He was no more sure when the knights finally rode past the Great Redoubt.

As they did, horns and drums signaled another enemy attack.

Rick watched helplessly as the cavalry rearguard, two cohorts of the Fourth Legion, dissolved under the massed enemy cavalry. If they'd had room to maneuver or arrows to shoot, they might have made a fight of it. Backed against the forest they couldn't maneuver, and they'd emptied their quivers covering the retreat of the Drantos ironhats. The Tamaerthan archers in the forest and the star weapons in the Great Redoubt had plenty of ammo, but no clear targets.

A couple of centuries of the *cohortes equitates* came pelting down the hill, but all they could do was drag a few wounded out from the fringes of the battle. That was one legion that was going to have a blood debt to settle today. Rick only hoped they weren't too weakened or shaken to take it when they had a chance.

When the cavalry action petered out, Rick saw that the enemy was now across his line of retreat up the hill. Ganton needed him as a Captain General, the Tamaerthans and the city-state infantry needed him as a CO. Neither needed him as a casualty.

"Let's move, Top!" he called to Elliot.

"Sir." Elliot waved commands.

Twenty Guardsmen moved ahead. Rick had long since got used to that: the elite troopers weren't about to let him lead the way into combat. They rode across the leading skirmishers of the Prophet's army. Lances dipped, and rose dripping red. Sabers flashed. Rick, Elliot, and the fifty Guards of his headquarters troop rode through the enemy foot at a gallop.

When they were past they saw the cavalry.

"Damn all!" Elliot shouted. He raised his Ingram. "Going to take shooting to get through those."

"Right as usual," Rick said. And we're getting low on ammo. Should be more in the Redoubt. He smiled to himself. The Great Redoubt. Like Borodino. Ring it with artillery. Fill it with star weapons. And wait. The Prophet would send his troops charging toward it, to be cut down in thousands.

Good battle plan, Rick thought. *Good enough? What the hell is a track star doing in a place like this?*

Elliot's Ingram sounded like tearing paper as he fired off a full clip into the lancers blocking their path.

Trouble with those things. Easy to shoot up too much ammo for too little effect. And we're getting low on nine mm parabellum— He raised his automatic and shot an approaching cavalryman out of the saddle. *How casually you do that. Having fun, Galloway?*

Then they were past. A dozen Guardsmen wheeled behind Rick to cover his retreat. He turned to urge them to follow him, but saw they were needed. The enemy cavalry wasn't retreating at all. *Fanatics. They all fight like fanatics. I guess the rumors are true, the Prophet holds all their families hostage.*

Another fifty yards. He spurred his horse forward. The Guards shouted behind him. "Cover them!" Rick shouted to Elliot.

"Roger." Elliot wheeled and rammed a new clip into the Ingram.

Rick came to the ditch and abatis of the Redoubt. Larry Brentano waved, something like a salute.

"Help Elliot," Rick ordered.

Brentano waved again and ran to the edge. After a moment his H&K chattered. Then Elliot rode in followed by the rest of the Guards.

"Who'd we lose?" Rick demanded.

"None," Elliot said proudly. "Two wounded." He pointed to the hospital area at the rear. "Get 'em up there, Sarkas."

"Sir." The Guards lieutenant shouted his own orders.

"Colonel!" Brentano shouted. He pointed downhill.

The Prophet's army was moving forward in one vast wave of infantry.

"You taking command now?" Brentano asked.

"Right. Just give me a moment to have a drink." He reached for the wineskin attached to his saddle and tried to look casual as the Prophet's drums and horns sounded again and again.

Rick hitched one leg up to sit casually atop his horse as he watched the enemy boil forward. Somebody had finally got them organized. As organized as that outfit would ever be. "Forty thousand?" he asked Elliot. He tried to keep his voice calm and casual.

"Maybe that many," Elliot said. "Maybe even a few more. How close you going to let them get?"

"Not much more," Rick said. He signaled to his signalmen. "Trumpeter, sound the General Alert, then All Units."

The notes sang out.

Gunners stood to their guns.

"Sound Fire On Command," Rick said. He reached out to his signalman and took the red and white striped flag, raised it high, and waited as the enemy infantry moved forward. When they reached the clump of brush he'd mentally selected he brought the flag sharply down.

The Redoubt erupted in fire. Bombards, musketeers, all the mercs, including the mortars and the crew with the Carl

Gustav. The mortars were right on target: Rick saw whole squads fall in the center of the enemy ranks. Meanwhile twenty-pound stone balls from the bombards cut lanes from front to as far as Rick could see into the enemy formation.

The one-oh-six blazed again. White phosphorus exploded just at the enemy first rank. Men screamed in horror and ran trailing smoke.

"That ought to stop them," Elliot said.

"Yeah, it ought to, Sarge," Brentano said. "But it don't look like it did." He raised his H&K and fired slowly and deliberately. "And I don't reckon we're going to stop them."

"Fire in the hole!"

The one-oh-six roared, and more of the Prophet's army died.

Not enough. Rick raised his own H&K and fired carefully and deliberately. Men fell.

"They just keep coming," Elliot said. "Goddam, Colonel, I could sure use troops like that."

"Yeah." With competent leadership those men could take any army on Tran. Fortunately they didn't have competent leadership.

"Defenders," Elliot muttered. He pointed to a formation at extreme range. "Six thousand, I hear. That's the damned secret. Everybody in that army knows them Defenders will kill anyone who runs. And go back and mop up the village he came from to boot." Elliot rose in his saddle. "Ernikos! Keep them musketeers loading properly. That last volley was ragged."

"Aye my lord!" came the reply.

"They're going to get in here," Elliot said. "Dismount?"

"No. We'll need to fall back."

Elliot looked at him quizzically but said nothing.

"I remember a Korean vet," Rick said. "He said watching men try to put out a fire by jumping into it will give you the willies if you let yourself think about it."

"Right," Elliot said cheerfully. "So don't think about it."

"Sure." But it took a very experienced soldier not to think

about what would happen if that kind of man reached you. Most of the locals weren't that experienced.

What the hell, Rick Galloway? Are you that experienced yourself?

"Sappers," Elliot said. He pointed. "Masked by the first wave. I thought them infantry wasn't supposed to get here. Good planning."

The leading infantry had taken the casualties. Now, behind them, were several compact formations of men who carried brushwood fascines and axes.

"They'll sure as hell get in here, Colonel," Elliot said. "We got maybe five minutes. No more. And I better see to my gunners."

"Right."

Elliot rode off. The Guards officers were chanting orders as the Guards musketeers loaded in unison. "Bite your cartridge. Spit. Ram. Return ramrod...."

The artillerymen were struggling to lower the aim points of the bombards. They'd never been intended to be depressed that low. Then from the center of the Redoubt the LMG opened up. Pfc. Arkos Passovopolous had it, with Gardner as his number-two; it was in good hands. Ben Murphy would have been even better, but he had to ride with the Drantos ironhats if he wanted to hold on to Westrock.

For a couple of minutes the battlefield was almost silent, except for the mortar and recoilless rounds falling into the sappers and the boss gunner, Pinir son of the smith, roaring at his men. Then the sappers hit the ditch and the abatis, and what they lacked in skill they made up for in numbers. The logs of the abatis seemed to dissolve like the cohorts of the Fourth Legion, and suddenly the whole southern end of the Great Redoubt was open to the enemy.

"Fall back in order!" Rick shouted. There wasn't a trumpet command for that. He backed his horse away from the oncoming enemy. At intervals he fired his H&K. *Set an example. About all you can do.*

"Get First Pikes up to the northern end of the Redoubt,"

Rick shouted to a staff officer. The man rode off and another took his place next to Rick. "Vis infantry to connect with First Pikes. Move them north, and have them connect First Pikes to the Tamaerthan archers. And keep the archers supplied."

"Aye my lord."

And did you understand? I should write orders, but there's no time. Not with the enemy fifty yards away and closing.

He fired again and again. Then trumpets sounded behind him. He stood in his stirrups, then turned back with relief. First Pikes hadn't failed him.

"Close on First Pikes! Retreat behind the pikes!" He sent messengers down both sides to repeat the orders.

Elliot rode up. "They're keeping better order than I'd have thought," he said. He gestured to indicate the Guards musketeers, who had loaded while retreating and now turned to deliver another terrible volley at point blank range.

The battle dissolved in confusion. For a while it seemed that the Redoubt was full of people with every kind of weapon or none at all, trying to run in three directions at once. Rick's Guardsmen had to draw their swords and hack their way through the enemy's skirmishers, then prod their way through the retreating musketeers and gunners.

Gunners drew swords and prepared to die by their bombards.

Rick rode down the line of gunners. "Retreat! Fall back behind the pikes! We'll take the guns again, and you'll use them again! Fall back!"

They did, although they wouldn't have if anyone but Rick had ordered it.

Close one, that. Even my middle class gunners get the ironhat mentality. Never retreat. Never budge....

A mob of half-naked men, heads shaved, wielding long knives, poured over the LMG's pit. Rick mentally awarded the Great Ark and Gardner posthumous Medals of Honor; they'd stayed on the gun long enough to take a big bite out of the enemy.

Then the mob stopped, churned, and went abruptly into reverse as the Great Ark erupted out of the pit. He held the LMG under his arm and swept it back and forth until the belt was gone. Then he tossed it to Gardner, drew a short sword with one hand and a long-handled mace with the other, and waded into the enemy.

From the speed of their retreat, it looked as if they'd finally found something that scared them more than the Defenders.

Gardner and Passovopolous fell back. Halfway to the pikes, Gardner went down with an arrow in his leg. The Great Ark picked up his number-two, machine gun and all, slung the whole load over his shoulder, and kept on going.

Rick mentally erased the "posthumous" from the Medals of Honor and added an unlimited line of credit at Madame Echenia's for the Great Ark and a case of McCleve's Best for Gardner. They'd probably enjoy that more than the medals.

Everyone cheered as the Great Ark carried his load into the ranks of the First Pikes. Then they cheered again as Lord Rick rode up. Rick waved his binoculars to acknowledge the cheers, but it took an effort to hold his hand steady as he did. "No battle plan ever survives contact with the enemy," but this one had been a little too short-lived for his peace of mind.

Or had it? The enemy had spent his energy and most of his ammunition. He held much of the Great Redoubt, but it was a pit of carnage, worthless to the enemy—and they'd made no progress against the pikes at all.

"Mortars," Rick called. "Make them regret being in the Redoubt."

"Roger," someone shouted. A pair of mortar bombs fell among the enemy. Dead and living men were tossed about. The one-oh-six added white phosphorus. The interior of the Redoubt was a scene from the Inferno.

"City infantry's holding."

Rick turned to see Elliot on his right. The Sergeant Major looked as calm as he did on parade.

"And the Guards." Elliot raised his hand and brought it

sharply down. A volley crashed out from among the pike-men. More of the Prophet's troops fell.

The city infantry on the left were indeed holding, but the enemy was doing no more than skirmishing with cavalry there. The allies' own cavalry was out of danger too, both the Drantos knights and the two mounted legions, the Eighth and the chewed-up Fourth.

The trouble was that the enemy's infantry had pushed so far forward and was massed so solidly that Rick's cavalry didn't really have room to charge. Rick had hoped the enemy would jam themselves between the river and the forest like a cork in a bottle; what he hadn't expected was that they'd do it so fast they immobilized most of his own cavalry. Now the two armies were like two porcupines facing each other in a sewer pipe, neither able to back up without giving the other an advantage.

"Damn Rudhrig," Rick said. "If he'd stayed a bit farther back—"

"Sure," Elliot said.

No point in if. "The key is those Defenders," Rick said. "Eliminate them and the Prophet's whole army comes apart." *I hope.*

CHAPTER FIVE

Art Mason looked at the map and nodded. "No question, Colonel. Them Defenders are the key. Get them out of the way and all that infantry will run like blazes. They're only holding on because they got no place to go."

"Good. Glad you agree. Top?"

"Looks that way to me, too," Elliot said.

Mason stood and swept the area with his binoculars. The Prophet's infantry must have taken at least fifteen percent casualties; in places the ditch was solid with bodies, some of them still moving. They'd all run if they could.

"So what do we have to hit the Defenders with?" Colonel Galloway asked.

Mason thought fast. *Good question.* "Well, we can't use the Romans. Or Drantos heavies, for that matter. The only way in there would be the High Road."

The Colonel nodded. "Bottleneck. We hold it with minimum forces, but that works both ways. We'll never get through their blocking force. Unless we can lure them off?"

Mason shook his head. "Tried. Didn't work. Whoever's holding that area knows what he's doing and has steady troops."

"Damnedest thing," Elliot mused. "How did a madman like the Prophet get first-class troops?"

Who cares?

"It's messed up from here to the Lynos River," the Colonel said. "But south of there is Herdsman's Ford."

"Herdsman's Ford. Right!" Art said. "Wide enough to

send cavalry across in column of squadrons. If—" He frowned.

"I think we can do it," the Colonel said. "If we can clear off that blocking force on their side of the river and push a couple of thousand horse across we can sure give the Defenders something to worry about. Now who do I send?"

"Reckon I know," Mason said. "I'll round up volunteers. What can I have?"

"The Carl Gustav for one thing."

"Right, I'll need that. And enough more firepower to clear the river guards. Say a squadron of Guards. Two troops anyway. And for the main body—Colonel, can we borrow some Romans?"

"Doubt they'd follow you, Major," Elliot said. "Or that we can get Publius to lend them."

"Not without being here until the True Sun comes up," the Colonel agreed. "They used to teach us that 'unity of command' was a major principle of war. Hah."

"Worse down there," Elliot said. He waved toward the enemy.

And that's for damned sure. Now, who can the Colonel order directly? Hah. "Sir, what about Gengrich's troops?"

"Nowhere near enough," Galloway said. "They're not very reliable just now, either. Need rest and training. No, Art, there's only one group we can send. Drumold's Tamaerthan chivalry. There's close to three thousand of them."

"It's also the whole nobility of Tamaerthon," Elliot said.

"Objection, Sergeant Major?"

"No objection, Colonel. Just reminding you. Sir."

"Thank you. It's a chance we'll have to take. Mason, I'll give you a written order to Drumold. Take your Guards, and our people, and get moving."

Ganton made a point of studying the messages from the balloon, then scanning the battlefield with his binoculars, before turning back to the Imperial headquarters staff. "The enemy does not know what to do," he said. "While they argue, we should strike."

"How do you know they are confused?" Publius demanded. "If your knights had withdrawn when ordered we would have no doubts about this battle."

"We have none now," Ganton said. "Yet certainly I have cause to be displeased with my knights and barons." *As perhaps you have to be displeased with the Fourth Legion. The legion that hailed me as worthy to lead Romans.*

It had been a heady moment, there after the battle of the Hooey River, when the Roman soldiers hailed him as *Imperator*. *Worthy to command Romans, but not a Roman. I am no threat to Publius Caesar, but can he believe that?* Ganton stole a glance at Titus Frugi, who was pointedly studying the battle.

"Patience is a Roman virtue that I wish my barons would learn. Ever do we seek to ride to the battle and trample our enemies beneath the hooves of our horses. Sometimes that is the best way. Often it is not."

"It would seem, Titus Frugi, that my son-in-law has learned much."

"Thank you, Caesar," Ganton said. "Would you care to instruct me further today?"

Publius looked at him sharply, but Ganton showed no expression at all. *It's true. I have much to learn. More from Titus Frugi than from Publius, but—*

"The High Road," Publius said finally. "It is the key to this battle." He gestured, and a headquarters optio came forward with maps pinned to a board. "The balloon reports that five thousand horse and nearly that many foot hold the High Road. They have been blocked by the Tamaerthan archers."

This time Publius did wince. It wasn't hard to know why. Tamaerthan archers and pikemen, aided by no more than two starmen, had defeated a Roman legion and sacked a Roman town. That was years ago, but it was not easily forgotten.

Ganton pretended to study the maps, but in fact he had memorized the terrain. He had found that Romans were not so well trained as he in that art. They didn't have to be. They always had maps.

"Bad ground for cavalry," Ganton said. He indicated the area along the High Road. "Narrow. Best for foot."

"Agreed." Titus Frugi pointed to the massed troops milling around the Great Redoubt. "You see that Lord Rick sends the chivalry of Tamaerthon toward the river ford. It is easy to guess his plan."

"And there is a rider coming to tell us anyway," Ganton said. "I do not doubt that, even though the Lord Rick commands Tamaerthon independent of me."

"You have a plan, Frugi," Publius said.

"Yes, Caesar. Send the foot to menace the High Road. I will keep the survivors of the Fourth, and the *cohortes equitates*, to support Wanax Ganton. The Seventeenth will stay between under your command, ready to move either way, and we will see who first can advance."

"A good plan," Publius said. "I agree."

"Thank you, Caesar," Ganton said. *And you too, Titus Frugi. I reward my friends, and you are a true friend.*

Three arrows thrummed past Matthias. Two of them found targets, one in a centaur's belly and a second in the thigh of one of his guards. The man reeled in his saddle but said nothing. The centaur screamed until its rider dismounted and cut its throat.

"Retreat," Matthias ordered. "Fall back. Carefully, carefully." He rode up and down the line, making certain that this was a retreat and no rout. Whatever the skills of the Tamaerthan hillsmen, whatever Ganton of Drantos had learned, the Romans at least would know the value of the High Road, and must have troops poised to take advantage of any disorder here.

I could lose this battle in an hour, and Phrados the False Prophet does not even know. A fool. He looked to the sky for a sign from Vothan. *Am I to be chosen today? Or have you more work for me?*

They withdrew out of bowshot from the forest. For the third time they had ridden up the High Road to test its defenses, and for the third time the Tamaerthan archers had warned them against going too far.

"It's hopeless." The mercenary captain spoke in a low voice so that only Matthias could hear. "We need infantry to clear out those woods." He pointed to more than three hundred bodies, men, centaurs, and horses, that littered the road and its ditches. "Cavalry will never get through alone. We need infantry."

"We have none, Captain Marikos. The Prophet, praise his holy name, has ordered the foot he sent here to stand fast and protect the road."

"If they'd attack, they could keep the damned kilties busy enough—"

"But they cannot attack. They have orders from the Prophet himself. Praise to the gods."

Marikos looked at Matthias quizzically. "As you say. You could ask for a change in orders. Or more infantry."

"I have sent messengers to ask that," Matthias said.

"But they have not returned," Captain Marikos said.

"Yes—"

"Killed by the Defenders as deserters."

Matthias frowned. "I would hope not—"

"You know they were. The Defenders are mad, and the Prophet as well. A child could have won this battle, but instead of a child we had Phrados."

"That is blasphemy—"

Marikos waved airily. "My troops are closer than yours. But you're no believer. You never have been. You're an orthodox priest of Vothan."

"Why do you say that?"

"I have eyes. I see where you look for signs. And what you wear under your armor. I've heard how your servants address you. Honorable, I'm surprised the Defenders didn't find out."

As am I, perhaps. "I see. And what now?"

"We save what we can. I've got men watching behind us. When the Defenders are engaged—and they will be, today or tomorrow—I'm taking my troops out of here."

"Where will you go?"

"Anywhere. North. I've heard Prince Strymon can use good soldiers. I've got two thousand cavalry."

"And their families?"

"Already alerted. Unlike yours, my messengers really were deserters. They got through. And one returned. He saw your messengers killed by the Defenders. No message you sent the Prophet ever got to him."

"How do you propose to get past our own foot soldiers, who stand between you and freedom precisely to keep you from running away?"

"That's my business."

"I see. And what do you want of me?"

"Nothing. Stay out of my way. But since you've been a friend, I'll give you warning. Three blasts of the trumpets followed by two more. If you hear that, save yourself, and your men. If you can."

"Thank you." *What more can I do? It would be folly to warn Phrados. There are no Defenders here, and Marikos is surrounded by his officers and loyal men. It was the act of a friend to warn me. Now I must think how to make use of that warning.*

A cloud of dust rose from the hill beyond the narrow area of the road. A sizable enemy force was approaching. He turned to see that the commander of the foot soldiers had seen it also and was placing his men.

The horseman spurred straight at Art Mason. He wielded a heavy battle-ax and was screaming praises to the gods. Mason shot him twice with his .45 Colt, and even then had to dodge the ax. One of the Guardsmen brought his own ax solidly onto the man's head, and another seized his horse.

"No ransom for these fanatics," the Guard sergeant said contemptuously. "But some of them have good horses."

"Yeah, sure. Now let's ride." He signaled Teuthras to advance with the light cavalry.

Amazingly, the enemy melted away into the cultivated land west of the river.

"From that last chap I'd have thought they'd fight like tigers," Mason said aloud.

"My lord?" his orderly prompted.

"Nothing."

The enemy light cavalry retreated, with Teuthras and the Hussars in pursuit. Mason was about to signal recall when he saw that Teuthras had halted his pursuit, set pickets to watch to see that the enemy didn't return without warning, and was coming back.

Well done, Mason thought. More locals learning to think ahead. Not long ago they'd have chased that enemy cavalry forever.

"Messenger from the balloon," his orderly called.

"Right."

The man had ridden hard. Both he and his horse were lathered. He held out a square of paper.

"Thank you. Orderly! Wine for the messenger. A groom to walk his horse."

"At once, lord."

Art read the message aloud as Teuthras rode up.

WARNING TO BATTLE GROUP DRUMOLD; ENEMY CAVALRY PRESENT ON WEST BANK OF RIVER CLOSE TO HERDSMAN'S FORD.

Teuthras grinned. It probably would have hurt too much to laugh; he was riding in a sort of corset of bandages to keep his cracked ribs in place. The priests had wanted him to stay in bed, but nothing short of a direct command from Yatar could have kept him out of this battle.

"Was it not Lord Rick's intention, that the men in the balloon should see what others could not and give warning? If all they can tell us is what we have seen for ourselves..."

"Yeah, that can happen. But remember Pirion. The balloon saved our asses there."

"I do. I also remember the Hooey River."

So did Mason, and so did the Captain. That was why the balloon was so far back, so its anchor and ground crew wouldn't be overrun. The Westmen had done that, killing not only the ground crew but the aeronauts. It took a long time to train those crews, not just technicians for the balloon but competent observers.

All very well, but it would be nice to have more information. And who was antsy about being an officer? Yeah. A corporal who got promoted over his head, and too late to think about that now.

The rest of the Tamaerthan arrived at a fast walk. Drumold was in sight, and so was his son Balquhain, in that tent-sized green cloak he'd adopted in order to be recognized in battle.

Just as important, so was the Carl Gustav recoilless and its crew. Time to get the troops deployed.

"Stand by to fire," Mason said.

Rudolf Frick grinned like a wolf. He knelt, and Doug McQuade knelt behind and to his left. Three Guards brought ammunition from the pack mules.

Mason stood in his stirrups and looked up and down the river line. The Tamaerthan chivalry were arrayed three deep, lances erect, armor gleaming.

They looked more impressive than they were. Tamaerthon was mountainous land, poor horse country at best. Its real strength was in its infantry, especially longbowmen, and now the disciplined pike formations Colonel Galloway had trained. And none of that made any difference. The nobility of Tamaerthon wore armor and tried to make believe they were as good as the Drantos ironhats.

"All I got," Art muttered to himself.

After it crossed Herdsman's Ford the road led through a draw between two low but steep-sided hills. The enemy cavalry commander had bunched up his forces there. He'd also put archers on the hilltops, and in front of the archers was a line of infantry forming a shield wall. It wasn't a very solid shield wall, but it would be good enough to shake up Tamaerthan cavalry.

Well, first things first. That enemy cavalry force made a beautiful target. Hadn't those idiots ever heard of star weapons? "Six for effect, Rudy. Concentrate on the cavalry. Fire when ready."

"Yo!" Frick took aim.

"Stand clear behind!" McQuade shouted and rammed a load into the small shoulder-fired recoilless.

"Fire in the hole!" The Carl Gustav roared, and flame belched from both ends of the recoilless. The shell slammed right into the middle of the enemy horsemen, twenty yards to the right of the CO's banner. The second shell took out the banner.

By the time the fourth shell was on the way, the first rank of the enemy cavalry had broken. They turned on the troops behind, so that the entire force was in disarray. Mason turned to his trumpeter. "Sound the charge."

He was only just in time. The sight of enemy backs was too much for the Tamaerthan heavies, and not even Drumold and Balquhain could hold them. They'd already begun to move when the trumpets sounded. In seconds they were waist-deep in the water.

Two upstream cavalrymen suddenly screamed as translucent tentacles reached up and around them. The men slashed wildly with their swords as their horses bolted in panic. The other cavalry spurred onward. Some emerged with half a dozen foot-long hydras clinging to the horses. Their comrades smashed at them with sword flats. The hydras dropped off and were trampled.

Now the heavies were in extreme archery range of the troops on the hilltop. They hadn't lost a man crossing, but now Mason saw three fall. Then two more horses were down.

Frick slammed four more rounds into the retreating enemy cavalry, then turned to harass the shield wall on the hill to his left. Three rounds, and the first of the infantry threw down their weapons and ran. By the fifth round they were all running, and carrying the archers with them.

Teuthras was just crossing the river. He saw the hill cleared and led his light cavalry across the rear of the charging heavies and up the left side hill. It was tough going on the steep hillock but there was no opposition and soon he'd outflanked the enemy cavalry in the draw below.

On his own initiative, too, Mason thought. We got ourselves some decent officers, by God!

The Tamaerthan heavies lowered their lances and charged home into the enemy cavalry in the gap. The enemy was already in retreat. Now it became a headlong rout. The infantry on the right-hand hill threw down their weapons and knelt. Some held up charms, of Yatar and Vothan, as tokens of surrender. A quarter of an hour after the first round was fired there wasn't an armed enemy to be seen.

Drumold and Balquhain held up their banners, waited until their troops had rallied and were in formation, and led the way into the gap.

And that tears it, Mason thought. We're well beyond any intelligence I've got. There was supposed to be one hell of a lot of enemy here. So far it's been easy. Too damned easy.

Drumold's banner had reached the head of the draw when Mason saw it stop. Art spurred his horse ahead along the column, but the rough ground on either side of the road slowed him. As he came in sight of more open ground the Defenders began their move, but between them and the Tamaerthans was a solid mass of cavalry coming on at a trot.

Drumold stood in his stirrups. "Spread out! Get in line!"

"That's where they were," Mason muttered. "Frick! Follow me! Guards, rally here!" He turned to scramble up the left side hill. "Get up here and set up! Your target is the oncoming cavalry. Fire at will!"

We're in time, he thought. Just. But they sure act like nothing can stop them—

Skin-clad figures seemed to sprout like mushrooms from the scrub to Mason's left. He shot one, hacked through a spear-wielding arm with his sword. He caught a flicker of motion out of the corner of his eye, then a sling stone smashed into his helmet. He saw blood-red fireworks against a black sky and barely had time for one thought as he toppled out of the saddle.

Maybe that enemy commander was right in thinking he couldn't be stopped.

Ganton focused the binoculars, and the banner on the hill by Herdsman's Ford sprang into clear sight. Lord Rick's plan had worked well so far; the Tamaerthans were in the rear of the Defenders and in no small strength.

Yet the Defenders had cavalry aiding them. Together might not the enemy's strength be too much for Drumold and Lord Mason? It very well might be, and then whether the battle was won or lost, Tamaerthon would be a long time recovering from the loss of its knights and archers.

I owe Titus Frugi much, and that is good and sufficient reason not to shame him without cause. I owe the Tamaerthans more—my very throne, indeed. But is that cause enough to risk shaming Titus Frugi, to say nothing of quarreling with my wife's father?

Only Yatar or His Son could be certain. I only know this: I will not have it said that the Wanax Ganton of Drantos was like his father, without honor. That he let the chivalry of Tamaerthon be cut to pieces when his aid could have saved them.

"Morrone!"

"Majesty?"

"Sound the trumpets and advance the banner of the Fighting Man. We ride to aid the Tamaerthans!"

If Morrone's grin had been any wider it would have met at the back of his head. "As you command."

"Oh, and send a messenger to Lord Rick."

"And one to Publius?"

"To Publius, of course. But send the one to Lord Rick first."

The Drantos heavy cavalry took up all the space between the hill and the forest, so the Romans had to follow them. Rick saw that Ganton was taking his time, too. The heavies moved at a walk until they were on level ground, and even a little farther, until they were on ground that wasn't littered with bodies from the earlier attacks.

Then the knights of Drantos shook out their lines, and even from the top of the Great Redoubt Rick could see Ganton's golden helmet take its place in front. They worked up to a trot, and at a trot they rolled across the rear of Phrados's host, straight toward the Defenders and the cavalry around the Tamaerthans.

That solved one of Rick's biggest headaches, and without his having to say a word. Just as well, because Publius must be about ready to have a stroke. He might not risk insulting his son-in-law, but his son-in-law's Captain General?

And isn't that thinking a lot like a medieval politician— like your wife, in fact?

A moment later he saw the Romans move out. The Praetorian Eagle led the way, but the Fourth was close up behind it, and the Eighth brought up the rear in a really beautiful formation.

A messenger rode off, with a signal for the balloon to send: TO TAMAERTHAN ARCHERS ON HIGH ROAD; PREPARE TO ADVANCE DOWN HIGH ROAD IN SUPPORT OF SEVENTEENTH LEGION WHEN SEVENTEENTH ADVANCES.

If Publius had the brains God promised little white mice, he'd move his own pikemen and foot archers out of cover to stiffen up the cavalry cordon he would soon have drawn around the enemy's infantry. Then the Tamaerthan archers could leave their cover and stiffen the Seventeenth, and the enemy's whole center would be surrounded—Tamaerthan and Romans on two sides and the river on the third.

Close off the Redoubt and they'll be surrounded—provided of course, that I can retake the Great Redoubt. Time to fight again.

Rick sent off another messenger to the heavy weapons, then rode down to First Pikes and stood in his stirrups. "First Pikes, Guardsmen, gunners! Follow me! Let's clean these vermin out of our house."

He drew his sword to signal the advance. Suddenly the men to either side dropped their pikes and bows and ran forward to grab his bridle, his stirrups, even his horse's tail. Shouts rose.

"Go back, Lord Rick!"

"Stay back, Lord Rick!"

"We won't advance until you're safe, Lord Rick!"

Then:

"Lord Rick to the rear!"

—and everybody picked up on that and shouted it until Rick's head ached.

Elliot rode up grinning like an idiot. "Captain, looks like you're outvoted. They think you're their good luck charm. Maybe you are."

"Elliot—"

"Think about it, Colonel. They'll follow you, all right. But if you buy it, this outfit's finished, and we all know it. For Christ's sake, sir! You don't have to prove anything."

I don't have to prove anything? "All right, Sergeant Major. Carry on."

"Sir!" Elliot rode out in front of the pikemen, fired a burst into the air from the Ingram, and shouted, "Okay, you crazy bastards! Do you want to live forever?"

Cheers rose, pikes followed, and the counterattack charged down the hill. Mortar and recoilless rounds fell among the enemy. In the center of the line rose two giant figures, the Great Ark swathed in ammo belts and Gunner Pinir with a barrel of powder under one arm and a rammer over his shoulder.

The enemy troops in the Redoubt stood for a moment. Then someone raised a shout. "The Defenders! The Defenders are running away."

It was true enough. Ganton's chivalry had struck the Defenders in flank even as they were closing on the Tamaerthan knights, and the Defenders dissolved into uncoordinated groups. Some stood and fought like demons. More turned and ran as they realized their gods had forsaken them.

"They run! The Defenders run!" The shout rang through the Redoubt.

First Pikes came at a steady lope, pike aligned into a forest of advancing points, in step as if on parade. A few of the bombard gunners ran ahead of the pikemen to beat the last of the Prophet's men from their guns, then wrestled the bombards back into action. Three were actually firing at the retreating enemy when the Seventeenth Legion marched out of the forest followed by Tamaerthan archers.

Art Mason woke to a thundering head and a sharp pain in his leg. He tried to sit, but was restrained. It was a struggle to open his eyes. Somewhere nearby a man was screaming. Many men.

The first thing he saw was the smiling face of Yanulf's sidekick, Apelles.

"Praise Yatar the Healer," Apelles said. He turned and shouted to an apprentice. "Carry the word to the Lord Rick."

"At once."

So the Colonel's alive too. We're getting too old for this. He listened, and heard distant sounds of guns, but not nearly enough.

"Can you count the fingers I hold up before you?" Apelles asked urgently.

"Fingers? Four. No." He tried to shake his head and that hurt. "Two."

"Good." He wiped Mason's face with a wet cloth. "The Lord McCleve has been summoned."

"To hell with McCleve. Who's winning?" Mason demanded.

"All is well."

"Talk, damn your eyes!"

"You should rest—very well." Apelles wiped Mason's forehead again and held a cup of water to his lips. "Drink. Then I will talk."

The water was bitter.

"Where to begin?"

"The goddam cavalry was about to grind up my troops!"

"Ah. The captain of that cavalry had arrayed his men without telling Phrados. Phrados thought he was deserting. He ordered the Defenders to attack.

"When the Defenders advanced, Lord Balquhain held his forces and waited until the Defenders had finished their work. Then he charged."

"Good man." Mason tried to grin, but it hurt.

"Then our gracious Wanax Ganton most honorably led the host of Drantos against the Defenders! He smote them to the ground! They never rose again!

"Publius Caesar, envious of our king's glory, led his legions against the enemy's center, and the Lord Rick retook the Great Redoubt and the Guns.

"The day is ours."

The day is ours. His head buzzed. There had been something in that water. He closed his eyes to sleep, and a smile drifted to his lips. *Survived again.*

The Prophet's tent stood. The interior was stripped bare. The great wheeled altar lay on its side. Holes gaped where there had once been bronze handles and silver fittings.

Matthias turned away. He handed his torch to a guard and mounted.

Captain Pharikos rode up. "It's like this everywhere, sir." He shrugged. "At least one thing's for the best. If they don't find Phrados's body, anyone can claim to be him. If Drantos has to fight a new Phrados every year, they'll get a bellyful of fighting. If we send all those Prophets silver and arms—"

"Peace. The gods have judged Phrados. It is not for us to question their judgment."

Matthias knew that he had spoken sharply, but not why. He turned his horse away and waved his band forward out of the camp.

Screams echoed behind him. Screams of both men and women. Matthias was glad of his two hundred armed and mounted men. *Men I can trust. There are few enough honest men left here.*

It was not until the camp was several stades behind that Matthias thought of his harsh words to Captain Pharikos. *The strategy is sound. It would rob the starmen of much of the profit of today's victory.*

He rode on in silence. *No. To harass the starmen with false Prophets will strengthen their alliance with the city-states. The men who would rise in that alliance will not be those of the old blood who honor the old ways. Mercenary captains, merchants. New men who will multiply like lamils in the breeding time.*

And that is what I must tell Issardos, yea, and the High Rexja Toris himself.

He would not speak of the judgment of the gods to any but Vothan.

CHAPTER SIX

Gwen dismissed her servant, then helped Siobhan lift Art Mason's injured leg onto the carved ironwood table.

"And Publius Caesar took back not one word of what he said to the knights of Drantos?" asked Siobhan.

Art Mason grunted as she loosened the binding holding the poultices Apelles had applied from ankle to midthigh. "Not that I heard, but then he'd hardly do it in public. Maybe to Ganton, in private—"

Siobhan bristled. "Then the knights of Drantos have known great insult, with no redress. Will the Wanax let matters rest there?"

Mason and Gwen Tremaine exchanged smiles. Earthmen against locals, but also discreet age against hotheaded youth. Getting any kind of smile from Art—and from Sergeant Major Elliot, Larry Warner, and Rick—was lifting Gwen's spirits more than she would have believed possible. Whatever had been making all four of them look through her, then shy away from any explanation, the victory over Phrados's host and the end of the southern war had helped a lot.

Helped, but hadn't ended it. *What do they know, and why won't they tell me?*

Siobhan saw their conspiratorial glances and laughed softly. Gwen smiled to herself. Mason was going to have his hands full with that young lady after they were married—and that seemed certain now. There was no mistaking Siobhan's reaction when she heard that Mason had been wounded, or when she saw his troops bring him through the

University gate on a horse litter. *Chalk up another arranged marriage that's turning into a love match. Hah. Les intended that for Rick and me.*

"Publius Caesar drips insults like a hydra feeds. It doesn't mean all that much," Mason said. "I think we're just going to have to live with it."

Siobhan frowned.

"Ganton will probably give Rudhrig an important post next time," Mason said. "I just hope Rudhrig's learned enough that a lot of good men don't get killed for his damned honor. Anyway, that'll have to do. Ganton has a few other things on his mind." He grinned. "Like becoming a father."

"It's official then?" said Gwen. "Octavia's pregnant?"

Siobhan looked intently at the fire.

"The priests say so," Mason said. "I hear the formal announcement goes out over the semaphore in a couple of days. When the Roman bishops say the signs are right."

"Hallelujah!" said Gwen. *I hope I sound surprised.* She thought of the letter Octavia had written to her ten days ago.

"A good thing," Siobhan said. She sniffed. "Lady Prygisia has told the entire court that our queen is barren. And some listened, too."

"This should help," Art said.

"I'd think so." Gwen brushed back a wisp of hair. "The great ladies of Drantos weren't too pleased that our Wanax went to Rome to find a queen." *Poor Octavia. Hardly any friends at all, so when Ganton isn't home she broods.* "This will put a stop to that particular gossip anyway."

"Especially if it's a boy," Siobhan said. Then she giggled.

It was Art Mason's turn to look at the fire.

Siobhan had finished with Art's leg and was trimming his hair.

Art Mason reached up to take the scissors from her, and looked at them closely. "Steel?"

"Sort of," Gwen said. "Something between a good tempered iron and real steel. The University makes them. Actually we were looking for better ways to make swords and bayonets, but one of our apprentices made scissors, and now we make a good profit selling them."

"Much to the annoyance of the Guild of Smiths," Siobhan said.

"Yes. I've been thinking of some way to license our inventions. Patents. Something—"

"Far as the Captain is concerned you can give it away," Mason said. "Spread the knowledge—"

"Yes, but if we can't afford to do the research, how will we have knowledge to spread?" Gwen demanded.

"Hmm. Budget time again?" Art grinned.

"How did you know? But seriously, we need to get along with the locals, but we need to reward our people for doing good work, too."

"Right. I'll bring it up next staff meeting." Mason took a folded sheet from his pocket and made a note with a ball point pen. "Sure wish your husband would bring us proper notebooks."

"Daytimers, adjusted for the Tran calendar! Art, not to change the subject, but did any of the Defenders escape?"

"Not many. Once the Prophet's people saw they could surrender to us without being killed, a lot of the infantry— ours and theirs—settled their scores with the goon squad. It wasn't pretty. A lot of the Prophet's main body got away, though. Ten, twelve thousand, maybe more."

"Hah. I wondered why Publius accepted Rick and Yanulf's terms on the disputed lands."

"Hadn't thought of it, but I guess Rome would have a problem with that many of the Prophet's people running around. 'Tween them and the just honest-to-Yatar bandits, it'd need at least two legions to tame that area. And they ain't got any legions to spare."

"Not if they want to resettle their old Southern Provinces." Gwen looked thoughtful. "That's going to be a powder keg pretty soon."

"Yeah, until everybody starves."

"Starves, or gets killed by refugees from the far south." Gwen shuddered. "And next year things get really bad."

"The city-states are what really worried the Colonel," Mason said. "Not too much off the top, where—"

"My lord?" Siobhan asked.

"Nothing. Joke that doesn't translate."

"My lord, why was the Lord Rick so concerned about the city-states? Are they not loyal to the alliance?"

"They are now." Mason reached out to touch Siobhan's hand. "But they're short of troops, and sure don't have enough cavalry to spare to police the disputed lands. Only somebody's got to hold that territory to keep the refugees from streaming through."

Gwen smiled to herself. Siobhan was hanging on every word Art said. *But she's really interested, too. She'd better be. We'd all better be.*

"Anyway," Art said, "that's how Morrone wound up as Protector of the Southern Marches. Gives him the same rank as an Eqeta, and he gets a little army of his own with everybody chipping in to pay for it." Mason laughed. "Damnedest little army you ever saw. He's got hill tribes, some of those outlaw Tamaerthan Gengrich brought north, a lot of younger sons, a bunch of mercenary cavalry from Phrados's horde, and Vothan only knows what else."

"Even so, I should think the Lord Morrone would be pleased," Siobhan said.

"Oh, he's happy as a grig. The only man who even raised an eyebrow was Eqeta Rudhrig. He said that Lord Morrone's great and undoubted gifts seemed to fit him better for a place closer to the throne."

Siobhan smiled. "Does he wish the Protectorship for himself, or does he think Morrone less than fit?"

Hah. She's pretty when she smiles. And that's a sensible question. Mason could do a lot worse.

"Damned if I know. His Lordship of Harms is like Publius these days. He's got it in for the whole world, so you don't know how much he really means. On the other hand—I like

Morrone, but I've never seen him with an independent command."

Gwen nodded. *And maybe Ganton is being bought off from doing something about the Roman insults to his knights—Rudhrig's knights—by a Roman gift to his Companion.*

The thought disturbed Gwen. Was Ganton letting the Romans bribe him? One compromise didn't make a pattern, but—She remembered King Stephen of England. *He couldn't say no to anyone. And brought on one of the worst civil wars in English history. A king who will blow this way and that is bad news.* "Can Morrone do the job?"

Mason shrugged. "Personally, I don't think he's much of a diplomat, but it'll be a year before he'll be out of the saddle two days running. By then we'll have him fixed up with somebody like Apelles. Or maybe that oddball Vinicianus."

"I see." The haircut was nearly done. Gwen stood. "If you will excuse me, I have work. Ring for anything you like. I will be in my study."

She climbed the spiral staircase to her loft. It was the only spiral staircase on Tran, and she'd had it and the little study built during the nesting stage of her last pregnancy. Being a noblewoman with a lavish supply of cheap labor had its advantages. *Of course it spirals the wrong way. How did I know you want to hamper a swordsman by putting his right side against the core of the stairs? Oh, well. Nobody else knew, either. Except Rick. And I have my pistol.*

The window of the studio was only an arrow slit, but it gave her a good view of the west wall of the University and the cemetery beyond it. There were a lot of new monuments there; the bodies of the dead at Vis had been burned or buried where they fell, but the Romans who'd returned had been busily carving monuments to the comrades who hadn't.

They bought us time. They deserve their monuments.

A shift of the wind brought a cloud of stone dust from where the Roman masons were building the new workers' quarters and a block of shops. Mortimer Schultz had his eye on that block as just the right place for Tran's first printing press.

The clink and rattle of masons peaked, then gave way to the shouts of drill sergeants. The University's immigrant craftsmen were getting their basic training. Elliot wanted to train them all with the Tamaerthan longbow. Gwen couldn't convince him it took years to train a competent longbow-man, especially since Elliot had learned to use one well enough to win prizes.

There was another problem. The Tamaerthans wouldn't much care for foreigners learning their national weapon.

If it isn't one thing, it's another. Which would cause the more trouble, trying to teach foreigners to use the Tamaerthan longbow, or teaching them musketry? Either way some of the Tamaerthan clans would be unhappy.

But we have to do something. Suppose the Romans abandon us? This place can't be defended. And it damned well is going to be!

First things first. She'd need both archery and target ranges. Gunpowder. Carronades. How did that Kipling poem go? No, said the cannoneer, shooting from the wall. Iron, cold iron shall be master of you all.

Damned right, provided I get all that brush cut away from around the walls. Fields of fire—

First I'm a medieval politician, now a medieval general. Next?

Whatever. Tran is changing us as fast as we're changing Tran, and neither of us is going to recognize what we were before Rick Galloway came here with that flying saucer full of mercs.

Interlude
D'JORR

The viewer on the polished wood table was as plain as everything else in the chamber, but it was of high quality. The Guides of the Way of the Warrior did not live luxuriously, but they lived well.

Right now it showed Les's head silhouetted against the main screen on the bridge.

"You will note that his screen is off," Agzaral said.

The robed man seated behind the table nodded. "His third visit to Tran, did you say? Then why does your pilot wish to conceal his location from you?" A faint smile came to his lips. "Agzaral, I think you have not told me everything."

Agzaral returned the smile. "Everything of importance. Watch his report."

Les's image continued unemotionally. "Captain Galloway continues to work toward raising a professional standing army loyal to its commissioned officers, in place of a medieval host loyal to feudal lords. He has to move slowly, for many obvious reasons, not the least of which is to keep the support of the Wanax Ganton.

"Ganton feels much more secure on his throne now that he has a male heir, but he always remembers that his father lost his crown by ignoring the advice and the interests of his nobles, and he's determined not to make that mistake. As a practical matter he hasn't much choice. Any of his nobility who get sufficiently annoyed can always side with the High Rexja Toris when the war with the Five Kingdoms begins.

"Meanwhile, Captain Galloway does what he can with the Mounted Archers and the Guards. This is not much, because the Mounted Archers ultimately follow him because he is War Leader of Tamaerthon, and the Guards because he is Great Captain General of the Realm of Drantos. Were he to lose either post, he might have some difficulty commanding the allegiance of anyone not sworn to him as Eqeta of Chelm."

Agzaral's companion chuckled. "Not entirely unlike Council politics, my friend."

"Precisely. It is one reason I find Tran such a fascinating place." Agzaral adjusted the gain on the viewer.

"War with the Five Kingdoms is inevitable. In my opinion it will come next year. The High Rexja has recovered from the Sarakos war, and commands considerable resources. He has a popular and damned competent leader in Crown Prince Strymon of Ta-Meltemos. Strymon's armies turned back the Westmen quite effectively. There are still a lot of Westmen, but I doubt they can make much trouble for a couple of years."

"Victory feeds victory," Agzaral said. "The High Rexja has a leader and a proven army. He will certainly use it."

"The weapons I delivered on this trip could be decisive, but Galloway won't trust many locals with modern weapons."

"Wise of him," Agzaral's companion said.

"He hasn't got enough mercenaries, and now they're growing *surinomaz* in several places besides the fields around Armagh. That all has to be defended, along with the stockpiled food and the bricks of processed *surinomaz*."

The robed man frowned. "I think that is not all Captain Galloway may care to defend."

"Perhaps not," Agzaral replied.

"—more decisive will be the role of the two northern city-states, Nikeis and Margilos. Nikeis will surely be neutral. Most of their trade depends on peace with the Five Kingdoms. So does their mainland rice crop.

"Margilos will probably stay neutral, but may ask a high price. They haven't forgotten that the Drantos-Roman alliance drove the Westmen north and forced the Margilans to fight a sharp campaign against them. They bear no love for the Five Kingdoms and never have, but Drantos has most recently offended them."

"Who will win this war?" Wilno asked.

"I don't know. For all our sakes, it had better be Captain Galloway."

"You cannot give him greater resources?"

"Not more than I have already sent. His problem is that he casts his nets very wide indeed. He is not content merely to secure a small area and grow *surinomaz*. He seeks to spread civilization across much of the planet."

"This Galloway is not a typical mercenary soldier."

"Obviously."

Agzaral and his companion watched in silence until Les finished with technical details of the status of his ship, and a polite farewell. The screen went gray and the robed man turned to Agzaral.

"He is being rather discreet."

"I imagine there had been some developments which he did not wish the *Shalnuksis* to know about at this point. I can hardly imagine anyone of Les's intelligence trusting their judgment. Can you?"

The other man smiled faintly. "Hardly. But I can hardly imagine anyone of your intelligence not trusting a classmate with the information needed to carry out his assignment. Yet it has happened. So perhaps Les—"

"Wilno, what makes you think I am not trusting you with necessary intelligence?"

"What makes you think I've forgotten the time you wanted me to make a diversion while you reprogrammed the mess computer? I might have been thrown out of the Academy for that!"

"True. But you were not, and you must remember why?"

"Indeed, you retrieved that situation in your inimitable manner. As you always do. But this time you will be light-years away during the crucial moments of whatever it is you want me to do."

Wilno was smiling, but Agzaral was not deceived. Wilno

was trying to keep the atmosphere pleasant out of old friendship, not out of weakness.

He would have to put the full details of the Tran situation in the hands of someone not already part of his plans. This was a moment he'd known for some time would come; he could not regret too much that it had come so soon.

"It is important, what I am asking of you."

"I suspected as much. You aren't the sort to spend your leave traveling a hundred and seventy light-years on four different ships over a trivial matter."

"It is also secret."

"If it involves the *Shalnuksis*, how could it be otherwise?"

"Very well. What I want you to do is serve as weapons officer aboard the *Shalnuksi* ship they will send against Tran when they believe they will obtain no more *surinomaz*. It may be a crucial task."

"As usual, the Council knows nothing of this?"

"As usual, some know and some do not. Wilno, we are both committed. The future of our species is no small matter."

"No. But why do you believe we are crucial to that?"

"Because we are." He handed Wilno a plastic envelope. "Put this in water for a minute, then play the disk inside. It will tell you most of what you need to know. If you need any protection for your viewer—"

His companion laughed. "Thank you, but there is no need for your skills. Confederate Intelligence pays little attention to the Houses of the Guides. If we were annoyed we would not be so useful."

The controlled anger in Wilno's voice and the eager way he reached for the envelope gave Agzaral more hope. He let none of it show on his face as he walked to the door of Wilno's chamber.

The red dwarf sun of D'jorr was touching the peaks of the mountains on the horizon. The valley below the viewing gallery was already in shadow, but sun still blazed from the snow near the summit of the great triangular peak across the valley. A dancing plume of snow trailed from the summit like a feather from a war helmet.

Higher still, a vapor trail crept across the sky, with a golden glint at its head. Human or Confederate? At this distance it was impossible to tell. Agzaral decided to have his eyes examined soon. He would not again need the keen sight of his youth, but he would need every year left to him. It would be as well to lose none of them getting new eyes.

Probably Confederate, he decided. Few humans came to these mountains, which ranked above the Himalayas for both height and splendor, except the Guides and some hardy climbers. Both came on the ground. On the other hand, the flying city of Nesha was barely an hour's flight beyond the horizon. Doubtless there would be some Galactics aboard it who had never seen the mountains and would now be taking the chance to fly over.

"A beautiful view," said a soft voice behind Agzaral.

He turned to see Wilno. The Guide had taken off his red robe and boots and wore only undertunic, kilt, and sandals. His expression was unreadable.

"Very. Earth's Himalayas and Chrin's Giants are almost as splendid."

"I have never seen either. Nor do I really need to, after seeing these. I fell in love with this view when I was only a lay servant. I think I would have stayed on in the House even if I had never risen higher, if only to look at the mountains at sunrise and sunset.

"Let us go to my quarters."

When they were alone, Wilno's smile broadened, until it was an old familiar grin. Agzaral had seen that look when Wilno took a choice assignment from a rival.

"I would judge that you find the mission worthy of your attention?" Agzaral asked.

"You'd have to shoot me to keep me off it now."

"Our *Shalnuksi* friends may yet save me that trouble."

Wilno shrugged. "Then I die in battle. Better than dying here as Chief Guide, and a damned sight better than dying in some Slave hospital or by my own hand!"

Agzaral could find no reply to that. He knew even better than Wilno the toll suicide took among the Slaves of the Confederation. However light his chains, a Slave was still not a master, even of himself.

"Questions before we settle details," Wilno said. "I think I understand why you don't want Les for the job. Even a *Shalnuksis* might be suspicious of his presence on the bomb ship. Also—I can see circumstances under which our interest lies alongside the *Shalnuksis*. You may wish Tran bombed."

"Reluctantly."

"I would be as reluctant as you. Let us not think of such unpleasant things."

"And your other question?"

"Is there any chance that our gray-skinned friends will be able to come up with someone for the job themselves?"

"A small chance. If their Intelligence somehow concludes that the secret has leaked out, they may override the Council of Merchants."

"Why don't I believe you've told me everything?"

"I have told you all I know. Wilno, I am doing all I can. All that anyone in my position can do."

"And you fear it is not enough."

Agzaral spread his hands. "There may be ways to obtain more resources."

"My friend, it is no great matter to deceive the *Shalnuksis*, but robbing them is something else entirely."

Agzaral smiled.

Wilno shrugged. "Since I have known you, Agzaral, I have had many complaints, but boredom has never been one of them."

PART FOUR
The Royal Sacrifice

CHAPTER ONE

Gwen Tremaine's Diary

Almost summery weather today, even by the standards of Iowa. By the standards of Tran, it's a blistering heat wave. I'd try introducing the bikini or at least the sunback dress, but who's going to spend money on clothes useful maybe ten years out of every six centuries?

Lunch with Larry Warner, who turns out to be riding off on the mission to Margilos with Rick and a whole bunch of the other rough-and-tough types. I asked him why, when the Margilans are supposed to be hostile and the rule is 'No University People in Combat.'

He said the Margilans have promised the mission safe-conduct, and by all reports they have an ironbound sense of honor that won't let them do anything to guests who don't insult them. I asked him if he knew all the things Margilans consider insults, and he decided he'd better keep his mouth shut. As if he could.

Apparently having the Westmen dumped on them was more of a fight than the Margilans liked, and they want to find out if this was part of some new policy toward them, or just the fortunes of war. So maybe the Margilans aren't so dangerous, but then there are stray bands of Westmen. Larry says the expedition will be armed to the teeth. I hope so. We need Rick. For that matter I need Larry.

Even if the risk was a lot greater, Larry says it would be worth it to visit Margilos. Apparently they have some very unusual methods of gold-mining, plus hot springs where they can dump the gold if the city is in any danger. Also, they can do things with centaurs nobody else can, like teaching them to use simple weapons.

After the second cup of wine I realized that I was going to miss Larry a lot. So I kissed him good-bye. He turned red and didn't kiss me back, but he didn't back away either. I have the feeling that Larry is settling into kind of a brotherly attitude toward me, which is better than nothing. Besides, suppose he was just as indispensable to Rick's plans but a real slimeball like Alex Boyd? Boyd's going to Margilos, and if the Margilans want to string that one up for messing with their women I hope somebody invites me!

LATER—A letter from Octavia, sent from Benevenutum. The visit to show Publius his grandson Adrian was a great success. Maybe that will mellow Publius. I know Rick hopes so.

Rick. What's wrong with him? The servants tell stories. He hasn't been alone with Tylara for a year. A year. Rick's a normal man, he must hate that. And don't get ideas, Tremaine....

Of course the Roman matrons are tongue-clucking the way the Drantos ladies used to, only it's "Octavia's barbarian husband" instead of "the Wanax's Roman wife." At least Octavia has learned to laugh at the old biddies.

Old. None of them are really old. This place ages people. It hasn't done that to me yet. Has it?

Publius is quite the proud grandfather. I wouldn't have thought he had it in him. I guess knowing his line won't die out makes a big difference to him. Even if it does have to be passed on through his daughter. Note: be even more careful with Catwin than with Les and Caradoc. As long as Caradoc's only legitimate child is alive, that family has got an obligation to help you, or at least not help your enemies.

Still Later—Mortimer Schultz dropped in. He says Diana is doing fine; Campbell expects the kid any day now. Mostly he wanted to talk about printing presses. I admit I groaned when he started off, because he's kind of obsessed with getting moveable type introduced before the *skyfire* falls, but this idea made a lot of sense.

He thinks we should make up several portable presses, with all the metal parts bronze so they won't rust, and train a couple of dozen acolytes of Yatar as printers. Then we store the presses in the Caves of the Preserver along with everything else we want to keep safe from the bombs. When the fallout's gone and it's safe to come out, we can start on printed books. The *Shalnuksis* won't be back for a long time....

I suspect there are a few holes in that plan, and it probably gives the priests of Yatar a monopoly on printing. Does that matter? Schultz is right, moveable type is one thing that's *got* to survive the Time, however we manage it. I asked him for an estimate on labor and materials, and I'll write to Yanulf as soon as I get it.

And now Rick is gone to Margilos, Larry with him, and Les is God knows where, and Caradoc's dead. When will Rick be back? And when he comes back— enough. Back to work.

Elliot reined in close and spoke low. "Colonel, something's got Sam spooky." He indicated the older of the two centaurs the Margilans had given him as goodwill gifts.

Larry Warner eyed the sling hung round Sam's neck. "Still don't know if I want to trust those things with weapons."

"My problem, Professor," Elliot said.

It could be bigger than that, Rick thought. Most of the Guards felt the same way Warner did. But no doubt about it, Elliot was proud of Sam and wasn't going to part with him. And we trust dogs with teeth, don't we?

Sam wrinkled his nose and swung his graying head from

side to side. His hands clenched into fists. Pete, the younger centaur, wasn't sniffing the air but Sam's nervous excitement had made him skittish.

"Badger-bear? Cat?" said Rick.

"This isn't cat country. Or wasn't last year."

"Yeah. A lot of the wild herds have come north. If the cats have followed them..."

The greatcats were larger than mountain lions and would attack a mounted man if they were hungry enough. "Okay. I don't want to stop, this close to Westrook."

"Sir!"

Rick lifted his canteen. Nearly empty. Well, it wasn't far to Westrook, and there were streams. He shifted in the saddle. Twenty-five miles a day in armor. But tonight he'd be in Murphy's castle, with bath—hot water! And maybe Murphy had some Preparation H left—

Sam screamed and reached for his sling. He plucked a stone out of the cloth bag hung below the sling. Pete threw up his head, and waved his arms. He backed away to give his mentor and friend room to use his sling.

"Sam! Hold!" Elliot shouted.

Dust rose at the crest of the next hill. Half a dozen leather-armored men on scrubby ponies rode into view.

"Westmen!" one Guardsman screamed. Another nocked an arrow and started to draw before his sergeant stopped him.

"Skirmishers left and right!" Elliot commanded. "Colonel? How you want to handle this?"

"Hold what you've got," Rick said. He pointed. The Westmen hadn't moved from their hilltop, and no more came to join them. The Westmen held at the hilltop until it was clear that everyone had seen them. Then they came down at a fast walk. Just beyond long bowshot they stopped and waited again.

"Odd enough," Elliot said. He lifted his binoculars.

"You know it." *And thank God there aren't more of them.* In the previous Time six hundred years before, a Westman army washed clear across Drantos and almost to the gates of Rome itself.

"The one in front's got his hands out. And Colonel, none of them have drawn weapons."

"I see that," Rick said.

"Big wads of turf on their lanes, too. I got no experience with Westmen, but these sure don't look hostile."

Mason rode up. "Cap'n, I think they want to parley."

"Looks like it."

"But what about?" Elliot demanded.

"I don't know, but it can't hurt to find out," Rick said.

Mason frowned. "Okay, Captain. Not you. I'll go talk to them—"

Three more horsemen rode over the crest of the hill. They were mounted on full-sized horses and wore Drantos clothing and armor. The leader carried a Westman bow, and reined in to speak briefly with the Westmen before he rode on toward the column.

Curiouser and curiouser, thought Rick.

"Those are Murphy's troops," Mason said. "He got Westmen for allies?"

"Sure like to ask him a couple of questions," Elliot said.

Me too.

The three men rode up to Rick. "Lord Murphy bids you welcome to his lands and hopes you will avail yourselves of the hospitality of Westrook."

"Now just a goddam minute—" began Art Mason. Rick raised a hand.

"Perhaps you would be kind enough to tell us who you are? And of your friends there."

"I am Etro, son of Panar, headman of Irakla, steward to Lord Murphy. This has been my reward, for fighting well when the Westmen came to Irakla in the year of the Wanax Ganton's great victory on the—"

"Who the hell are those Westmen?" Rick didn't realize that he'd shouted, but Etro looked stunned and Sam reached for another stone for his sling.

Elliot gentled the centaur. Etro stammered, "My Lord Eqeta, they are not enemies! These are warriors sworn to the chief Mad Bear. Mad Bear found enemies among his own people and fled here."

The Guardsmen who weren't looking at each other in confusion were glaring at Etro.

A strange enough story, Rick thought. A Westman chief seeking sanctuary? Or alliance? There's more to learn about Tran than I thought. Or Ben Murphy's a damned fool. Or both.

Only one way to find out. Rick waved the column forward.

Mad Bear stood a bowlegged five and a half feet tall. His skin was the color of the leather trousers and tunic he wore, and his head was bald except for a single gray-shot scalplock. Bone and gold wire ornaments dripped from both tunic and belt, and a Drantos-style dagger rode on his right hip in a gilded horsehide sheath.

He looked as if he could have been dropped into the front rank of one of Genghis Khan's armies with nobody the wiser.

Rick couldn't help wishing that when Mad Bear was putting on all his finery for the Great Chief of the Iron Houses, it had also occurred to him to bathe. Or else that this meeting was taking place outdoors with Mad Bear downwind, instead of in Ben Murphy's study. At least Westrook's thick stone walls kept out the worst of the heat. *I could use a bath myself.*

Mad Bear was speaking through an interpreter. Rick recognized the Margilan priest of Vothan. He'd been a slave among the Westmen for ten years until Ben Murphy rescued him during the Hooey River campaign. Since then he'd served as a combination of chaplain, administrative assistant, and translator to Murphy. *Ben reports everything, but I could sure use that man back at Armagh. Oh, well.*

"So it came to New-Grass Time," Mad Bear was saying. "Once more I was hailed as chief of all the Silver Wolves. So by the gods and the laws I could do nothing but what I did, when the warrior Chintua slew a man of the tent of Walking Stone. He slew the man honorably, for the man had said Chintua was not father of his sons, and then struck the first blow.

"Yet Walking Stone would not come forth to avenge his tent-man. Instead he sent a hand of men against Chintua by night and slew him, then carried away his body so that his kin could not honor it. Chintua's spirit and body alike died that night.

"I went to Walking Stone and demanded that he face me, or be known evermore as a man without honor or shame. Walking Stone said that he and those chiefs who had sworn to him were now the judges of honor among the Horse People. They judged that there was no honor in such as Chintua, and that such men as Chintua were no better than weakling foals, to be cast out lest they breed more weaklings.

"I could not believe that any of the chiefs had sworn to follow such a man. Yet it was so. I will not name them, for they may still return to the way of honor. But there were so many that I was fortunate to pass alive from the tent of Walking Stone.

"Walking Stone could not fall without warning on the Silver Wolves as he had fallen on Chintua, but yet we could not stay close to him. If we moved swiftly, the gods might yet grant us a life with our kin and our herds, and without shame. So we rode to the Green Lands, and sent messengers to the Great Chief of Westrook. He gave us honor in our need, as he had given it in our defeat."

Mad Bear sat down cross-legged on the floor, arms folded on his chest.

"Great Chief, eh, Ben?" Elliot said.

Murphy shrugged and turned to Rick. "Mad Bear brought the message himself, Captain, him and six others with turf on their spears.

"He swore a whole bunch of oaths that he'd keep the peace. I called up enough of the ban to keep them out of mischief, and gave them a campsite and some food. The crops were real good last year."

And the surplus should have gone to the Caves of the Preserver, but let's not get into *that* now. "Have they behaved themselves?"

"Far as I can tell. There've been a couple complaints of missing sheep, but a little silver took care of that. I sent a report, but I reckon you were on the road out of Margilos by then. So I had to sort of make do."

Make do. And it's always easier to get forgiveness than permission. Rick was certain that despite Murphy's elaborate politeness, Ben had decided to make alliance with Mad Bear no matter what Rick Galloway might want.

Typical Drantos nobleman. But dammit he reports to me. . . .

"All right, Sergeant. How many warriors does he have?"

Mad Bear clearly understood the question. He made rapid gestures with his hands. Rick noticed that he had a long scar across the knuckles of the left one.

Baldy, the interpreter, nodded. "He says—call it three hundred and fifty. He speaks the truth, for I have seen the camp and counted that many but no more."

"Okay. I suppose something can be worked out, if he's telling the truth about wanting—"

Mad Bear glared and his hands twitched. Then he snarled something Rick hardly needed interpreted, and went on with a speech that made Baldy turn pale under his tan. The priest could barely keep up with the flood of words.

"He says that he has already taken all the oaths before all the gods that a warrior may honor. If the Great Chief of the Stone Houses doubts him, then let the Chief Murphy take those oaths. Better, let the Great Chief take those oaths himself—or if he is too much the coward to bear the fire, the sun, or the wind, let him come against Mad Bear with a warrior's steel. Mad Bear will meet him with no more weapons than his knife and his honor, and let the gods judge who lies."

Suddenly Rick was glad of the .45 in his shoulder holster. "I meant no offense. Tell him that. Offer him whatever is customary."

Mad Bear spoke again. This time he seemed less angry. The priest translated. "I hope the Great Chief of the Stone Houses is wise enough to see how much he may win by friendship toward the Silver Wolves. Sooner or later, Walking Stone will drive other clans to do as we have done. If they may hope for friendship among the Stone Houses, they will come in peace.

"If they cannot do this, then they may yet follow Walking Stone's banners when he marches again. We fought well when our horses were thin. Think how we shall fight when our horses are fat." He sat down again.

Murphy shrugged. "It's pretty much as he says, Captain. The grazing is getting a lot better out to the northwest. If Walking Stone can unite all the Westmen, they'll really be a handful. From what Mad Bear says, they weren't exactly driven out of the Five Kingdoms. Walking Stone and some other big chiefs ordered a retreat, and made the order stick."

It made sense to provide a way out for the chiefs and clans who didn't want to follow this self-proclaimed Genghis Khan. *But do we want any Westmen allies at all? Mad Bear came south because Walking Stone had the sense and the muscle to try sitting on blood feud. What will the chiefs say when they find out they've got less freedom to follow their old customs in the south?*

He wants an answer. Think fast, Galloway.

Mad Bear grinned. "I know that there may yet be a blood price we owe you, for the last time we came. I will ask the gods. If they say so, my warriors and I will swear to ride with you against your enemies in the north. We know they dream of avenging their defeat upon you. The prisoners we took said as much. If the gods will it, we will shed our blood in battle at your side."

That sounded a lot like an offer of alliance—gods permitting. "Will the other chiefs do the same?"

"I can bind no other chief. Each must call upon the gods himself. Yet surely if the Silver Wolves are bidden to swear oaths of friendship with the Chiefs of the Stone Houses, it will be a sign to others."

Which, freely translated, hinted that Mad Bear might twist a few arms.

Ben Murphy looked expectant. So did Baldy. Mad Bear had no expression at all.

I'd hate to play poker with him. Man for man the Westmen were the best light cavalry on Tran. They weren't all that bad in bunches, either, if they could get behind a single chief. *Damn Ben Murphy and damn Mad Bear. I want a bath and Preparation H, not decisions—*

"Surely Mad Bear must seek the will of his gods. No man of honor could do less." *And just hope that doesn't mean human sacrifice or I'm for it with the Yatar people. But I think they just sacrifice horses.* "If the gods wish that the Silver Wolves ride with us against our common enemies, they will be greeted with honor. If that is not the will of the gods, the Silver Wolves may depart in peace."

Mad Bear grinned widely as Baldy finished the translation. So did the other two. Rick wished he felt as relieved as they did. He'd committed not only himself but the whole alliance to friendship with rebels against Walking Stone. *Serves me right for praying for a chance to make a decision without having to consult everyone and his fifth cousin's steward.*

Rick recalled a Chinese proverb. "Be careful what you wish for. You may get it."

The anticlimactic council of war took place after the dinner Murphy hosted on the roof of the keep of Westrook. Murphy had had a table, benches, and several kegs of beer lugged up, then dismissed the servants and sat down at the foot of the table. Rick took the head and Bisso, Elliot, Warner, and Mason ranged themselves along the sides.

Rick had drunk too much beer and eaten too much beef and venison. He felt a little groggy, and knew only part of it was a proper meal after too many days in the saddle. The rest was trying to forget what he might have let his friends and allies in for, and particularly what Tylara might say. *You've allied with Westmen and traitors to boot.*

It was that way every time they tried to talk. Within seconds she had found something to resent. Or he had. It was easier to avoid each other. *It can't go on like this. The kids aren't old enough to know what's happening, but I think they feel it, and I know that damn clanswoman nanny of hers hates my guts.*

When I get home we're going to have it out. I tell her what I know, and she tells me why.

Clouds hid both the Firestealer and the Demon Sun, but Murphy had laid out lanterns, and the bonfire in the courtyard added more light. Rick glanced over the battlements at the dancing figures around the fire. It was amazing how much noise two drums, a lyre, and a set of pipes could make.

Alex Boyd reeled through a patch of firelight, a woman on each arm. Tonight all the unattached females of Westrook seemed to be making themselves available. *Alex shouldn't have to take "no" for an answer tonight, and that's one less damn thing to worry about. It sure wouldn't hurt if somebody's husband or father did pound on Volunteer Boyd good and hard.* Rick blearily realized that the others were waiting for him to speak.

"All right. We've got Westmen whether we like them or not. Like fleas. Murphy, what do the people around here think?"

"Well, some think the only good Westman is a dead one. Sir. But they don't all feel that way. Mad Bear did his oathswearing in front of a couple dozen village headmen and knights. Baldy did the interpreting. They trust him, you know. I taught him a lot of 'star medicine' and he's delivered a lot of babies who wouldn't have made it."

"So they're willing to let things ride as long as the Westmen behave?"

"That's about it, sir. They will behave, too, while Mad Bear's running things."

"Okay. Next question. Suppose he dies. Or suppose his gods tell him not to make an alliance with us. What then?"

Murphy shrugged. "If Mad Bear dies, the Silver Wolves elect another chief, and we start over again."

"The new chief wouldn't be bound by Mad Bear's oaths?"

"No, but he wouldn't start a fight unless he was real dumb. Any new chief has to be an experienced warrior, and I don't think any of them are stupid enough to fight star weapons or a castle."

"And if the gods don't come through?"

"Captain, your guess is as good as mine. One thing, though—I'm not going to force him and his people back to Walking Stone. We couldn't if we wanted to, and they'd fight to the death if we ever tried."

"Murphy—," Elliot began ominously.

Rick shook his head. "I wasn't thinking of doing anything of the kind, Sergeant. Being a bheroman doesn't give you the right to assume your CO's an idiot."

"Yes, sir."

"Still, we can't keep him and his people around here forever. Not enough good grazing land, for one thing. Besides, some hot-headed warrior or a villager with a grudge would make trouble sooner or later."

Warner frowned. "Captain, I don't know what your lady would say to giving away Chelm land—"

You certainly do, but thanks for being polite. "Depends on what land."

"Way down south. I went through there when I ran away from Parsons. That area's going to get pretty warm, but there are springs. The land's too rocky for farming but not for grazing. A bunch of hills, but nothing those little scrubs the Westmen ride couldn't handle."

"I know that area—is there Earth grass there? Horses can't eat Tran scrub—"

"Westmen horses can," Elliot said. "Have to have some grain too, but they make out."

"Genetic drift?"

Elliot shrugged. "Don't know, sir. But it's for sure Westmen ponies can live awhile on Tran plants."

"There's Earth grass anyway," Warner said.

Probably scattered broadside by the *Shalnuksis* a thousand years and more ago. They seemed to do that: bring in Earth plants and animals and turn them loose. It made a goofy ecology, but there's always *some* kind of ecology. "That's near the city-states," Rick mused. "What the hell, if the city-states can't handle three hundred Westmen, what are they good for?"

The others laughed. A servant filled their glasses again.

It's still alienating Chelm land. Poor land, but Chelm land. I'll have to get Tylara to buy off on that. Anything else and there'd be trouble with the bheromen and knights. Not to mention Companion Morrone; his claim to Chelm was just as good or bad as ever, and now he had an experienced little army of his own. Making him a Marcher lord had made him tougher but not a whole lot smarter. He'd listen to an appeal from any bheromen who claimed the Eqeta was violating his oaths. *Another reason Tylara and I have to talk, if we didn't have enough already.*

"Okay, I can agree. In principle, anyway." Rick shrugged. "We have to settle Mad Bear and his people somewhere safe." *Don't even think the word "reservation," and maybe you can avoid what usually happens when a nomadic people runs into a sedentary one. If civilization survives and spreads on Tran, the Westmen are doomed; but maybe we can give them a more dignified end than the American Indians got.*

And maybe Tylara will get down on her knees and beg your—

"Excuse me, Captain." A servant stood at the head of the stairs. Murphy went to him and came back with a sealed message paper. Rick broke the seal.

"Christ!"

"Sir?" Elliot prompted.

Rick read the message aloud.

SUTMARG REGION INVADED BY HOST OF TA-MELTEMOS UNDER PRINCE STRYMON. HOST OF DRANTOS ASSEMBLING TO MEET IT. HAVE SUMMONED THE BAN IN THE NORTH. UNIDENTIFIED HORSEMEN IN HIGH CUMAC MAY BE SCOUTS FOR SECOND HOST OF HIGH REXJA. WANAX RETURNING FROM BENEVENUTUM. I LEAD THE VANGUARD OF DRANTOS NORTH TO

MEET STRYMON. WITH RESPECT SUGGEST YOU
REMAIN IN WEST TO MEET INVASION THERE.

> MORRONE, PROTECTOR OF THE
> SOUTHERN MARCHES
> ACTING CAPTAIN GENERAL`

> TYLARA DO TAMAERTHON, EQETASSA OF
> CHELM
> JUSTICIAR OF DRANTOS

"Has that little bastard gone crazy?" Mason said.

"No. At least not yet," Rick amended. "With both me and
Ganton away from Edron and Armagh, he's the highest-
ranking officer around. He's sure got the authority to summon the host and lead it north." Rick thought for a
moment. "Fact is, I think he's right. Strymon moves fast.
Give him half a chance and he'll be through the Sutmarg
and into the south in no time. If Morrone moves fast
enough he may be able to bottle him up long enough for us
to get the Romans into the picture."

"If they'll help," Mason said quietly.

"Yeah." *They have to.* "Sergeant Major."

"Sir."

"There's a hell of a lot we need to know. What's Strymon
got? How did he get into the Sutmarg without any kind of
fight?"

"Maybe—"

"Maybe. Exactly. Everything's a maybe. We need information. Now."

"I'll get patrols out."

"Send enough that they can leave messenger relays. I
want to know things fast. This is a good time to try that new
heliograph system."

"Sure," Elliot said. "I'll send back to Armagh to have a
team meet us north of here."

"Right. We're going to have to make a visit to Armagh
ourselves, but it's best to get them started. Murphy."

"Yes, sir—"

Rick stood up. His head felt clearer. "Murphy, Westrook is now the Captain General's temporary GHQ. I want the semaphore manned around the clock. Ban and arrière-ban, and full patrols north and east. Look for these 'mysterious horsemen.' They may be garbled reports of your Westmen, and they may be some of Strymon's light cavalry. Find out. Send steady troops. We need live witnesses, not dead heroes."

"Sir! Uh— Cap'n?"

"Yeah?"

"Ban and arrière-ban, and I've got nobody to plow and plant."

"Christ, Murphy, you think he don't know that?" Elliot demanded.

"It's all right, Top. Murphy, I don't expect you to keep everybody mobilized all summer, but it can't hurt to muster them and see what they've got."

"Yes, sir."

"I have to get back to Dravan. This place is too far west for a main base. When you get organized here, send me what you can spare. I'll have to leave that up to you."

"I'll have a lot after we get the crops planted," Murphy said. "Not much I can send you until then."

"Yeah, I know that. Next. If the gods tell Mad Bear he can join us, send him as escort for some of our hussars. If he doesn't join up, you'll have to escort him out of our territory. South. Be polite when you tell him, but he joins us or he goes."

"Yes, sir."

"Bisso, Warner, you take five troopers and half the Guards back to Edron. Make sure that you take Sniper MacAllister and at least one more of Gengrich's men. Not Boyd, he stays here."

Elliot looked pained.

"Okay, I know you rely on Bisso, but it can't be helped."

"Yes, sir."

"Warner, when you get to Edron, assess the strategic situation. Consult Gwen. You're authorized to evacuate the University and escort what you can to Edron. Use the Guards, and if you can get any of Drumold's people to help, do it. Bisso, you're field commander. Warner calls the shots, but you're in charge outside the walls. You'll also be Acting Provost of the University."

Rick watched Larry Warner for signs of resentment, but saw none. *Maybe he's learning*.

"Yes, sir." Bisso didn't look too happy.

Rick suppressed a grin. Independent command was always a nice dream until it turned into a real hot potato. *And it's time we promoted some more NCOs to officer status*.

Of course they already were, as far as the locals were concerned. Star Lords. Brave wise men from the sky. Hah.

"Do the University people fight?" Warner asked.

"Not unless you have to, but it's likely you'll have to," Rick said. "You know the situation better than me, but I'd guess some of the minor clans are going to see this as a great opportunity."

"I hate to abandon the place—"

"Warner, the University is its people. Buildings are easy to come by. Trained personnel aren't. And Gwen's not replaceable at all." *There. I've said it*.

No one argued with him.

"And me, Colonel?" Art Mason asked.

"Stand by. We'll all be going to Dravan as soon as possible, and after that somebody'll have to collect the ammo from the dump at Armagh. And see to the *surinomaz*."

"That's you or me, Colonel," Mason said.

"Yeah." Rick thought of the long ride to Dravan, and even farther to Armagh, and shuddered.

"Anything else?" Mason asked.

"Not that I think of." For the moment he needed to hit the latrine. As he headed for the stairs, he heard Warner tell Murphy, "Hey, Ben, it just hit me. Once we've won, we give Mad Bear land in the Five Kingdoms."

Bloody hell, he thought. They all have such complete confidence in me. Yeah, and sooner or later my luck will run out, and what then?

What now? Everything's hanging on a thread, and Tylara acts like she's afraid of me. That's a mess that can still wreck everything.

What's a hero? A track star with no place to run. That's me, all right.

CHAPTER TWO

The wind moaned across the hilltop and the corpses swung from the long gallows erected there. Some of the corpses still had faces—faces as gray as the sky overhead. Tylara shivered. The wind seemed to blow through her, and the corpses seemed to beckon her to join them.

Wait a little, my friends. The gods will give their judgment soon enough. Do not do what I have done. Do not think that you know better than the gods.

"The one in chains is Carlga the Smith," her guide said. "He tried to send warning of Lord Ajacias's treachery, but was caught and tortured for the name of the message-bearer. He died rather than betray the man."

And Carlga's son rode in the Guards. He would have a bleak homecoming.

"He will be avenged," Tylara said, the same way she might have said, "It is raining." The Christians spoke of leaving vengeance to God, but there were some things honorable men could not entrust to God or Vothan. One was to leave Ajacias unhanged and his sty of a castle standing.

Tylara's resolution faltered. If she submitted to the judgment of the gods, she might not live to see the Wanax's punishment of the traitor.

That might be the only pleasure life still held for her. Yet the blood guilt on her would grow no less, and the gods' judgment was certain. If not on her, where would it fall? Perhaps on Drantos. Perhaps it had begun when Ajacias turned traitor and allowed Prince Strymon to cross the border.

No. The blood guilt was hers and hers alone, as surely as if she had thrust the knife into Caradoc with her own hand. She alone must answer for it.

"Have them taken down and buried with reverence," she said. "Now let us rejoin Lord Morrone."

Her Tamaerthan archers drew around her. She turned and rode back down the hill.

Morrone had ridden ahead to scout when Tylara reached the campfire. She was eating porridge and sausage when he returned.

His grin was wide. "Either the tales that put Strymon's host at above ten thousand are lies, or else he has divided his forces most unwisely. Our scouts have found no more than three thousand of his horse and a thousand foot. They are drawn up on the flank of Piro's Hill. I will order our men to eat, then advance straight to battle."

That was wisdom, if four thousand was truly Strymon's whole strength. Seven thousand against four. A thousand of the seven were Tamaerthan archers. It promised victory. But—

"Might Strymon have hidden part of his host to tempt you into just such action, my lord? Or perhaps he can hold until *reinforcements* can be summoned?"

Morrone shrugged without altering his grin in the slightest. "If he can hide more than three thousand men, Strymon is a wizard greater than any starman. My scouts turn over every fallen leaf. As for his calling up his—*reserves,* the faster we strike, the less time he will have to do so."

Tylara did not share Morrone's confidence in the irregular light infantry levies he'd brought from the south. They were certainly loyal to their lord, tough, enduring—and as good at looting inns and farms as they were at fighting. Tylara would have had more confidence in half as many Guards or Mounted Archers, but the Guards were with Rick and Ganton.

Moreover, Morrone resented the least criticism of his faithful levies. Did their loyalty flatter him out of all judgment? Tylara only knew that she had twice come close to quarrels with him over the levies' poor discipline. A third on the day of battle would only hand Strymon the gift of a divided enemy. Morrone did her as much courtesy as she could expect by listening to her at all in matters of war.

"I await your orders, Lord Morrone."

"I would order you to keep yourself safe, but I know what you would say to that." Tylara forced a smile. "Your archers are on our left side. That is good. Bring them forward to extreme bowshot and harass the enemy's infantry until my knights are set to charge, then guard our left flank. If Strymon does launch an attack from that direction, I can trust you to keep your head and not see fifty men as five thousand."

"Thank you, my lord."

Morrone waved to his squire and vaulted into the saddle without touching the stirrups. Another wave of his hand, and he was off at a brisk trot, followed by the cheers of everyone around the campfire.

Tylara cheered with them for a moment, then turned away. *He can win the hearts of fighting men. Yet can he win battles as well as the husband I have betrayed? Or does he crave a victory of his own? Crave it so greatly that he sees nothing that he does not wish to see? And if that is so, and I accept the gods' judgment, who will be left to lead the host of Drantos until the Wanax rides north?*

No. These are only more excuses. I have sworn to submit to the gods. I broke my oath to Caradoc; I will not break this one.

The host of Drantos closed with the enemy as the True Sun touched low hills at the horizon. There was not enough time or light to lure the enemy from his chosen position, nor to maneuver behind him. The attack must go straight in, and the gods grant victory to boldness.

She led her archers forward and halted them a full three hundred and fifty paces from the enemy's infantry. Her arm swept up, then down.

"Let the gulls fly!"

The Tamaerthan arrows did their terrible work against the enemy's shielded warriors. Arrows flew in flights, half shot high to fall against those who raised their shields, half lower to strike those who held steady. Infantrymen fell. Some turned to run.

Rick always said that frontal attacks on a prepared enemy were wasteful, yet perhaps Vothan will favor us today. Now, Lord Morrone! A charge of chivalry has won more than one battle for Drantos.

Morrone's forward battle came into sight. The sky was the color of old lead. The True Sun was half out of sight when the Drantos vanguard broke through the enemy's screen of light cavalry. More trumpets sounded, and the Drantos horse parted, turning to either side to chase Strymon's skirmishers from the field.

The main body of Drantos heavy cavalry moved forward.

The Tamaerthan archers could no longer help for fear of striking their own men, but that did not matter. The enemy infantry broke and ran. The way lay open for a single grand charge to sweep through the fleeing infantry and crush the knights who stood behind them. The day might be won in an hour.

Grant that it be so. Tylara did not know to whom she prayed, and turned her mount toward the several stades of hills and scrub oak that she and her archers watched over. There were enemies there, but in no great force, certainly not enough to break through a thousand Tamaerthan archers who could shoot a man out of his saddle at four hundred paces.

The horns signaled for the charge; Tylara turned in her saddle to watch it. The steel-clad knights rode in a solid formation, banners in line as on parade. As they lowered their lances they looked fit enough to carry all before them. The trumpets signaled the trot. Then the charge.

The steel lance points reached the fleeing enemy foot-soldiers—and suddenly half of Morrone's line was in chaos, horses screaming and falling, knights toppling from the saddle. The enemy foot turned from fleeing rabble into deadly foes. They ran in among the horses to slash with long knives and thrust with short spears.

Pits. Morrone's right had been lured into a chain of pits dug in front of Strymon's shield wall. Those knights would be lucky to save their lives, let alone carry their charge home. But the left was still intact—and now Strymon's horse were wheeling, to fall on Morrone's left with equal numbers and the advantage of the higher ground.

No, superior numbers. Over the crest of Piro's Hill came a solid line of horse, light and heavy mingled together but coming on at a good pace, with the Great Banner of Ta-Meltemos in its chariot in the middle of the line.

Trumpets sang, and the Drantos left slowed, then re-formed to receive charges from two directions. Morrone was not such a fool as to hope for victory now. He galloped up and down the line like a maniac. Tylara could not hear, but she could imagine what he was saying.

He might yet save much of the host.

If Morrone could stand off the first charge until his right untangled itself from the pits, he might yet manage an orderly retreat. Then superior numbers would tell—

"Ho! Archers! Look to your front! Let the gray gulls fly!" The cry went up and down the Tamaerthan line and Tylara whirled. Light cavalry were pouring out of the scrubby oak forest. Some of the horsemen were already falling to arrows but more took their place every moment. Tylara's mind had room for only two thoughts:

I have seen a good captain routed by a great one.

The gods have given their judgment. Now—how best to submit?

It seemed wisest to stay where she was and let the enemy come to her. Soon her archers would retreat before the press of Strymon's cavalry; then if she rode forward only a few paces she would be beyond the protection of her own troops. *So be it. The guilt is mine alone. I will take none of them with me.*

Some of the enemy cavalry were horse archers. Their light bows could not match the range of a Tamaerthan long-bow, but that was no handicap for Strymon's archers. They used the cover of the scrub oaks to slip close. *They can shoot from horseback, or lying on the ground, while my archers must stand.* Tamaerthans fell, and arrows whistled around Tylara. *If my horse is killed—*

"Lady, time for ye to be out of here," an archer captain said. He gripped her bridle and turned her mount away from the line.

"Thank you, but it is better that I stay."

"Lady, ye'll be goin', if I have to—"

Tylara never knew what the archer captain would have done. An arrow pierced his face and he fell, his fingers still clutching the bridle. Tylara's horse shied and reared.

With perfect clarity she saw herself draw her light battle-axe and strike with the flat of it until the dead man's hand slipped from the bridle. She urged her horse forward, and the animal leaped over the captain's body. Other archers ran toward her and she drove her spurs in hard. Her gelding bolted past the approaching archers and through the fighting line.

Tylara whirled the axe as she rode. Tamaerthan oaths and Drantos cheers came to her lips. The hail of arrows from both sides slackened as the Tamaerthons held their fire and the enemy used the pause to rally. A mass of horsemen took shape ahead of her. She settled into the saddle and rode straight at them.

Two arrows hit her horse in the flank. He reared, screaming. She kept her seat but the battle-axe slipped out of her hand and hung by the thong around her wrist. A horseman rode down on her, and she saw the gods' judgment coming toward her in the steel tip of his lance.

"For Caradoc! Vothan!"

The lance tip drove into her horse's chest. The gelding stumbled and she tried to throw herself clear. Too late. The stirrup leather was wound around her leg and her horse was falling. The gelding rolled over her and the eye of her battle-axe struck her on the forehead. "I've failed," she thought, and the blackness took her.

Apelles had put his field hospital near good water, on a rise with a good view of the battlefield. He would have preferred a site that his handful of men could defend. He didn't fear the enemy so much as Morrone's southern levies once their lord was too busy fighting to watch them.

He cheered with the rest as the host of Drantos drove forward. After that he had a fine view of the defeat, and the horror of Lady Tylara's fall.

Light horse from behind the hill swept around to surround the Tamaerthan archers. The clansmen drew into a square. The light cavalry charged once and were driven back by flights of arrows, then withdrew to beyond bowshot, where they stood watchful. The Tamaerthans were no longer a danger to Strymon's main battle. Apelles wondered if they could withdraw, or if they would stand, never to leave the field unless Prince Strymon granted them quarter.

On the right Morrone's levies were scattering. The Drantos knights formed into groups and began a more orderly retreat. Apelles hoped they would win free, but they were not his concern. He had known what he must do from the moment he saw Lady Tylara ride into the ranks of the enemy.

Her futile charge had not greatly surprised him. Thrice since the host of Drantos rode north he had seen Lady Tylara when she thought no one was watching. Each time, her eyes seemed those of one who had gazed into the Christians' Hell.

If Lady Tylara had found what she sought, he could at least bring out word of her death, so that her kin would hear it from a friend. If she yet lived—she might think herself in Hell while still in this world. No one should have to face that alone.

"Culin!"

"Yes, Father Apelles?" That was not yet the accepted title

for priests of the Dayfather, but the boy could not be broken of using it.

"I am going to ride down and surrender to the enemy."

"You cannot—"

". . . to assure honorable treatment of our wounded prisoners. You will bear a message to Yanulf. Ask him to care for Maev and our daughter."

"Fa—you cannot command me to do that. It would be turning my back on the enemy." He looked indignantly at Apelles.

Apelles noticed that Culin's eyes were now on a level with his. Soon he would be taller, if he lived. Apelles remembered the scrawny, gawky boy he'd found at a House of Vothan and taken as his servant a year ago. Now Culin could read and write, his clothes would not have disgraced a yeoman's son, and he had his whole life before him.

He would not lose that life, if Apelles had aught to say about it.

"Culin. If you do not go to Yanulf, he will think I have gone mad. That would take honor from me. And from you as well. Besides, if Yanulf thinks I have gone mad, will he care for Maev and our daughter? Would you have them begging their bread, with the Time approaching?"

"No, Father."

"And you have sworn obedience. Was that a false oath?"

"No, Father."

"Then be off. I will wager you a meal in a good inn that we shall see each other again."

"How shall I pay if I lose?"

"By selling the horse you will need to steal to reach Yanulf."

Culin's mouth opened, but no sound came out. Then he knelt, kissed Apelles' hand, and ran off.

Apelles watched him go, glad that he had no running to do, in search of a horse or anything else. His knees seemed to lack the strength they'd had this morning. His mouth was dry, and his breath came quickly as if he'd been running.

Now he might never have to choose between his family and a bishopric in the united faiths. Certainly he would have liked to see Maev again. Or discuss the Act of Union with old Polycarp. It would be pleasant to sleep in his own bed in his own chambers once again, and drink a cup of the good wine he could never have afforded as a swineherd's son....

None of that mattered. His god had called him to Lady Tylara. He strode down the slope and never looked back.

PART FIVE
Affairs of Honor

CHAPTER ONE

Rick reined in at the top of the small hill. Castle Armagh was visible ahead. He dismounted. Time to walk the horses. Ten minutes every hour. Every moment was an effort, and he felt as if someone had been standing on his back.

Only ten more miles, he thought. We've made good time from Dravan in the last week. Ten more miles. Fifteen minutes in a car. An hour in a four-wheeler with no roads. Half a day's ride for us. Silently he cursed the *Shalnuksis* and all their works. *But if they hadn't taken you off that hill, where would you be, Galloway?*

Dead, I expect. But I wouldn't be responsible for saving civilization for a whole planet.

Fields of young wheat filled the valley between the road and the hills. It looked like they'd have a good crop, enough to feed the region, with a lot left over to be stored in the Caves. *If we can keep Strymon's army from trampling it. Or burning it. Or burn it ourselves, only I won't do that. Sure, we'll have plenty for a couple more years. But then the Time will come, and the Shalnuksis...*

Rick couldn't see the fields on the other side of the hills, but he knew what they held. Tangles of *surinomaz*—madweed, as the locals called it—tended by convicts and slaves under the watchful eyes of armed guards. *I wouldn't blame the slaves for running. Cultivating madweed's hard work. Dangerous, too. But if we don't grow the stuff, we'll have nothing for the Shalnuksis, and they'll bomb the planet just to keep it in the Stone Age. And if I tell myself that often enough, maybe I'll believe it's all right to be a slave master. Maybe.*

* * *

As they approached Castle Armagh the gates opened and four blue-robed priests of Yatar rode out. When they were closer, Rick saw that their leader was Yanulf.

What's he doing here? Rick wondered. His place is at Edron. Or with the Wanax. There's not much here but mercs and madweed, and those are my job, not his.

"Hail, Lord Rick."

"Hail."

Yanulf gestured, and the junior priests and apprentice who'd ridden out with him drew away. "I would speak with you alone," Yanulf said.

Rick waved his guards back and rode on with Yanulf. "Bad news?"

"The worst," Yanulf said.

Worst. "Tylara's dead."

"No, my lord. Captured by Prince Strymon. Morrone lost half his force, and both he and the Eqetassa were taken."

"But she's alive."

"Yes, when last we heard. But there is more you should know."

Rick studied Yanulf's expressionless face. "If she's being mistreated—" He shuddered. Yanulf would remember what Tylara had suffered from Sarakos as well as Rick did. Better.

"It is not that. My lord, she rode out through the lines of her archers, and alone charged the enemy cavalry."

"That doesn't make sense—"

"She is the leader of a clan of Tamaerthon. Could she believe she has lost the favor of God?"

Rick glanced at his watch and reined in. "Time to walk," he said.

"My lord—"

"Give me a minute." He dismounted carefully and walked ahead.

Lost the favor of God. Yeah, and her husband, too. And all her husband's friends. And—

Damnation, she tried to talk to me. Why didn't I give her the chance?

"Who brought the news?"

"The boy Culin. When Apelles saw the Lady Tylara captured, he sent his servant to me, and followed his lady into the camp of the enemy."

"Good man. I owe him. I suppose he's getting messages out through the priests of Yatar in Strymon's army?"

"Of course. Those who serve Yatar know that the Time approaches, and who their true friends are."

Rick glanced at the front of Yanulf's robe, where a pectoral cross lay over the circled thunderbolt of Yatar. "How do you feel about the unified faith?"

"Some accept, some do not. Those who accept help as best they can."

"Strymon permits the new faith in his camp?"

"A quarter and more of his soldiers have accepted it. How could he not?"

"Oh. Thanks. I didn't know you'd made that many converts." He walked on a few paces, then turned. "If the priests can get messages out, I can get one in."

Yanulf nodded. "It can be done."

"Thank you." *And what in hell will I say to her?* He laughed bitterly. *"Come home, all is forgiven." Now how the hell do I say that in a message that half the priesthood's going to read?*

"What will you do?" Yanulf asked.

"Get the hell up there and see how many of Ganton's people will help me get her out."

"Calm. I know you wish to act, but think first. Prince Strymon has a reputation for honor, and surely will not demand excessive ransom. If you attempt a rescue, she may be killed. I am no soldier, but most battles hastily begun are easily lost."

Rick was silent for a long moment. "All right. I'll get the stuff I came here for and go back to Dravan. By then we'll know more. If that— If you can send messages into Strymon's camp, send him this one. If he harms her in any way,

by spring a year from now there won't be a living thing left
in his kingdom."

"I will send the message, but I doubt it will be believed."

"Tell him anyway."

Gwen and Siobhan acknowledged the sentry's salute and
turned down the hall toward Octavia's chambers. Voices
reached them before Gwen was close enough to knock at the
door of the royal apartment. *If Octavia ever finds herself at the
head of a legion, she'll have no trouble making herself heard. That's
for sure.* She motioned Siobhan behind her and stepped
close to the door.

"—abandon Edron, which has never fallen save by starva-
tion or treachery? We have provisions for at least two
winters. If you know of traitors among us, tell me now lest I
suspect you of being one of them!"

Octavia's command was answered by an incoherent
chorus of protestations. *She must have half the ladies of the court
in there. This sounds interesting.* Gwen glanced back down the
hall. The sentry was out of sight. She waited, one hand
poised to knock.

"...much of Morrone's host escaped Piro's Hill and will
soon fight again. The Wanax will take the field against Strymon with the knights Morrone couldn't muster. Tamaerthan pikemen will join him. Tamaerthan pikes and
archers alone once defeated a Roman legion! And then
there are the star weapons— God knows how many *guns* we
can field against Strymon. It is the host of Ta-Meltemos that
should be thinking of fleeing to safety! Not us."

"But, Your Majesty—you cannot—"

"Your son, Prince Adrian—" This round of protestations
was slightly more coherent.

"No. I am the daughter and the granddaughter of soldiers, who held their posts where God and Caesar sent

them. Can I do less? What honor does it bring them or your Wanax if I teach my son to flee at the first sign of danger?

"I cannot. I will not. Enough of this nonsense. I will hear no more." Octavia's tone held all the finality of the headsman's axe.

"That's our cue." Gwen took Siobhan's hand and led her down the hall away from the sentry. They turned the corner and flattened themselves against the wall as ladies-in-waiting bustled out of Octavia's apartment. *Not this way, ladies. You're already annoyed that Octavia booted a couple of you out of your rooms for me when we evacuated the University. You don't need to know that I've heard the queen dressing you down like raw recruits.*

Gwen waited until the ladies had left the corridor, then motioned to Siobhan to follow her back down the hall. She knocked at Octavia's door and a maid admitted them. Octavia was sitting on a window bench, pretending to knit. Gwen had taught her Earth-style knitting, and the queen was quite good at it—when her hands weren't shaking.

Octavia turned a pale face to Gwen as the Earthwoman entered. "I expected you earlier. Did you hear those mewling biddies? Do they think they can find any place that's safer than Edron? Strymon will never get this far. Ganton will see to that."

Octavia's smile was strained. Gwen realized that the girl was as scared as any of her ladies. *She's just hiding it better. Goes with being queen, I guess.* Gwen smiled. "Forgive me. I don't doubt the Wanax will make short shrift of Strymon."

"I'm glad to hear you believe that. But... I'm frightened. We will surely win, but at what price? We've already lost four thousand good men slain or taken, and Lady Tylara and Lord Morrone are prisoners."

What price indeed. If I had the answer to that question, I'd be Yatar or some other Higher Authority. As it is— "I'm scared too, Octavia. But we'll just have to do the best we can. One thing, you might admit to your ladies that you're worried about your husband. Most of them are probably scared for their men too."

"Thank you, Gwen. Will you—will you give me advice and counsel? Yanulf returns today. When he rides north with the host, you'll be the only one I can talk to."

"Of course." Gwen realized she was thinking of the power that position would give her. *What's worse is that I don't despise myself for it. Is this what they mean when they talk about doing well by doing good?*

A faint knock sent Octavia's maid to the door. "The Lord Chancellor of the University, Lord Warner, craves audience with the Wanaxxae Octavia and the Lady Gwen."

"Come."

Octavia and Gwen sat side by side to receive Larry Warner's graceful bow. *He's becoming quite the courtier. I wonder how many ladies he's courted into bed?*

"Your Majesty. My report on the University's contribution to our coming victory. With your permission?"

Octavia laughed. "Lord Rick has made it *very* clear that the University is no part of either Drantos or Rome. You need make no report to me."

"Well, Majesty—" Warner was obviously amused. "That's true, but I am supposed to report to Gwen, and besides, I've brought some troops to add to the defenses of Edron."

"Ah. Proceed, then." Octavia smiled. "You may speak to Gwen or to me, as is most appropriate." Then she laughed.

"Yes, ma'am," Warner drawled. "All the essential records and equipment from the University are safe in Edron now. The Romans withdrew most of their University cohort to support the defense of the south, but since most of the threat is from the south, that's not as bad as it sounds. Still, it left us with not much more than Rustengans and other craftsmen too old or too young to go to war, and some random Tamaerthans from the major clans."

"All the clans?" Gwen asked.

"Most of them."

Gwen nodded in satisfaction. "Good. Then any clansmen who attack the University will be at blood feud with their own relatives."

"Right. Anyway, the Roman tribune wanted to take the

whole cohort, but Lucius convinced him he'd better leave some of them with us. So he and his centurions rolled dice to see who'd get to leave. I think he used his own dice, because he got to go himself."

"Larry, what's the bottom line?" Gwen asked in English.

"Yes, ma'am. Well, the University is defended by the Tamaerthan clansmen, the worst half of the Roman cohort, the city militia, and God Almighty. I've brought a token century of Romans, a company of Tamaerthan archers, all the University craftsmen who think they're militia and volunteered to travel, and the First Balloon Squadron, commanded by Your Servant Warrant Officer Warner."

"Balloon? Larry—"

"Well, I admit it'd do more good out west, but it'd take forever to get it there."

"The Wanax wishes each to fight whatever enemy is closest," Octavia said. "I think you will soon find many of them close enough."

"Yeah—Yes, Majesty. I'm afraid you're right."

"That's good strategy. It's even better politics," Gwen said. "Fighting the enemy where he is has got to be better than just defending your own land. Drantos has no national army. Rome sends troops where they're needed."

"Maybe the ironhats will learn and maybe they won't," Warner said. "Anyway, we're here, and I no sooner got here than we were ordered to join Ganton's army. We move out tonight. What am I getting into?"

"I don't know how many troops the enemy has," Gwen said. "But I can tell you what the Wanax's forces are." She looked to Octavia and got a tiny nod of approval. "With your people—and I expect he can use your aeronauts—he ought to have nearly ten thousand, plus the field guns, and seven mercs with rifles. Eight, counting you."

"No Romans," Warner said.

"Caesar will send aid," Octavia said.

"Majesty," Warner said gently, "I am certain that Marselius Caesar would like to send aid. I also know that even a single cohort is valuable to him at this moment. The turmoil in the south grows worse each ten-day, and as the weather improves and the Demon grows closer, Rome will need even more legions to hold the southern borders."

"They disbanded two legions after the last southern campaign," Gwen said.

"Sure," Warner said. "And they'll probably call them up again, but it sure won't be until they've got crops planted. Otherwise, what'll they eat this fall?"

And it takes time to assemble militiamen, Gwen thought.

"Whatever the Romans can do, they won't be sending any legions tonight," Warner said. "And that's when we march. Your Majesty, my lady. This is farewell, until we come back with Prince Strymon's head."

"God be with you," said Octavia.

Gwen fumbled for words. "Come back safe" didn't sound right, but what—? "Good hunting," she said, grinning.

Warner embraced her and kissed her on the forehead, in a less brotherly fashion than usual. Gwen felt Octavia's eyes on her and blushed. She was still blushing when the door closed behind Warner.

"Lady Gwen," said Octavia, carefully looking at her knitting.

"Yes, Your Majesty?"

"Is Lord Warner your—lover? He has a reputation—"

"Almost as bad as Lord Morrone's?"

"I wasn't going to insult him, but..."

That came close to confirming the rumor that Morrone was jealous of Octavia's being both wife *and* confidante of his friend Ganton. It also suggested that Octavia's watching her father be the Don Juan of Rome had given her a distaste for unchastity in others.

If I want to be Octavia's friend and confidante, does this mean I have to keep my pants on except when Les visits?

Probably. And now the sixty-four silver question: can I do it?

Maybe. If Rick's not interested. Meanwhile, I can tell Octavia the truth....

"Lord Warner is not my lover and never has been. If Caradoc had not offered first, I might have married Lord Warner, as we have much—much in common. But I have been faithful to Lord Les, and pray only that Yatar, Christ, and all the Holy Archangels bring him safely back to me at the end of his travels."

That last part, at least, was the truth and nothing else.

"Please be seated, my lords. Wine?"

Murphy and Bheroman Traskon sat down at the big table in Rick's conference room at Castle Dravan. Rick noted that Murphy sat down as quickly as Traskon. The first time he'd addressed a group of nobles that included Murphy, Ben had glanced behind him to see who was being spoken to. Now Murphy wore the title as easily as his Tran clothing.

Rick sat at the head of the table. The noon sun lighted the white plastered walls covered with maps drawn in charcoal. Murphy kept glancing at them.

"They're current as far as I know," Rick said. "After lunch you can help update them."

"Main thing is we haven't found any new threats."

"Good."

"On the other hand, everybody agrees on the twelve thousand we know about." Murphy pointed to the arrow indicating a detachment of Strymon's army marching toward Dravan.

"We can hold those." Rick kept his voice even, and turned to Traskon. "My Lord Bheroman."

"My Lord Captain General," Traskon said. "My knights and I await your orders. I have assembled the ban and arrière-ban to hold our lands, and my knights are ready to ride. Tell us how we may avenge the dishonor to our Lady Eqetassa."

"Thank you. I expected no less." Rick swallowed hard, as he always did when he thought of Tylara in Strymon's hands. *Tylara might have been Traskon's stepmother, if Sarakos hadn't thrown his father off Castle Dravan's battlements. And I'd never have met her. Would that be better? No. But—Traskon wants something. What?*

Murphy cleared his throat. "My Lord Captain General, it has come to my ears that you plan to arm the villagers, that they may defend themselves as they did against the Westmen."

"Yeah, Sergeant?"

"Captain, they say you're going to give them guns—nothing big, maybe, but *guns!*"

"So have I heard also," said Traskon. "When the Westmen came, Hilon the blacksmith of Clavton, a town in my lands, proposed that the town buy guns to defend itself. I asked then, and I ask now, how can we be sure that villages and towns so armed will defend themselves only against our common enemies, and not their lawful lords? How shall a bheroman do his duty, if his towns can refuse theirs? It also seemed to me—and forgive me, my lord, if this grieves you —but the Lady Eqetassa seemed willing to hear me."

Damn right. Tylara isn't about to arm towns against the nobility. And now what? Rick laughed aloud.

"My lord?" Ben Murphy asked.

"Nothing. Your pardon." *And one thing's for damn sure, Ben Murphy's gone native. The great-grandson of a man hanged for shooting a landlord's rent collector is trying to keep people from shooting his rent collectors!* Rick spoke quickly in English. "Found out being boss man isn't all that easy, right, Sergeant?"

"Sir!"

And now for my stuffiest shirt. "My lords. I will never arm rebels. Moreover, our guns are too few for me to allocate them to the villages. That is true also for our firepowder."

"Thank you, my Lord Captain General," said Traskon. "And—may I say that our thoughts are with you, in your grief for the Lady Eqetassa?"

"Thank you." Rick forced a smile. "It could be worse. She's alive, so we should see her again once the ransom's paid. She'll probably throw a pot at me for spending so much."

The two noblemen laughed dutifully and bowed themselves out. Rick sat motionless until the door closed. Then he got up and poured himself a cup of the wine the others had refused.

I didn't talk to her for a year, and now she's a prisoner. That has to be a nightmare all by itself.

It was hard to think like the Tamaerthan nobility, but couldn't she think that was punishment enough? He had no way of knowing. *She thinks every bad thing that's happened in the last year is her fault. Everything from crop failures in the south to Morrone's defeat.*

The only good thing about the situation was Apelles. *I'm glad he went with her. He's no psychiatrist, but he's smart, and she listens to priests. If anybody but me can talk her out of the crazy notion that she's got the world on her shoulders, it'll be him.*

And meanwhile he had eight thousand men to command and twelve thousand enemies to face, and despite his assurances to Murphy and Traskon he was pretty sure the enemy's strength was growing. He went to the map and stared at it. It had cost good men to fill in the information there, but now he knew that Strymon held all the roads north into the Five Kingdoms, and could bring down reinforcements as needed.

The only thing to slow them down would be the remnants of Morrone's force, and the sheer logistics of marching an army in the spring when there wasn't much grass and granaries would be empty. A quart of wheat a day for each man. A bushel for each horse. It all added up to a *lot* of transport, and the transport horses had to eat, too.

If that damned Ajacias had kept all the grain supplies in his goddam castle, Strymon wouldn't have—

If wishes were horses, beggars could ride.

"Jamiy!"

His orderly opened the door.

"Officers' Call in one hour."

The Death Wind Bringer hung low on the horizon, bloated until it looked more than ever like the evil eye. Around it the stars were coming out, as Mad Bear walked out of the Silver Wolves' camp toward the vigil hill.

He walked slowly, according to custom, but his thoughts ran on ahead of his feet. The sacrifice was ready at the hill-top.

It had never before occurred to him that he should defy the gods. Yet now he thought he would aid the Stone House Chiefs no matter how the sacrifice went. The thought was frightening.

If he didn't stay with the Stone House Chiefs, there would be no home for the Silver Wolves. Without a home, they would perish, Walking Stone's work would be done for him, his enemies would lose heart, and all this without costing the dung-weaned son of a diseased mare a single warrior!

This was the truth, but not all of it. The rest of the truth was that Mad Bear had begun to see that the sky-wizards themselves might be the sign from the gods. If they were indeed wizards. Mad Bear had begun to doubt even this. Certainly they had wizardry at their command, but they bled and died like men—and when they died, they died like warriors.

It seemed true, what he'd thought first in the tent where he awoke a prisoner of the wizards. Nothing among gods or men would ever be the same again, and a wise man would do what his own wisdom told him to do, not wait for signs that the gods might have already given.

Mad Bear knew that he himself would not live to see all that would come of the rule of the wizard-warriors. Still, he might get sons who would, and *their* sons might stand beside the wizard-warriors as blood brothers and fight among the very stars.

He would have to be content with drinking his death toast from Walking Stone's skull.

The path began to climb the hill. Mad Bear slowed further and raised his spear to the Child of Fire. He would keep the vigil according to custom, give judgment likewise, and make the horse sacrifice afterward.

He would make the horse sacrifice alone, though, with no one aiding him. If by some chance he *had* angered the gods, let their punishment fall on him alone.

CHAPTER TWO

Tylara awoke with a headache that felt as if Great Guns were being fired inside her skull. Dull knives stabbed her in the ribs every time she breathed. Her left wrist and right ankle throbbed so hard she was glad she was in bed with no reason to move them.

It wasn't much of a bed—she felt straw under her and smelled damp fleeces piled over her—but it was a bed, inside some building with whitewashed plaster walls around her and a thatched roof overhead. The knowledge that she was safe in a bed, out of the weather and perhaps in the hands of friends, made her groan in a way the pain could never have done.

She had given herself into the hands of the gods as a sacrifice, to turn away their vengeance from her husband and children, from Chelm and Tamaerthon and Drantos. She should not be alive. She *could* not be alive unless the gods had rejected her sacrifice.

What she felt now was worse than the pain of her wounds, although she had not endured such pain since she bore Isobel. It was despair, which she had not felt since she crouched in Sarakos's bedchamber, wondering who would come next, Sarakos or the crone with the whip?

The despair was not so much for herself, although she knew that if the gods had not allowed her to offer her own life in return for Caradoc's they would demand something worse. The despair was for those innocent men and women who would now be dragged down with her into the gods only knew what pit of demons.

Except that in a pit of demons, one could at least be sure that one was already dead, and that matters could grow no worse. Tylara knew that her husband's punishment, her children's, Ganton's—all would begin like hers, while they were still alive to taste the worst of it.

Pride still forced her to cram her right fist into her mouth to stifle another groan. A moment later she saw faces looming over the bed. A woman and two men. One of the men was armed, while the other looked vaguely familiar. She knew she ought to know him, but she could not remember his name. The woman washed her face and neck, and the man held a cup of cool water that tasted of wine and herbs to her lips. They did things to her wrist, ankle, and head that both hurt and soothed at the same time.

She was still trying to put a name to the man when her eyes grew too heavy to be worth the trouble to keep open, and she let them fall shut.

The second time Tylara awoke, the pain in her head was only muskets firing, not Great Guns. She realized that her ankle was twisted and swollen, that her wrist and at least two ribs were probably broken, and that her stomach was dreadfully empty.

The idea of food still made her gag. The sound and movement brought her three attendants to her bedside again. This time she recognized the one who'd seemed familiar. It was Apelles. He had washed his face and found a clean robe somewhere. He smiled as he lifted her wrist to study the bindings.

"Greetings, my Lady Eqetassa. I rejoice to see you awake. It is a good sign."

Tylara tried to turn her head. This set the muskets to firing volleys, but she saw that the opposite wall was now hung with a tapestry of dragons hurling *skyfire*. The floor was a finger's length deep in fresh rushes, and the damp fleeces piled over her had given way to dry furs.

Tylara wasn't sure that her healing was a matter for rejoicing. It seemed not unlikely that she would save everyone a great deal of trouble by dying. She also knew that she was most unlikely to die of these wounds even if she refused further care—and if she did that, they would doubtless only treat her as a madwoman and take her fate even further out of her own hands.

Her thoughts must have shown on her face. Apelles frowned, then gestured toward the door. The woman and the armed man went out. Tylara caught a glimpse of the ragged and mud-smeared surcoat he wore over his short mail coat. It had once been white and green—the colors of Ta-Meltemos.

"Apelles," Tylara said when they were alone, "who is the prisoner here—that soldier of Prince Strymon or—?"

Apelles did not meet her eyes. This time she had the strength to weep, but pride kept her eyes dry.

"Morrone led a final charge when he saw the archers breaking," Apelles said. He still couldn't meet her eyes, and busied himself washing her hands and feet. "He caught Strymon's knights unready. They thought the battle already won. The host of Drantos drove many of the Meltemes from the field."

"Then we won?" Tylara asked wonderingly.

"No. Strymon rallied his forces and held Morrone's charge. Drantos was already defeated when he challenged Morrone to single combat. Bards will sing of that fight for a thousand years! Morrone fought most valiantly, but he was unhorsed, then stunned. Then our knights who remained on the field yielded on the customary terms of ransom. The Fourth Pikes also yielded, on terms of life and limb."

"And—the Tamaerthan archers? Morrone's levies?"

"Most of the levies did not wait on the outcome of the charge, but fled the field. The Tamaerthans—they advanced—they advanced—"

"They advanced too far trying to save me, and could not make a safe retreat?

"A good ten-score did, my Lady."

Ten-score, out of more than eight hundred. Once again she had led the clansmen to slaughter, as she had done against Sarakos. Would they have been able to escape and go on stinging at Strymon if she hadn't dragged them after her?

Only the gods could know the answer to that. What she knew was that her people had already suffered part of the punishment she had hoped to turn away by her sacrifice. She had betrayed them as she had betrayed Caradoc, and their blood was on her hands as surely as his was.

Worse, she had blundered. Rick had defeated a Roman legion with nothing more than Tamaerthan pikes and archers! *If I had used them properly, we might yet have saved the day for Morrone.*

She made an animal noise in the back of her throat, tried to swallow, and found that an iron band seemed to have tightened about her neck. Then Apelles was beside her, a surprisingly strong hand gripping her right wrist.

"My lady. It is not quite unknown—what you tried to do. I do not know why you passed such a judgment on yourself. I do not wish to know, unless you choose freely to tell me. Although you might do well to speak of it to Yanulf, if it lays such a burden on you and for some reason you cannot speak of it to your lord and husband."

Tylara's eyes filled with silent tears.

"I can say this. You fear that the gods have judged you unfit as a sacrifice, and have some further punishment—"

"Isn't a lost battle, thousands dead or taken, and all of Drantos open to Prince Strymon punishment in the eyes of any god or man?"

Apelles' face told her that she'd cried out loudly enough to be heard outside the chamber. She went on more quietly. "Apelles, don't treat me like a child."

His face now told her that he would not give her the comfort of losing his temper. Then he smiled.

"My lady, I am only a consecrated priest of Yatar, so I am not as sure of His will and that of Christ His Son as you seem to be. I suppose it is possible that horrors beyond belief await you and yours because you were not a fit sacrifice.

"Yet I think it likely that whatever your sin, it was not one for which Yatar asks the lives of you and your people. Few sins are as great as that! And beware of assuming that the judgments of the gods are always so simple that men may easily understand them."

"Small comfort—"

"Hear me out. My lady, I know that will be small comfort to you. What you would consider a true comfort, my oaths as a priest of Yatar forbid me to offer, even if common sense did not. Will you swear by Yatar, Vothan, Hestia, and your own honor to lay no hands upon yourself nor to contrive that others aid you in so doing? If you will not, I must lay this matter before Prince Strymon."

Tylara now realized why Apelles had gripped her good hand before beginning to speak. If it had been free, she would certainly have thrown something at him. With steel in her hand...

Yet whether or not he was right—and perhaps the will of the gods *was* harder to guess than it had seemed to her when she rode toward the enemy—he had certainly bound her as tightly as a babe swaddled in a cradle. She had to live. Her only choice was whether she lived with her secrets still hers, or with her shame brought before a mortal enemy.

"By Yatar, by Vothan, by Hestia, and by the lives of Mikail my son and Isobel my daughter, I swear to do myself no harm while I—enjoy Prince Strymon's hospitality."

"Yatar and Christ bless you, my lady."

Tylara could not quite keep from smiling. "I think we have spent time enough guessing what the gods may wish. Would it be possible to bring me a meal? I did not swear not to tear your arm out of its socket and start gnawing on it if I am not fed!"

"Prince Strymon has ordered that you and Lord Morrone be fed from his own table. I shall bring something immediately."

"I thank you, Apelles."

The priest was out the door and the woman and the guard were coming back through it before Tylara realized that she hadn't asked about Lord Morrone. Well, Morrone's skull was thick enough. *He'd few enough wits to begin. I hope no more were knocked out of his head.*

Her meal was meat broth thickened with barley and a small piece of bread. Apelles cheerfully ignored her demands for three times as much, but at least allowed her to feed herself. As she ate the guard unshuttered the room's one window. Tylara saw a manure pile, a pigsty, and beyond it the True Sun setting. Apelles brought her a larger cup of the same sleeping draught—a silver cup with Prince Strymon's stylized megaron device on it—and from somewhere a thin brown and white cat appeared and curled up at the foot of the bed. She drank the sleeping draught thirstily and stretched out under the furs.

As she did, she realized that since her talk with Apelles she had been behaving as if the gods would allow her to put both Caradoc's death and the battle behind her. Those debts were still unpaid, and now she had new ones to the kin of the archers who'd died trying to save her.

That was at least one good reason for staying alive. Another was to learn about Prince Strymon's camp, his host, perhaps even his plans. There should be a way to send word to her husband and Wanax Ganton.

Have the gods judged that my punishment is to leave me alive to undo the damage I have done?

The motion of Tylara's litter changed as the bearers broke step to cross the wooden bridge over the stream known as Sigbard's Run. Tylara parted the side curtains and looked out. The water level was lower and the current was slower than seven days ago when she was first carried out of the farmhouse they'd given her.

This was no surprise; there'd been no rain for twelve days, and the mud that had held up the baggage trains of both sides was now gone except in low-lying spots. In the hills, the survivors of her Tamaerthans and Morrone's levies would no longer be eating cold food and sleeping fitfully in sodden rags. They would be preparing to ambush the Melteman patrols, loot Melteman supply wagons, drive off cattle and even horses, and slit the throats of unwary Melteman sentries.

They'd done plenty of that already using the weather for cover. *Tamaerthan clansmen and southern outlaws. It wasn't so long ago that Drantos considered all of Tamaerthon as no more than a home for bandits. But it is no wonder that I get black looks from Strymon's officers. They must have lost much to our raiders.*

Rick had once called it "guerrilla warfare." Chivalry and peasantry alike had harassed Sarakos and Parsons. Now it would be Strymon's turn. Doubtless there would be a reckoning for this, but until then Tylara could take comfort both in her own returning health and strength and in the knowledge that her people were helping Rick win this war.

She had no doubt at all that he would win. *The gods do not hate him. He had no part in my sin. And only the gods could best him.*

It was barely a hundred paces from the bridge to the wealthy peasant's house that had been turned into quarters for her. Strymon had offered her hospitality in Bheroman Ajacias's castle, but the idea of accepting so much as a crust of bread from that traitor revolted her.

That would be reason enough, but she also suspected that Ajacias was more the ally of Prince Teodoros, Strymon's younger brother, than Prince Strymon. Strymon deserved his reputation for honor and chivalry. She was not so certain of his brother, and she feared the men around Prince Teodoros. She was particularly concerned about a burly Vothanite archpriest who spoke like a king's councilor and moved like a warrior. The little she'd heard him say showed that he knew far too much about Drantos, Tamaerthon, and even Rick's star warriors.

The litter bearers had brought her nearly to the house when half a score of riders reined in. The helmeted axemen surrounded a tall bareheaded man in silvered mail. His fair hair seemed to glow in the light of the rising True Sun. He wore a surcoat of Nikeian red, and an amber-hilted sword of state. Jewels flashed at his ear lobes. Tylara smiled; Prince Strymon could not be called vain about his good looks, but he did not exactly try to hide them either!

Tylara's smile faded when he dismounted. Prince Strymon's face was as friendly as a battle-helm.

"Welcome, my lord," Tylara said. "I bid you enter, but will you give me a moment?"

He nodded curtly and paced while Apelles helped Tylara inside to a settee and arranged a bright silk coverlet over her legs. When the bearers left, he stormed in unasked. "Leave us," he commanded Apelles.

"Your Highness," Tylara protested, "Apelles is a consecrated priest of Yatar. His oaths—"

"I know the oaths of a priest of Yatar. I also know that his master is Yanulf, Chancellor of Drantos, and that half the priests of Yatar follow him no matter what land they serve in."

Tylara bristled. "Do you doubt my honor?"

Strymon returned an encouraging ghost of his usual smile. "No more, my Lady Eqetassa, than I doubt your beauty or the sharpness of your tongue. Do you doubt my wits? I wish to speak to you alone."

Tylara sighed. "Apelles, if you please—"

"Certainly, my lady. I will wait outside."

Apelles went out; two of Strymon's guards brought honeycakes, fine bronze cups set with seashells, a jug of water and another of wine. Another brought a small folding table fitted with ivory and silver. Strymon on campaign seemed half a Roman. He carried the luxuries of a Praetor, but he also fortified his camps, sent out scouts, paid attention to sanitation—and mixed his wine half with water.

Strymon did that now and filled their cups. Tylara sipped at hers. The brown and white cat who had adopted Tylara jumped up on the settee. Strymon absently broke off a piece of honeycake and gave it to the cat, who took it and jumped to the floor.

"My lady. I cannot imagine that you do not know that the survivors of your—of the Host of Drantos—continue to fight in the hills around us. Supplies and messengers are not safe unless they are escorted by five-score and more armed riders. Men have been sent gull-feathered to Vothan's House without ever seeing an enemy. Others have gone to sleep three under a blanket, and in the morning the one in the middle has awakened to find his comrades lying with their throats cut."

Tylara recalled hearing Rick speak of such a trick used on Earth, by warriors who swam into battle in the country called Vietnam. "Surely you do not complain that my people are teaching yours the folly of sleeping on watch? When they have done their work, you will have a smaller host, but most assuredly a better one."

"This is not a matter for jesting. I want it stopped!"

"That is easily done. Release us and return to your own lands. Do that and we will harry you no more."

"There could be a blood price for such obstinacy. Not your blood alone, either."

"Threats, Highness? Against your prisoners? I take it you are not satisfied with the songs the bards will sing of your combat with Morrone. You wish them to sing of your dishonor as well."

"Lady—"

"Your Highness, you can do nothing to me, or Lord Morrone, that will win you the smallest victory over the men in the hills. What you can do is make certain of war to the knife. You believe you have won a victory because you bested a foolish King's Companion and a woman. Wait until you face not the chivalry of Drantos, but Romans, Tamaerthan pikes and archers who have bested Romans, Great Guns and muskets—and star weapons. Wait until you face the Wanax Ganton who is your equal, and my Lord Rick who is the master of us all! When you have bested *them* you may proclaim victory."

"Enough!"

Tylara smiled. "Forgive me, Your Highness. I do not

doubt your courage. I only warn you that if any harm comes to me, my Lord Rick will defeat your armies, and turn loose the clanless ones of Tamaerthon to pick Ta-Meltemos to bare bones, and this is as certain as anything mortal man can know."

"Your lord or the Wanax Ganton might not place so small a value on the lives and limbs of those I hold. Are you sure that you can speak for them?"

"Hah. Who can speak for a Wanax? But do you think I have married a fool, or that I have lived with him these years and borne him his children, and yet do not know him? For him may I speak; and I tell you, he knows terrible things, and in his anger he will use them against all of you. You have doubtless heard that he and his men are not of this world. I tell you that is true, and I tell you beware harming what little he holds of value here lest he let this entire world go to its doom."

Strymon looked thoughtful. He took a paper from his glove, glanced at it, then returned it. "My Lady, many have marched against me. None have returned. I stand on your land, not you on mine—"

Tylara laughed. "Forgive me, Highness. Again I do not doubt your skills. Yet ask yourself this. Sarakos with the aid of the traitor Parsons was able to conquer Drantos, yet he could not hold it. Three days after Lord Rick killed Parsons he drove the host of the Five Kingdoms from our land. What can my husband do now that he has gathered his strength? I tell you that you do not know what you face.

"Consider the star weapons, the least of which can strike down a man four stadia away. There is another, named for a king from another world, and with that Lord Rick can tear a castle gate to splinters from twice bowshot. How long can your castles stand against that?"

"That will depend, I suppose, on whether there are more gates than this—Carl Gustav—has bombs."

Tylara's bowels went cold. Strymon knew the very name of the star weapon! What else might he know? And from what source?

For a moment she toyed with the idea of attempting Strymon's life herself. *Ridiculous. It is dishonor, and what he knows, his brother knows.* "That is one of my husband's weapons. He has more. Many more," Tylara said. "Your spies have told you truly, that the star weapons are like bows—useless when there are no more arrows. It is even true that we do not have so many arrows as you have castles. We do have quite enough to batter down any castle unfortunate enough to shelter you or any of your family. And surely you have heard—no. I have said enough. But consider all these things, before you lift a hand against any of your prisoners." She laughed. "My Tamaerthans in the hills will be flattered, that you have found them so great a menace that you contemplate dishonor."

Tylara sipped wine and watched as Strymon poured more for himself.

He took his time doing it, and when he turned, his face was expressionless. Then he smiled. "I knew it would not work. Matthias thought it worth trying. My lady, I contemplated nothing dishonorable, but could I have persuaded you I did, you might have given orders to your men." He shrugged. "I owed the attempt to my soldiers."

Tylara began a smile, then wondered. Would this work against Morrone? But there was nothing she could do about that, at least not while Strymon was watching. Tylara sipped more wine and reached for a honeycake. She had not quite touched the plate when Strymon laid a hand on her wrist.

"A moment, my lady. Where is the cat?"

"You gave her a piece of cake, the shameless little beggar! I have not seen her since."

"Nor have I." Strymon put the plate of cakes on a bench out of Tylara's reach, looked around the room, then knelt down and looked under the settee. A moment later she heard a muttered oath, and he straightened up, holding the cat in both hands.

The cat hung limp, eyes closed and bloody foam dripping from her mouth.

CHAPTER THREE

Strymon stared at the dead cat in horror. "Guards! To your prince!"

The door crashed open and five of Strymon's guards tried to come through a door that would have been snug for two. They regrouped and entered, Apelles behind them. One of the guards raised his axe and stared around the room for the threat to his prince.

"Hold! Guard this lady!" Strymon gestured and the guard lowered his weapon. Two of the guards took positions at the head and foot of the settee. Two others ranged themselves on either side of the door.

"Send for Gythras," Strymon snapped. The fifth guard saluted and ran from the room. Apelles knelt to examine the dead cat.

Tylara watched Strymon pace furiously up and down the room. *He must be innocent. No man is that good an actor. Besides, he knows my death would not drive my archers from the hills. I am in danger, certainly, but not from him.*

The fifth guard returned with a blue-robed priest of Yatar. "Ah, Gythras." Strymon gestured toward Apelles and the cat. "Find out what killed it."

Gythras knelt besides Apelles. The two healers poked at the cat and exchanged a few muttered words. Then Gythras rose and sniffed at one of the remaining honeycakes.

"Goat's-ear root, most probably, Your Highness. Its flavor is musky, but sweet enough to blend well with honey."

"Indeed," said Strymon. Gythras picked up the dead cat and the plate of honeycakes and went out. Strymon nodded to his guards. They left, taking Apelles with them. The prince closed the door, pulled the bench close to the settee, and sat down.

"My lady. I ask you to believe that I would not dishonor myself by an act such as this."

"I never doubted that," Tylara said. "But I think less honorable men have power over one of your cooks."

Strymon smiled grimly. "The cooks will be questioned." He motioned to one of his guards. "Put all the camp cooks under guard. Bring the Master of the Kitchen to my tent and wait for me there."

"Your Highness." The man saluted and left.

"And until the cooks are questioned, you'd prefer that I not ask questions that you cannot honorably answer? Very well, Your Highness," Tylara said. "But I urge you to take some thought for your own safety. Do we know whether the poison was meant for me or for you?"

Strymon's expression softened, and Tylara smiled back. *No man, prince or not, can entirely resist hearing that a fair woman prefers him alive.*

"Both of us, I think. Last night I made no secret that I would visit you this morning."

Tylara nodded slowly. "Your Highness, if it is in your power, will you return my star weapon to me? The next attempt on my life will probably come with steel. I am a bedridden woman with only one hand fit for use, but with the star weapon in that hand I may give a good account of myself. Its—magic, let us call it"—he lifted one eyebrow at that, and she answered with a grin—"its magic is too weak for me to harm anyone outside this chamber. I could hardly injure your guards, let alone your host, and as for fighting my way out of the camp—I could sooner fly to Castle Dravan by waving my arms!"

"You ask much."

"You risk much. If I am killed, you will never be free of suspicions."

"True." He thought for a moment longer. "Very well. You may have your star weapon. With my thanks for the opportunity to examine it."

Of course Strymon would have taken the Colt apart. *And ten crowns says it'll come back with seven cartridges instead of eight. Ah, well.* Rick always said it would not be very long before everyone knew the secret of firepowder weapons, and victory would go to whoever made the best use of what everyone had!

Tylara spoke with elaborate casualness. "I trust you did so with due care."

Strymon tilted his head in an ironic little nod. "I am as you see intact.... Would you convey to Lord Rick my request that such a star weapon form part of your ransom?"

"Yes, I can convey that request. But only Lord Rick can grant it."

"Of course."

"By Yatar and Vothan, Your Highness, I swear that none but your enemies shall face the magic of the star weapon as long as I am in your camp."

Strymon raised Tylara's hand to his lips. There was a knock at the door. Strymon dropped her hand and stood, one hand on the hilt of his sword.

"Come." The door opened and Apelles came in.

"My Lady, I—," he began.

"It's all right, Apelles. His Highness will grant us a few minutes so that you may tend my wounds." She smiled up at Strymon. "He will bring my star weapon to me after I have dined."

"My lady." Strymon nodded and left, and Apelles began to loosen the bandages on her leg.

"Tell me, Apelles. How soon will I be able to walk again?"

"At least seven days, my lady. Perhaps sooner, but I doubt it."

Tylara sighed. She might need the Colt as more than just a symbol of Strymon's honorable intentions.

The lamp hanging by the door had long since burned dry. Tylara's searching eyes found only darkness, yet she was sure she'd heard a sound, either from above or from outside the door.

The sounds came again. Above *and* outside. Tylara drew

the Colt from under the furs and snapped off the safety. A round was already in the chamber. She had only six others. Yatar grant that she should need no more.

The sound from above now sounded like the scampering of rats. Then she smelled smoke. Had someone fired the roof thatch?

A moment later—

"Fire! Fire! Guards, save Lady Tylara!"

The sounds outside turned into stamping feet and fists pounding on the door. Then—

"No, Lady Tylara! Treachery, treachery, treach—!" Apelles shouted from outside.

She could not let herself think of what might have happened to cut him off. She had the Colt raised and aimed as the door flew open and two men in the colors of Strymon's guards plunged through.

She shot the first man in the stomach and he slammed backward into the second to knock him off his feet. Outside the door a third man was gathering himself to leap over the two fallen ones, when yet another man seemed to fall from the sky onto him. The last man left on his feet was unslinging a short bow when Tylara shot him in the face.

Apelles staggered into the room. Blood streamed down one arm but he held a knife in his good hand, and swore terrible oaths in most unpriestly language. A dozen and more of Strymon's host ran up to the door. Apelles examined each before letting him in, but even so the room was suddenly full of people. Tylara snapped the safety on the Colt. Her hand was shaking so badly she was afraid she might fire by accident.

She did not stop shaking until Prince Strymon appeared in a sleeping robe with a sword belted on over it. Gythras was behind him, followed by two servants laden with bottles and instruments. From overhead the crackling of flames gave way to the hiss of water, and Tylara smelled steam instead of smoke.

The three would-be murderers who could walk were led away. As Gythras examined Tylara, Strymon kneeled over the two she'd shot. He frowned at the man with the belly wound, then went over to the one shot in the head.

"All the gods be merciful! I did not think..."

Two of the guards held up the dead man. He looked as Rick had told her to expect—a bloody hole in front, and the back of his head nearly blown away, so that blood and brains oozed down onto his clothes.

Gythras turned away from his examination to stare. So did Apelles. Then Apelles took a stumbling step forward and toppled to the floor. Gythras turned to him, and muttered imprecations about priests who thought they were knights and didn't have the sense to admit they were wounded.

When Gythras had finished, litters were brought from both Tylara and Apelles. Gythras mixed a sleeping draught and handed it to her. As the bearers carried her out of the house, she fell asleep—but it was a sleep troubled by nightmares, in which Prince Strymon kept turning into the High Rexja Toris, into one of the *Shalnuksis,* and worst of all, into the Wanax Sarakos!

It was the last that made her wake screaming and stay awake until just before the rising of the True Sun.

When Tylara awoke, the walls around her were canvas without windows and the door was a hanging now tied half back. It revealed a patch of trampled bare ground with Strymon's guards standing practically shoulder to shoulder. Beyond them she could see another tent striped in Strymon's colors.

It was clear that she had been moved into the royal compound. She might not be as safe here as Strymon hoped; not unless Prince Teodoros and his people had been moved out of the compound. Still, this was more evidence of Prince Strymon's concern.

Gythras arrived with a speed that suggested he had been waiting outside for her to awake. He and a priestess of Hestia examined Tylara from head to toe.

"By the mercy of Yatar, she is unharmed," Gythras said.

"I thank my Lady Hestia—"

It seemed to Tylara as if they were trying to reassure themselves as much as her. Well, they had some right in the matter; their fate would not be pleasant if she died, and her waking screaming must have been heard from one end of the camp to the other.

They took their time, and when they left, Prince Strymon himself entered. His hair was uncombed and he had not shaved. There was both soot and blood under his nails.

He drew a stool close enough to the bed so that he didn't need to speak above a whisper, and sat without asking her leave. After a moment he got up again and untied the hanging to close the tent door.

"Your priest Apelles lives," Strymon began. "He has a long and deep cut in his shoulder and arm, and has lost much blood. He has already told Gythras how to drive out the fester-devils from water, wounds, and bandages, and his wounds seem the better for it. He will still be writing left-handed for a time, though—unless his wounds fester after all."

"That is with Yatar and Hestia, is it not?" said Tylara. She sensed an uneasiness in Strymon that went beyond the danger to his honor.

"It is, if Apelles and the other healers who have dealt with your wounded have been told the truth by the starmen. It is said that in casting out the fester-devils as Apelles taught us, we let in other and worse devils."

No need to ask who said that. She shrugged. "It is the way he treats me. Do you see me infested with devils?"

"No— My lady, why would you allow your enemies to learn this great secret? If this is true, many soldiers will live who would have died. My soldiers."

"My Lord Rick has commanded that this wisdom—and much other that he knows—be given freely to all on this world," Tylara said proudly. "He says that knowledge is not to be hoarded as a miser hoards gold, but spread to the winds."

"I—see," Strymon said. "Now, my lady, are you well enough to discuss serious matters?"

"I am quite well. Haven't the healers told you?"

Strymon reddened. "Forgive me, but in the night we heard you screaming—louder than the wretches we were questioning about the attempt on your life. Gythras would not tell me, but it seems to me—"

"It was a nightmare, Your Highness. An old nightmare, from a time I thought I had put behind me—"

The wide gray eyes were suddenly as cold and hard as the stones of Castle Dravan. "Then the tales of how Sarakos dishonored you are no tales." It was not a question.

Tylara swallowed twice before she could say, "No. But he is dead and food for worms."

"Worms that fed on Sarakos's corpse probably died of it." His face twisted. "I have never been wholly easy in my mind, over refusing to serve under Sarakos. Had I been there, I might have prevented— My lady, I can only beg your pardon. I gave too much thought to defending my own honor, and not to how I might defend that of others."

"You could not have known that Sarakos would be a fool as well as a brute—," she began, but Strymon raised his hand to stop her.

"I cast nothing on the High Rexja, but his eldest son always behaved like one begotten in a kitchen-midden. I cannot in honor say that I should not have known better."

"Your own honor is pure as fire, Strymon. That makes you less than the best judge of those who have none."

Unbidden and surprising, but not unwelcome, an odd thought entered Tylara's mind. How would matters have gone, if Strymon had been willing to march against Drantos as a captain under Sarakos?

Rather ill for Drantos, she suspected; the horse and foot of Ta-Meltemos would have given Sarakos a third again his strength, apart from Strymon's skill. The contest in the field would have been foreordained. Yet without Sarakos free to indulge his bloodlust and treachery, might not more of the men of Drantos have seen surrender as an honorable alternative?

And her own fate—what of that? She might not be a widow at all, for Strymon would never have done to her Lamil as Sarakos did, cutting his throat like a pig while a dozen men held him. Strymon would have faced Lamil in single combat, almost certainly defeated him, but left him alive if he was prepared to yield at all.

If by some chance Lamil had still died—Strymon would hardly have slaughtered the men of Castle Dravan. That would have left Bheroman Trakon alive to press his suit. Or perhaps Strymon himself would have courted her. His first wife had died bearing him a daughter, the year before the war began. She could see herself captured a little at a time by his charm, his grace, his good looks, his concern for her honor as well as his own....

And then what would have happened to the starmen, if she had not been in need of an ally to destroy Sarakos and regain Chelm, and if Sarakos had not been in need of someone like Colonel Parsons to put down the guerrillas in Drantos?

Were the gods as capricious as that, in sending fates to men and women? And if they were that capricious, how could anyone be sure what they demanded?

Another question for Yanulf—and now she realized that Strymon had begun an account of the night's events, while she was lost in dreams of how things might have been.

"—was able to buy men, but not men brave enough to simply storm into your room and shed your blood with their own hands. Had they done that, some would surely have died from the star weapon, but the rest would have killed you.

"As it was, they conceived an elaborate scheme and divided themselves into three parties, all disguised as my guards. One party set fire to the roof. The second would rescue you from the fire, and when you were safely out of the house the third would dash up and stab you. Even with all these foolish complications, they might have done their work if it had not been for Apelles. He saw that the second party were not the new watch of guards, but impostors, and gave the alarm. The man who wounded him also knocked down the ladder in the struggle. One man fell from the ladder and the other man was trapped and burned to death on the roof."

Tylara could not keep back a smile. Her would-be murderers seemed to have been a pack of prize fools. Had Yatar addled the murderers' wits to save her?

"Have you—is there anything you may tell me of who hired those men?"

"Matthias, priest of Vothan, fled the camp before True Sun-rise," said Strymon. "Several of his men went with him. They passed the northernmost of our outposts before the alarm, and told the officer of the guard that they were on urgent business for the High Rexja."

"I suppose that can be called the truth," said Tylara. "Fleeing from the headsman is certainly best done in haste."

Strymon's smile was forced. "My lady, how much do you know of Ta-Meltemos?"

She shrugged. "We hear stories—"

"Yes, yes. Stories you are too polite to repeat. They are true. My father seems in good health, and has a sweet and forgiving nature. But—" Strymon swallowed hard. "He cannot find his way from bedroom to throne room without a guide, and lately we do not even dare have him appear on state occasions."

"I had heard," Tylara said gently.

"The last time, he rose from the throne to question the High Marshal of Ta-Boreas about sweets and children's toys."

"Then you govern the land."

"I confess I do not. I have always been a soldier. You must understand, until recent years Wanax Palamon was as good a king as ever ruled our land. It was only when he—changed that Toris took new advisors, and the first wars between Drantos and the Five Kingdoms began."

"Your brother—"

"Was much younger then. Lady, Ta-Meltemos is ruled by Chancellor Rauros. He was sent to us by Issardos, and found much favor with my father during his declining years. Now he is sometimes— Lady this is not easily said. There are times when Palamon recognizes no one but Rauros. Not even his sons."

"It cannot be easy, living in such a court. I see now why you and your brother would prefer the field. In your place I would do the same. Prince Strymon, do you believe that Rauros knows of this plot against your honor?"

Strymon pressed his lips into a thin line. "I do not know. But I will know."

"How?"

"Yes. That is the question, is it not? The only men I can trust are soldiers with no more skills at intrigue than I have."

You need a woman. I will find you one. But for now— "There are priests of Yatar whose loyalty is to honor and the gods. They might serve you well."

"Priests of this new religion?"

"It is not *new,* Highness. It is the religion of the starmen. We—New Christians—honor all of the commandments of Yatar. We also recognize His Son, the Christ."

"I must think on this."

"Of course. For now, we must think again who is behind this plot. The High Rexja—"

"Again, I do not know. I can say nothing against the High Rexja. Nor can Teodoros."

"You asked him?"

"Yes, my lady. My brother says he doesn't know anything about plots." Strymon shrugged elaborately. "I would be surprised if he did. It is not in his nature."

"Issardos," Tylara said carefully.

Strymon nodded. "It would not surprise me if Chancellor Issardos had a hand in this. It would insure war to the death

between Ta-Meltemos and Drantos. If half what you say of
Lord Rick's abilities is true—and Matthias has, it seems,
seen Lord Rick in battle—then I might well die in such a
war. That would leave Teodoros on my throne."

"As Issardos's puppet," Tylara said softly.

Strymon sighed. "I love my brother, but—yes. I can trust
Teodoros, but without me to guide him, he would be no
match for Issardos. I doubt Issardos would care if Teodoros
ruled over ruins and beggars, so long as he could not disturb the peace of the Five Kingdoms."

"Issardos is a fool," said Tylara. "The Time will disturb
everyone's peace, and the skyfolk will do worse."

"Perhaps a fool, but a dangerous one." He straightened
and squared his shoulders. "You will sleep and wake surrounded by my guards, and eat and drink nothing that has
not been tasted first." Strymon raised his voice. "The baker
who prepared the honeycakes and those who sought your
life last night have an appointment with the headsman.
Their bodies will be cast into the middens and their heads
borne through the camp by heralds crying out 'Here be
hardy traitors, who sought the lives of the Crown's prisoners.'"

Strymon looked around the tent, then lowered his voice
to a true whisper. "That should discourage the faint-
hearted. With Matthias gone the stouter spirits have no
leader. If these measures are not enough, I swear by Yatar,
Vothan, and Hestia that I will release you without a ransom
and send you to your husband.

"Yet I would not do that before we have talked further. I
have thought on what you said yesterday, and I have listened to my own priests of Yatar tell about the Time. It
seems it has never been easy for the Five Kingdoms."

"This my husband says."

Strymon fell silent. Then he turned and paced the length
of the tent. For a moment he stared at the tapestry of
dragons spitting *skyfire* onto a melting city. Then he took a
deep breath and turned to Tylara. "My lady, there may be

ways to bring peace to the Realms of Drantos and Ta-Meltemos."

Tylara caught her breath. She was not wholly surprised. *But I thought it would take much longer.* Inwardly she thanked Matthias and Issardos for making her work easier.

Now I know why the gods spared me. Am I fit for this task? Dayfather, Warrior, Mother, you have given me back my life. Now give me strength and wisdom to use it in your service.

CHAPTER FOUR

Rick Galloway looked at the map on the camp table in front of him. An inkwell, a dagger, and a pair of gloves held down the corners and kept the hot wind off the Westscarp from blowing the map as well as the dust all over his tent.

If maps had faces, Rick decided, this one would be wearing a sullen frown. He remembered telling his "General Staff" classes that you should always look at a map when you couldn't think of what to do next. The map would almost certainly tell you something.

The problem was that the map wouldn't always tell you anything you didn't already know. The map in front of him was a case in point. The blue pins showed the twelve thousand men of his Army of Chelm exactly where they'd been the day before, and the day before that, and the day before *that*. Same thing with the red pins for the twenty-odd thousand men in the High Rexja's Army of the West.

It wasn't the odds that bothered him. Two to one wouldn't be enough against star weapons and Tamaerthan archers. Some of the enemy captains were veterans of Sarakos's campaign, of course; they would have seen the archers and the weapons in action, and might have worked out tactics to make them less effective. Still, tactics wouldn't hold troops together if the one-oh-six started dropping WP into their formations from five stadia away. Black magic did a lot to wreck morale—at least the first time around. Rick was pretty sure that if he was willing to use up most of his ammo, he could keep the Army of the West from fighting again, at least for another six months.

The problem was, the High Rexja's captains had learned something even more important than how to meet star weapons—they'd learned scouting. Maybe they'd always known something—a lot of their cavalry was light stuff, mounted on centaurs or scrubby little hacks like Scots border horses. Those ponies could scatter across country and live on forage where heavy cavalry mounts would starve.

Certainly they'd learned a lot from a year of fighting the Westmen. The ones who'd survived were light cavalry of a quality that Rick had hoped he wouldn't see on the other side for quite a while. A dumb hope, he now realized—nobody but Yatar could make sure that your enemies would always learn slower than your friends, and Yatar seemed to be sitting this one out.

So he couldn't hope to take Captain General Ailas by surprise and defeat him in detail. Ailas would get word in time and pull his three "divisions" together. Or maybe he would hold with two and send one around Rick's rear. He might even just stay where he was, with his army divided into three for better grazing and water supplies, and wait for Rick to move—forward or back, it didn't matter. As long as Rick and his men were here in the west while the main army of the Five Kingdoms crunched into Drantos farther east, cutting it off from Rome, Ailas was helping win the war for his king without killing a single enemy!

It didn't help that only half of Rick's army was cavalry, and their mounts weren't in the best shape. The rains had stopped and now the streams were drying up. Before long Rick might have to move his army just to stay near water.

What I need is the Tamaerthans. Pikes and archers. Then I could move them up, and to hell with Ailas. He can attack good pikemen with heavy cavalry and get his lunch, or he can hang back and let the archers have at him. Either way—

None of it mattered though, because he didn't have the archers and pikemen. Ganton did. *And I hope to God he uses them better than Morrone did.*

I've got to get up there where the real action is. This is nothing but a holding operation.

As for here, he'd have to do something soon enough or withdraw without a fight, and that would lose him his reputation for invincibility. When that went, a lot of men would go with it, some because they wouldn't follow a leader who wasn't lucky, but a lot more because they didn't want to abandon their lands and would swear fealty to Toris to keep them.

Tylara wouldn't like that. *Wouldn't she ever.* If they ever sat down and had it out over what she'd done with her junior-grade ninjas, she'd be able to claim that he'd betrayed his own men and her just as badly. Stalemate—and from there Rick could see things going in a lot of different directions, most of them labeled "from bad to worse."

He looked at the map again. Lost reputation or not, he'd better put the army on the move before it *had* to move to stay near water. Then there'd be too good a chance of Ailas cutting him off from water and doing to at least part of his army what Saladin did to the Crusaders at the Horns of Hattin.

The key to the campaign was that damned light cavalry. Ailas had been using it to scout in front of his army. Suppose he had to watch his rear? "Damn right," Rick said aloud. "Now who do I send?"

There weren't many candidates. The striking force had to be all cavalry, and there was a good chance it wouldn't be coming back soon. That ruled out leading them himself, but the leader would have to know modern tactics and weapons. Somebody who would be obeyed by both mercs and Tran soldiers, and knew the territory well enough to make a small force do the work of a big one.

Exactly one man matched that description.

"Jamiy!"

His orderly appeared and saluted with a click of heels. (Rick wondered how much of his income from bribes Jamiy spent on new boots that would click properly.)

"My compliments to Lord Murphy, and I'd be pleased to see him at once."

"Sir!"

"—stays dry for another couple of days, the water in Dead Gunkel Lake will be down enough for us to march along here." Ben Murphy traced a line on the map with a forefinger.

"That's pretty close to Ailas's Second Division, isn't it?"

"There's a couple-three klicks of scrub and thicket just above the shore, between the lake and the camp. Even bandits don't go there very much. It's full of patches of quicksand and something that must be a wild cousin of madweed. Stinks like it, thorns like it, and it makes you crazy if you put the sap in booze."

"They could still get wind of your movement, and put an ambush at Gorgon Pass to cut you off."

"Not if we have a couple of heavy weapons along. Blast 'em out with a mortar or the Carl Gustav, and pick 'em off with one of the LMGs as they run." He frowned. "Mortar'd be better, I think. We don't have to have it in line of sight, now that I've taught some of the local kids flag signals."

"Sergeant Murphy, what the hell makes you think you're going to have any heavy weapons at all?"

"Captain, I've been thinking it over. I know there's a risk of losing them. But if I don't get some of the big magic, my people might start wondering if they're being sent on a suicide run. I may not be able to get them out of the camp, let alone keep them from running away if it hits the fan. And look, we can do a lot more damage with some heavy firepower. I think you want to stomp the bastards, not just tickle them!"

"What you really mean, Sergeant Lord Murphy, is that you *won't* order your people out without heavy-weapons support."

"Yeah, I guess so."

Sure. And now what? I don't need a crisis just now.

Jamiy's blank expression matched Murphy's. Rick hoped no one could ever pry this story out of him. It would make a story to tell, all right, one of the starmen bargaining with the Lord Rick. Shades of Parsons' and Gengrich's mutinies!

Not really, though. This wasn't an officer dealing with an insubordinate NCO, it was the Captain General of Drantos dealing with a bheroman who owed it to his people not to put them in needless danger. Murphy couldn't really do much else. *But I bet the S.O.B. is having fun.*

"Okay, Lord Murphy. You can't have the Carl Gustav anyway, and I'd rather give you some rifle grenades than an LMG. You shouldn't have to face a massed attack. We're damned sure going to have to if it comes to the crunch."

"Captain, if you give me an LMG I think I can beef up my force with Mad Bear's Westmen. They're used to raiding, and if they think they have some really big wizards on their side . . . Besides, I think they're not too happy sitting around camp half the time."

True enough. Despite Mad Bear's oaths, his three hundred warriors weren't really pulling their weight in the campaign, because nobody except Ben and a couple of his men-at-arms knew how to handle them. Not many in the army trusted them, either. There'd been a few nasty incidents—not too many, considering that a lot of men in the camp had lost homes and kin to the Westmen, but enough to worry about.

"I'm going to have to be sticky about the LMG, Lord Murphy. What about some rockets?"

The bargaining went on long enough for Rick to send Jamiy for more wine. They compromised: a section of First Rockets with twenty-five rounds, and Second Engineer's portable ballista with twenty bombs, but no LMG. Ben would take two hundred and twenty-five Westman warriors; the rest would stay in camp to protect the women, children, and remounts.

"That's five hundred men, near enough," Rick said.

"Yes, sir—"

"It's enough. During the Civil War Ben Grierson covered Grant's advance on Vicksburg with not many more, and he had to face a lot better men than Ailas has."

"That right? Yes, sir. I'll try. There is one more thing—"

"Yeah?"

Murphy poured himself more wine. "I want your permission to swear blood-brotherhood with Mad Bear."

"Holy hell—why?"

"Captain, the thing is, if I'm blood brother to Mad Bear he can never fight against you again unless I release him from his oath to me. Or you release me from mine to you."

Better not ask what else Murphy might feel released him from his oath to his Captain General. "You've got a point. Go on."

"It'll also help in picking the men to go, 'cause they'll all want to, and I may have to order some to stay behind. They'll take it better if I'm sworn to Mad Bear. Besides, I may have to order night marches. Mad Bear doesn't worry about demons as much as he used to, but a lot of his people do. If I've sworn never knowingly to put a warrior in the path of demons..."

"Okay, okay. Swear anything you think you can keep without having to rebel, only tell me about it afterward. Fair enough?"

"Sure thing, Captain."

After Murphy left, Rick considered the new lesson he'd just learned. It wasn't the stupid mercs who were dangerous. There were some who thought modern weapons could let them live as petty kings, but they weren't the problem. It was the smart ones, like Gengrich and Murphy. The ones who knew how to give loyalty as well as take it.

The ones who knew how to be feudal lords.

Ben Murphy scrambled out of the warm, muddy stream. Rough-barked branches and sharp blades of grass scraped and pricked his bare skin. *Hell of a skinny-dipping party. Not a girl in sight. And Dirdre wouldn't like it if there was.* It was funny how possessive she was now that they were hitched. Even funnier was the fact that he didn't mind. Dirdre was a damned fine woman, even if she probably wouldn't ever forget Lafe Reznick. Reznick had been one hell of a good man. One of the happiest days of Ben's life at Westrook was the day they dedicated the shrine to Lafe, so that all the young men could come ask his spirit to bless their weapons and give them courage in war—

"Come, brother-to-be." Mad Bear's voice broke into his thoughts. "It is time to run."

They loped up the north side of the little valley. Ben gritted his teeth as the stones and scrub punished his bare feet, but pushed himself as hard as he could. He didn't want Mad Bear to have to hold back for him.

By the time they reached level ground, Ben had worked up enough of a sweat to satisfy any reasonable god. *Wouldn't old Father McCarthy have a fit if he heard that!*

He stumbled and nearly fell as a root snagged his left foot. He didn't need Mad Bear's warning cough to remind him that falling on his face now would bode very badly for their blood-brotherhood. Murphy emptied his mind and settled down to the run.

The Firestealer silvered the water of the stream behind them and gave enough light for Murphy to find a path through the scrub. Night birds called, but Murphy couldn't hear anything but his heartbeat, his pounding feet, and the rasp of his breath. *Benjamin Murphy, you're too damned old for these barbarian rituals.* It was too late now. Murphy realized that he'd been heading toward this oath and tomorrow's raid ever since the day Mad Bear and his tribe rode into Westrook.

It was the wives and kids that had done it. Murphy couldn't send them back with their men to be slaughtered by Walking Stone. He couldn't do that, any more than he could have said "Sure, and I'll be glad to blow up a store full of grandmothers and children, as long as some of them are

Protestants," when the two Provo gunmen came to reason with him.

He was three-quarters through the run. Another half-klick, then jump over the bonfire and enjoy the applause. Sure. *I never was much for jumping. Hope I can get over it without losing something Dirdre might miss.*

Closer up, the fire was less intimidating. It was burning in a little hollow, and the light reflected from the sides of the hollow made it look bigger than it was. Murphy flexed his knees as he reached the raised lip of the hollow. *Holy Geronimo! Here goes*— He sailed over the fire and landed on his feet. But the grass was slippery and the hill sloped away under him. He overbalanced and went down on hands and knees in front of two dozen Westmen.

Mad Bear landed on his feet beside him, but the tribesmen were already hissing and muttering. *Not too swift, Murphy. Now what? Ah.* He remembered one of the Captain's history lectures. He pulled up a clod of earth and grass with each hand, and held them high as he got to his feet.

"I hold this land I have taken with both hands," he shouted. "None of the High King's dogs will drive me from it. With my brother-to-be, I will whip them all back to their kennels." From the corner of his eye he saw Mad Bear grin. The hisses and mutters died away.

They drank water from the same cup, and sipped fermented mare's milk mixed with blood from the same bowl. They ate from the same piece of bread sprinkled with salt. It was lousy bread, but Murphy didn't care. The ritual had called for him to fast from the setting of the Father Sun, and now he was hungry enough to eat a lamil raw.

Murphy took out his knife. *Mad Bear's knife, actually. Arekor gave it to him while he was a prisoner.* He held it high, then laid its blade against his wrist. A moment later he handed the blade to Mad Bear, who did the same. They pressed the cuts together while someone started beating a drum. Someone else piled more branches on the fire, and Mad Bear began to chant.

"Father Sun, Father Horse, Father Grass, see us."

"They see us," responded Murphy.

"We have crossed the water."

"This we have done."

"We have shed our sweat in the running."

"This we have done."

They recited how they had jumped over the fire, drunk water and milk, eaten bread, and mingled their blood. Finally Mad Bear shouted:

"Are we not brothers?"

"We are brothers!" Murphy yelled, and the Westmen joined in. "They are brothers!" A young boy handed Murphy another bowl of fermented mare's milk. *Even without blood in it, it'll never replace Tullamore Dew. But at least this time I don't have to hold my nose.*

Elliot was playing the part of Murphy's kinsman. He came forward with Murphy's coveralls and rifle. Elliott wasn't going on the raid; Jack Beazeley, newly promoted to corporal, would be the senior man. *Jack's a good guy. If it comes to a fight, he's got his head screwed on with the nose to the front.*

Elliot handed Murphy his M-16. He slung it, sat down, and started in on a bowlful of raw horsemeat and wild-grass stew the youngster handed him. *The Savoy Grill this ain't. But we won't leave camp until just before True Sun-set tomorrow, and I'll probably be too busy to sit down and eat during the day.*

"Colonel—"

"Damn it, Art, I'm going. I don't give a damn what they say about Prince Strymon's honor, he's got my wife and I'm going to go get her back."

"And just how are you going to do that?"

Rick laughed. "Good question, but look, I'm not doing a damn bit of good here. You can handle this situation as well as I can. Wait until Murphy draws off some of that cavalry, and keep the pressure on to take up the slack. This is a holding operation. We can't win the war out here."

"No, but we can sure lose it here, Colonel."

"Can, but won't. The worst that happens is you withdraw to Dravan. You can do that. *I* can't, without everybody thinking I've lost my touch."

Mason looked thoughtful. "You know, that just about makes sense."

"I'll tell you something else that makes sense. I know how to handle Tamaerthan pikes and archers. Ganton doesn't, but he's got them."

"Yeah. Okay, I buy that. But damn all, Colonel, those ironhats won't obey me—"

"Sure they will, for all you have to do. Look, we sent all the big cheese types off to Ganton. All you've got to deal with are some minor barons and city fathers. They'll *want* somebody to tell them what to do. If you can't do that as chairman of a council of war, I've promoted the wrong man."

"Maybe you—"

"And don't give me that crap. Look, Art, all we're doing here is keeping Ailas from coming into Drantos by the back door, and at the same time making him keep his army here instead of going over to join Strymon's force headed for Edron. He wins just by existing, but so do we! And don't tell me you can't do that as well as I can, because I don't want to hear it."

"Colonel—"

"Art, I'm taking a couple of squadrons and getting the hell out of here, and you're going to shut up and soldier."

CHAPTER FIVE

The Wanax Ganton reined in at the foot of the gallows. He looked up as a gust of wind rattled the dangling chains. *Ajacias will be hanged here. I think I shall build a new gallows for him. Then his ghost will not trouble the good men he killed here.*

Of course the Christians said that a man like Ajacias would go to Hell and suffer torments from the Devil until the end of time. It pleased Ganton to imagine Ajacias spending eternity in the hands of a being like the Roman *quaestionarii. But does that mean I may take no vengeance on the wretched traitor myself? I shall have to ask Octavia or Archbishop Polycarp.*

The Demon Star silhouetted horsemen on the crest of the hill. Lord Enipses and Lord Hilaskos were forming up patrols. Each led a hundred lances, charged above all things with the Wanax's safety. With Strymon's camp only fifty stadia away and his scouts perhaps no farther than the other side of the hill, a century of lances was none too few.

A voice called the challenge and Lord Drumold replied. Someone else observed loudly that if a certain misbegotten son of a she-goat was late serving the Wanax's dinner, in the morning he'd find himself serving the Wanax's hounds.

Ganton called a squire to hold his horse and dismounted. He wanted to set a good example for those of his knights whose pride in their shiny-bright armor kept them in the saddle, never mind how their preoccupation with their looks wearied their horses. Hadn't the bheromen and knights of the Wanax of Frankia lost a great battle to the Wanax of Angeland by doing just that? Lord Rick had told him such a story, and his tales of battle rang true, even when he himself had not been in the field. To be sure, Lord Rick spoke of battles as though he had been in all of them. *To have been in so many he would have to be three hundred years old. No matter. Those are fine stories for a winter night, and they give soldiers courage and trust in our Captain General.*

The Lord Rick is as wise in war as if he really had been a soldier for centuries, and so far he has freely given his wisdom to the Realm of Drantos. Yatar, Vothan, and Christ grant that he continue.

Food and Lord Drumold arrived at the same time. Ganton and Drumold drew a little apart and ate their sausage, bread, and cheese in silence. It was a cold meal. Ganton had forbidden fires with the enemy this close, at least until the Second Division arrived tomorrow and the army was complete.

"Mergil," Ganton called softly.

"My lord?"

"Go to the duty commander and have him send two squadrons of Hussars to patrol the roads between the First Division and the Second."

"Ye suspect my son may have forgotten?" Drumold asked.

Ganton listened for any tone of resentment but heard none. "Well, my lord, with the enemy so close in front, perhaps my Lords Balquhain and Teuthras have not given thought to the rear. We are all still learning the new ways of war. But I am Wanax, and if any important thing is left undone, it will be on my head."

"Aye," Drumold muttered. "We all learn from my daughter's husband." He went back to his sausages and cheese.

And I thank Yatar for this alliance. We need the clansmen in this war. "Not that Strymon can place any great force between Balquhain and Teuthras," Ganton said. "Our scouts will warn us if Strymon sends out a troop of any size."

Drumold grunted.

"But it does not take any large force of cavalry to ravage our supplies. We will need all our firepowder, and fodder for the horses—"

"Aye, lad—Majesty," Drumold said. He chuckled. "And I too have commanded on nights before battles. 'Tis no easy thing."

They heard the staff officer ride away to carry Ganton's orders to the Hussars, then moments later the sound of galloping hoofbeats reached them from the far side of the hill. Ganton stood and lifted his battle-axe. Drumold continued with his sausages.

"Who is there?" the sentry demanded.

"Messenger from Lord Balquhain, for the Wanax Ganton!"

Indistinct mumbling, then several horses moved on at a trot. Ganton laid down his axe and sat again on his saddle as the messenger reached him.

"Majesty, Majesty! A message for you. An urgent message! I am bidden—"

"You are bidden to stop stammering and give me the message. The sooner the better." Out of the corner of his eye, Ganton saw Drumold trying not to smile.

"Yes, Majesty. Prince Strymon has released the Eqetassa Tylara do Tamaerthon and enough of our captive knights to form an escort of honor. They have met our scouts. Lord Balquhain will furnish them fresh mounts and send them to you guarded by a squadron of his Hussars."

Drumold opened his mouth and dropped a piece of cheese. The Wanax smiled to himself and turned away. Give him a moment to compose himself. He has known for some time that his daughter was alive, and we heard from the priests of Yatar that she is well, but who can know? And there is the evil rumor that Tylara went alone to charge Strymon's cavalry at Piro's Hill. That must be a lie, but it also must have given her father many sleepless nights.

"My Lord Mac Clallan Muir. Will you ride with me to greet the Eqetassa?" Drumold's face gave Ganton his answer.

"Was there any word of Lord Morrone?" It was said he'd survived the battle, but wounds and captivity might have done for him.

"I am bidden to tell you that the Lord Morrone is alive

and well and giving honorable service to the Realm." The messenger looked at Drumold, then at Ganton. "Your Majesty, this was for your ears only—"

Drumold swore and Ganton glared. "Pray cease insulting Lord Drumold. Or have you some reason to suggest that his son should not trust him?"

The messenger gulped. "Pardon, Majesty. Lord Balquhain says further that the Eqetassa brings an urgent message from Prince Strymon, heir to the Wanax of Ta-Meltemos."

"Indeed." Ganton spoke to keep his mouth from gaping open in a manner quite unfitting to a Wanax. What could his enemy want? "Then it is all the more important that we bring the Lady Eqetassa safely home." He took a deep breath and squared his shoulders.

"Squires! To horse!"

Ganton, Drumold, Balquhain, and Tylara huddled near the tiny fire. A score of bodyguards stood just beyond earshot, and the others patrolled farther out.

"Peace," Ganton said. "On what terms?"

"Aid in surviving the Time," Tylara said. "Alliance against invaders, and a promise of aid after the Demon has withdrawn from our skies."

"And in return?" Ganton prompted.

"Ta-Meltemos withdraws from Drantos. Majesty, Prince Strymon may even lend his personal aid to Drantos. He has no love for Chancellor Issardos and his agent Matthias."

"You speak of Prince Strymon's promises. He is not Wanax of Ta-Meltemos. Not *yet*."

Tylara forced a smile. "Majesty, Prince Strymon betrays neither Wanax nor father. The stories we have heard are true. Wanax Palamon has the mind of a child."

Ganton shivered. "Yatar grant me death before that. It

seems that we must meet, Prince Strymon and I, and soon. The loss of Prince Strymon's army will do great harm to Toris."

"Losing Strymon as a general will do even more," Balquhain said.

"That is so. Now tell me, Lady Tylara, why was Morrone not released?"

Tylara sipped hot tea and brandy. "He did not wish it, Majesty. Lord Morrone said that my own release might be managed without offending the High Rexja's captains or exposing Strymon's suit for peace with Drantos. But Lord Morrone could not honorably accept his own unransomed release without that of all the other prisoners. That would surely give the enemy more than a hint of our plans."

"Arrh. We could do wi' a bit less honor an' a bit more common sense." Drumold spat into the fire.

Ganton's face was unreadable. Tylara decided it didn't much matter whether she knew what he was thinking. *One thing's certain. There's very little of the boy about our Wanax.* She found that thought oddly comforting.

"I continued to talk with Strymon," Tylara said. "He fears no man, but he truly fears the Time."

"As he should," Ganton said.

"As he should. Then we received word that the vanguard of Toris's great host was on the march to join us. We had also heard that the Host of Drantos was on its way north. Prince Strymon feared that battle was inevitable, and once our forces were engaged, peace might be impossible."

"Then Morrone escaped."

"Escaped?" Ganton asked. "Surely he had given his parole—"

"It seems he had not. It had never been asked. From the moment they lifted him from where he fell he had been treated as guest, not prisoner—"

Balquhain chuckled. "An easy mistake."

"So where is Morrone?" Ganton demanded.

"I know only the plan he told me," Tylara said. "He intended to gather as many of his southern forces as he could, and any clansmen who might follow him, and go north to harass Toris and delay his march."

Ganton smiled for the first time. "There are places north of the Sutmarg where fifty archers can stand off an army for a whole day. Perhaps we should send reinforcements."

"Aye," Tylara said. *And I did that once, in the war against Sarakos. Long ago.*

"Indeed," said Balquhain. "But how should we make our way back across the Sutmarg, if the rains come again and the rivers rise?"

Tylara looked at her brother with new respect. He would not have asked that question two years ago. *My lord husband, you will have more and stranger monuments than you can imagine.*

"All the better, for neither the enemy's host nor Morrone's men will be able to cross the Sutmarg," Ganton said. "We shall have all the time we need to parley with Strymon, and prepare a warm reception for the enemy when they *do* cross."

"And it were me of the older days, I'd not be returning at all wi'out a victory to dim the memory o' Piro's Hill," Drumold said.

"So Morrone has ridden north, then?" Ganton asked.

"Three days ago. His escape delayed my release. Prince Strymon was not pleased to have a wolf free behind him. But then the Prince realized that if we waited any longer, Toris might send south a band of horse too strong for my escort. We rode out of the camp as the Demon Sun was rising."

"And Apelles? Yanulf will ask after him," Ganton said.

"He is in no danger now that Matthias and his minions have fled. He stayed to tend the sick and wounded."

"And to send us information as he can," Drumold said. "'Twas how we knew ye'd not been harmed."

"Then we must act swiftly," Ganton said. "Before Toris merges his army with Strymon's."

"Majesty, there is more you must know—"

"My lady, it will wait until morning. Your rest cannot."
Ganton stood. "Lord Enipses!"

"Majesty!"

"Take your lances and join the scouts. Our patrols must
be able to fight an enemy as well as to find him. For the next
three days you must prevent any enemy spies from leaving
our realm alive. This is most important."

"Majesty."

"Lord Hilaskos, you will ride north with me tomorrow to
view the battlefield my rangers have chosen. We must be
able to fight either, neither, or both of the foreign hosts in
the land of Drantos. That will mean bringing up the Great
Guns as well as the Musketeers—yes, Lord Enipses?"

"Surely Your Majesty will not ride north with less than the
entire host? At least let me come with you."

"I have given you your task. Do you refuse it?"

"No, Majesty."

"Good."

"And what of treachery?" Balquhain asked quietly. "I
have never met the man who could deceive my sister, but
there is always the first time."

Drumold glared at his son, but his frown showed his concern.

"I know I was not deceived," Tylara said. "In any event I
will go with Your Majesty."

"That you will *not*," Ganton said. "I will be surrounded by
the best fighting men of Drantos and Tamaerthon. Nothing
that can catch us can beat us. Now, peace. Unless there is
more—discussion?"

No one spoke. Whatever doubts remained, no one would
give them tongue in front of a Wanax who had clearly made
up his mind.

Ganton called his staff officers to arrange foraging parties
and other details of battle. Tylara drew her cloak more
tightly about her.

Drumold stood. "You're exhausted, Lass. Come."

She remembered her father leading her·from the tiny

council fire to a tent that seemed miles away. She remembered his laying her on a bed as if she were a child, and pulling furs over her until at last she stopped shivering. She remembered swallowing most of a cup of hot wine. Then she remembered nothing more.

The True Sun had risen and nearly set again when Tylara awoke to see her father sitting beside her bed. His eyes were red with lack of sleep, and for the first time she saw how much of the gray in his beard had turned to white.

She smiled. "Thank you, Father."

He smiled back. "And what good would I be, lass, if I couldna help ye in a time of need? The gods willing, I'll be ready to hand for many a year yet." He handed her a bowl of porridge and watched as if determined to force it into her by sheer will. When she had emptied the bowl, Drumold took it from her, stood up, and went outside briefly. When he returned, the smile was gone.

"This is the Wanax's own tent, so I much doubt there'd be any ears about that shouldna be. Still, best to be sure...."

The frown deepened. "Daughter, there have been rumors of what ye did near the end of the battle. Or rather, rumors of what ye wouldna do, which is to let yourself be saved to fight another day. I ask ye for the truth."

Tylara wanted to weep with sheer relief, to learn that her father had guessed so little of the truth, and that little something she could talk about freely. A moment later she was weeping in her father's arms.

When she was done, he found a cloth to wipe her face and pulled a stool close to the bed. "I willna say that a lost battle is nothing. But no orders of yours began that battle. 'Twas Morrone, who never did know the value of the clansmen. I am thinking that the Wanax will have aye to say to him on that."

"But, Father, I obeyed him."

"I should hope ye did! Would ye be like Dughuilas, always disputing orders until someone sent him to dispute wi' Vothan?"

Tylara shuddered, but Drumold did not notice. "I'd disown ye, an' ye did that! Daughter, I've gone myself where you went the day of Piro's Hill. Aye. Long before you were born, I led the clansmen against Roman slave raiders. I led them back too, but many fewer than I led out.

"I thought the gods had turned from me, and long I stood on the great cliff looking down at the sea. But I could no hear the gods' voices clear, only my own shame, and it seemed a coward's deed, to run away from only that.

"So I walked away from the cliff, and when next I led the clansmen forth, the Romans bled as much as we. That was when I fought side by side with your mother's kin, and how ye came to be."

"But—"

"Hush. Your luck's better than mine. I had to wait half a year to know my luck had turned. Ye charmed the very man who took ye prisoner, until now he's thinking after giving away his whole victory!"

"It may be a false promise."

"Hah. Your brother said it. Who last fooled you? Lass, lass, you must no think less of yourself than you are worth. Modesty is no virtue for those who lead good men to war."

CHAPTER SIX

The wide valley was green with maize not yet high enough to form ears. Tents stood at each end, green and white at the north, blue and gold to the south. As the True Sun stood high overhead, a single trumpet sounded in the southern camp, to be answered by one from the north.

Ganton mounted carefully. *Vaulting into the saddle is all very well, but this is no time to break a leg. Or be in pain.*

Drumold was helped to his saddle by Balquhain.

"I like this not," Hilaskos said. He glared at Drumold.

Ganton ignored him. He signaled to his squire to raise the banner of the Fighting Man and ride ahead. Ganton and Drumold followed.

"Be careful of the corn," Ganton said.

Drumold nodded. "Aye. An' this goes not well—"

If this doesn't go well, there won't be anything standing here, or in a dozen other valleys.

A party of three rode toward them from the other end of the valley.

"We're out o' range o' *their* bows," Drumold said.

And the center is beyond range of both. But Drumold has a point. I wonder what orders he has given those clansmen of his? "By Yatar, he's brought Apelles!"

"So 'tis no trick," Drumold said. "Or Strymon's the greatest fool in nine kingdoms."

Ganton's squire reached the tiny flag the scouts had set twenty paces short of the field's center. He halted, and Ganton rode on ahead. Drumold waited with the squire.

"Hail, Prince Strymon."

"Hail, Wanax Ganton."

He dresses well. Ganton smiled grimly. His own armor was still stained with dust from the trail, and the golden helmet tied to his saddle had dents from battle. Despite the protests of his bodyguards he'd left his axe and carried a jewel-hilted sword of state, not really fit for war, but otherwise he looked very much the commander of an army.

If Strymon wore armor, it was concealed under his green and white surcoat and scarlet silk cape. His sword was hilted in amber, and he wore gold rings on fingers and ears.

No helm or shield. Ganton relaxed. He unslung a flask from his saddle horn. "Wine, My Lord?" He poured into the goblet that hung from his saddle, drank, and turned the goblet over to show it was empty.

Strymon grinned. "With pleasure, Majesty." They came closer together. Strymon accepted the flask, drank deeply, and returned it. "Excellent wine. I should have my vintners speak to yours."

"Thank you."

Strymon's grin faded. "If the Time leaves any grapes at all in our lands. Your pardon, Majesty, but we have little time this day. The High Rexja's army approaches, and much of his vanguard will be in my camp by tomorrow night."

Ganton shrugged. "Highness—your army is in my lands, not mine in yours."

"Yes. I received my orders, and I obeyed them—"

"Whose orders?"

"Yes. You know, then. Orders signed by Wanax Palamon, but never written—never *understood* by him."

"In a word, orders from Toris."

"Or Issardos." Strymon shrugged. "Does it matter? The question now is, can we come to terms we can both accept? I confess, Majesty, that I have always been a simple soldier. I am not accustomed to thinking like the Wanax of Ta-Meltemos. War has been my profession. Now I must think of my people."

"I see you have brought Apelles."

"Yes. He has much experience at—what he calls *administration*. I have learned much from him. Majesty, I know his true loyalty is not to me."

"Nor to me," Ganton said. "Apelles serves Yanulf, who may be my Chancellor, but who is first and always Highpriest of Yatar. You could have chosen a worse advisor."

Strymon shrugged. "Except for military officers, there is no one in my camp I can trust not to give first loyalty to Chancellor Rauros or his master Issardos."

"Highness, if you wish the services of Apelles for the future, I am certain Yanulf will give his consent." *He'd better!* "This is an odd moment. We each have an army. We each believe we would win victory were we to fight."

"And we would each lose no matter who has won," Strymon said. "Were it not for the Time, it would be—interesting to see whether your *guns* could make the difference. I tell you this, no army of mine is going to ride down this valley against nine of those monsters."

Ganton grinned wryly. "Your scouts are better than I had thought. But we have eleven."

"Nine. One has lost a wheel, and another was overturned in a river last night."

Yatar, Christ, and Vothan! "I—see. Thank you, my lord. Battle between us might very well be more—interesting—than either of us would like. But your army must leave my Realm!"

"Of course. That will not be as easy to accomplish as I would like." Strymon's voice dropped even lower. "Majesty, less than half my troops are of Ta-Meltemos."

"Issardos again."

"Yes. I see now that he schemes to make the High Rexja into a Great King of Kings, and I have been his catspaw. Majesty, all of the chivalry of Ta-Meltemos will follow me north, but the rest probably will not."

A problem I cannot solve for you, my friend. "Where will you go?"

"To the Green Palace, to send Rauros packing! I see my duty is to take the throne, in fact if not in name."

"A hard decision."

"Not so hard. My father will not know the difference."

"I grieve for you." *My father knew he had been cast out. You're lucky, my friend.* "Now to terms. You will withdraw your army. Ta-Meltemos will give no more aid to the Five Kingdoms in war against Drantos, and will send aid to Drantos in war against anyone *but* the Five Kingdoms."

Strymon considered. "I can agree to this. In return, you seek no reparations for damages done in this campaign, and you will share your knowledge of the Time with us."

"That is easier to agree to than you think," Ganton said. "Even if we all stand together, few enough will survive the Time and the *skyfire* that follows."

"Those stories are true, then?"

"You will learn." Ganton raised his voice. "Apelles."

"Majesty?"

"Prince Strymon, may he approach?"

"Certainly. Apelles, if you please."

Apelles rode up to join them. "Majesty. Highness."

"Apelles, from the moment that Prince Strymon's army marches northward and out of Drantos, you will share with him all your knowledge of the Time, and of our preparations for it, saving only what you may know of our recent troop movements."

"All." Apelles tilted his head to one side. "All?"

"All. Including the sky box that talks, and the great sky-ship you have seen. All."

"I gather I am not to go home so soon as I thought," Apelles said dryly.

"I am certain that Yanulf will consent," Ganton said.

Apelles grinned. "So am I. Majesty, I must send letters—"

"Of course. We will send apprentices and a priest to aid you, as befits your new station." *And Yanulf will make you a bishop at least, or he's going to find it harder to collect his tithes.*

"May I offer advice, Majesty?" Apelles said.

"Why do you think you're here? Speak!"

"I do not care for the reports I receive from the Green Palace," Apelles said.

"What do you know of my father that I do not?" Strymon demanded.

"Only that Rauros grows more bold. Highness, think upon what might happen if a messenger brings a Royal Writ under the Great Seal, accusing you of treason. Or accusing Wanax Ganton of atrocities and demanding that his lands be laid waste. Or—"

"I see. I must return at once."

"Highness, you cannot," Apelles said. "Without you, your army will put this land to the sword."

"Then what must be done?"

"Send Prince Teodoros. At once."

The lady Tylara does not think much of Teodoros. How can I say this?

"Apelles, my brother is loyal, but he—"

"Is no statesman," Apelles said. "True. He will need good advice, which we must be at pains to send often. But I see no other way."

Strymon looked thoughtful. "It may be enough. I suppose you can suggest an advisor to accompany him?"

"Prakes, priest of Yatar," Apelles said.

"Um. I would have thought him young, but yes, he has my brother's respect if any churchman does. A convert to the new faith, I believe—"

I would wager half a kingdom he is a convert, Ganton thought. "Highness, I see we must move swiftly. Shall we bring witnesses to our agreement?"

"I am ready. Yon squire is Bheroman Tarmon do Karimos. I am afraid I cannot trust many more of my officers to know our terms."

"Bring him then. I will summon Drumold, and we five will be witness enough."

"You are mad!" Bheroman Darkon pounded on the council table. "Withdraw? Nonsense. We lost time while you were enthralled by that highland witch, but we can still thrust to the walls of Edron in a ten-day!"

Strymon stared at the map on the table, then lifted his eyes to scan the faces of the dozen lords and officers around him. He thought most approved of Darkon's speech. "Perhaps, if the weather holds," Strymon said. "And what then?"

"Then we will have won!"

"We will have won nothing. Edron will not fall to threats. Let me remind you, my Lord Darkon, it is they, not we, who have the *guns.*"

At least two barons muttered approval.

"Then we must destroy them in the field. Kill or capture that boy king of theirs. That will certainly bring us victory."

"It is easy enough to speak of destruction, and I do not doubt we could hurt Ganton badly. But my lords, the trick is to avoid being destroyed ourselves. You've heard the reports of our scouts. Before he left us so strangely, Matthias told us what *guns* and star weapons can do. Ganton seeks no battle. He will choose a strong position and make us come to him. My lords, I doubt no one's courage, but this is no way to make war."

"If you hadn't stopped here," Darkon said.

"My lord," Strymon said gently, "I was ordered to remain here to await the High Rexja's army."

"So we serve fools—or—" Darkon caught himself.

Pity. Had he said 'coward' I could have killed him with honor. "I will not hear that said of our High King," Strymon said. "Nor yet of me, and I would *be* a fool to remain here facing the host of Drantos on its own terms. Captain Ninas, how long will the fodder last?"

"Highness, no more than a ten-day. Even now we feed the horses but seven pecks of the eight they need."

Bheroman Abados grunted. "And meanwhile Ganton's tame wolf Morrone rages through *my* lands. Whatever the rest of you do, I want permission to take my forces home and put a stop to that."

"Granted," Strymon said.

Some of the others glared.

"My lords, many of your homes are far from here. Think upon the Time."

"Legends," someone said.

"It is legend that the seas rise? That the rains come late, then beat the crops into the ground? The Demon Sun is no legend." Strymon shrugged. "I do not know what the other kingdoms will do, but Ta-Meltemos cannot afford war with men when the very gods war with one another across our lands!"

"You seek peace without the High Rexja's permission!" someone shouted. "Treason!"

"The High Rexja is not *yet* Great King," Strymon said. "And who here wants him to be? My lords, do you all wish to be slaves to Issardos?"

"By Vothan, it *is* treason!" Darkon shouted. "Guards! Treason, treason!"

"My lord, I think you do not wish to shout so loud, lest *my* guards believe you threaten me," Strymon said carefully.

Darkon dashed to the tent doorway. "Soldiers! Hear me! Prince Strymon abandons the High Rexja!"

A dozen troops in the green and white of Ta-Meltemos charged forward with drawn swords. Strymon held up his hand. "Let him speak," he said.

Darkon opened his mouth to shout, and saw that everyone within earshot wore green and white. "I see." He turned to Strymon. "Will you let me address the troops in assembly, then?"

Strymon grinned. "Certainly, my lord. As soon as we are across the border."

Interlude
LUNA

Agzaral sat across the table from the three *Shalnuksis*. "My thanks, Excellencies, for setting the cabin temperature for human comfort."

"You are welcome," Karreeel answered.

Agzaral had dealt with *Shalnuksis* long enough to recognize the tone. They wanted something. It would take some time to find out what. *Shalnuksis* were long-lived and had a great deal more patience than humans.

They had arrayed themselves in their traditional pattern. Karreeel, the only one Agzaral had much experience of, sat in the middle chair. That meant the others outranked him. The *Shalnuksis* to his left wore the silver-blue tunic of the Council of Merchants. Badges of civic achievement decorated his collar. Agzaral knew nothing else about him except that his name was Lyaaarin.

The third *Shalnuksis* was Tsirovv, one of the nine members of the committee known as the Sentinels of Governance. *Shalnuksi* government was complex, with a multiplicity of officers and officials, and a Grand Council that was in theory supreme. The Sentinels were something between Ephors and ombudsmen, and were supposed to represent the best of *Shalnuksi* business ethics.

Agzaral smiled to himself. The best in business ethics did not prevent the Sentinel from coming to Luna to negotiate what was, after all, if not a criminal activity, then certainly one the *Shalnuksis* did not care to have come to the attention of the Confederation and its Council.

Tsirovv was nearing the end of a long career, begun in

the year Louis XIV of France died. He was one of the few living *Shalnuksis* with a reputation for statesmanship. His presence on this unexpected delegation to Luna could mean anything. *The matter is more important than I had thought.*

Agzaral's smile was exaggerated. *Shalnuksis* did not easily read human expressions; best to make them unambiguous. "Excellencies, how may I serve you?"

Karreeel made some entries in the portable computer on the table in front of him and inclined his head toward the Councilor. The Councilor contracted his nasal slit, the *Shalnuksi* equivalent of a frown.

"Do you wish to claim that the additional heavy weapons and ammunition were procured and shipped to Tran by the Slave Les without your knowledge?"

"Should I? Excellencies, my time is yours, but surely you have not come all this way to discuss trivia. I sent Captain Galloway most of the equipment he requested, including ammunition, toilet paper, a product known as 'Preparation H,' and cartons of a particular brand of cigarette. I believe you have an inventory. If not, I can provide one. Are you suggesting I have overcharged you?"

"Do not be hasty," Karreeel said. He exchanged looks left and right. "We must be certain you are in control of what can be—a delicate situation."

Delicate. If the Council officially hears of what you're doing, 'delicate' won't begin to describe the situation. For you or for me. "Excellencies, many matters demand my attention, but be assured that I am fully aware of Tran and what happens there. As witness the fact that I have, here on Luna, more and better *surinomaz* than you have seen in your lifetimes."

"Ah." The three exchanged looks again. "We knew we had made a good choice in you, Inspector."

"Thank you. You have arrived just in time. I was about to send the *surinomaz* to the usual place. Now you may collect it and save us all trouble."

"Thank you. That is however not why we have come."

"Indeed. Excellencies, I forget my manners. Will you have refreshment? I have a well-stocked bar, and the kitchen staff has been informed of your arrival. Luna is not the Capital, to be sure, but I think our provinces are not entirely barren. There is an ethanol-based drink known as 'Grand Marnier' which I think you might enjoy."

"Perhaps a sip," Karreeel said. "After our talk."

"As you wish, Excellencies."

"Inspector, I believe you are often invited to attend meetings of the High Commission."

"I have been, Excellencies. Not since I was sent to Luna, of course."

"You have agents there." Tsirovv spoke for the first time.

Agzaral kept his smile tiny and ambiguous. "Excellencies, I have many friends in many places."

"We know the ways of Important Slaves," Tsirovv said. He looked again at Karreeel.

"Inspector, we have also heard disturbing rumors of the actions of the Council," Karreeel said.

Time to get down to cases. "Yes, Excellencies?"

"Actions that may affect our trade."

"Ah. Excellencies, are you not aware that no one of my rank is ever truly alone?" He looked exaggeratedly at the walls.

The three exchanged glances again. "We trust your—discretion," Tsirovv said. "We will speak if you will."

"How may I serve you?"

Karreeel flared his nasal slits, and the color of his eyes changed to a deeper shade of blue. "Inspector, we are told that the Council is contemplating decisions regarding the development of Earth. Meanwhile, they have become much more strict about contact with humans. We have heard there was a motion to bombard Earth."

"Tabled by a large majority," Agzaral said.

"But the suggestion was made. Inspector, how many in the Council know of the existence of Tran?"

And now we have come to the point. "More than one. Not all."

"That is not a satisfactory answer."

"It is all the answer I have, Excellencies. I have given no information to the Council. I know that at least one group of the Ader'at'eel is thoroughly aware of Tran, but they seem as determined to keep that a secret as we are."

This time the silence was long. Agzaral had long wondered whether the *Shalnuksis* were telepathic. If so they were unique. *On the other hand, it may be equipment. Transceivers in their heads. That never worked for humans although it should have.*

"We thank you," Karreeel said.

Agzaral bowed to acknowledge the compliment. *Threw you, didn't it? You're not in a position to take on the Ader'at'eel. That would take a bigger coalition than you'll ever build.*

"What is the Council likely to do about Tran?" Karreeel asked.

"Excellencies, I do not know."

"We wish you to find out. We will not be ungrateful."

"It will not be easy. It takes—resources—to keep my friends in the Capital."

"We know this," Tsirovv said.

"I believe we may be able to help," Karreeel said.

"Excellencies, I shall endeavor to give satisfaction." *You cannot possibly have read Wodehouse.* "Now shall I send for refreshments?"

PART SIX
Church
and State

CHAPTER ONE

Castle Fasolt rose proudly from a low hill at the border between Drantos and the Five Kingdoms. Ganton reined in at the top of the path it guarded, and looked down at it with his binoculars. Details were easy to see in the midmorning sun. The ground around the castle had been cleared and plowed for a Roman mile. The gates were closed, and the only road up the hill was blocked with stakes and barbs.

"I see no streams," Lord Enipses said. "Perhaps thirst will force Ajacias—"

"There are both cisterns and a spring," Ganton said. "I've been there."

"Ah. Majesty, may I?"

"Certainly." Ganton didn't like parting with his binoculars for even a moment, but the request was reasonable. He put the strap over Enipses' head before letting go of them. The University craftsmen were making single tubes they called *telescopes* that worked much as the binoculars, but the images were never as clear. Some of them even turned things upside down!

Ganton waited until Enipses had finished his examination and he had retrieved his star gift. "Well?"

"It will be no easy task," Enipses said reluctantly. "Even with the Great Guns."

Only one of the field pieces was really suitable as a siege cannon. The others could not fire heavy enough balls far enough to be useful against walls. Ganton had been told this often enough that he believed it, although he still did not understand why. Artillery remained a black art practiced by wizards, mostly the sons of craftsmen. *I should have paid more attention to those classes at the University. I know this now. Why didn't I then?*

"Still, we must take it," Ganton said. "We cannot leave open this gate to Drantos."

"Majesty," Enipses said, "without disrespect—can we not take that castle in the same way that we drove Prince Strymon's armies from Drantos?"

"What do you know of this?" Ganton demanded.

"Majesty, it is common knowledge! The Lady Tylara—somehow enchanted Prince Strymon. The highpriest Apelles brought him to the knowledge of the New Christ, and Your Majesty showed him that his invasion of our lands was a sin. Everyone knows this."

"Everyone knows this. I see." *Not only do they not give me credit for victory, I have the least part of this matter. Lord Rick once said there is no limit to what you can accomplish if you do not demand credit for it. I see I am learning this lesson better than I wanted to.* "Does everyone also know how we are going to rest tonight in that castle?"

"No, Majesty, but I am certain you do."

Yatar's Teeth. Ganton lifted the binoculars to study Castle Fasolt again. *A third or more of those I see on the walls wear green and white.* Ganton smiled. "Perhaps I do, my lord. Only perhaps."

Rain beat down on the encampment. The Guards had erected enough shelter to keep the royal campfire burning, but it didn't keep out all the rain.

"Perhaps," Enipses muttered.

Ganton laughed. "Not even kings have their own way all the time. At least we have a fire."

"And they have the castle."

"When I invited you to take Lord Morrone's place as Companion during his absence, it did not occur to me that you would adopt his manners. May I have more wine, please?"

"At once, Majesty." Enipses poured from the pewter flagon heating near the fire.

Someone shouted from the distance. "Stand! Who is there?"

"Balquhain do Tamaerthon and guests."

"Stand and be recognized!"

Enipses jumped to his feet. "Guards—"

"That was Balquhain," Ganton said. "Didn't you recognize his voice?"

"Yes, sire—"

"And he would not come here without reason. Sit down before you insult him."

"Guests, you said." Ganton looked at the cloaked figures around his campfire. "Guests. Prince Strymon, what are you doing here?"

Strymon laughed. "Majesty, I am a fugitive."

"You?"

"My choices were to flee or continue a civil war within my own army." He glanced nervously at the others around the fire.

"I think it matters little who hears us and who doesn't," Ganton said. "Still—" He sighed. "Lord Enipses, if you please, I would be alone with Prince Strymon and Lord Balquhain."

"Majesty—"

"And Apelles, of course." Ganton poured wine while Enipses led the others out of the shelter. "Now, Highness, if you are comfortable—"

Strymon sat on the log nearest the fire. "Majesty. The vanguard of the High Rexja arrived as my rear guard crossed the border. Matthias led the Royal Bodyguard. He carried a direct commission from Toris relieving me of command, and ordering my arrest for high treason."

"I—see." Ganton sat heavily on the log across the fire from Strymon.

"I had sent home most of the Melteme troops as escort

for my brother. Only my personal Guard remained. They were sufficient to prevent Matthias carrying out his order immediately, but he and Bheroman Darkon then appealed to the soldiers from the other kingdoms. The host of Ta-Boreas rallied around Darkon, and the others were ready to follow."

"Highness, could you not have sent for your Meltemes?" Balquhain asked.

"Perhaps, my lord, but it seemed better to let them ride on. I would rather see my brother secure in the Green Palace than have more of my Meltemes killed in a hopeless civil war."

"Then I confess, Highness, I do not know how you got here alive," Ganton said.

"My Lord Father Apelles," Strymon said. "He did what I never could have. As Darkon and Matthias sought to rally the troops against me, and I saw to arming myself, Apelles rode up and down the lines of the army shouting to all the New Christians. 'Brothers! Will you fight your Brothers? Will you take arms against the Nuncio of Archbishop Polycarp and Highpriest Yanulf?'"

Ganton looked quizzically at Apelles. Apelles' face retreated deeper into the cowl of his robe.

"Great Yatar," Balquhain muttered.

"His speech was—heard, then," Ganton said.

"The army dissolved. Some came to me. Some threw their weapons down. Many rallied around my Lord Father Apelles, to stand between him and any who would do him harm."

"Apelles—"

"With apologies, sire, he deserves his titles," Strymon said.

Ganton gulped. "My Lord Father Apelles—"

"Majesty?"

"I think we will speak later. I also think Highpriest Yanulf will have something to say."

"I make no doubt of it," Apelles said. "But Majesty—I could think of nothing else to do. And soon Bheroman Darkon approached Prince Strymon, to offer him safe conduct from the camp—"

"He ordered me out," Strymon said. "And I was glad to go."

"How much of your army came with you?" Ganton asked.

"Perhaps one part in ten. At least that many more simply went home."

"He has lost a quarter of his strength, then."

"Of Prince Strymon's own soldiers, Majesty," Apelles said. "And one part in ten of those who came with Matthias have seen the True Light. They await Your Majesty's inspection at the perimeter of this camp. Lord Drumold is with them."

Lord Rick always said there are better ways to conquer than battles and war. I should have believed him. "My Lord Father Apelles, you have done well indeed. Prince Strymon, who will command their army now?"

"They have sent for Prince Akkilas."

"The Heir himself? Sarakos's brother?"

"I think the army would follow no one else."

"He is said to be hotheaded," Ganton said. "Is this why his father has kept him from command?"

"Hah. High Rexja Toris sent the boy to me to learn the art of war. I think he has listened to too many of the tales of the prowess of his name hero. After a month I sent him back to Teveron to organize reinforcements and supplies. He is intelligent enough, but young and impetuous. It is dangerous to trust such a one with soldiers who will follow without question."

Something to remember. Lord Rick would do much with this knowledge. Perhaps I can as well. "Well. In any case, Highness, welcome to my hospitality, such as it is."

Strymon laughed. "Why, Majesty, I thank you, but will you allow me to offer you mine? I know a much dryer place we can sleep tonight."

The stamping feet of Guardsmen sword dancers and the drone of pipes made the Great Hall of Lord Ajacias's Castle

Fasolt as noisy as a battlefield. The Wanax Ganton watched from the High Table. Prince Strymon sat at his right, and the Lord Highpriest Apelles at his left. Stewards filled their wine cups as fast as they were emptied.

Ganton remembered the last time he had sat at this table in this hall. *Well over a year ago. I received a letter from Octavia. I think it was then I knew we'd marry.*

On Lord Rick's advice he had honored Lord Ajacias with a royal visit. It had been intended to uncover any plots Ajacias might contemplate, and strip him of the gold he needed to carry them out.

Perhaps the High Rexja Toris sent more gold. Perhaps Ajacias was a greater fool than anyone could imagine. For whatever reason, this was one plan of Lord Rick's that hadn't succeeded. Ajacias had gone on plotting until he admitted Prince Strymon's army into Drantos.

Thanks to Prince Strymon, the traitor cannot be hanged. It was a bitter thought. Before Strymon would order his men to eject Ajacias and open the castle gates, he had made Ganton swear to exile Ajacias.

In his place I could do no less. But the Lady Tylara is not pleased, and I think Lord Rick will be no more so. Yet what choice had I? It would take half a year to reduce this castle. My people are better employed growing food for the Time.

Ganton gulped wine, then grinned. *Only five companions chose to go with Ajacias. He will live without gold, wi'hout friends, in a foreign court. He may yet wish he had been hanged.*

At that last banquet the Lady Cara, Ajacias's daughter and heir, had partnered the Wanax at dinner. Now she was in the custody of Lady Tylara. Morrone had been King's Companion and carved the stag. Now he led a ragged band of *guerrillas* Yatar alone knew where. And Lord Rick had watched from his own table, instead of commanding the Army of Chelm somewhere in the west.

The shaggy head of Master Gunner Pinir loomed through the candle smoke. Prince Strymon stood and raised his wine cup. "Ho, Pinir son of the smith!"

Pinir made his way around the dancers and approached the table. He looked like a full-grown war horse passing through a herd of yearlings. Even when he knelt, his eyes were on a level with Ganton's.

"Your Majesty, Your Highness. I am at your service."

"Indeed, and good service it has been. A full day of instructing me in the mysteries of the Great Guns. You have my thanks."

"Highness, you are most welcome."

Strymon laughed. "Matthias has left me little enough, but you deserve more than thanks."

Strymon rose, and his chair went over backward with a clatter. He took a ring from his finger and gave it to Pinir. "Wear this, in token of my gratitude."

Pinir stood and took the ring. It would barely pass the first joint of his smallest finger. "With your Majesty's permission . . . ?"

"Oh, have it, have it." Ganton waved his hand. "But I ask you, Prince Strymon, why do you presume to reward *my* Master Gunner?"

"Is it so great a presumption?"

"Great enough that I must demand satisfaction."

Strymon laughed. "Indeed, we never broke lances against each other. I rather regret that."

"I am as sorry as you. But I think that is a pleasure we need not be denied. One course with the lance, then on foot with my axe against whatever you choose?"

"My sword, I think. Ah, what a grand spectacle it will be! We can have three knights from each host as judges, with Chancellor Yanulf to cast a deciding vote if need be. We—"

"You will not have Yanulf, Highpriest of Yatar and Co-Vicar of Christ on Tran, to judge this foolish combat," came a voice from behind Ganton. Strymon tried to turn around, caught his feet on his fallen chair, and fell on top of it. Ganton jumped, knocking over his wine cup. The wine dripped from the table onto his robes.

"I will not judge this combat. If you are determined on

this folly, I shall stand in the middle of the lists, and you will have to ride me down!"

Ganton felt about six years old. Without turning around he said, "My Lord Chancellor, you presume rather greatly."

"You may have that office." Yanulf snatched the chain of office from his neck, threw it on the table, and stalked away.

"My Lord—Father Apelles, reason with him!" Ganton said. "Tell him I—tell him any damned thing you like, but give him back this chain!"

"Sire." Apelles took the chain and followed Yanulf toward the back of the hall.

"He'll do it," Strymon said. He tried to get up and fell against the table. "Majesty, I think we had best postpone this tourney."

"I have pondered the matter, and I agree," Ganton said. He looked up. The first eyes he met were Pinir's. The Gunner was still kneeling, with the ring in his hand. His face was the color of dirty chalk.

Ganton hiccoughed. "Master Gunner, I think you will have tales to tell. Tell them well. You are dismissed."

"Majesty—"

"Go!" He looked down and smiled. "Send Prince Strymon's body servants to carry him to his chamber. And when you tell this tale, be sure you say that Wanax Ganton walked to *his* chambers on his own legs!"

"Enter," came Yanulf's voice through the heavy oak door.

Tylara took a deep breath and opened the door. Rusty hinges screamed like demons; her carefully gathered composure weakened. She walked into Yanulf's chamber and pushed the door shut behind her.

Yanulf sprinkled sand on the letter he'd been writing and capped his inkwell. "Greetings, my lady. How can I serve you?" A second look at her face and he rose, pushing a stool toward her. She sat down heavily.

"How fares the Lady Cara?" Yanulf asked. His tone was casual. "We are grateful to you for taking her as your ward."

"You may be," said Tylara, amused in spite of herself. "She is not. She has refused everything this 'hill-robber's daughter' has offered her. Besides, she giggles. I beg you not to speak of this to anyone else," she added. "My brother would be furious, and my father might not hold him back."

"I see." Yanulf pursed his lips. "I think I shall propose that the Lady Cara marry a loyal knight whose lands lie far from the Sutmarg. Perhaps you know of one."

"No." Tylara knew she'd answered too abruptly. "I am glad to see that you wear the chain of the Lord Chancellor."

Yanulf smiled. "Men will be boys. But I doubt you came to me to inspect my attire."

Tylara's mouth was dry. She shook her head.

"I thought not. Daughter, I know that matters have not been easy between you and your lord. You have come to talk to me. Speak."

"It—I—Apelles—Yanulf, I am dishonored in the eyes of the gods. Caradoc's blood is on my hands."

Her words came slowly at first, then faster. "The Lady Gwen had married Caradoc, truly married him before all the clans, yet she could not resist her—former husband— when he returned from the stars. She lay with him. She was not even discreet. Caradoc would learn of it, and when he did, all that my husband had built, all that we had planned, would be lost. In the Name of Yatar, what could I do? The instrument lay in my hands. Father Yanulf, I swear, I had not planned that the Children of Vothan be used that way!"

The candles on Yanulf's table had burned to stubs before she finished.

"Come, my child." She knelt with her head on his knees. Yanulf laid his hand on her shoulder and cleared his throat. "I have no easy answers. Nor do I think you expect one. Indeed, I think you decided there was no answer save your own death. Is that not so?"

Tylara shuddered. "Yes, Father."

"Is that still your belief?"

"As Yatar is my witness, I do not know. I am alive when I expected to be dead. I may even have done some good for my people."

"It is plain to all that you have done much good for your people."

"If you say so. Truly, I do not know. I don't even know whether my life offends the gods."

"Apelles said that you swore—"

"Not to lay hands on myself while I was in Prince Strymon's custody? That is so, and I kept my oath. Now I am free again."

Tylara stared into the fire. Yanulf's silence stretched on for minutes. *I can't look at him. My fate will be written in his face.*

"Penance."

"What?"

"Penance. A rite of the Christians. One confesses one's sins to a priest, who is sworn never to reveal what he hears. The priest then orders one to perform certain—charitable works."

"What—what sort of works?"

"Prayers, pilgrimages, offerings...as he may discover through his own prayer and meditation. One performs them, and thereby is freed of one's guilt, in the eyes of man and the eyes of God."

"In God's—Yatar's eyes."

"Yes. Tylara, your fear is not for yourself. What you fear is the wrath of God against your husband and your children. It was fear for others that drove you to ride against the enemy. If you were as evil as you seem to think, you would be thinking only of yourself. You are not a monster, and neither god nor man will call you such if you open your heart to them."

All the tears Tylara had been holding back flowed in a rush. "But how can my husband forgive me? I never told him what I did. And now he seeks heirs by another."

"What makes you think this?"

"He is cold. He is never alone with me."

Yanulf wiped her eyes. "Tylara, have you never thought that he has discovered your secret? And that he is cold because he believes you do not trust him?"

"I— No."

"I would be amazed if he had not. As to seeking heirs by another, there is little I do not hear, and I have never heard that."

"Never?"

"Not one word."

"Then what must I do?"

"Tell him everything."

"After the best part of two years?"

"Yes. It is only your pride that fills you with doubts. The Christians show great wisdom when they call pride one of the Seven Deadly Sins. Where is the sense in thinking the worst of your husband when you will not speak to him? Can speaking to him be so much harder than speaking to me?"

"You have learned much of the Christians' ways. Father Yanulf, have you yourself been baptized?"

"Child, I have told you nothing tonight that is not written in books."

"This—penance. Can it be offered to those who have not been baptized as Christians?"

"Christians or New Christians? The Faith of the New Christ holds confession and penance as sacraments."

"Then can you—"

"You have already made your confession."

"Then what is my penance?"

"Child, it is my turn to confess. This is new enough to me that I must meditate and pray. I know this much. You must make amends."

"I have stood as godmother to Caradoc's child—"

"Not to Caradoc. To the Children of Vothan. You have robbed them of their innocence."

Tylara turned away from him. Tears streamed unchecked. "I had—I had not wanted to. They were lost, and—" She waited, hoping that Yanulf would interrupt, but he said nothing. "They were lost, and I used them for my own ends! Father Yanulf, what must I do?"

"You must see that they learn new trades. Trades of honor. You cannot restore their innocence. What you can do is give them, not pride, but faith in themselves."

"Trades of honor? They know no skills but death— Wait! Father—those who know the skills of assassins can also protect! What better dog to guard sheep than a wolf? Would that fulfill this penance?"

"Lady Tylara, what are you thinking of?"

"Prince Teodoros. I do not believe he will long be alive in the Green Palace. Unless—"

Yanulf was silent for a moment. He fingered the Great Seal of Drantos on its chain. "You still command the Children?"

"Yes, Father."

"Then—I lay it upon you. A portion of your penance shall be to send those Children to protect Prince Teodoros. Go. Go quickly. And go with God."

CHAPTER TWO

Ben Murphy dipped his pen into the ink horn.

Task Force Murphy War Diary. Mission Day Twenty-three. Position seventeen kilometers WSW of Shora's Rift, northern portion of the Sutmarg.

Day's march fourteen kilometers. Day's casualties one dead (sunstroke), one MIA, six horses disabled and abandoned. Strength seven officers, four hundred sixty-eight men. Twenty-nine WIA, twelve fit to fight. Five hundred thirteen horses. Ammunition remaining: twenty-two percent for star weapons, forty percent for rockets, fifty percent for arrows. Recovery of arrows is running well ahead of estimate.

Comments: Looks like we've outrun all of the High Rexja's western army. Estimate three regiments were chasing us. I make that "Mission accomplished" for drawing off their cavalry. The problem is we've run into the rear of Prince Strymon's army, and they're between us and Drantos.

So far we're all right. We have good water and there are meadows of Earth grasses scattered through the Tran scrub. Between that and the oats we've captured we have fodder.

I plan to rest up the horses for a couple of days. Once everybody's fit to move I'll decide whether to raid Strymon's rear or head south and join up with Ganton.

Morale solid. Minimum tension between our people and the Westmen. I still try to keep Westmen and Drantos fighters in separate units because of language problems, but pretty much everybody on either side trusts the other now. They've been saving each other's asses a couple of times a day for nearly three weeks.

"Sarge?"

Murphy looked up to see Hal Roscoe dismounting. "Yeah?"

"Scouts just rode in. There's a big supply convoy laagered up about six klicks ahead."

"Fortified?"

"Just a wagon circle. Some VIP's banner over the CP."

"Whose?"

"Damfino."

"Yeah." Most of his rangers were former poachers, and wouldn't. And the Westmen scouts sure didn't know heraldry.

"Want to go after it, Sarge?"

"Does the bear shit in the woods? Tell 'em 'Well done' and I'll be along in a few minutes."

"Okay, Sarge." Roscoe remounted and rode off.

"Lucky break," Murphy wrote. "VIP banner means food. Remounts, and maybe some decent loot. We'll take this thing just after the True Sun sets. The Demon will give us enough light."

The Father Sun had set, and the Child was only a crimson smear in the east. The baleful eye of the Death-Wind Bringer cast a red glow over the clearing. All was deep shadow near the woods where Mad Bear's people waited.

The wizards' firesticks—the *rockets*—soared up from behind the line of Horse People and arched across the sky. Two, three, four of them plunged down onto the enemy camp.

Mad Bear saw warriors making gestures against evil spirits. Others struggled to control jittery horses. He himself no longer feared the wizards' firesticks, any more than he feared fighting at night. Clearly the wizards' magic was stronger than that of the night demons. Therefore it must be stronger than that of the men in the camp, who had not dared to move by night.

Only one fire sprang up where the rockets fell, but it was enough to show horses and oxen milling in panic. Mad Bear grinned and drew his sword to await the signal from his chief and blood-brother.

Murphy's trumpet sounded and was followed by a long, shrill blast on his iron whistle. Mad Bear rammed his heels into his mount's flanks. The pony leaped forward like a maddened ranwang. Mad Bear swept his sword down the way he had seen Chief Murphy do it, then reined his horse aside to let the archers sweep past.

The archers were a hundred paces ahead of Mad Bear when they came within bowshot of the wagons. A few arrows arched out to meet them. Two of Mad Bear's warriors fell from their saddles.

There were two Horse People for every archer in the wagon circle, and the Westmen's arrows carried farther and struck harder. Soon the screams of men joined the screams of the horses, and fewer arrows flew from the wagon circles.

Mad Bear rode up to the line of archers. There was movement in the enemy's camp. Torches glowed, and armored men mounted their horses. A squire handed a banner to one of the knights. The banner bore the same device as the one that had flown over the tent. *Ah. The chief of the camp would do battle with us. Father, Thunderer, grant that he may be fodder for my lance.*

Mad Bear sheathed his sword. It was an iron sword, a gift from his blood-brother, and in more skilled hands no doubt it would be a match for the armor of any Ironshirt. It was well to have an iron sword, and to learn the Ironshirt way of war, but the Horse People had trained with the lance from the day they had been set in the saddle. It would always be Mad Bear's first choice. Mad Bear's steel lance head had been passed down through five generations.

The enemy horsemen rode out in fours. Some of the archers began shooting at them. Mad Bear shouted. "The camp. Leave the horsemen to us!" Without the Ironshirts to defend it, the camp would certainly fall, and it was the camp they wanted. That was another thing Mad Bear had learned from Murphy. Do not swerve from your target. Do not be deceived by the prospect of easier prey.

The archers turned back toward the camp and advanced slowly, followed by the dismounted troops who would storm the wagons.

The enemy horsemen massed for a charge. Mad Bear led a hand of hands of lancers to meet them. Enemy horns sounded. Mad Bear's hand of hands faced no less than five times their strength. "The darkness must be our friend," he shouted to his band. "When they come close, run away, and lead them far from here!"

He urged his pony forward. One Ironshirt rode far ahead of the others. Mad Bear whirled his pony to the right, as if to avoid the man. His enemy followed, but his heavier mount was not as agile as Mad Bear's pony. As he turned, Mad Bear whirled back and thrust his lance into the man's throat. His fall twisted the lance from Mad Bear's hands.

To his left a man in silver armor slew two of Mad Bear's people. Mad Bear pivoted toward him, but a dozen enemies came between. Mad Bear drew his sword and shouted at them. He waited until they were close enough to hear his insults, then spun away. He kept his pony at a slow gallop and stayed just far enough ahead to lure them farther away from the camp.

When he'd led them far enough he turned to his right, riding past the older warriors who waited in the darkness at the edge of the woods. Then he gave them no more thought, and wheeled back toward the camp.

Most of the Ironshirts had halted at the edge of the firelit circle, but two had ridden farther on. One was the man in the silver armor who had slain Mad Bear's kinsmen. Mad Bear felt the blood lust rising in him. Such feelings were always dangerous. The Horse People had long ago learned that it was better to tire your enemy, and kill him in your own time, than to fight him when he had his full strength.

The silver-armored Ironshirt shouted and rode toward Mad Bear. He was followed by another, a mere boy, who carried a banner. *A chief,* Mad Bear thought.

Mad Bear dashed toward his enemy, then halted three lance lengths away and wheeled to his left. He dashed forward ten lengths and stopped again, to let the chief hear his laughter.

The Ironshirt shouted curses. Mad Bear could not understand them all, but he heard the Ironshirt word for 'honor.' He grinned and rose in his stirrups. "You have no honor!" he shouted.

The Ironshirt chief cursed louder and spurred his horse toward Mad Bear. Mad Bear grinned again. He had learned that phrase from Murphy. *And my brother wondered why I wanted to know that!*

Mad Bear let his pony dance across the field, staying always three lengths ahead of his enemy. The Child had risen enough now to show the lather on the flanks of his enemy's horse. *A little more,* Mad Bear thought. *Just a little farther.*

"Coward!" the Ironshirt screamed, and reined in. He looked back, and saw that he had been led far from the battle. His banner-bearer was fifty lengths away.

Now!

Mad Bear galloped up behind and to the left, and struck with his sword. His blow landed on the Ironshirt's shield. Mad Bear galloped past and wheeled twenty lengths beyond his enemy. The banner-bearer was coming up fast. Two Ironshirts together would always be a match for one warrior of the Horse People. This must be done quickly.

Mad Bear rode forward, and suddenly the man spurred his horse at him. It was a better horse than Mad Bear had ever seen. Lathered and snorting, it yet dashed forward at the chief's command. The Ironshirt lance came down and thrust deep into the throat of Mad Bear's pony.

As the Ironshirt let go the lance to draw his sword, Mad

Bear leaped leftward over his dying mount's neck and rolled to break the fall, then dived over his fallen pony and rolled on his back to thrust his sword upward deep into the belly of his enemy's mount.

The horse screamed and reared. The Ironshirt chief kicked free of the stirrups and leaped backward over the horse's rump to land on his feet. Mad Bear tore out a handful of turf and threw it at the Ironshirt's visor. Then he dashed to his left and rolled to kick the man's legs from under him, then stood and pushed him down. As the Ironshirt thrashed, Mad Bear tried to drive his dagger through the eyeslits of the visor. The Ironshirt smashed at his head with his steel gauntlet, and sparks flew in Mad Bear's vision. He leaped to his feet and jumped backward. The Ironshirt rose to his knees and lifted his sword to slash at Mad Bear, then got to his feet as Mad Bear leaped back. Mad Bear circled toward the fallen horse, and the man turned to face him. When Mad Bear struggled to pull his sword from the horse, the Ironshirt retrieved his shield.

The banner-bearer rode down on them. He had dropped the banner and held a sword. As he rode past, Mad Bear dove to the ground, then leaped up before the dismounted Ironshirt could strike. The banner-bearer halted and turned. His Ironshirt master shouted commands that Mad Bear could not understand.

Where are my clansmen? Mad Bear turned to run away. As he did, a mounted starman rode up. The starman shouted, and the banner-bearer turned toward him. The small star weapon they called the "Ingram" made its sounds of tearing cloth.

The Ironshirt chief's chest turned from silver to red. He crashed to the ground and lay still. The banner-bearer tried to raise his sword to strike, but he had no strength, and toppled from the saddle. Mad Bear dashed forward to grasp the horse's bridle to secure it for the star warrior.

The star warrior shouted something and rode away. Mad Bear turned back toward the camp. The circle of archers had grown tighter around it.

Mad Bear turned to his dead horse and took off saddle and bridle, then cut loose the feathers and claws woven into the top of the mane.

It had been a tougher fight than Murphy wanted. *Sure were a lot of guards for one goddam wagon train. And not all that much loot, either. Glad we had the Westmen, instead of Drantos ironhats, or we'd never have beat that many heavies.*

Murphy sent a scout platoon to chase the enemy survivors farther from the camp. *And that's funny too. One minute they fought like tigers, then all of a sudden they couldn't run fast enough.* He didn't expect to catch the survivors. Hell, he didn't *want* to catch them, just keep them from regrouping to launch a counterattack.

Murphy went with the detail guarding all the prisoners who could walk. It was the only way to make sure the Westmen didn't cut their throats. Westmen didn't believe in prisoners, and they believed even less in leaving live enemies behind them.

The camp and the wounded were left to what might loosely be called the mercy of the Westmen. The only way the Drantos men could stop them if they wanted to cut throats was by a fight. If it came to that, Murphy would rather lose sleep over dead prisoners than over a task force that chewed itself to bits in enemy territory.

Besides, we got no doctors. Anybody hurt bad enough he can't walk and unpopular enough his friends won't carry him isn't going to make it anyway.

He stood watch until the prisoners built a camp outside the wagon ring. They'd been stripped of their weapons, and footgear, and despite Murphy's best efforts, most of their valuables as well. *I cannot make these damn fools understand that it's better to carry oats than gold.*

Murphy heard snatches of bawdy songs coming from the wagons. Somebody had found the wine. He sent two sergeants to be sure the duty platoons stayed sober, and prayed there wasn't an enemy reaction force anywhere near. *Bit different when* we're *the Viet Cong. . . .*

Discipline was holding pretty well, though. Probably everybody had filched one choice piece of loot to hold out from the general division of the spoils, but that was nothing new. What mattered was that the horses and the wagons were in good shape.

A man-at-arms met Murphy as he rode up to the wagons.

"My lord. Arekor wishes you to speak to Mad Bear and Lord Roscoe before they slay each other. He says it is a matter of honor."

"Oh, shit. Okay, I'm coming."

Murphy found the three men standing beside a camp bed in the former CP tent. On the bed lay the body of a tall blond man of about twenty-five. He'd been shot at least five times in the chest with a nine-mm weapon. *Ingram. Roscoe's kill. So?* "What's the problem?"

Mad Bear promptly burst into a torrent of words, so fast that Murphy couldn't understand more than one in four. Arekor tried to translate, then gave up and started again after Mad Bear ran down.

"He says that the Lord Roscoe insults him by giving him Prince Akkilas's head when he did little to—"

"What the hell—? Hal, is this Prince Akkilas, S.rakos's kid brother? Really?"

"Sarge, he wore steel armor with silver inlays. Toris's griffin defaced on his shield, and on the camp banner. He's got a birthmark on his left ear, and wears a silver griffin earring. Who the hell else could he be?"

"Holy Mother of God," said Murphy softly. "No wonder the prisoners are acting spooked. That's why they all ran, once the banner was down! Jenri, go get me a couple of the prisoner officers."

"Sir." His orderly went out.

"Now, assuming that's who we've got—"

"It is," Roscoe said. "Believe it."

"I do. Which still doesn't answer the question. Why the hell do you want to give Mad Bear a head he thinks you should have?"

"Mad Bear did most of the work. He'd got him off his horse, and in another minute he'd have killed him. I just speeded things up. Hell, Sarge, I was trying to be friendly!"

"Yeah," said Murphy. They all looked at him. "Gimme a goddam minute, will you?"

Mad Bear muttered something Murphy didn't understand.

"Arekor, be real careful when you say this to Mad Bear. Tell him Lord Roscoe offered the head to Mad Bear as brother to his chief. Tell him that Lord Roscoe did not understand that this is not the custom of the Horse People. Roscoe, you nod like anything, you hear me?"

"Yes, *sir!*"

Arekor spoke rapidly. Mad Bear glared, then looked at Murphy, back at Roscoe, then at Murphy again. He grinned and spoke.

Arekor translated. "He says he has been with you long enough to know something of the ways of starmen, and it will not be necessary for you to swear this is true."

"Good. Now somebody send for some of that goddam wine. And some of that mare piss my brother drinks."

His orderly came in with two of the prisoners. Murphy pointed to the body. "Is this Akkilas Son of Toris?" he demanded. He waited a moment. "I see. Take them out. Fellows, we got ourselves either an opportunity or one hell of a problem."

When the others had left, Murphy poured drinks for himself and Corporal Roscoe. "It all comes down to this," Murphy said. "Kings don't like people killing kings and princes unless they do it themselves. I'm going to buck this one up the chain of command."

"How in hell are you going to do that when we can't even get home?" Roscoe demanded.

"For starters, we take off this guy's head and pickle it.

Keep the shield and banner, too. Then we give the whole goddam mess to the first senior officer we find, and hope like hell that turns out to be Captain Galloway."

"I'll buy that one," Roscoe said. "But it ain't likely. Ganton's army is a hell of a lot closer."

"Yeah, I know," Murphy said. "I've just been studying the best way to join up with him. Of course it'd help if we knew exactly where he was."

"You could send the Westmen out looking."

"Could, but won't. We all came in together, and we'll go out together." Murphy unrolled a map. "Look, the last we heard, Ganton was just south of Castle Fasolt. It ain't likely he's moved too far away. Tomorrow we'll go looking for him."

"About time. Even with the stuff we took tonight, we're gettin' low on everything. Especially horses. And your buddies have used up a lot of those ponies of theirs, too." Roscoe scratched his head. "Sarge, you gotta teach me more about getting along with those touchy little suckers."

"Hah. When I learn, I'll tell you. I know one thing. You and Mad Bear did a hell of a night's work. You could get a goddamned knighthood out of this. You realize that with Akkilas dead, Ganton's the nearest male heir to the High Throne?"

"No shit? But I thought it wasn't exactly hereditary—"

"Yeah, yeah, I know. That's so if the blood heir's an idiot they can pick somebody competent to hold things together. So who's a better candidate than our Wanax, especially with his Roman connections? And he's got the Captain on his side, too."

"You mean, Ganton could be High Rexja because we zapped Akkilas?"

"May gunkels eat my underwear if I kid you."

"Shit." It was nearly a prayer. Roscoe shook his head.

"I wondered where Akkilas was," Murphy said.

"Eh? Yeah, I keep forgetting you've gone native, Sarge."

"Ah, cut the crap—"

"Well, maybe I didn't mean it quite like it sounds. You

think like the Captain does. Like these people do. Me, I just go where they tell me. You're a goddam officer, even if I don't have to say 'sir' every two minutes."

"Yeah, sure. Thanks. Anyway. I did wonder where they were keeping Akkilas."

"Now we know," Roscoe said. "Where they thought he was safe. Guy sure had more *cojones* than brains."

"So it goes." Murphy looked at the body. "He had *some* smarts as well as guts. He got those troops mounted up and riding out damned fast, and was ready to take the mounted archers in the flank. He could have done some real damage if Mad Bear hadn't held them up till I threw in the cavalry reserve."

He shook his head. "Hal, sometimes I have nightmares about the grayskins cutting off our ammo right when somebody has really learned how to fight us. Combined-arms army, gunpowder and guns, professional soldiers, logistics, the whole bag. You ever heard the definition of the Second Law of Thermodynamics?"

"Can't say I have."

"'You can't win, you can't break even, and you can't get out of the game.' Sometimes this whole mess seems like that. Not that it isn't better than being dead, but still..."

"Sarge, you've been listening to the Captain too much and drinking too little. Mind if I break out some of Akkilas's private stock?"

"Go ahead."

Mad Bear walked until the fires around the camp faded in the light of the rising Child. He took bow, quiver, sword, and dagger, for this was not a true vigil in which a man had to trust to the protection of the gods. Some of the camp's Ironshirts might have had the courage to lie in wait in the darkness. He did not care to be easy prey for them.

At last he reached a grassy hummock, drove his sword

into the ground so that it might drink the strength of the earth, and sat cross-legged beside it. It was as well that this was no vigil, because for once in his life Mad Bear did not even know what to ask the gods, let alone what answer he wished to hear.

By all the laws and customs in war Mad Bear had ever known, the kill of Prince Akkilas belonged to the warrior Roscoe. Yet it seemed his dearest wish to give it to Mad Bear, for all that this was taking honor not only from himself but from his sons.

Perhaps he had no sons? Some warriors took vows to lie apart from women until they had accomplished some great deed or sworn vengeance. They accepted the danger that their line might die with them, if they died before fulfilling their vow. Certainly not all the wizard-warriors were like that. His blood-brother had been married twice, as well as having concubines in between.

Roscoe might be such a man—if such oaths were known among the wizard-warriors. Mad Bear did not know, nor did he have much hope of learning soon. The gods had sent the wizard-warriors and made them—or at least some of them, for now—friends of the Silver Wolves. That was enough. A warrior who had sworn to aid these—whatever they might be—whether the gods said yea or nay—well, he had small claim on the gods for easy answers to hard questions.

Mad Bear decided that the gods had given him enough and more than he had any right to. He had his life, his wits, his eyes, ears, and tongue. If he lost none of these, he might in time know all that he needed to know of the wizard-warriors.

The wizard-warriors were like a great storm, blowing *mekar* seeds across the land. They blew some men to victory, others to defeat. Tonight they had blown him to victory.

Mad Bear laid a captured sword on the earth beside his own, raised his arms to the sky, and began to sing his victory song.

CHAPTER THREE

Chief Captain Volauf entered the tent as Matthias was pulling on his gauntlets.

"Good day, my lord. You are awake early."

"I have been at my prayers, that Vothan may grant us his favor."

In truth Matthias had barely slept. Many things could happen in battle, and Vothan One-Eye was notoriously fickle, even toward those who defended his honor. He had always been so. Yet the cause of the High Rexja had prospered under the House of Vothan.

That was not all. This mad new religion, this fusion of the ravings of Roman scholars and the worst of the preachings of the House of Yatar, had driven many of the priests of Yatar to alliance with Vothan. Matthias had seen that happen in the Five, and even in Drantos. If they did no more than send information, they served. When the Ottarn bridge gave way and carried off three pack mules, Matthias had learned almost as soon as Ganton.

"Captain, have you new reports?"

"Only one, Honorable. In addition to Morrone's band in the north, we have heard that a small band of raiders has come from the west. My scout officer believes it is the remains of a force sent to harass Captain General Ailas."

"Ah." Ailas held Ganton's western army in check. Poised to threaten the High Road past Dravan, Ailas was doing greater service by existing than most generals could give by a victory. "Nothing more on Morrone?"

"No, Honorable. Our supply trains now require heavier

escorts, but Morrone's raiders are more an annoyance than a real threat."

"Good. When we have won this battle we will deal with him."

"Otherwise, Honorable, all remains as it was last night. We have twice Ganton's strength. Our light horse is spread across his rear. A mixed blessing, Honorable. We cut into his supply, and we can turn any retreat into rout, but the knowledge that we have forces behind him will make his men fight all the harder."

Matthias smiled grimly. "They do not know how much strength we have behind them. I had rather have my enemies looking over their shoulders. And now that one of the greatest of their star weapons lies at the bottom of the Ottarn to amuse the hydras, they have even more to fear."

"I have never faced the magic of guns before," Volauf said.

"I have. In the south. Captain, guns need firepowder. That is not made by magic, and without firepowder the guns are as useless as unstrung bows or empty quivers."

I also have friends who went with the traitor Strymon, but that is no concern of yours, Captain Volauf.

"Your pardon, Honorable, but it is my duty to ask. Are you certain we should begin this battle before Prince Akkilas comes to lead the host?"

"It is your duty to ask. A moment." Matthias went to the chest that stood at the foot of his bed, and took out a parchment. He unrolled it. "You see the Seal of Issardos. See this."

Volauf read. "I see. He shows great confidence in you."

"You mean that he shows less in the prince. Captain, we carry Prince Akkilas's banner before us, and we give our orders in his name. The bards will say that he won this battle. You and I will know different."

"You and I," Volauf said. "And Chancellor Issardos."

"Yes, of course. You will not be forgotten, Captain Volauf."

"I thank you, Honorable."

Matthias waved his hand in dismissal. "Is my horse ready?"

"Yes, Honorable."

"I will be there presently."

Ganton was watching the Second Division move into position when the messenger reached him.

"Majesty, a bheroman of Toris's host has ridden close to our front and challenges you to single combat."

"Indeed," Ganton said. "And who might he be?"

"Majesty, he gives his name as Roald of Caemoran. He says that you are no true Wanax if you refuse him battle to hide behind wizards' magic."

"Indeed," Ganton said in a tone that made the messenger flinch. "Lord Hilaskos, have my squires bring my warhorse to Prince Strymon's banner." He put spurs to his palfrey. After a moment he swallowed his rage and reined in the horse, so that his guards would not have to tire their own mounts to keep up with him. The fate of Drantos today might rest on how many fresh horses the host could command at the end of the battle.

When Ganton reached Strymon's banner he reined in and used his binoculars to inspect the area between the two armies. An armored man on a bay gelding walked his horse in a large circle. The red and white of his shield matched the pennon on his lance. Every time he completed a circle he shouted. "I am Roald of Caemoran. I call the Wanax Ganton of Drantos to honorable single combat. If he comes not, I denounce him as no true Wanax, but a coward who hides behind godless wizardry!"

Ganton listened to this three times while waiting for his warhorse to arrive. Finally he pulled out his battle-axe, his only weapon, and wrapped the thong around his wrist.

"Your Majesty!" exclaimed Strymon. "You are not going down there as you are, with neither armor nor weapons nor warhorse, to fight a full-armed—"

Ganton whipped the battle-axe up and in a circle over his head. "This is enough weapon for any man."

"Your—" Strymon lowered his voice. "Ganton, my friend, it is not well done to call a Wanax and ally a fool, but—"

"The more reason, then, for not doing it. I know what I am about, and I do not think Roald of Caemoran does."

"At least let me take the challenge as your champion!"

"No. It is not you that Roald calls a coward who hides behind wizards."

"My friend, you have told me that when one becomes Wanax, one can no longer act as one wishes. I believe this. Are you not being foolish, to endanger the day in this way?"

"I thought on this as I rode here," Ganton said. "The Lord Rick is not here. We lost a star weapon when the bridge collapsed. The clouds are low, so that the balloon will not be useful. The army knows that we have little enough of wizardry today, and we face forces larger than our own. I think it can do no harm to show our men that their Wanax has not forgotten the old ways."

"Then be careful, my friend."

"I will. Be ready to avenge me if I fall." He turned to his staff officers. "You will follow Prince Strymon as you would me."

"Sire—"

"Silence. You have your orders." He kicked his horse to a walk.

"Go with—Yatar and Christ," Strymon said.

As Ganton rode down the hill, he shifted his Browning so that he could draw it with his left hand, and clicked off the safety.

Tylara could not hear the conversation between Ganton and Strymon, but she could see Ganton ride out to accept the challenge.

He is no foolish knight, yet he acts like one. This is not the act of the Wanax I saw in Council. Her heart turned to lead. For a moment all the assurances of Apelles and Yanulf seemed vain lies. Not given the sacrifice they demanded, the gods *were* striking at those about her, starting with the Wanax, whom they had just afflicted with madness....

The moment passed swiftly. *He is in range of my best archers. No. Half our knights would ride away if it appeared that the Wanax had so little honor. I cannot even avenge him that way.*

She watched with dread as Ganton rode down the hill.

When Ganton rode out into the circle Roald had trampled, the bheroman shouted and spurred his horse to a canter.

His horse is tired, she thought. *And Ganton has a fresh mount.*

The Wanax rode directly toward Roald. Roald's lance came down. The bheroman spurred his horse into a lumbering gallop. Three lengths before they met, Ganton swerved sharply to his left. Roald's lance tried to sweep in a circle to follow, but Ganton was already out of reach of the point. Then he turned to his right and rode directly at Roald.

Ganton passed just behind the bheroman, and as he did he swept his axe in a backhand blow at Roald's neck. As Roald crumpled and fell, Ganton rode back toward his own lines without looking back.

There was a moment of silence, then the deafening cheers of the army.

The ridge was low, but high enough to overlook the battlefield below. When Tylara rode up to Ganton's banner, she saw that the staff had placed a low trestle table there for Ganton's maps.

She was the last to arrive. The most senior officers were

seated at the table. Other staff officers stood behind them. At the foot of the table Apelles looked uncomfortable in robes hastily altered to show his new station. Drumold indicated a place to his right, where she could look across the maps to the battlefield.

It had taken years of Rick's instruction, but she was now familiar enough with maps that she needed only a cursory glance at the field below to see what was represented on them. Still she took her time with her binoculars, looking at the field and then back to the map.

The army was divided into three Divisions. Each Division had horse, foot, and guns, and was a small army complete in itself. Ganton had heard Rick say that was the way armies were organized on his home world. Tylara wondered if that would be so appropriate here, but the Wanax was proud of what he had done. She looked beyond the host of Drantos to the enemy.

"Griffin," she said almost to herself.

"Yes," Ganton said. He nodded to acknowledge her arrival. "They raised the banner of Prince Akkilas an hour ago. Your pardon, lady, if I do not begin again. I do not think we have much more time."

He pointed again to the map. "It is called *echelon,*" he said. "Each Division supports the others."

Tylara remembered Rick's lectures on the formation. A Wanax of the Germans, one later called Great, had used it. Each of the three Divisions could attack or defend, and each guarded the flanks of another. There was no way an enemy could crush one Division without fighting at least one other. No way that the host could be defeated *in detail*.

Ganton had also held back what Rick called *reserves*. They stood behind the Second Division: the starmen and their weapons, more guns, the Tamaerthan chivalry, Nikeian city militia who fought with great axes, and the handful of Romans who had come with Larry Warner from the University.

The balloon was nowhere in sight, and Tylara guessed

that the clouds were too low for it to be useful. The air felt heavy and smelled of coming rain.

"Are there to be no Romans?" Hilaskos asked.

"No, my lord. Our Roman allies do us good service in keeping safe our southern borders. How long has it been that the host of Drantos can be sent north without a care for south and east? If we cannot defend one of our borders without crying for Legions, we are poor allies indeed."

"What is the signal for the advance?" Rudhrig asked.

"We will not advance," Ganton said.

Rudhrig growled. "I feared as much."

"My lords," Ganton said. "We have no need for battle at all. We stand at the very border of our lands. We are well supplied. Our enemy is deep in Ta-Meltemos, a land turning more hostile to him each day. Lord Morrone harasses his rear—"

"We've taken our share of that," Rudhrig said. "Your pardon, Majesty."

"When you have matters to say in Council, say them," Ganton said. "I did not call you here to be silent. I am as aware as you that half a thousand of enemy horse are in our rear. They are pursued by the local levies and our Mounted Archers, and I do not think they will be a threat for long. Certainly they are not as great a danger to us as Lord Morrone is to Akkilas."

Rick always said the defense is stronger, but it seldom wins decisions, Tylara thought. I hope that Ganton is right today, but I have doubts. She raised her binoculars to study the enemy.

Their heavy cavalry alone outnumbered Ganton's entire army. The enemy had dismounted well beyond range of bowshot. They stood or sat on the ground, waiting, and did not seem to be impatient. Small blocks of infantry, mostly crossbowmen, filled gaps between the blocks of enemy cavalry. The enemy line stretched beyond Ganton's on both the left and right. On the Drantos right were four stadia of swampy lowland, then the Ottarn River. Any of Akkilas' cavalry who waded through the swamps would not be in good formation to receive a charge from the reserves at the top of the hill.

The Drantos left rested against a bluff. Tamaerthan archers and Drantos levies held its top, and in any event the sides were too steep for cavalry.

If we must defend, it is a good place for it. Still, I wish he had kept the pikes and archers together. Rick always does. And where are you, my husband? I think we need you.

And if we do not, then Ganton will soon prove that he can win battles without the War Leader of Drantos. How long before Ganton takes that post for himself? Or gives it to another?

Horns sounded across the quiet field. The enemy soldiers stood. Cavalrymen began to mount.

"My Lord Father Apelles," Ganton said. "But—please be brief."

Apelles looked out at the bustle of activity below, then stood and raised his hand in blessing. "Go with Yatar and Christ His Son."

"Thank you. Now to your posts, my lords. My lady. Go with Yatar and Christ." Ganton raised his hand high and brought it down sharply. The Great Guns roared.

Before Tylara reached her Hussars, the battlefield was dimmed with smoke.

As the third charge retreated, Volauf rode up to Matthias. He plucked an arrow from his saddle and another from the gambeson covering his mail.

"Are you wounded?" Matthias asked.

"I have felt worse from bees. No, Honorable, the Chooser has not yet called me to his Hall."

"He has called more than I like." A thousand and more of the host lay in heaps between the three great battles of the enemy. They were hidden by the sharp-smelling smoke that covered the low areas.

"Or I, Honorable. This formation of theirs is damnable. We advance against one group, and the others fly on our flanks, or shoot us down with arrows. And always there are the *guns.*"

"At least we know this much. The guns are not wizard weapons. They are only machines. You saw it as I did. They are served by men, who fill them with firepowder and stones, and bring torches to make them shoot. Kill those men and the guns are as useless as any other weapon."

Volauf frowned in thought. "Honorable, I believe you. But what of the star weapons?"

"I believe they are the same," Matthias said. "Nothing but more powerful guns. They need—arrows, stones, firepowder as guns do, and they must be wielded by men."

"But what can we do? Honorable, I believe the men will charge once more if I lead them. I cannot guarantee you twice."

"Wait. Refresh yourself, and see that your officers are ready. I will not send you forth again without a plan."

"All is ready, Honorable," Volauf said. "Have you commands?"

"I believe so. Captain, what makes archers cease shooting?"

"They cease when they have used all their arrows. Or when the enemy is amongst them."

"Nothing else?"

"Ah! When friend and foe are so mixed that they cannot be sure who they will hit."

"Exactly so. The guns and star weapons must be much the same. Captain Volauf, ride to those captains of horse and foot you trust most. Say that if they will follow me even to Vothan's Hall, we may yet bring home victory to the High Rexja!"

"The Council of Captains—"

"Demons fly away with the Council of Captains! This must be done quickly or not at all!"

Larry Warner and his aeronauts were held in reserve at the command post. The balloon was useless, and now smoke lay so heavy across the battlefield that it was rare to get a semaphore message through. No one had any orders for him, so he watched the battle.

Larry had a bad feeling about the enemy charge the minute he saw it was led by that crazy with the Vothanite robes over his armor. The guy might be crazy, but he had guts, and his men stayed with him.

The charge came right at the corner of the Third Division.

Smart, Warner thought. The corner of a square is always the weakest point.

The archers and musketeers in reserve in the center of the square ran to support the corner, but before they could arrive the enemy cavalry struck home. The cavalry were followed by infantry, then more cavalry, and it looked to Warner as if the entire enemy army was ready to pour into that one area.

The corner broke. Pikemen tried to close around the point without breaking ranks. Warner mentally crossed his fingers; that was the Fourth Pikes, who'd been a little shaky ever since they'd been forced to surrender at Piro's Hill.

The pikemen held for a moment. Then the sheer weight of the enemy's numbers tore two holes in the line. Cavalry and infantry poured through. Third Division's archers tried to loft their arrows over the pikemen and into the enemy cavalry, but they were harassed by arrows from horse archers.

The musketeers formed ranks. Warner held his breath. If there was any way to get a message to the musketry captain—

The muskets ripple-fired, more than a hundred going off so fast they sounded like one enormously loud and long shot. Enemy cavalry and friendly pikemen took the bullets in about equal proportion.

The ranks of the pikemen bulged inward. More pikemen turned and ran away, running into the Tamaerthan archers and upsetting their aim or just getting in their way. The Tamaerthan officers screamed curses, and some of the pikemen stopped to try to hold with the archers, but not enough.

The pike wall was broken. More enemy cavalry poured into the gap. By now the entire corner and half the sides of Third Division was crumbling. Light cavalry charged through the gaps and laid about with saber and lance.

And now somebody on the other side had seen what was happening, and was bringing up the goddamned infantry! Warner thought up two interesting new punishments for the son of a bitch who'd lost the LMG and prayed Bisso would let the mortar open up. They'd been waiting for a good target, because they only had fifteen rounds and some of those not too good. That infantry would be a mortarman's dream, though.

By the time the infantry got into safe mortar range, the Third Division was no longer a square but a slightly ragged rectangle. Where the enemy had hit first was an almighty brawl, with everybody hacking and poking at each other for dear life.

The CO of the Division—Eqeta Rudhrig, Warner remembered—seemed to have his act together. He was pulling cavalry over to stiffen the pikemen who'd lost their nerve and help the archers and musketeers who couldn't shoot without hitting friends. They were slinging their bows and muskets and wading into the fight with cold steel, and maybe they would be enough.

Maybe not, too, because more enemy cavalry was working around the Division's right flank, where it didn't have any support. Time to commit the reserves, Ganton old buddy old pal, and where the hell was that mortar . . . ?

The 81-mm coughed. Smoke sprouted just short of the

advancing infantry. A second round landed right in the middle of them. Three more rounds did the same. Warner breathed easier. The infantry and more cavalry were pushing into the gap between the Third and Second Division, where they could also be hit by the Second. That was Teuthras', and with a little help from the mortars he could—

"Oh, *shit!*"

The fifth round from the mortar was a short. It didn't touch the enemy, but it landed right in the middle of a battery of four-pounders. From the amount of smoke, it must have touched off some of the ammo.

Warner snapped off the safety on his G-3 and chambered a round. He wasn't completely sure who he was going to be shooting at. Probably Toris's people, but no way you could get around the fact that all of a sudden the battle had got a whole lot hairier, and if somebody started looking for scapegoats, the starmen were going to be well up toward the head of the line....

Rudhrig, Eqeta of Harms, saw the corner of his Division crumbling. He shouted for archers and musketeers from the *reserve* in the center of the square. Then he remembered to send messengers as well. The starmen's way of war called for armies so large and battlefields so noisy that a captain's voice could not always reach those who must hear it.

Some of the musketeers and more of the archers didn't wait for orders. They hurried toward the corner of the square where the enemy charge had struck. Rudhrig waved to his house knights, urging them to one side so that his foot could shoot freely.

It was unknightly that his best men should be reduced to guarding the flanks of the sons of Drantos peasants and Tamaerthan hill-bandits. Yet there was no other way to keep the enemy from crushing his Division. Saddles fell empty swiftly, but two men took the place of each fallen rider.

Rudhrig shouted. "Raise high the White Hawk, Guy! Let them know whom they face!"

His son grinned and raised the great banner of Harms with both hands, then waved it back and forth. Rudhrig prayed that Guy would have no more dangerous work this day. When Sarakos's host had marched into Drantos, the Eqeta of Harms had had three sons. When it marched out, he had only one.

The guns hurled stones into the enemy's ranks. Men toppled, headless. Horses screamed. An angry din grew behind Rudhrig as the musketeers joined the shooting. More enemies fell.

Pikemen fell too. Rudhrig looked for the enemy's archers and cursed. The musketeers were hitting their own comrades as well as the enemy! Gaps appeared in the pike ranks as men fell. Enemy shortswordsmen swarmed into the gaps, slashing and stabbing. The gaps grew wider as Fourth Pikes gave way.

"Death or glory!" A high-pitched young voice gave the battle-cry of the Eqetas of Harms. Rudhrig's bowels turned to ice. The White Hawk swept down the hill. Guy held the banner-staff in one hand and his sword in the other. "Men of Harms! To me!"

The boy reached the fleeing pikemen just as the enemy horsemen poured through the gap in Fourth Pikes' line. Guy laid about him with his sword, trying to rally the foot soldiers. Then he vanished among the enemy.

Rudhrig had no breath left to give orders or even to curse. He needed none. His men surged as one toward the enemy. Riflemen ran, holding their empty weapons like clubs. Archers ran, slinging their bows and drawing swords. The Eqeta's house knights charged toward the White Hawk banner before their lord could put spurs to his horse.

Three horsemen rose from the ground at Rudhrig's feet. His lance flung one out of the saddle and broke. Rudhrig carved the second man's shield with a blow from his sword, then slashed the man's face. The third enemy rained stout blows on Rudhrig's shield and mail. A knifeman slipped closer.

Two archers ran up to Rudhrig's side. One clubbed the knifeman with his bow, and the other slashed at the last horseman's mount. The horse reared, giving Rudhrig an easy target. He ended the fight with a sword cut to the man's neck.

"My thanks!" Rudhrig gasped, and charged down the hill.

The archers and riflemen had closed with the enemy before the knights reached them. The fleeing pikemen were thick enough to block a horse, but men on foot could slip through. Now the archers forced the pikemen back into ranks at the point of their swords. The riflemen ran to either flank. The White Hawk was nowhere in sight.

Dayfather, grant me Guy's life, and you may have anything you ask of me.

More enemy horse rode toward the Eqeta, but this time his knights were there to meet them. Two knights and six of the enemy went down. Tamaerthans ran in to slit the enemy's throats almost as fast as they fell.

Rudhrig saw the enemy foot pressing up into the gap between the remnants of his Third Division and the Second Division to his left. The guns fired faster, flailing the enemy with stones that cut great swathes through the ranks. His pikemen reformed their ranks. Riflemen and archers joined them, and the enemy cavalry gained no more ground. Rudhrig shouted for a messenger. If the Wanax threw his reserves against the enemy's horse and foot—

Three archers and a musketeer ran out of the press, carrying a limp figure. The banner of the White Hawk was still in his hand. Rudhrig suddenly lacked the breath even for a prayer.

The limp figure raised its head and shook off the hands that tried to hold him down. Rudhrig found himself at his son's side. "Guy—my boy! How is it—"

"I'm not hurt, Father. Please tell these sons of swineherds to stop stepping on my hands!" His voice held both indignation and affection. "I'm sorry the White Hawk's been muddied."

"They could have used it to wipe Toris's arse!" Knightly language be damned, Rudhrig thought. Thank Yatar, my son is safe. "Guy, you must take a message to the Wanax Ganton."

"Father, I *won't* be sent away like a disobedient—"

The Great Gun of the starmen opened fire. Rudhrig counted five shots from the—the *mortar.* There was a crashing explosion, and a great cloud of white smoke poured up beyond the enemy. Rudhrig scrambled into the saddle.

The smoke cleared and he saw that the barrels of firepowder must have exploded. Had the starmen's mortar by chance struck at friends? Certainly something had destroyed two of the guns. The ground was littered with the bodies of the men who had tended the guns.

Three of the guns remained, and the men who served them were still alive. Limping, black-faced, half-clothed, they took their places. Rudhrig remembered what he had heard of the fight at the Great Redoubt: how the gunners had charged with Lord Rick himself to take their weapons back from the enemy.

Courage comes in many forms. As does honor. And there were things not even knights or Eqetas could face undaunted.

Ganton saw the enemy thrusting into the gap between the battered Third Division and Teuthras' Second. A messenger rode off to Lord Drumold to bring up the Tamaerthan horse. Then Ganton spurred toward the gap.

Hilaskos and the Guards had just caught up with him when the starmen's mortar opened fire. The first four rounds gave Ganton hope the enemy attack would never reach the guns. The fifth round dashed that hope. When the smoke cleared, two of the five guns were overturned, and many of the gunners lay on the ground. Ganton cursed.

"Guards, halt! First Squad go tell the starmen—" *Tell them what? Not to kill our own people?* "Tell them to be careful. I am going to rally the gunners." He sent a messenger to Lord Clavell and his Nikeian axemen: rally at once at the banner of the Fighting Man.

"Where will that be, Majesty?" asked the messenger.

"Among the guns," said Ganton, pointing downhill. The messenger swallowed but his Wanax's glare froze any argument on his lips. He rode off as Bheroman Hilaskos raised the Fighting Man and the royal party trotted downhill.

They reached the rear of the guns just as the enemy's foot recovered their courage and came on. The Guards musketeers fired from the saddle, a ragged volley that still couldn't miss a target the size of the oncoming foot. Their wine-colored tunics identified them as spearmen of Ta-Kartos.

The enemy surged forward, the Guards dismounted to reload, use their bows, or hold horses. Master Gunner Pinir ran about, using a rammer to prod reluctant gunners back to their duties. The gunners seemed more afraid of him than of the enemy.

From behind the enemy's foot horse archers began shooting. With the short northern bows, few of their arrows reached hostile targets. A good many struck their own foot. The attack wavered again, then wavered still more as the musketeers of the Second Division opened fire.

Ganton's horse was spent. He dismounted. Moments later he was in the middle of another battle. Enemies were all around him. He drew his sword and lashed out. *Lord Rick would never approve. I am no more than a common foot soldier. And who commands now?* He tried to hack his way to the rear so that he could return to the command post. There was nothing to be done here.

Hilaskos fought beside him, holding the Fighting Man. A spearman ran at him and thrust him in the thigh. Hilaskos brought the banner pole down on the attacker's head. A Guardsman cut the spearman down, just as Hilaskos staggered, then fell. A squire ran forward to lift the banner.

"Hold it high! You are a knight as of this moment!" Ganton shouted.

More enemies, with swords and ironbound clubs for close work. Ganton's sword broke on the head of a club but his Guards were all about him, throwing their shields in front of him until they made a wall. Ganton drew his Browning and fired between the Guards' shields. Five of the enemy went down. Others heard the thunder of the star weapon and held back.

More of the host of Drantos rallied to the Fighting Man, until his friends were causing as much confusion as enemies. Rudhrig brought up the last of his cavalry reserves. They began their advance into the gap, not in a solid line but picking their way forward in twos and threes. With swords and lances they cleared the rear of the guns of enemies, then formed into two columns. One to the left, one to the right, they passed through the guns and into the enemy's foot.

The Ta-Kartos spearmen were neither armed nor trained as well as Lord Rick's pike regiments; they could not stand against cavalry and did not. They would have fled, except for their own horse pressing hard against their rear. So most of them died where they stood. Those who did not die under Drantos steel died from the arrows and bullets of both Divisions; the archers and musketeers of the Third had rallied.

At last there was nothing in front of Ganton and the guns save dead men or wounded that the cavalry were finishing off with lance-thrusts from the saddle. Rudhrig had his knights well in hand; Ganton had no fear of their charging too far. When he'd seen Hilaskos bandaged and carried off the field, he remounted and ordered the Nikeian axemen to the right of the Third Division. Their long-handled axes would do well against either horse or foot, as long as the Fourth Pikes did not give up the fight.

The Guards reformed their shield wall. Some time before the low clouds had broken into misty rain. One after another the guns fell silent. Ganton had time to pull out the arrows stuck in his gambeson. None had penetrated the mail beneath. He reloaded the Browning.

The rain would silence guns and muskets alike. Thick smoke from the firepowder lay across the entire battle area. Archers could not see a hundred paces into the gloom, and had no targets.

The battle would be won by whoever could bring home a charge, infantry or cavalry. There could be no strategy, and in this smoke weapons that struck at a distance were useless.

Vothan favors the side with the greatest numbers. Ganton had heard that as a child. Today it might be true.

The enemy trumpets sounded again.

CHAPTER FOUR

Tylara watched the battle until the rain and smoke closed in. Then there was nothing to see.

Balquhain rode up. "Mac Clallan Muir sent me to ask if you know who commands this army."

"It is certainly not me." She pointed down the hill into the smoke. "The Wanax Ganton rode that way with the Banner of the Fighting Man half an hour ago. I have not seen him since."

"I think our father knows this."

"So do I. Why did he send you here?"

Balquhain shook his head. "You always did know him better than me. But I think he wants you to take command of the army."

"Take command—"

"Tylara, you are Eqetassa of Chelm and Justiciar of Drantos. The Wanax has vanished. Someone must command—"

"Brother, the knights will not obey me. I am Eqetassa, not Eqeta—"

"Drantos knights would obey you more than me, or Mac Clallan Muir."

Yatar, is this part of my penance?

"Father says we must do something or the battle is lost."

Tylara peered into the smoke. The sounds of battle flowed up the hill. Screaming horses and men, the clash of swords and shields, and other sounds she did not recognize. None of them told her what was happening. Just as the weather closed in completely she had seen Akkilas's forces rally and attack once more. She had no guess as to their progress, but many of them had moved against the weakened Third Division. *Without orders the other Divisions will not move. They cannot support each other if they cannot see. We may yet be defeated in detail. Rick says that is nearly always how battles are lost or won.*

"He may be right. Do you wish me to command?"

"Mac Clallan Muir does."

"Then ride to Prince Strymon. Offer to take command of his Division, or to serve him in any other way, and beg him to come here and take command of this army."

"Tylara—"

"You wanted orders, Balquhain. You have them."

"You always did get your way. Yes, sister. As to my squadrons—"

"Send them to me. Tell them to obey me. I have work for them."

"May I ask what?"

"Balkie, none of us do any good here, and in this rain the guns cannot defend our right flank. I am afraid the enemy will come through there. I will take the clansmen to stopple that hole."

Balquhain grinned. "Hurrah for Tilly! I'll tell Father." He turned his horse, then stopped and looked back. "Tylara—"

"Get out of here!"

"Yes, my lady."

The sounds of battle came over the hill. Rick stopped for a moment to listen. "That way!" he shouted. He spurred his horse forward.

"Colonel," MacAllister shouted. "It ain't going to do nobody any good to get there with dead horses!"

"Sh—" Rick caught himself. "Right, Corporal." He reined his horse to a walk. "Who's got the best mount?"

"You do," MacAllister said. "Colonel, we're *all* wore out, and you got to know it."

Which didn't help a bit. Somewhere ahead was a battle. Rick looked at the sheaf of semaphore messages he had received. Tylara's ransom. Tylara's release. Strymon an ally. Castle Fasolt taken. And now a battle in the Ottarn Valley, only that wasn't in any message. "What in hell is going on?" he said aloud.

"Beats me, Colonel," MacAllister said. "I just know it's time to walk the horses."

"Oh, shit. All right, Corporal." As Rick dismounted he wished for a Honda Tricycle.

Tylara waited impatiently for Balquhain's squadrons. The rain was falling more heavily. It washed away the smoke from the guns, but still she could not see into the valley below. There were no more sounds of gunfire anywhere, but the other noises of battle were undiminished.

Where are the starmen? More important, where was the king?

Hoofbeats. Drumold rode up through the rain. "I've brought the clansmen, Daughter. Your brother said you had need for us."

"That may be. Certainly we do no good nere." She pointed to her right. "There is a gap yonder between the Third Division and the village. Guns were to protect it, but in this rain they cannot fire."

"Does the enemy advance there, then?"

"Father, I don't know. I only know that we do no good waiting here, and if Akkilas brings his cavalry through there we are lost."

"What is the ground there?"

"Solid down the slope. Then mud."

Drumold grinned. "So they come from mud to face us on solid ground?"

Before she could answer, two of her cavalrymen rode up the slope. They reined up and the older one said, "We have heard horsemen in the swamplands."

"How many?"

"We cannot tell. The noises of battle are too great. But horsemen are advancing."

"Well done," Drumold said. "My lady, should we not go to meet them?"

"Father—"

"Lass, I am Mac Clallan Muir, but you are Justiciar of Drantos. I wait your command."

She wheeled her horse and beckoned to her light cavalrymen. "Follow me." She led the way down the slope.

The sounds of battle grew louder. *To hell with the horses.* Rick remounted and spurred his mount into a trot. As the slope grew steeper the beast dropped back into a walk. Rick cursed. *One consolation. A walk's easier on my arse than a trot. And thank God Agzaral sent the Preparation H.*

A banner showed in the gloom. Green and white, a stylized megaron device— "Ta-Meltemos?" He took the sheaf of semaphore messages from his belt pouch and read again. There was no ambiguity.

STRYMON OF TA-MELTEMOS JOINED TO HOST
OF DRANTOS AS ALLY

First time I've ever worried that somebody cracked the semaphore code. "Let's go."

"Who is there?" someone challenged.

"Eqeta Rick, Captain General of Drantos." *And I ought to have your arse for letting me get this close.* "Take me to the Wanax."

An officer rode up hastily. A dozen Guards scrambled

after him. The officer stared. "My lord. Your pardon. You were not expected."

"I sent the message by semaphore."

"We have received no semaphore messages for two days. Prince Akkilas's cavalry destroyed the station south of Castle Fasolt."

"All right. I'm here now. Where is the Wanax?"

The Guard officer turned away, then stammered, "My Lord Rick, we do not know."

"What? How in hell can his Guards not know where he is?"

"My Lord, he told us to wait, and rode down into the battle."

"Does he live?"

"We have not heard."

Oh shit. "Who is in charge here?"

"Prince Strymon, my lord."

"Take me to him." *Holy shit.*

Rick clasped hands with Prince Strymon.

"My lord," Strymon began. "I—I am pleased to meet you, and apologize for any trouble I may have caused your lady—"

"We haven't a lot of time, Highness," Rick said. "I've already heard that Lady Tylara is safe. Now what's going on here?"

"I wish I knew."

"Jesus Christ. You're in command!"

"My lord, a quarter hour ago I was summoned by Lord Balquhain to assume command of the army. It took nearly that long to give Lord Balquhain command of my Division and come here. I arrived to find that the Wanax Ganton is there—" He pointed downslope into the rain and smoke. "I am told that the Third Division is in trouble, but I do not yet know what that means, or what to do about it."

"Christ on a crutch. Look, can you at least tell me where the Third Division is?"

"At once." Strymon produced a map from inside his surcoat. He unrolled it. Rain spattered and the ink began to smear.

Rick took the map and tried to orient it. *The enemy is that way. Ah. Here's the ridge we're on.* He turned the map so that it faced the same directions as the terrain. "Third Division. This one?"

"Yes," Strymon said.

"And the other Divisions? What's in them?"

Strymon shrugged. "Everything. Pikes, horse, archers—"

"I see." *Damn kid took my lesson in Napoleonic organization too bloody seriously.* "But First and Second are intact?"

"First certainly is. I believe Second is as well."

"Reserves." Rick pointed. By now the rain had half washed away the marks on the parchment. "Tamaerthans here."

"No longer," Strymon said. "They were brought around to secure our right flank. Your lady and her father lead them."

"Good." *Okay. Right flank secure. Maybe. No need to ask what's happened to the guns. In this rain we'll be lucky if they get off a round every hour.* "Highness, you had First Division?"

"Yes."

"Any action?"

"We were charged by cavalry earlier this morning. The guns dealt with most of it. I took few losses."

"Have you ever commanded pikemen?"

"Not until this morning."

Yeah. But as a distinguished ally, you had to have a suitable command. Holding the left flank. "Your orders were to hold?"

"Yes. I would have preferred a more active role."

"You'll get it." He rose in his stirrups. "Ark!"

Passovopolous rode a mule. Nothing else would carry him for long. "Sir!"

"Take the weapons squad down there." He pointed off to his right. "Go that way and down hill until you get to the village. Get through it and set up the weapons with a good field of fire."

"Colonel—"

"I know, I know, you can't see a damn thing. Just do the best you can. You go set up and wait. You're the anvil. Someone find me a fresh horse. I have to go get the hammer."

It took five minutes for the staff officers to find Teuthras and bring him to the rear of the Second Division. Rick kept glancing at his watch. *Tylara, Tylara. Are you safe? Where are you, my love?* It would do no good to go riding after her. The battle had to be won. *I heard she rode right into the enemy lines at Piro's Hill. Bull shit. She's not like that. So why do people tell me that?*

"My Lord Rick," Teuthras shouted. "Welcome."

"Thanks. My Lord, what is happening with your Division?"

"Little. We heard sounds of fighting in the Third, but we have had little of the battle for an hour."

"What are you doing to support Third?"

"What can we do? I have sent cavalry to stand ready in case we are ordered to attack, but—"

"I see." *Shit fire. For years I tried to get them to obey orders and not just go charging off to the thickest fighting. Now we'd have been better off if they'd never learned any discipline.* "Thank you. My lord, I intend to send First Division across your front, then pivot and move down toward the Ottarn. We will sweep the enemy before us into the star weapons I have placed near the river village."

Teuthras grinned widely. "How can we help?"

"Second Division will be vital. As we cross your front, the enemy's cavalry to the northeast will fall on First Division's rear. When they do, you must move forward to counter-attack and cover us."

"Ah! Gladly."

"I will also want your pikemen in the vanguard of that counterattack. It may be that I will assume personal command of those pikemen."

Teuthras frowned. "I would hate to lose them."

So you would. You know more about pikemen than any of the

other Division commanders. "Belay that. I'll leave you First Division's pikes," Rick said. "What you must do is use the pikes as a walking wall to shield the rear of First Division's sweep."

Teuthras looked thoughtful, then grinned. "Aye!" He looked up into the sky and blinked away the raindrops from his eyes. "Alas, we cannot support them properly with archers. But then the enemy cannot attack the pikes with archers, either. Lord Rick—where is the Wanax?"

Beats the shit out of me. "Rallying Third Division."

"Ah. That's Ganton. In the thick of the fighting." Teuthras grinned widely. "I had not heard you would be here, but well come, my lord. Well come."

Balquhain's shout of welcome left no doubt of its warmth. "You have come to take command!"

"More or less. I left Prince Strymon in charge at headquarters."

"Have you seen Tylara?"

"No, damn it! And I can't go looking for her until I get things moving."

"Aye. What must I do?"

Good man. Rick held out the rain-spattered parchment. The ink had long ago blurred to meaningless smears. He pointed to the top left blob. "We are here. We're going to take your cavalry straight east, across Second Division's front, then pivot on Second and sweep down toward the river. Lord Passovopolous and the weapons squad are set up there."

Balquhain frowned. "My lord—will the others not come through the gap I have left and attack the others from behind?"

"I was getting to that. You're making the sweep with the cavalry. As you advance, leave the pikes behind. Teuthras will add his pikemen to yours. I'm leaving two Star Lords with rifles. That's more than enough to hold this line."

Balquhain considered that for a moment. "Especially in this confusion. Akkilas cannot know more about this battle than we do. Good. Another question, my lord. We attack from one side, and drive the enemy toward the river, but what is to prevent them from running east?"

"Nothing. I want them to. My lord, we aren't trying to win any great victory here. Once those troops start running in this rain and mud it will take a ten-day to make a fighting force out of them again. By then the rest of the Drantos chivalry will be here."

"I see." Balquhain grinned. "And by then *you* will be in command."

Balquhain's trumpets sounded. His cavalrymen moved out in good formation at a slow walk. Pikemen marched to beat of drums to close across the front the cavalry had vacated. Archers stood behind the pikemen. Most had unstrung their bows to dry the bowstrings inside their clothing.

At first there was no opposition. The rain fell harder. *A hundred yards visibility. If that.* Rick looked around to be sure that a full score of staff officers, mostly young squires from the great houses, were following him. They didn't look happy to be left out of the fighting, although Rick had told them that communications would be the most important weapon Drantos had. He sent one officer out to the left side. "Just see what's happening, and be sure the formation's holding," Rick said. "And when you see the enemy, ride like hell back here. Don't get in the fighting."

"Yes, sir." The squire didn't look happy, but Rick thought he'd do it.

The right flankers reached the edge of Second Division. "Here's where it gets tricky," Rick muttered. He sent another messenger to the left flank. "Tell them to start the sweep." As the boy galloped away, he sent a third rider to the right.

"Slower, damn you!" Rick shouted at the troops in front of him. "Wait for the men on your left!" He turned to his messenger pool. "Ride down the line shouting that."

The trouble with great turning maneuvers was that the troops at the pivot had to stay in position while those at the end covered a large arc. Since everyone wanted to get it over with, there was a tendency for those nearest the pivot to move too fast. This could leave gaps in the line. Worse, the whole front might bow backward.

The first squire Rick had sent to the left galloped back. "Enemy in sight. Light cavalry ahead and to the left."

"Which way was that?"

The boy thought for a moment, then pointed.

"Good. Now go tell Lord Balquhain please to send a company of the reserves to watch them. Watch and nothing else."

They continued at a fast walk. Rick peered ahead into the rain. Suddenly a man on his left shouted. "There they are!"

They were dead ahead, a ragged line of heavy cavalrymen. They were nearly flank on to Rick. The far end of the enemy line was visible in the gloom. "Trumpeter! Sound the trot. Have at 'em!"

The enemy commander tried to rally his troops, but it was too late. Caught in flank, fifty men of the enemy right faced a thousand of Rick's heavies. Before Rick's cavalrymen could reach the enemy's right flank it dissolved as first individuals, then whole squads turned to ride away into the rain. Within minutes there wasn't an enemy to be seen. "Sound the walk," Rick said. "And get the goddam line dressed again."

"It's the waiting I hate," Drumold said.

"Yes." Tylara cupped her hand behind her ear and listened. Definitely closer, she thought. There were at least a hundred men out in the swamp. *Probably many more. It would be foolish to send only a hundred.*

"I'm thinking we may be too many here," Drumold said.

Tylara shrugged. "We can only guess."

"Aye. I know." Drumold pointed off to his left front. "And that way the ground is solid enough, if it's needed that we join the main battle. I think you've chosen well." He hunched his shoulders and drew his cloak closer around him.

He looks old today.

A rider came up behind her. "My lady! Lord Rick has come!"

"Rick!" *Prayers are answered, then.* "Where is he?"

"My lady, he asked after you, then took command. He goes to bring the First Division down to the aid of Third."

"I see." Tylara closed her eyes and brought up a mental picture of the battle front. She could see First Division sweep around Second, move down and to the right— "Where are his star warriors?"

"They were sent to hold yonder village."

Tylara frowned. Why would Rick do that? She brought up her mental picture again. *Ah. To be certain the enemy does not get past us.* "Well done, kinsman. Now, if you will, go find Lord Rick and tell him where we are and in what strength. Tell him also that Mac Clallan Muir and the Eqetassa of Chelm await his commands."

Rick rode up to Balquhain and drew his horse to a walk. "The tricky part's done," he said.

They'd run into three more enemy formations. Two had run. The third had a more able commander. He rallied his soldiers into something like a charge, but couldn't get them into a useful formation. They'd struck in driblets rather than all at once, and were driven away like the others.

Rick pointed ahead. "Now all we have to do is go forward. Teuthras can guard our rear. Our left is vulnerable, but not if we keep the reserves out there. The important thing is not to use up the reserves chasing shadows."

A messenger rode up. "Lord Teuthras says that the pikes are now in line."

"Good. Now go up and report to Prince Strymon. Tell

him where we are, and where the pikes are, and anything else you know."

"Yes, sir—" The boy rode away.

"He'll be thinking this a strange kind of war," Balquhain said. "All riding and no fighting."

"I'll be glad enough if we've done all the fighting we're going to do." *We haven't, though. When we start closing this box—*

Another messenger came up. *Ha. That's the boy I sent looking for Rudhrig.* "Report, lad!"

"Lord Rick! I bring commands from the Wanax."

Well I will be go to hell. "Uh, what would His Royal Majesty like us to do?"

"He said to greet you welcome in his name, and say that you should come to his aid."

"Thank you."

"Generous of him," Balquhain muttered.

"I expect he's in trouble," Rick said quietly. He raised his voice. "Where is the king?"

"He said to say: 'I stand where the banner of Third Division stood as the day began. There are enemies a hundred paces away.'"

Aha. "That would be near the center of the old square. Lord Balquhain, I think we must shift to our right."

"I agree."

On a parade ground I'd just say 'Right Oblique, March.' This is going to be a bit tougher. Rick called his messengers together.

"Enemy in sight!" The shout went up from a dozen men at once as the rain slacked off.

"Well, my lord, we have found the fighting you wanted," Rick said.

Balquhain grinned. They had reached what had been the corner of Third Division. Now it was covered with enemies, thousands dead but many thousands more still alive and fighting. None faced Rick's force.

"Sound the charge," Balquhain ordered.

"Damn right! Go like hell." *Nothing like surprise.* "Messenger, ask Lord Teuthras to send any cavalry he can spare. Have them come directly here." He drew his sword and rose in his stirrups as the trumpeters sounded the charge.

Tylara heard the trumpets sound charge just as the rain stopped. "To your horses!" Drumold shouted. "Ah, lass, now I truly believe your husband is here."

Ha! I had not planned for our first meeting to be on a battlefield, but now I think it is well.

Minutes later enemy cavalry galloped into view. They veered off at the sight of the Tamaerthan chivalry.

"Should we not charge?" Drumold asked.

"I think not yet." *Rick, where are you?* "I think there will be more, soon, and it is best we wait."

The enemy was out of sight in moments. Then, suddenly, Tylara heard the sound of star weapons to her right. "The —*light machine gun!* Lord Rick must have brought another."

Drumold raised the nasal bar of his helmet and grinned. "Whoever was thrashing about in yon swamp will have good company I'm thinking. I doubt we've aught to fear from that place now."

Tylara smiled agreement. Few captains could get men to go forward through retreating comrades. None could make them do it against star weapons. "It means, I think, that we are free to do whatever we think best," Tylara said.

The rain had stopped, but she still couldn't see much. Far ahead and to her left were the pickets marking the rear of Third Division's area. Off to the right was the village, and somewhere beyond it were Rick's starmen.

More trumpets sounded far to the left. *That must be Rick. It must be! Who else could win the day two hours after he came to the battle?* She turned to Drumold and grinned. "Is it no time that the clansmen had their wish? Yonder trumpets signal the charge. Shall we no obey?"

Drumold drew his sword and stood in his stirrups. "Aye, Lass. Forward!"

Tylara spurred her horse to a trot. Soon enough the thin mud of the slope changed to the deeper mud of the valley. The Tamaerthan forces angled off to their left, trying to stay on more solid ground. They had gone a quarter mile when Tylara remembered to send messengers, to Strymon, and to Rick and Ganton if they could find them.

The rain began again as they passed the corner of Third Division's old square. Now the wind came up from behind her. *A good sign. It drives the rain into the enemy's face, not ours.* The sounds of battle were louder.

She turned to one of her officers. "Go and find Lord Rudhrig. Be sure he knows that we are here. I would no care to be charged by his horsemen."

"There, lass." Drumold pointed.

A gust of wind blew away smoke and rain for seconds. The enemy was ahead.

"We can no do a proper charge in this mud," Drumold said. "But we can try." He stood in his stirrups. "Charge!"

Someone behind shouted "Mac Clallan Muir!" A thousand more took up the cry. Kettledrums and horns sounded. The clansmen spurred forward.

Matthias cursed the rain. Victory lay less than a hundred paces ahead, where Ganton stood in his golden helmet beneath the banner of the Fighting Man. They had only to kill Ganton and the war was over. Akkilas would have no difficulty persuading the barons of Drantos that this was no time for an infant Wanax.

Men fell all around him, but he was untouched. "Forward! Forward to victory!"

The spearmen of Ta-Kartos advanced. They struck the shield wall of Ganton's bodyguards, and the battle held there. Whenever a man fell on either side, another replaced him. The rain cleared for a moment. Matthias looked around for more forces to throw into the attack. He had waved a new group of infantry forward when he heard horns.

Drantos horns. "What call is that?" he demanded of an acolyte.

"Honorable, it is their charge."

Matthias cursed. "They have brought up the others at last." Where were the blocking forces he had set to watch the enemy's middlemost battle? No matter. Clearly they had been driven away without even sounding an alarm. "Captain Volauf! Press forward here! I go to meet this new attack."

"As you will, Honorable."

His spirit is broken, I think. Better to leave him here than to let him run away. Matthias signaled to his personal guards. Many of them were veterans of the southern wars. There were only two hundred, but they were all he had left. "Follow me! Find the enemy commander and slay him." *It is all we can do. It may be enough.*

Matthias mounted. He thought it would not be easy to get through his own troops, dead and living, but he found the Drantos forces were much closer than he had expected.

The day is lost. Why has Vothan given victory to our enemies? The wind blew into a real storm, but through the gusts of driving rain he caught sight of banners ahead. The leaders of this new attack.

Could we yet win? We still have more strength than Ganton. Kill these leaders and this attack comes to naught. Then I can return to kill Ganton. We have not lost yet. "Forward!" He galloped toward the banners, and rejoiced to hear the hoofbeats of his men following close behind.

The fury of his charge carried him through the first of the enemy's line. "Ignore those!" he shouted to his followers. "Ride for their banners! Kill the leaders."

Now he was close enough to see the banners clearly, and he rejoiced. The War Lord of Drantos led here! His death would harm the Drantos cause nearly as much as Ganton's.

Matthias's horse was tiring. A dozen of his followers came

level with him, then passed him. They dashed on toward the banners.

Tylara's light cavalry dashed ahead of Drumold's heavy chivalry. The surprise was total. Much of the enemy cavalry was dismounted, and their infantry faced Tylara's left. In the distance she could see the shield wall of Ganton's Guards, and behind that his banners. She rose in her stirrups to look back at Drumold, and pointed toward the Fighting Man with her axe.

She couldn't hear his acknowledgment, but he waved to his left and his heavy cavalrymen struck the Ta-Kartos spearmen from behind.

Tylara nodded in satisfaction and waved her own men ahead, toward where she had last heard Rick's trumpets. *They must be his. And I will go to him.*

The Tamaerthan Hussars swept through the disorganized enemy. None fought, except to defend their own persons, and as soon as they were not threatened they ran away. A whole block of cavalry led by a great banner crossed just behind Tylara. Infantrymen clung to the horsemen's stirrups. All fled to the east. Others ran behind them, some calling to their comrades to hold up.

"We have won!" Tylara shouted. "Victory! For Yatar and Christ!" Rain swept across the field. She could see nothing, but ahead she heard sounds of fighting, swords against shields. Then the rapid fire of a battle rifle. Pistol shots.

"Rick!" She waved toward the sounds and spurred her horse on. She slapped him gently on the neck. "On! On my wonder!" *If you live through this day, I will see you have apples every day forever.* "Drantos! For Yatar, Christ, and Drantos!"

There were cavalrymen ahead. A solid formation, in line—

"Drantos!" she cried again.

They answered. "Drantos!"

More rifle fire to the right, and now three pistol shots, rapidly.

Rick took out a flask of brandy and drank a hefty shot.

Done, he thought. The enemy ahead couldn't run away fast enough. First Division's charge carried right through the enemy lines, such as they were. Anyone who didn't run away could be left for Teuthras's cleanup squads.

Now to find Tylara. Oh. And the king. He waved the troops forward at a walk. "Save the horses," he called. "Pass it on."

The line was stretched too thin, but that couldn't matter. The only opposition was from disoriented enemies who couldn't see that the way east was clear and thought they had to fight to escape. It didn't take long to kill them or chase them off.

The wind came up from the southwest and turned the squall into a real rainstorm. Gusts drove cold rain into Rick's face. Rick wiped his eyes. "I won't be sorry for a fire tonight."

"Me either, Cap'n." MacAllister rode alongside. "Any chance there's more in that flask, sir?"

I don't really encourage— "Sure." Rick took out the flask and handed it over. "You didn't get much action today."

"All I want, Captain."

"Me too—" Rick lifted his helmet and listened. "What in hell is that?"

"Cavalry—" MacAllister unslung his H&K battle rifle. "Coming right at us, I'd say."

"Who in hell?" Now he could see the galloping horsemen. Rick stood in his stirrups. "Drantos!" he called.

"Holy shit!" MacAllister shouted. "They sure ain't ours!" He shouldered the weapon and fired, slowly and deliberately. The oncoming cavalrymen dropped one by one. Still they charged onward. "Jesus Christ, Cap'n, it's *US* they want!"

Rick shifted his sword to his left hand and drew his Colt. He thumbed off the safety. *Wish I'd kept a rifle for myself. Never was much good with this—*

MacAllister fired the rest of his clip. The oncoming enemy was no more than ten yards away now. One group dashed at Balquhain. Henchmen rallied to him.

Rick's first round took the lead man full in the chest. He wheeled to his right to avoid the second, then shot the man as he came closer. He wanted to use a two-handed grip, but he didn't dare let go of the sword in his left hand, and there was no time to sheathe it.

He fired three times, rapidly, and prayed that MacAllister would be able to reload in time. Then he was surrounded by enemies, and his pistol was empty.

He managed to thrust the Colt back in its holster and shift his sword to his right hand. As he did, his orderly spurred forward to take his place on his left. "Your shield!" Jamiy shouted.

Before Rick could take it, another horseman was on him. Rick parried the sword thrust and the man swept past. Rick had no chance to see what happened to him.

Ahead were half a dozen more of the enemy. The one in the center wore the robes of a priest of Vothan over mail, and carried a sword. He was screaming curses.

Rick looked around for MacAllister but couldn't see him. He heard more riders coming up fast from his right front. *Looks like this is it.*

"For Yatar and Christ!"

What? Who says that?

A rider in flowing cape appeared out of the rain beyond the enemy cavalry. The rider's cape and long black hair streamed in the wind. A woman. She whirled an axe over her head, and screamed war cries. *My God, a Valkyrie!*

The priest of Vothan turned to look. He stared, then slumped in his saddle. His sword fell forgotten as he turned to face the oncoming apparition. "Father Vothan! I come!"

Good God, it's Tylara!

She rode past the mailed priest and struck at him with her

axe. It knocked his helmet askew and he fell. His companions halted. One dismounted, and with the aid of another lifted the priest so that he lay across the saddle of his horse. They led him away.

Two of Balquhain's henchmen rode after him, but the priest's companions turned to fight.

"Let be!" Balquhain shouted. "There's few enough with that courage."

Tylara reined up alongside Rick. "My husband. I have come."

Rick drew a deep breath. "So I see. What kept you?" He stood in his stirrups to look around the battlefield. The last of the enemy were riding away to his left. Behind him MacAllister was getting to his feet beside his fallen horse. "But just in time. Well come." Rick sheathed his sword and drew the Colt. "Do you have any ammunition?"

"Why—yes."

"Then why the Hell didn't you use it instead of that goddam axe?" He leaned closer and touched her hair. "And for Christ's sake, you're not even wearing a helmet!"

She gripped his hand and held it against her cheek. "Forgive me, my lord. My husband. I did not think—"

"Yeah. Neither one of us has done much thinking for a while." He squeezed her hand and let go, then leaned back and whacked her horse on the rump. "Race you back to Ganton's tent!"

She steadied her mount and grinned back at him. They spurred their horses and galloped together into the storm.